MORE PRAISE FOR JOAN HESS AND HER MAGGODY SERIES

"Successfully combines Murder and Mayhem with the most bizarre goings-on east of the Rockies."
—*Library Journal*

"Jolly, raunchy.... More than entertaining.... Hess knows how to plot a fast-moving whodunit and create an engaging heroine."
—*Chicago Sun-Times*

"As rowdy and funny as Mark Twain ever dared to get.... Hess's books are also rather profound social satire, but most readers will be too busy laughing to notice."
—Charlotte MacLeod, author of *The Odd Job*

"A highly entertaining book!"
—*Chicago Tribune*

"Spicy ... a toothsome holiday treat with a bite of its own."
—*Arkansas Democrat Gazette*

"Joy to the world! Another delightful installment in a superbly comic series."
—*Booklist*

Other books by Joan Hess

The Maggody Series
MALICE IN MAGGODY
MISCHIEF IN MAGGODY
MUCH ADO IN MAGGODY
MADNESS IN MAGGODY
MORTAL REMAINS IN MAGGODY
MAGGODY IN MANHATTAN
O LITTLE TOWN OF MAGGODY
MARTIANS IN MAGGODY
MIRACLES IN MAGGODY

The Claire Malloy Series
STRANGLED PROSE
MURDER AT THE MURDER AT THE MIMOSA INN
DEAR MISS DEMEANOR
A REALLY CUTE CORPSE
A DIET TO DIE FOR
ROLL OVER AND PLAY DEAD
DEATH BY THE LIGHT OF THE MOON
POISONED PINS
TICKLED TO DEATH
BUSY BODIES
CLOSELY AKIN TO MURDER

The Maggody Militia

An Arly Hanks Mystery

Joan Hess

AN ONYX BOOK

ONYX
Published by the Penguin Group
Penguin Putnam Inc., 375 Hudson Street,
New York, New York 10014, U.S.A.
Penguin Books Ltd, 27 Wrights Lane,
London W8 5TZ, England
Penguin Books Australia Ltd, Ringwood,
Victoria, Australia
Penguin Books Canada Ltd, 10 Alcorn Avenue,
Toronto, Ontario, Canada M4V 3B2
Penguin Books (N.Z.) Ltd, 182–190 Wairau Road,
Auckland 10, New Zealand

Penguin Books Ltd, Registered Offices:
Harmondsworth, Middlesex, England

Published by Onyx, an imprint of Dutton Signet,
a member of Penguin Putnam Inc.
Previously appeared in a Dutton edition.

First Onyx Printing, April, 1998
10 9 8 7 6 5 4 3 2 1

This book is dedicated to the memory of Ellen Nehr,
who was a treasured friend and confidante.
Her perspicacity, wit, and boundless knowledge
of the mystery genre will be missed.

A great deal of my information came from *Armed and Dangerous: The Rise of the Survivalist Right* by James Coates (Farrar, Straus and Giroux, 1987; revised edition 1995). Mr. Coates was gracious enough to consent to a telephone interview and answered a lot of really stupid questions. Margaret Maron generously shared her impressive array of research material. Other information was unwittingly provided by pawnshop owners, dealers at my one and only gun show, and such publications as the Paladin Press catalog and books written (I use the term loosely) by devotees to the cause.

From *The Starley City Star Shopper,* November 1:

What's Cooking in Maggody?

BY RUBELLA BELINDA HANKS

I'd like to thank the wonderful folks at the *Star Shopper* for asking me to write a weekly column about happenings here in Maggody. It'd be nice if they were paying me more than $15.50, but I reckon it's better than a kick in the backside, as my great-aunt used to say before she had that stroke that froze up her face like a dried apricot.

For starters, the Four-H Club at the high school took second prize at the county fair for their display on kitchen appliance safety. Lottie Estes asked me to remind you all of the bake sale next Saturday in the home ec room right across from the welding shop.

Last Sunday afternoon Eileen Buchanon hosted a baby shower for her daughter-in-law, Dahlia, who's expecting toward the end of the month (although it's hard to tell on account of her being on

the large side to begin with). At the shower were myself, Estelle Oppers, Elsie McMay, Millicent McIlhaney, Joyce Lambertino, Mrs. Jim Bob Buchanon, and Edwina Spitz and her sister Teddi Witbreed, who's from Hagerstown, Maryland. Eileen served spicy cider and sponge cake, and a good time was had by all.

A warm Maggody welcome to our newest addition to the community. I suppose someone ought to go out to the edge of town and change the sign to "Population: 756," one of these days, but then when Dahlia and Kevin's baby comes, it'd have to be done all over again. Anyway, for those of you who've been off visiting kin, Kayleen Smeltner will be opening a pawnshop in the old hardware store. She bought the Wockermann property out on County 102 and is staying at the Flamingo Motel while she's having the house remodeled. Kayleen tells me she's originally from Dallas, Texas, and was living over near Malthus when her husband was killed by burglars that broke into the house. Kayleen's hobbies include needlework, fishing, and gardening. She hasn't decided which church she'll attend. Everybody's invited to drop by and get acquainted. I don't want to name names, but I've been told one local resident has been spotted at the doorstep with flowers and a box of candy.

Edwina Spitz had herself a real nice trip to Branson, where she attended three shows and ate lunch at the Country Catfish Café.

Leslie and Fergie Bidens will attend Fergie's sister's wedding in Kansas City the day after Thanksgiving. Leslie will preside over the guest book at the reception.

Elsie McMay is visiting her niece in Blytheville for ten days. Lottie Estes is dropping by Elsie's house every day after school to feed Stan, Elsie's cat.

Estelle asked me to announce that she'll be running specials all this month, including a ten-percent discount on perms and festive holiday tints. Give her a call at Estelle's Hair Fantasies.

The Voice of the Almighty Lord Assembly Hall will be the site of a Thanksgiving pageant presented by the Sunday school. Brother Verber's not real sure of the time and date yet but is leaning toward the Wednesday prayer service the week before Thanksgiving.

Bismal Buchanon is home from the hospital after having surgery of a personal nature. His wife wants to thank everyone for the cards, casseroles, and prayers. Bismal expects to be back at work by the end of next week, as long as his hemorrhoids don't flare up.

Until next time, God bless.

EILEEN'S SPICY CIDER

1 cup packed dark brown sugar
1 cinnamon stick
1 tablespoon whole cloves
2 cups water
1 ½ quarts apple cider
⅓ cup lemon juice
4 cups orange juice
1 lemon, sliced
1 orange, sliced

Put your sugar, spices, and water in a saucepan and heat to boiling, stirring until the sugar dissolves. Simmer for about ten minutes, then strain the syrup and throw away the spices. Add cider, lemon juice, and orange juice, and when it's back to simmering, garnish with the fruit slices.

Chapter 1

"You didn't say anything about the sale on beauty accessories," Estelle said as she tucked the *Star Shopper* into her purse. "I just got in three dozen bottles of fingernail polish in an exciting variety of colors." She held out her fingers. "This is Pumpkin Patch Pizazz. I think it'll be my best seller."

Ruby Bee finished wiping the bar and dropped the dishrag into the sink, where the water was as dingy as the sky outside. Her face, normally pink and plump as a baby's bottom, was puckered with some unexpressed worry. "I'm not supposed to be giving folks free advertising," she said with a shrug. "I'd end up with a whole column of nothing but used pickup trucks for sale. Raz would expect me to announce his moonshine prices, and Jim Bob'd start telling me about his two-for-one specials on paper towels."

"Well, excuse me, Miss Lois Lane," Estelle finished her sherry and picked up her purse, but put it back down. It didn't seem neighborly to leave Ruby Bee all by herself in the gloomy barroom, especially when anyone with eyeballs in the front of their head could see how blue she was. "Maybe I'll have another piece of apple pie," she said, just so Ruby Bee would have something to do.

Ruby Bee gave her a sharp look, but obliged without commenting on certain people's gluttony. After all, Estelle was as skinny as a fence post, although darn few fence posts had bright red hair in a beehive teased a good eight inches high. You didn't see many with violet eyeshadow and cherry-colored lipstick, for that matter. Imagining Estelle out at the edge of a field, holding a strand of barbed wire, brought a flicker of a smile to Ruby Bee's face.

Estelle mentally congratulated herself on the success of her ploy. "So who's this mysterious suitor sniffing around Kayleen?" she asked. "I'd have thought you might have told me right away instead of leaving me to read it in the newspaper. Didn't I tell you when Millicent McIlhaney let it slip that Darla Jean came home drunk and threw up in her pa's boot?"

"I don't want to be accused of spreading gossip. The woman's only been in town for a week, and she might get her feelings hurt if she finds out everybody's talking about her behind her back."

"So who is it?"

Ruby Bee leaned forward like she thought a tabloid reporter was hunkered down in the booth in the corner, taking notes. "I just happened to be setting out the garbage when I saw Brother Verber come sneaking around the corner like a schoolboy with a toad in his pocket. He liked to drop the box of candy when he saw me standing there. He stammered out some foolishness about how he was calling on Kayleen to invite her to go to the Assembly Hall this Sunday. Maybe he thinks I'm as near-sighted as Lottie Estes."

"Brother Verber?" said Estelle, stunned.

"I was a little surprised," admitted Ruby Bee, "but if you think about it, why shouldn't he come courting? He's a bachelor, after all, and it could get a mite lonely over there in the rectory. Kayleen's been widowed for more than a year now. There's nothing unseemly about her entertaining callers."

"But he's so . . ."

"I'll be the first to say nobody's gonna confuse him with Rudolph Valentino, not with his red nose and squinty eyes and flabby lips. It's not hard to guess who's first in line for dessert at the Wednesday night potlucks, either."

Estelle took a sip of sherry while she considered all this. "I suppose there could be another side to him, although he sure keeps it hidden behind his blustery, self-righteous sermons and unhealthy interest in exposing depravity. What's Mrs. Jim Bob got to say?"

"Nothing as of yet, but you can bet the farm we'll hear something before too long,"

"Amen," said Estelle with a snort.

"The woman is nothing but a common tramp," Mrs. Jim Bob (aka Barbara Ann Buchanon Buchanon) told her husband as he came through the back door. "Did you wipe your feet? The last thing I need right now is mud tracked all over the house. Edwina and Millicent are coming over in the morning for coffee, and Perkins's eldest hasn't been here to clean in a week. She says she hurt her back, but it's more likely she's pretending to be poorly so she can collect welfare checks and sit around all day in her bathrobe."

Jim Bob froze in the full wattage of her glare, even though he was carrying two hefty bags of groceries. "Is that why she's a common tramp?"

"I was not referring to Perkins's eldest." Mrs. Jim Bob opened the oven door to check on the pork chops, then slammed it closed and resumed glaring. "It's that woman staying in the motel out behind Ruby Bee's Bar and Grill. A good Christian would never open a pawnshop."

"Why not?" he asked curiously.

"Because it is not the Christian thing to do." She shifted her attention to a saucepan on the stove while she searched her mind for a more insightful explanation. She knew perfectly well that there was something sinful about pawnshops. She finally thought of an old movie she'd watched a few weeks ago when Jim Bob had claimed he was working late at the supermarket. "Pawnshops lure in criminals who want to get rid of stolen property. We've had more than our share of wickedness here in Maggody since Arly Hanks took over as chief of police. I told you when you hired her that it was not a suitable job for a woman, especially one that struts around in pants and has a smart mouth."

Jim Bob set down the bags on the dinette and ran a hand through his stubbly gray hair. As far as Buchanons went, he was on the more perceptive end of the continuum. "Did you and Arly have another run-in today?"

"No, and I don't have any more time to waste trying to help her get back on the right path. I can't count the number of times I've prayed for her, tried to counsel her, and invited her to attend church and join the Missionary Society. Living in New York City swelled her head and corrupted her soul. If she doesn't mend her ways, she and that Smeltner woman will be on the same express train to eternal damnation."

"If you say so," he murmured, wondering if there was any way he could slip back out to his truck and sneak a swallow of bourbon from the pint bottle in the glove compartment. Probably not, he concluded. Mrs. Jim Bob's piety had given her a keener sense of smell than a bloodhound's. He didn't have any idea why she was so fired up, but he sure as hell wasn't going to give her another reason to lecture him. Not when he and the other boys on the town council were planning to play poker Saturday night.

"I may have to work late this weekend," he said as he started for the living room. "I was gonna have Kevin do it, but the boy's just too stupid to trust with the receipts. I caught him this morning on the loading dock, staring into space like one of those department store dummies. I had to whack him upside the head with a broomstick to get his attention. You'd think he was pregnant instead of that cow he's married to."

"I will not have that kind of language in this house, Jim Bob. What would someone walking by think if he heard that coming from the mayor's house? We have an obligation to the community to maintain the highest standards." She came to the doorway, her beady eyes narrowed and her mouth pursed. After a moment, she said, "I assume you'll be working late this weekend in Jim Bob's SuperSaver Buy 4 Less instead of in the backroom of Roy Stiver's antiques store."

He snatched up the remote control and aimed it at

the TV set. "You get the craziest ideas of any woman I've ever met. What would I be doing at Roy's on a Saturday night?"

Kevin was no longer on the loading dock, but he was far from being bright-eyed and bushy-tailed. He'd been mopping the same square yard of linoleum for the best part of ten minutes while he dreamed about fatherhood. Back when Dahlia had first told him she was in the family way, it had seemed so far-fetched that it hadn't sunk in. Now, with less than a month to go, with the crib in the room next to theirs, with the stacks of nighties and diapers and cotton blankets on the dresser, with the smell of baby powder in the air, he was beginning to realize that he, Kevin Fitzgerald Buchanon, was gonna be a father. He was gonna be presented with a warm little bundle to love and protect.

Without thinking (which he rarely did, being on the opposite end of the aforementioned continuum), Kevin dropped the mop and cradled a four-pack of toilet paper in his arms. Babies were soft and squeezable. They arrived all pink so you'd want to kiss their tiny toes and tickle their little noses.

"Excuse me," said an old lady with a cane, "but could you tell me where you keep the toothpicks? I've been up and down all the aisles."

Kevin replaced the pack and gallantly escorted her to the right spot. Rather than return to the mop, however, he dug a dime out of his pocket and went to use the pay phone in the employees' lounge.

He waited patiently for a dozen rings, imagining his beloved heaving herself off the couch and moving majestically across the room. A stranger peering through the window might not guess she was within weeks of having a baby. What weight she'd gained blended right in with the three hundred odd pounds there'd been of her to begin with, and she'd refused to wear outfits with storks and cute messages about the current location of the baby. Kevin's ma had found one that might have fit, but Dahlia'd turned up her nose and kept on wearing her regular clothes.

"What?" she growled into the receiver.

Kevin realized he might have interrupted her in the middle of one of her soap operas. "Nothing, my sweetums. I just wanted to call and ask how you was doing. Is there anything I can bring home this evening?"

"You know darn well I'm on this awful diet. What are you gonna do if I ask you to bring home two gallons of ice cream and a carton of Twinkies?"

He gulped unhappily. "I was thinking more of crunchy celery and that real tasty low-fat yogurt." His beetlish brow, common in varying degrees to all members of the Buchanon clan, crinkled as he struggled to make amends for setting her off again. "Or a magazine! The new issues just came in this morning. I don't recollect exactly, but I think there's one with ideas to decorate a nursery."

"When am I supposed to sew curtains and paint stencils on the wall?" she said with a drawn-out sigh of pure misery. "I have to poke my poor finger four times a day on account of this diabetes. The sight of my blood bubbling up makes me sick to my stomach, so I have to get a sugar-free soda pop and lie down until I stop feeling queasy. Then I haft to listen to that tape they gave us and make silly noises. When I'm not doing that, your ma's hauling me to the clinic so I can put on a paper dress and wait until that weasel of a doctor finds time to pull on plastic gloves and smear petroleum jelly on—",

"I gotta get back to work," Kevin said as his knees buckled and sweat flooded his armpits. "Why don't you have yourself a nice nap on the sofa? After all, you're sleeping for two."

He made it back to the mop and bucket, but it was a long while before he started sloshing dirty water down the aisle.

"Am I disturbing you?" asked Kayleen Smeltner as she came into the PD and paused, her expression cautious.

I put aside my pocketknife and the block of balsa wood I was trying to coerce into resembling a marshland mallard. I keep it in a bottom desk drawer for those stretches of time when the rigors of upholding the law in Maggody are less than burdensome. Some peculiar things have happened since the day I arrived home to pull myself back together after the divorce, but mostly I run a speed trap out at the edge of town, pull teenagers over for reckless driving, beg the miserly town council for money, and try to stay in my mother's good graces by pretending that my only goal in life is to acquire another husband, a vine-covered cottage, and a lifetime subscription to *TV Guide*.

In her dreams, not mine.

"Have a seat," I said to Kayleen. "The bank robbery's not scheduled until five o'clock, and the extraterrestrial invasion won't start until midnight."

She sat down on the edge of the chair across from my desk and unbuttoned her coat. "Maggody doesn't have a bank."

"I know," I said. "It doesn't have a landing pad, either." I'd met Kayleen at the bar, of course, in that I was in there two or three times a day, sometimes four if I made happy hour. She appeared to be in her early forties, maybe ten or twelve years older than me. Her makeup might have been a tad heavy-handed, but it went well with her long, wavy blond hair and slightly masculine features. She was nearly six feet tall and carried a few extra pounds beneath well-tailored silk and linen dresses. The leers and wolf-whistles that greeted her in the barroom implied the overall effect was that of a 1940s Hollywood sex goddess.

She finally gave up trying to figure out what I'd said and relaxed. "I want to give you a copy of my license to buy and sell firearms, just so you'll know everything's legal. I applied for it a few months after Maurice was killed."

"Maurice?" I echoed.

"Everybody called him Mo, but I always called him Maurice on account of how sexy it sounded, like he was from France instead of Neosho, Missouri." She took a tissue out of her purse and dabbed the corner of her eye. "He left me his gun collection. I had to sell it, and I found out real quick that dealers end up with most of the profit. Pretty soon I had a brisk business going, some mail-order but most of it out of my home. When I got tired of having strangers tromp through my living room, I decided to open a pawnshop. This way I can keep my private life separate from my business one."

I leaned back in the worn cane-bottomed chair and asked the question that had been buzzing around town like a deranged hornet. "Why Maggody? Wouldn't you do better in a larger town? The only walk-in trade you'll get here is from the drunks across the street at the pool hall, and I doubt any of them owns anything of value. Traffic consists of tourists heading north for the country music halls of Branson, or heading south for the self-conscious quaintness of Eureka Springs. The only reason anyone slows down going through here is to throw litter out the car window. If anyone actually stopped, we'd all go outside to stare."

"I stopped here once upon a time," she said in a dreamy voice. "I was on my honeymoon. Jodie and I were fresh out of high school, driving an old car his grandfather had given us, down to our last few dollars. We didn't care, though. We were heading for Texas when we had a flat tire four or five miles down the road from here. It turned out the spare tire was flat, too, and Jodie was setting off to walk back to Maggody when this man pulled up. He drove Jodie to a gas station to get the tire fixed, then brought him back and insisted we stay for supper. It was the kindest thing anyone's done in my whole life. I guess I've thought about coming back here ever since then."

"What happened to Jodie?"

This time she put the tissue to serious use. "We scraped together enough money to put a down payment on a little farm west of Texarkana. Less than a year later, Jodie was killed when the truck he was working on slipped off the jack and crushed his chest. I was pregnant at the time, and miscarried the next day. I couldn't stand living in the house filled with his memories, so I sold the property and moved to Dallas. Sometimes I pull out my old high school yearbooks and look at his picture, wondering what my life would have been like if . . ."

I was touched, although not to the point of asking to borrow her soggy tissue. "I still think you may regret opening a business here," I said to change the subject before she whipped out wedding pictures (or an urn filled with ashes). "And you may regret buying the Wockermann property, too. The reason the house is in such disrepair is that it's been empty for a couple of years. The real estate market's not booming in this neck of the woods. It's not even pinging."

"Maurice left me enough to get by on," Kayleen said with a small smile. "I'll have my mail-order business, although I guess I'll have to drive into Farberville to use the post office there. Besides, big cities are frightening these days. You don't know your neighbors. If you need something fixed, you have to let a stranger come inside your house. He could be a rapist, or a psychotic, or even a government agent."

"A government agent?"

"You never can tell. These are dangerous times we live in, Arly. Don't think for a minute that the government doesn't know how much money you make and how you spend it down to the last penny—and I'm not talking just about taxes. They know who you talk to on the telephone and get mail from, and which organizations you belong to."

I raised my eyebrows. "There're more than two hundred and sixty million people in this country. I can't imagine the government keeping tabs on all of them. Mobsters and drug dealers, maybe—but not ordinary citizens. Why would they bother?"

She gave me what I suppose she thought was a meaningful look, although it didn't mean diddlysquat to me. "Keep in mind that the media are regulated by the government, so they can't say things that might expose what's happening in this country. Come by the shop and I'll show you some interesting material about what you can expect sometime down the road."

"Okay," I said uneasily, then took a shot at changing the subject once again. "Maurice was your second husband?"

She promptly teared up again. "He was murdered a little more than a year ago."

"Murdered?" I said, mentally kicking myself for bringing up another painful topic. "What happened?"

"One night we heard glass break downstairs. Maurice took the thirty-eight from the bedside table and went to investigate. Three shots were fired. I called the police, then went to the top of the stairs. I saw men run out the front door, but it was too dark to get a good look. All I could tell the police was that there were three of them, wearing dark coats and ski masks. I've had some training as a practical nurse, but there was nothing I could do to help Maurice. He bled to death before the ambulance arrived."

"Were the men caught?"

Kayleen grimaced and shook her head. "The police interviewed all the local ne'er-do-wells, but nobody was acting guilty or bragging in the bars. I think the men must have been from Springfield or maybe Kansas City. Maurice was a well-known gun collector. He advertised in magazines, and we used to go to shows as far away as Chicago and Houston and Santa Fe. It wouldn't take a college degree to figure out there'd be valuable guns in the house."

I resisted the urge to launch into a lecture that would not amuse card-carrying members of the NRA. Sure, I have a gun (and a box with three bullets), but I keep it locked away in a filing cabinet in the back room. I'm a cop, after all, and may be called upon one of these days to shoot a rabid skunk or an Elvis impersonator. I can't imagine myself shooting much of anything else, even though Hizzoner the Moron has tried my patience on occasion.

I settled for a vaguely sympathetic smile. "It doesn't sound like you've had much luck with husbands."

"It's a good thing I'm not afraid of living alone,"

she said as she stood up, buttoned her coat, and pulled on hand-sewn leather gloves. "I need to run out to the house and find out if the electrician ever showed up. I just thought it'd be nice if you and I got better acquainted."

"Drop by any old time," I said, my fingers crossed in my lap. She seemed perfectly nice, if a little bit odd about wily government agents. A little bit odd barely rates a mention in a county with Buchanons as plentiful as cow patties in a pasture.

I watched her drive away in a creamy brown car, genus Mercedes, species unfamiliar. I turned off the coffee pot, collected my radar gun, balsa wood, and pocket knife, and was almost out the door when the telephone rang. Despite my instincts to keep on going, I turned back to answer it.

"Get yourself over here," whispered a voice I recognized as that of the proprietress of Ruby Bee's Bar & Grill.

"I can't," I whispered back. "I have to nab speeders at the edge of town so I can earn my minuscule salary at the end of the month. Maybe later, okay?"

"You got to come right this instant, missy."

I was going to inquire into the nature of the emergency when I realized I was listening to a dial tone. It could have been an armed robbery, I supposed, but it was more likely to be a mouse in the pantry or a snag in her panty hose. My mother dishes out melodrama as generously as she does peach cobbler.

I left the radar gun on the desk, and ambled down the road, pausing to wave at my landlord, Roy Stiver, who was hauling a spindly lamp into his antiques store. I live in an efficiency apartment upstairs, although I've begun to wonder if I ought to find something less cramped. It had seemed just fine when I first arrived from Manhattan, even though it was quite a step down from a posh condominium with a view of the East River and the Queensboro Bridge. My current residence has a view of the pool hall and a couple of vacant buildings with yellowed newspapers taped across the windows. It also has cigarette burns in the linoleum, mildew on the walls, and a toilet that creaks to itself in the night.

As a temporary refuge, it was adequate. I sure as hell hadn't planned to stay any longer than it took to let my bruised ego recover from the divorce. Now it seemed as though I'd never left town, that the blurred memories of cocktail parties and art galleries were nothing more than scenes from a movie I'd seen somewhere.

Shivering, I went into the barroom to find out what, if anything, had provoked the call. The provocation certainly had not come from the trucker snoring in the corner booth, or from the rednecks in the next booth, who were arguing about breeds of hunting dogs.

This narrowed it down to a lone figure on a stool by the bar. There were no antennas bobbling above his head, and he was wearing a camouflage jacket instead of a sequined suit from the Graceland souvenir store. Ruby Bee was standing in front of him, listening while she dried a beer mug with a towel. I couldn't quite decipher her expression; she was nodding politely, but there was a certain rigidity to her features that suggested she was keeping her opinions to herself.

Which was unusual, to put it mildly.

When she saw me, she dropped the towel and chirped, "Here's Arly. She took her sweet time getting here, but that doesn't mean she's not interested in meeting you. Did I mention she happens to be the chief of police here in Maggody? The mayor's wife was real annoyed when the town council hired her, but there wasn't a line of candidates begging for the job." She took a much needed breath as I came to a stop at the edge of the dance floor. "I was just telling General Pitts about you, honey. He's in town to visit Kayleen, but she's not out back in her room."

I crossed my arms. "If you'd told me you wanted to file a missing person report, I would have brought the forms with me. Before I round up a posse to search the ridge, however, I might mention that Kayleen left the PD about ten minutes ago on her way to the Wockermann place. Something about an electrician."

"General Pitts, this is Arly. Her real name is Ariel, which I chose on account of it having a nice ring to it. She used to be married, but when she got divorced, she decided to take back her maiden name, which is the same as mine. How long ago was that, Arly?"

The man slid off the stool and spun around in a neat, controlled movement worthy of a ballroom dancer. He had short gray hair, close-set eyes, and thin, taut lips. A jutting jaw gave him an air of belligerence. That, or listening to Ruby Bee dither about me as if I were the hottest thing since sliced bread.

"I'm Sterling Pitts," he said.

"Okay," I said, figuring he knew pretty much everything about me from kindergarten to court. "Would you like directions to the house Kayleen bought?"

"Eventually, but why don't you allow me to buy you a soda?"

I glanced at Ruby Bee, who was rolling her eyes and wiggling her mouth at me as though a bug was crawling up her back. "A beer sounds good," I said as I brushed past him and sat on a stool.

He frowned at the badge on my shirt. "Are you allowed to drink alcoholic beverages while on duty, Chief Hanks?"

"I'm not on duty," I said as I took off the badge and put it in my pocket. "My shift ended fifteen seconds ago when I decided to have a beer. I can deputize Kevin if the bank robbers show up."

Ruby Bee banged down a mug in front of me.

"Mind your mouth, Arly. General Pitts may not think you're as funny as you do."

"That's right," Estelle said as she came out of the ladies room and perched on her customary stool at the end of the bar, where she could eavesdrop without spilling her sherry. "What's more, you ought to take some interest in your appearance when you're on duty. I just got in a shipment of lipstick that might give you some color. Why don't you come by and let me give you a complimentary makeover?"

I ignored her. "You're a general?"

"It's really more of an honorary title," he said, flushing. "It was bestowed on me by the members of a group that I organized several years ago. We adopted military ranking in order to provide internal structure."

Ruby Bee gave him a disappointed look. "Oh, I thought you were a real general, like Eisenhower and Patton. Go ahead and tell Arly what you're aiming to do next week."

Pitts clearly was not pleased to have his rank dismissed so nonchalantly, but after a brief moment of pouting, he turned to me and said, "Please rest assured that our activities will take place outside your jurisdiction, Chief Hanks. Furthermore, we are law-abiding citizens with no desire to disrupt the community or cause alarm. We simply ask to be allowed to exercise our constitutional rights without undue interference."

It didn't sound as if he was planning to stage a beauty pageant to select Miss Stump County—or anything remotely that innocuous. Then again, he'd hardly tell me if he were plotting to overthrow the town council and put in a dictatorship (as if we'd notice).

"Just what do you have in mind?" I asked, setting down my beer in case I needed to put myself back on duty.

"I am the leader of a small group concerned about protecting the American way of life. We are preparing ourselves to fight back in the face of an invasion of foreign troops or even an attempt by the federal government to declare martial law and deprive us of our rights. Should push come to shove, we will not be led to the slaughterhouse like bleating sheep. We will resist."

"How are you preparing yourselves?"

Pitts gave me a smile that oozed superciliousness. "Through rigorous physical training, as well as education and networking with others who share our beliefs. We will establish an encampment at the far edge of

Kayleen's property in order to perform military maneuvers in the more rugged terrain on the ridge. We will perfect survival techniques in anticipation of the day when resources are controlled by the enemy. We will eat off the land."

Ruby Bee winced. "You're gonna eat roots and berries when you could have a nice blue-plate special right here? Wouldn't you prefer chicken-fried steak with cream gravy and your choice of three vegetables?"

"We are not ignorant savages," he said. "We will simply make do with game or fish, if necessary supplementing it with provisions brought with us. One of the women handles those duties while we focus on important matters."

"You can't make decent biscuits over a campfire," stated Ruby Bee, who clearly fancied herself to be an authority of the same stature as Julia Child.

He gazed coldly at her. "Sacrifices must be made in order to defend the Constitution of the United States of America."

When he didn't burst into the national anthem, I said, "I'm not sure it's wise to play G.I. Joe in the woods next week. Deer hunting season starts this Saturday. A lot of guys stick a bottle of bourbon in their pockets and go stumbling around, shooting at anything that twitches a whisker. There are one or two fatal accidents every year. I wouldn't set foot out there, even if Raz Buchanon offered to carry me piggyback to his still."

"You'd think so, wouldn't you?" I said without enthusiasm. After Ruby Bee had given him directions, no more complicated than left out of the parking lot, right on County 102, he marched out the door. I finished my beer and stood up. "Did Pitts say where

Pitts climbed off the stool and took a step back, his shoulders squared and that same damn smile on his face. "There are worse dangers than drunken hunters. Now, if you'll tell me how to find Kayleen's house, I will be on my way. I'm sure you have more important things to do than sit here and make idle conversation."

he lives when he's not stalking squirrels and godless communists?"

Estelle snorted. "Farberville. He owns an insurance agency."

"Then I hope he has a hefty life insurance policy," I said as I headed for the door.

"Do you think there's anything to what he said?" asked Ruby Bee. "Could the government up and take over the country?"

"About the time Marjorie sprouts wings," Estelle said with another snort.

I kept on walking.

Chapter 2

Brother Verber was slumped on the couch in the silver trailer that served as the rectory for the Voice of the Almighty Lord Assembly Hall. It was so small that it was a miracle he didn't run into himself in the hallway that led to the bathroom and bedroom. What's more, it lacked the cozy touches only a woman could provide, like doilies on the armrests and china knick-knacks on the table. The counter of the kitchen alcove was cluttered not with the makings for buttermilk biscuits, but with dirty dishes, crusted pots, and empty sacramental wine bottles.

It hadn't seemed so awful a week ago, when he was resigned to being a bachelor for the rest of his life. He had his pulpit and his congregation, his subscriptions to magazines that kept him informed of any new trends in sexual deviancy, and occasional trips to Little Rock to do personal research into such matters. Still, there'd been times when he wondered if he was missing something.

He put down the plastic tumbler to clasp his hands together and find out what, if anything, the Lord would think about all this. "Two are better than one because they have a good reward for their labor. For if they fall, the one will lift up his fellow, but woe to him that is alone when he falleth, for he hath not another to help him up.'" He paused, then added, "That'd be from Ecclesiastes, in case You couldn't quite put Your finger on it."

The Lord didn't seem to have a response, so Brother Verber went to the refrigerator and refilled his glass with the last of the wine. Rather than resuming his prayerful posture on the couch, he looked out the window at the Assembly Hall, a metal structure that bore a vague resemblance to the rectory. Kayleen had agreed to come to the Sunday morning service, but she hadn't promised to join his little flock on a permanent basis. He imagined her in the first pew, her face rosy with religious fervor and her skirt hitched up just far enough to permit a glimpse of her muscular thighs.

He took a handkerchief out of his bathrobe pocket and blotted his forehead. This wasn't anything to do with lust, he told himself. It had to do with warm, loving companionship as they traveled down the road to the Pearly Gates. There was nothing wrong with that, surely. They were both too old to go forth and multiply, but that didn't mean they couldn't partake in a few worldly pleasures of the flesh.

Sweat was dribbling into his ears and his eyes were glazed with the particulars of his fantasy when he heard a knock at the door. He shoved as many wine bottles as he could into the garbage bag under the sink, took a last swipe at his forehead, and opened the door.

"Why, Sister Barbara," he began in what he hoped was a voice of surprise and delight, "I wasn't expecting to see you this afternoon. Why don't you—"

"You're not dressed," Mrs. Jim Bob said as she swept past him. "Shouldn't you be out visiting the sick or over in the Assembly Hall working on your sermon? The devil finds work for idle hands, as you well know."

While she took off her coat, he snatched the tumbler off the kitchen table and stuck it in the nearest cabinet. "I was headed for the county nursing home this morning," he improvised, "but then I started feeling like I had a touch of the stomach flu. Not wanting to inflict my germs on those feeble old things, I came right home where I could pray for them without endangering their health."

"You do look kind of damp," she said as she sat

down on the couch. "If you're still feeling sickly tomorrow, I'll make a pot of chicken soup and bring it over here."

"You are so selfless," he said, sitting down next to her so he could pat her knee. "That's why you're such an inspiration to the congregation."

"I understand you've been doing some recruiting."

"It's my duty to bring sinners off the street and into the bosom of the Lord, Sister Barbara. I know for a fact that the angels burst into song whenever a lost soul finds salvation through prayer and Bible studies."

"I assume you remember how Jesus ran the moneylenders out of the temple, saying it had become a den of thieves. You wouldn't want that to happen at the Voice of the Almighty Lord Assembly Hall, would you?"

Brother Verber was more than a little mystified by her remark. "I should say not," he said, trying to sound emphatic. "In this sea of wickedness that surrounds us, the Assembly Hall is our lifeboat, and you, Sister Barbara, are right there at the helm beside me."

"I'm glad to hear we have an understanding." She removed his hand from her knee and picked up her purse. "I'll be by tomorrow with the soup."

"God bless you," he called as she went out the door, then retrieved his wine and watched her drive away in the pink Cadillac Jim Bob had bought for her after she found out about his relationship with a divorcée living at the Pot O' Gold trailer park.

Thinking about that reminded him of Kayleen, with her shapely figure and loving nature. He wouldn't rush her, of course, but instead give her time to learn to appreciate his finer qualities, like his compassion for the little heathen children in Africa, his spirituality, his sacrifices to battle Satan's soldiers.

Imbued with optimism as well as wine, he sat down on the couch and considered when it would be fitting for him to drop by the Flamingo Motel again. He'd give it a day or two, he decided as he took a swallow of wine and let it dribble down his throat like diluted honey.

* * *
* * *

The sun was shining the next morning, but the wind was frigid. I kept my hands in my coat pockets as I hurried across the road to the PD, accompanied only by skittering leaves and litter. As soon as I'd made coffee and was settled at my desk, I called the sheriff's department in Farberville and asked to speak to Harve Dorfer.

"Is there something goin' on out there?" asked La-Belle, the dispatcher. "More Martians?"

"No," I said, struggling to keep the irritation out of my voice. LaBelle covertly runs the department, deciding whose calls to put through and whose to leave indefinitely on hold. She was enough of a pain in the rear that I almost would have preferred voice mail: "If you're in the act of committing a felony, press one."

LaBelle sniffed. "Sheriff Dorfer's been real busy these last few days, what with the upcoming election and all. He's speaking at the Rotary meeting at noon about all the drug busts he's made in the last year, then he's supposed to—,"

"Just put him on, okay?"

"Yes, ma'am," she retorted, no doubt already plotting her revenge.

When Harve finally came on the line, he sounded as if he were rehearsing his speech. "Good to hear from you, Arly. It's important that law enforcement agents work together to keep crime out of Stump County so our children won't be sold drugs on the playgrounds and our senior citizens can sleep at night, knowing their houses won't be vandalized."

"Save it for the Rotarians," I said. "I need someone at your end to run a check on a guy named Sterling Pitts. I'd estimate his age at fifty-five to sixty, gray hair, a propensity for khaki. Purportedly, he has an insurance office over there."

Harve chuckled. "Sounds like a dangerous character. Did you nab him for running the stoplight?"

"He hasn't done anything—yet," I told him about the conversation in the bar the previous day, then added, "The last thing we need is a bunch of weekend warriors crawling around in the woods during deer season. You're not going to win any votes if half of them are carried out in body bags."

I heard the scritch of a match as he lit one of his infamously vile cigars. "You have a point," he said slowly, "but do we have a leg to stand on here? If they have the property owner's permission—and you're saying they do—I don't see what we can do about it. It may be stupid, but it's not against the law."

"Just check out this guy. Maybe we'll get lucky and find an outstanding warrant to dangle over his head. I don't care if they want to sleep in caves and eat bark for breakfast; I just don't want them doing it during deer season. We have to protect our reputation."

"Your reputation?" He guffawed as if I'd related a tasteless joke involving politicians and barnyard animals. "Are we talking about the same place that had Bigfoot sightings last spring?"

I waited until he quieted down. "Gawd, I'd forgotten about Diesel. The last I heard, he's still up on Cotter's Ridge, biting heads off rabbits and squirrels. He won't take kindly to being surprised by some wacko in an army helmet. And what about Raz? He keeps a shotgun in his truck in case he finds someone getting too close to his moonshine operation. How many stainless steel tables do they have at the morgue?"

"I reckon you've got yourself a problem," Harve admitted as he wheezily exhaled. "I'll check out this fellow when I get time, and I'll also have a word with the county prosecutor. It won't make a skeeter's ass of difference, but at least we'll have tried."

He promised to call me later, then barked at La-Belle to fetch him a fresh cup of coffee and hung up. I leaned back, propped my feet on the corner of the desk, and tried to remember if anybody else besides Diesel and Raz frequented the ridge. The high school kids preferred the gravel bars along Boone Creek for their beer binges; there were enough aluminum cans scattered in the weeds to support a recycling plant.

When the more mature philanderers desired privacy, they gravitated toward the trailers at the Pot O' Gold or the seedy motels at the edge of Farberville.

Cotter's Ridge was almost inaccessible by car; the steep, overgrown logging trails were rutted and often blocked by fallen trees. Robin Buchanon's shack remained standing (or leaning), and the odiferous outhouse behind it, but no one had lived there since she'd been murdered and her children dispersed by social workers. As far as I knew, Raz and Diesel had the ridge to themselves.

Until next week, anyway.

I shuffled through the mail, made a second pot of coffee, and examined the stain on the ceiling until my neck began to ache. I knew Harve wasn't going to call back anytime soon, but I wasn't in the mood to run a speed trap out past Purtle's Esso or lurk around the corner from our one and only stoplight. I wasn't in the mood to deal with Ruby Bee, either; she'd be in a dither because I hadn't shown up for breakfast. The last thing I needed was a lecture about common courtesy and the value of good nutrition (as if biscuits and sausage gravy were applauded by the surgeon general).

I finally decided to accept Kayleen's invitation to drop by the pawnshop and look at whatever material she claimed would lead to my enlightenment. The building that had once housed a New Age hardware store and then a short-lived "souvenir shoppe" was only a block away, but I took my car in case I spotted a getaway car idling in front of the charred remains of the branch bank. The radio rarely did more than snap, crackle, and pop, and the siren sounded like a dying donkey, but the heater was working for some mysterious reason.

I parked beside the Mercedes. There had been no grand opening as yet, but lights were on inside and presumably Kayleen was busily arranging her lethal display. In reality, the main room was barren and cluttered with the debris left by the previous occupant. I continued into the office, where I found Kayleen talking on the telephone.

"Hold on," she said into the receiver, then looked up at me. "Can I do something for you, Arly?"

"I'm hoping you'll answer some questions," I said.

"Sure." She told whomever she'd been talking to that she'd call later, then hung up and moved some files off a second chair. "I heard you met Sterling Pitts yesterday. Could that be why you have questions today?"

"You obviously have some sort of involvement with this paramilitary group Pitts mentioned. I'd like to know more about it."

"Sterling has an unfortunate tendency to get carried away when talking about what amounts to a small social club made up of people who enjoy camping. They don't exactly share the left-wing philosophy of the Sierra Club, but they're harmless. Otherwise, I wouldn't have agreed to allow them to use my property."

"Pitts was talking about military maneuvers," I said, unconvinced. "That tends to imply weapons."

"They use paint pellets instead of bullets. I've known Sterling for a good ten years, and I can promise you he and the others are no more sinister than your basic outdoors enthusiasts."

"Are you aware deer season starts Saturday?" I persisted. "Why is Pitts determined to do this at a time when the ridge is crawling with overgrown boys who can't see straight?"

"It's when most of them can get a few days off work. I'm not happy about it, either, but Sterling's the one who has to accept the responsibility if someone gets hurt. I'm just letting them use the back pasture."

"Then why let them use it?"

"Sterling can be as stubborn as a mule, and he kept badgering me until I agreed. In the past, they had a place over near Yellville, but the guy who owned the property got sent to jail for tax evasion and his wife refuses to let them come back. I don't think you should worry about this, Arly. They've been going out during deer season for the last five years, and nobody's ever had more than a bellyache from eating the wrong kind of berries."

"I wish you'd change your mind," I said. "They're risking not only the very real possibility of being mistaken for a buck, but also hypothermia, snakebite, and encounters with our local moonshiner and an unbalanced hermit—all so they can be prepared to defend themselves from a mythical foreign army."

"Sorry, but they're old enough to know their own minds, and they won't be breaking any laws. Sterling's always careful about that. Just ignore them. Nobody else in town will even know they're here, and at the end of the four days, they'll go back home to their microwave meals and warm beds."

I could tell I was wasting my breath, so I stood up. "You mentioned something yesterday about some material you wanted me to read."

She herded me toward the front door. "I do, but I forgot it's in a cardboard box in a storage cubicle over in Malthus. When I get everything hauled over here and sorted, I'll drop some tracts off at the police department." She accompanied me onto the porch and glanced at the silver trailer across the road. "He's an odd bird, isn't he?"

"Brother Verber? You could say that without any fear of being contradicted by anyone with a lick of sense, which includes everybody but the most witless of the Buchanons."

"He's kind of sweet, though," she continued thoughtfully. "Even though I was brought up Baptist, I said I'd come to the Sunday morning service. It's good to start putting down roots, meet my new neighbors, learn the local traditions. I'm glad I decided to move here. I think it's gonna work out real well."

It was not a sentiment often heard inside the city limits. I left her standing on the porch and drove out County 102 to make sure nobody had run off the low-water bridge or stolen the sign that continued to claim the population to be in the mid seven hundreds. It hadn't been changed since my high school days.

Not much else had, either.

Sterling Pitts was back in his office after lunch with his fellow Rotarians. Most of the time it didn't seem worth the trouble, but today he'd had a chance to get Lou Gerkin aside to discuss a group health proposal. Lou'd promised to think it over, which was all you could expect with a speaker droning on about drugs in the schools. As if drugs were the pivotal threat to society, Sterling thought with a sigh. One of these days the pudgy sheriff would be asking himself why he was living under martial law and taking orders from a member of an inferior race.

Missy came to the doorway. "Your wife called while you were out, Mr. Pitts. She said to tell you she's playing bridge tonight and won't be home till real late."

"Anybody else?" he asked, wondering what it'd take to convince the girl to write down messages on paper and leave them on his desk. She seemed to prefer to brief him as if she was a platoon leader.

"A man named Reed, but he wouldn't tell me his last name or what he wants. Is he a client?"

"No, Missy, he's a mechanic at the garage where I take my car. He's got an estimate for some repairs. Now go call the home office and find out what claims adjuster we're supposed to use while Durmont's laid up. And shut the door, please."

He waited until a button lit up on the telephone, then utilized a second line to dial a number that was answered not at a garage, but at a squalid apartment.

"I told you not to call my office," he began grimly. "Security is essential to our success. Your line could be tapped at this very moment."

"Yeah, but I got to talk to you, Pitts."

"I'll be home alone tonight. Park down the block and come in through the back door. I'm beginning to suspect my house is being kept under surveillance; an unfamiliar car has been parked across the street periodically for the last week."

"Then why don't we meet someplace else? My place, or at a bar or something? It's not going to help our cause if the feds link the two of us."

"Come to the house at 2200 hours." Sterling banged down the receiver, frustrated by the necessity of dealing with those of so little discipline. How many times had he stressed the need to follow the procedures laid out in the manual? Calls were to be made only from telephones known to be safe. Names were never used in communications, only designated code words, but Red Rooster had said Pitts's name in the course of the brief conversation. Of course the feds could figure it out without too much trouble, since Reed had dialed the number of Pitts's Tri-County Patriots' Insurance Services.

Instead of plunging back into group health policies or paperwork from the state commission, Pitts opened his drawer and took out a slim book. *The Ruger 1022 Exotic Weapons Systems* was as soothing as a glass of warm milk. Smiling, he flipped to the chapter on how to transform a Ruger 1022 into a selective-fire, close-combat gun—*all without modifying the receiver or trigger housing in any way!*

Reed "Red Rooster" Rondly was staring at the blank television screen when Barry "Apocalypse" Kirklin came into the apartment and dropped a six-pack of beer on the scarred coffee table.

"Thought you was supposed to work late today," Reed said as he leaned forward to wrench a beer out of the plastic holder.

"What the hell difference does it make to you? Oh, I get it—Martha Stewart's coming over to give you some decorating tips for Thanksgiving."

"Who?"

Barry opened a beer, then went into the kitchen to look for something to eat that wasn't covered in fuzzy blue mold. "God, you're a pig," he said as he came back to the living room with a bag of chips. "I don't know how Bobbi Jo put up with you as long as she did. You heard from her since she got to her parents', house?"

"I don't want to talk about her—okay? She's gonna be real sorry she went off like that, taking the car and the VCR. She probably would have taken the refrigerator if she could have figured out how to jam it in the backseat."

Barry flinched as his friend crumpled the beer can and threw it at the television set. Reed was a couple of inches shorter than he, but considerably more muscular and prone to getting into brawls with frat boys slumming at places like the Dew Drop Inn and the Exotica Club. They'd both gone into the army straight from high school; four years later Barry'd come out with a healthy regard for self-preservation. Reed had come out with a dishonorable discharge and the disposition of a junkyard dog. They were both pushing thirty years old. Barry worked at a bookstore, while Reed drifted from garage to garage, getting his sorry self fired for drinking on the job or coming in late. Or not coming in at all.

Reed opened another beer. "There's a new guy at the garage, name of Dylan Gilbert, not more than twenty-two or twenty-three years old, and scrawny as a free-range chicken. He doesn't know shit about American cars, but he's pretty good with Jap imports."

"Fascinating," Barry said as he moved a stack of old gun magazines from a chair and sat down.

"He needs a place to crash, so I told him he could stay here until he finds something."

"And?"

"And he says he was with that group in Colorado until a month ago when he heard a warrant had been issued."

Barry shook his head. "Did he just happen to tell you this when you two went outside for a smoke?"

"Yeah," Reed said grudgingly, "something like that. We was standing next to my pickup, and he took to admiring the modified shotgun on the rack. He was real impressed when I said I'd done the work myself, and then we got to talking about weapons in general. He converted an SKS rifle to an automatic that uses AK-47 magazines. He went on to say he'd had to sell it before he left town, and that's what led to him telling me about the warrant. Seems he sent an early Christmas present to a judge, but a hotshot at the post office called the bomb squad. Somehow or other they traced it back to Dylan."

"I hope you didn't reciprocate by spilling your guts to him," Barry said with a dark look. "He sounds like he's got a big mouth and a propensity for sharing secrets with strangers. The last thing we need is for him to have too many beers and start talking about our operation to anyone who'll listen."

"I didn't say shit about anything to him, but I'm going over to Pitts's house tonight to discuss this guy with him. Since Bradley got thrown in the state prison, Carter Lee upped and disappeared, and Mo got gunned down by thievin', mongrels, we're down to what—four members? The women are useful, but I wouldn't share a fox hole with either of them. A bed, maybe, but you can't trust women in combat. God put 'em on this planet to bear children, which is why they're as useless as tits on a boar hog when the going gets rough." He opened yet another beer and drained half of it, ignoring the dribbles on his chin. "I came home one night and found Bobbi Jo bawling on account of she'd spilled her fingernail polish on the bedspread. Jesus!"

"The manual says the optimum number for a cell is ten. That doesn't mean we ought to stand on the corner and pass out application forms to anyone who walks by."

"Yeah," said Reed, back to staring at the blank screen.

Barry left to find something to eat in one of the dives along Thurber Street. Although usually alert, he failed to notice the figure sitting in a small car parked across the road from the apartment building.

Chapter 3

Estelle pranced across the dance floor, her heels clattering like castanets, and fidgeted impatiently on the stool at the end of the bar while Ruby Bee finished filling two mugs from the tap and took them to Jim Bob Buchanon and Roy Stiver.

Ruby Bee was grumbling as she came back behind the bar. "I swear, I don't know how men can talk as much as they do about deer season. You'd think they were out to get a buried treasure instead of a flea-ridden old buck. Those two"—she jerked her thumb at the corner booth—"have been jabbering for more than an hour. If they'd spend half as much time earning a living as they do talking about dogs—"

"I had a real interesting letter this morning," Estelle said, unable to restrain herself. Beaming, she took a folded piece of paper out of her purse. "It's from a lawyer over in Oklahoma."

"Since when do you know any lawyers in Oklahoma?"

"Since I got this letter this morning." She paused while she unfolded it and smoothed it out on the surface of the bar. "His name is Chester W. Corsair, and his office is in Muskogee."

Ruby Bee gazed blandly at her, then shifted her attention to Jim Bob and Roy. "You boys want some pretzels or a couple of pickled eggs?" she called, knowing full well Estelle was close to bubbling over with excitement. However, it was *her* bar and grill, not Estelle's, and she could do as she pleased when it came to earning a living.

Instead of answering, Jim Bob dropped a few dollars on the table, and he and Roy walked out of the bar, still deep in conversation about how many bottles of whiskey and bologna sandwiches they'd need.

When the door closed, Ruby Bee said, "Does this Mr. Corsair want you to go to law school and become his partner, or is somebody suing you for wrongful hair?"

Estelle decided to be magnanimous about this petty display of poor manners. "Do you recall me talking about my Uncle Tooly?"

"I recall a little about him. Didn't he marry a one-eyed widow woman with a lot of money?"

"You'd think one eye would be enough to see he was nothing but a skinny old geezer with more hair poking out of his ears than on his head, but she married him anyway. They lived in her fancy house on Lake Eufaula until she died. Then he bought himself a farm way out in the middle of nowhere and took to experimenting."

"Experimenting in what?" asked Ruby Bee, thinking of Dr. Frankenstein's laboratory with its blinking lights and body parts scattered around the floor. "Why doncha stop telling me his life story and get to the point, Estelle? It's nigh onto three o'clock, and I haven't finished cleaning up the kitchen so I can sit a spell and work on my column. Writing a weekly column ain't like making a grocery list, you know, and I have to turn it in by noon tomorrow if it's gonna appear in the *Shopper* on Saturday."

Estelle folded up the letter. "Why don't I wait until tomorrow evening to tell you the rest of it? I'd feel just awful if I interfered with scrubbing pots and writing about who's been in the hospital. Maybe I'll run by Elsie's for a cup of coffee and a nice visit. She's not as busy as some folks."

"Just tell me."

"Well, the letter says how Uncle Tooly was attacked by sheep in his front yard. He—"

"Sheep?" said Ruby Bee, snickering. "That's the silliest thing I've heard in my entire life. It sounds like one of those yarns Samsonite Buchanon would spin to anyone fool enough to listen. He could have been a regular guest on the *Geraldo* show."

"While Uncle Tooly was trying to get away, he fell and broke his hip. Three days later a neighbor happened to drive by and spot him sprawled in the grass, but it was too late for Uncle Tooly. His mouth was full of fleece. He'd died of dehydration and shock not fifty feet from a telephone."

"I'd sure go into shock if I was attacked by sheep. Was it a flock—or a gang?"

Estelle gave her a reproachful look. "We are talking about my kinfolk, one of whom passed away in a most tragic manner. I'd appreciate it if you could show some respect."

"Sorry," Ruby Bee murmured, reluctantly forgoing a remark about a "drive-by bleating." "Does this letter from the lawyer mean your uncle remembered you in his will?"

"Yes, it does. It doesn't say exactly what Uncle Tooly wanted me to have. He gave all his money to charities, so all I'm expecting is an heirloom of some sort. It's kind of exciting, though."

"What's exciting?" Kayleen asked as she came across the dance floor and joined them at the bar.

Estelle explained about the letter, adding, "I don't recall him having a coin or stamp collection, so it's liable to be a mantel clock or a ship in a bottle or a carton of family albums. The letter said it'll be delivered next week."

"How's the remodeling coming along?" Ruby Bee asked Kayleen, since there wasn't much point in discussing Estelle's inheritance till they found out what it was.

"The walls have been stripped of that cheap paneling and some boards in the floor have been replaced. All the wiring will have to be redone, though, and a lot of pipes are so rusty the water comes out like silt. I have a feeling I'll spend a goodly part of the next six months in the motel out back. That reminds me, Ruby Bee—I need to book a room for Sterling Pitts."

Estelle cocked her head. "I thought he was all gung

ho about surviving in the woods. The Flamingo Motel's not much to look at, but it has your standard conveniences like hot water and clean sheets. The parking lot's hardly what you'd call rugged terrain."

"He needs a telephone and a place to set up a computer," Kayleen said. "Most of the time he'll be in the woods, but he likes to stay in communication with his office in case there's an emergency. To be honest, I don't think he's real thrilled about sleeping in a tent in this kind of weather. He's close to sixty and has spells of rheumatism."

Ruby Bee struggled not to sound sarcastic, but she didn't have much luck. "So he sleeps in a nice warm bed while the other fellows freeze their butts up on Cotter's Ridge? What do they think about it?"

"I don't rightly know." Kayleen took a pretzel from a basket and nibbled on it for a moment. "Can I ask y'all something of a different nature? I'm a little curious about Brother Verber. Is he originally from these parts? Do you know anything about his background and his family?"

Estelle and Ruby Bee smirked at each other, then Ruby Bee said, "He's been here for maybe ten years. Before that, I don't know where he was living, but you might ask Mrs. Jim Bob. You can be as sure as a goose goes barefoot that she knows every last detail of his life up to the time he moved into the rectory."

"I ran into her at the supermarket," Kayleen said with a wry smile, "and I have a feeling she won't tell me the time of day. She went right by me with her nose in the air and her lips squeezed tight, then made a production of telling someone in the next aisle that a pawnshop was nothing more than a gathering place for drug dealers and rapists. I can't imagine why she took such a dislike to me right off the bat, but she did. I felt like I had bad breath or oozing sores all over my face and hands."

Estelle decided to help out Ruby Bee, who clearly was having trouble finding a response. "Mrs. Jim Bob takes her role as the mayor's wife real serious, not to mention being president of the Missionary Society.

She thinks everybody should get her permission before they sneeze so she can make sure they have a clean hankie."

Ruby Bee nodded. "And she's suspicious of single women because she knows her husband strays with every hussy in Stump County. If he had a notch in his belt for every one of them, his trousers would be around his ankles and he'd be waddlin' like a duck."

"I prefer men with Christian values," Kayleen said firmly. "Men who come from solid Anglo-Saxon stock and are loyal and trustworthy, dedicated to their beliefs."

"Like Sterling Pitts?" suggested Ruby Bee. Matchmaking was one of her favorite hobbies, and she'd about given up on Arly.

"Sterling's married, so as far as I'm concerned, he's ineligible. There's no chance Brother Verber has a wife stashed away somewhere, is there?"

"I shouldn't think so," said Estelle. She stopped and thought for a moment, then said, "Unless she's in an insane asylum or prison. I don't suppose he'd say anything that might reflect poorly on him as a man of God."

Ruby Bee scooted the pretzels out of Estelle's reach. "That's hornswoggle—and you know it. Brother Verber may have his faults, but I can't see him leaving some pathetic woman locked up all these years. Why, he got all misty at Kevin and Dahlia's wedding, and had to stop and blow his nose at least three times before he pronounced them man and wife. He almost single-handedly raised the money to put a baptismal font in the Assembly Hall after one of the ladies in the choir got chased across a gravel bar by a water moccasin down at Boone Creek." She racked her brain for other examples of his worthiness, not because she had all that much respect for him but to impress Kayleen. "He collects discarded clothes and spectacles to send to a mission in Africa, too."

"That ain't all he collects," Estelle inserted.

"Hush, Estelle," Ruby Bee said sharply, possibly because she was still smarting over the comment about the Flamingo Motel not being much to look at. "Tell you what, Kayleen—if I run across Mrs. Jim Bob, I'll tactfully see what I can find out about Brother Verber's past. Are you planning to attend the Sunday morning service?"

"I said I would." Kayleen slid off the stool and waggled her fingers at them. "I'd appreciate it if y'all didn't mention that I was asking questions about Brother Verber. I've lived in enough small towns to know how tongues get to wagging. I need to run along and make some calls." She paused in the middle of the dance floor and looked back at them. "You two are just being so sweet to me. Once I get the house fixed up, I'll have you over for supper so we can get to know each other even better."

Ruby Bee and Estelle smiled brightly until she was gone, then set aside their differences and got down to business discussing how to find out whatall they could about Brother Verber's past. It had never before been of interest, but now it was downright intriguing.

As Eileen Buchanon drove out of the clinic parking lot and headed toward Maggody, she glanced at her daughter-in-law. Dahlia was downcast, but no more than usual these days. Being pregnant was harder on her than it'd been on Eileen, what with the strict diet and exercise program to control her blood sugar. They'd had a real scare when Dahlia had allowed a faith healer to convince her the diabetes had been cured, but his exposure as a quack had brought her to her senses. What there were of them, anyway.

"What did the doctor say?" Eileen asked as she slowed down for a chicken truck.

Dahlia sighed so gustily that the windshield fogged up. "Same as he always sez, I reckon. I got to keep pricking my finger and writing down the numbers in my notebook. I haft to come back next week so he can poke my privates. He's still harping about this test called a sonogram, but I ain't gonna allow it on account of it turns the baby into a mutant with the wrong number of arms and legs and eyes. No one's doin' that to my baby."

"The doctor wouldn't suggest something like that."

"He brings it up at every visit," she said, her chins quivering with distress and her placid expression turning fierce. "I signed a paper saying I refused to do it, and I meant it!"

Eileen finally got around the chicken truck and pressed the accelerator. "What makes you think this test would do the terrible things you said?"

"I read about it in the newspaper. Would you stop at that gas station over there? My bladder's liable to burst if I don't git to a potty real quick."

Eileen obliged, then glumly watched Dahlia disappear through a doorway on the side of the concrete block building. Other than the diabetes, which was under control, Dahlia seemed healthy and had gained no more weight than the doctor had allowed. Women had been giving birth for thousands of years without complicated tests, and a good number of them were doing so these days. It was probably better not to cause Dahlia more distress by pressuring her to have a sonogram or anything else she didn't want. It was hard enough keeping her away from what she *did* want.

Jake "Blitzer" Milliford opened the closet door and squatted down to paw through the shoes on the floor. "Where're my boots?" he shouted at his wife, who was in the kitchen.

"Wherever you dropped them," Judy shouted back, more concerned with the cornbread in the oven and the beans in a pot on the stove. "Did you leave 'em on the back porch?"

He slammed the door and started hunting under the bed. "When's the last time you cleaned under here—Easter?"

She gave the beans a stir, then turned off the burner and came to the doorway. She was small-boned and barely came up to his shoulder, but living with him for twenty-three years had thickened her skin. It had also etched some wrinkles in her pretty face and turned some brown hairs gray, as well as extinguishing a good deal of what had once shone through her eyes.

"Maybe you left them in the back of the truck," she suggested, "or in the toolshed."

"Bullshit."

"You ought to look anyway," she said, fully aware the boots were in the hall closet, where she'd put them after he left them on the kitchen table.

Jake got up off the floor and hitched up his worn, greasy jeans. "I ain't got time for a damn scavenger hunt. LaRue is pickin' me up as soon as he gets off work. He bought hisself a new laser sight for his Glock, and he wants to test it over at his brother's place."

"You don't need your boots for that, do you?"

He gave her a disgusted look. "No, I don't need my boots for that. I need 'em next week for the retreat. We'll leave for Maggody on Friday afternoon, soon as I can get away from the salvage yard. Shorty wasn't real happy with me missing work, but he shut up when I pointed out that everybody else'll call in sick all week long on account of deer season. At least I'm givin' him some warning."

"Were you aiming to mention this beforehand or was it supposed to be a surprise?"

He brushed past her and went into the front room to see if LaRue was out in the driveway. "Yeah, I was aiming to mention it beforehand," he muttered under his breath, then raised his voice. "When you find my boots, clean 'em up and set 'em on the back porch. While you're at it, see if the sleeping bags need to be hung out on the clothesline. Last summer I spilled some fish guts on one of them and it's liable to stink worse than a buzzard's roost by now. And check the cooking supplies. I ain't gonna be pleased if I have to drive back to Emmett because you forgot your pancake turner."

"What makes you think I'm going with you next week, Jake? I've got better things to do than sit around all day in a drafty tent and cook over a campfire. Friday evening I have a church bazaar committee meeting. I told Janine that I'd keep the baby on Saturday so she can get her hair cut and do a little shopping. She hasn't been out of the house in six weeks, and that fat lout she married won't even change a diaper."

"He puts groceries on the table, doesn't he? Janine's a whiner, same as you. It's gonna be cold and wet out at the campsite, and we need better than those gawdawful ready-to-eat meals. Janine doesn't have any call to waste her husband's hard-earned money on a hair cut. She can get a pair of scissors and whack it off herself."

Judy thought of something she'd like to whack off with a pair of scissors, but he most likely wouldn't appreciate hearing it. "Who all is going this time?"

"Who all is going?" he said in a falsetto, mocking her. "Do you think Pitts invited the cheerleaders over at the junior high and all the sumbitch politicians down in Little Rock? Same as last year, except for Carter Lee and Bradley. We figure we can dig up ol' Mo and prop him against a tent pole. It's not like we'd be able to tell the difference." He looked out the window, then took his jacket off a hook and made sure the can of Red Man was in the pocket. "LaRue's here. After we test the sight, we'll probably stop by the Dew Drop for a couple of beers. Don't wait up."

After she heard the truck back out of the driveway, Judy took the vodka bottle out from behind the cereal boxes, poured some in a glass and added a splash of orange juice, then returned to the living room to make a call.

She listened to the phone ring, instinctively smoothing her hair as if the person who picked up the receiver could see her. "Jake just now told me that retreat's set for next weekend," she began in a breathless voice.

On Saturday I could hear gunfire in the distance as I finished writing up a report for Harve about a motorcycle wreck out by what the high school kids called

"Dead Man's Swerve." The driver hadn't been wearing a helmet, but since he was a Buchanon, landing on his head had done no perceptible damage. I'd had to explain this to the paramedic, who was concerned when the cyclist couldn't say for sure how many fingers the paramedic was holding up.

Deer season had officially started. I put down my gnawed pencil and opened a drawer to ascertain I had enough blank forms to survive the next three weeks. The previous year there'd been two wrecks out by the low-water bridge, a half-dozen DWIs, three instances involving nonfatal shootings, and one fatal shooting. Harve and I had agreed the last was suspicious, since the victim had been dating his companion's ex-wife, but there was no way to prove anything.

Earlier in the day Harve had called with the scoop on Sterling Pitts, which amounted to zilch. No rap sheet, no outstanding warrants, no entanglements with the law more serious than parking violations. A year ago Pitts had complained to the police about a neighbor's dog, and more recently about black teenagers loitering in his parking lot in the afternoons. All in all, he was a law-abiding citizen and a successful businessman, and there wasn't a damn thing I could do to keep him out of Maggody.

I was getting ready to take the accident report to the sheriff's office (and maybe take myself to a matinee) when the door opened and in stalked Raz Buchanon, a successful businessman if not precisely a law-abiding citizen. As always, he was wearing bib overalls stained with tobacco juice and other unidentifiable substances. His whiskers were caked with the remnants of meals from the previous decade, and what remained of his gray hair glistened with grease.

"I got to talk to you," he said as he plopped down in the chair and scratched his chin.

"And how are you today, Raz? Enjoying the last of the autumn foliage?"

"That ain't what I come here to talk about."

I rocked back in my chair, but there was no way short of going out the door to avoid his sour stench.

"How's Marjorie these days? Is she snuffling up tasty acorns and hickory nuts?"

Raz let out a wheeze that engulfed me in a toxic haze. "Marjorie ain't doin' well. She's a pedigreed sow, ye know, and has a delicate nature. Lately she's taken to moping around the house, sprawled in the corner instead of in front of the television, turning up her snout at most ever'thing she used to gobble down. Why, yesterday evening she wouldn't take one bite of turnip greens."

"Did you fix them with ham hocks?" I asked.

He gave me a horrified look. "I'd never do something like that! That'd be like her eating kin. No, ma'am, I don't even use lard anymore." He resumed scratching his chin and sighing. "I reckon the problem she's bein' crumpy is on account of that dad-burned cousin of mine. You know about Diesel livin' up on the ridge?"

"Actually, I do."

"Well, used to be Marjorie'd wander around while I was,"—he hesitated, obviously not wanting to confess to a felony right there in the PD—"huntin' squirrels or pickin' poke salet, but the other day she must've got too close to Diesel's cave. The next thing I knew, she came trotting as hard as she could into the clearing, her eyes all round and her ears pasted back, and squealing somethin' awful. Afore I could figure out what in tarnation was goin' on, Diesel charged right into me and liked to knock me plumb out of my boots."

I clucked sympathetically. "I don't know what to tell you, Raz. There aren't a lot of veterinarians trained to deal with traumatized sows, pedigreed or otherwise. All I can suggest is that you leave Marjorie at home when you go fiddle with your still."

"Who sez I got a still?" he said, puffing up indignantly.

"Get off it, Raz. Everybody in the damn county knows you have a still up on the ridge. One of these days the revenuers are going to locate it and reduce it to a pile of scrap metal. Moonshining's a federal offense. That means you'll be up in Leavenworth instead of enjoying the company of your relatives at the state pen."

His rheumy eyes met mine. "I ain't got a still and ain't nobody gonna find it. What do you aim to do about Diesel? He's got no call to scare Marjorie like that, or me, fer that matter."

"I'm not going to do anything," I said, shaking my head. "If you don't have business on Cotter's Ridge, stay off it. You and Marjorie shouldn't be there during deer season, anyway. Neither of you resembles a buck, but that doesn't cut any mustard with a bullet fired from a mile away." I stood up in hopes he'd take the hint and leave, but he remained seated, glowering like a jack o' lantern well past its prime. "Something else?" I asked.

"I heard there's gonna be some fellers dressed in soldier clothes crawling all over the ridge."

"There's nothing I can do about that, either. It's going to be crowded up there next week, Raz. Take my advice and stay away."

I held open the door and tried not to grimace as he shuffled past me and climbed into a muddy truck. The thought of Sterling Pitts and his followers had given me the stirrings of a headache; Raz's redolence had escalated it to the quintessence. The report I'd planned to take to Farberville could wait until Monday. In the interim, I was going to crawl into bed, cram a pillow over my head, and imagine what it would be like to be somewhere else.

Anywhere else.

On the far side of Stump County, Sterling sat in his Bronco, drumming his fingers on the steering wheel and watching raindrops slither down the windshield like transparent slugs. He was parked at one of their carefully chosen meeting places, a farm that had been abandoned more than ten years ago. The windows of the house were as vacant as a dead man's eyes, and the rusted screen door groaned as the wind dragged it across the surface of the porch.

Sterling reminded himself he was not the sort to entertain irrational notions about ghosts. He was organized, efficient, decisive, truly a general's general. The fact that his underlings were so ill-disciplined was disturbing; he made a mental note to require them to study their manuals and the additional guidelines he'd typed up and stapled to the back covers. After all, the Second Amendment stressed the need for a "well-regulated" militia as necessary to the security of a free state.

He pulled back his cuff to look at his watch. Red Rooster had agreed to be there at 1700. It was now 1720, and Sterling was growing increasingly peevish. It was cold, damp, and getting dark. His wife was expecting him to come straight home from his office to escort her to some fool dinner party. She had no idea what he did in his free time, but it was getting harder to come up with lies about conventions in other cities and emergency meetings at the office.

Muttering to himself, he switched on the ignition and prepared to leave. Before he could back up, however, a pickup truck came up the weedy driveway and stopped.

Reed climbed out of the driver's side and came around to the car. "So, did you check him out?" he asked loudly.

Sterling could smell the beer on Red Rooster's breath. "I do not care to be kept waiting while you and your friend are drinking beer in a bar somewhere. Were you also shooting off your yaps about our activities? Should I expect a carful of ATF agents to pull up next?"

"Naw, we just stopped off for a quick one on the way out here. Wasn't nobody else in the joint except for a bony hooker, and she was talking the whole time on her cell phone." He put his hand on the roof of the car and blearily smiled down at Sterling. "Did you hear back from Colorado?"

Sterling glanced at the young man in the pickup who was staring at the ramshackle farmhouse. "Yes, I communicated with the second-in-command in their group.

He acknowledged that Dylan Gilbert had been with them for eighteen months before getting into trouble with the authorities in Denver. Apparently, he's quite adept with electronic surveillance equipment."

Reed turned and thumped the truck window. "Hey, Dylan, you fucker, you never told me you were a bug-meister."

Dylan rolled down the window, looked coolly at Pitts, and said, "I majored in electrical engineering for two years before I dropped out of college. What's the verdict? If I'm not welcome, I'll find another group someplace where the weather's not so shitty."

"Well?" Reed said to Sterling.

"The procedure," he said through clenched teeth, "is for the cell to interrogate a potential recruit before taking action. I for one have questions about why he came here and chose to make contact with you instead of having his former commander contact me through proper channels. I also need time to verify his credentials. Then, if we are unanimous in our decision to accept him, he will be inducted as soon as possible. Until that time, he can participate in the training, but he will not be present at sessions of a more tactical nature."

Reed grinned at Dylan. "That okay?"

"Exactly what I anticipated," Dylan answered without inflection. He pushed long black hair out of his eyes and stared at Sterling. "I've got some questions of my own, Pops. I don't want to get hooked up with a bunch of guys who are liable to spill secrets to the nearest undercover cop. I've got the FBI searching for me, and not so they can wish me a happy Thanksgiving. With my juvenile rap sheet and a few minor felonies since then, I'm looking at up to forty years."

Sterling bristled. "You have no fear of indiscretion from this group," he said sternly (if somewhat mendaciously, considering his previous thoughts). "We are highly disciplined and tight-lipped."

"Gotta take a wiz," Reed announced, then stumbled into the darkness.

Dylan waited until Reed was out of sight, then gave Sterling a contemptuous smile. "Then aren't you concerned about the informant in your group?"

From *The Starley City Star Shopper*, November 8:

What's Cooking in Maggody?

BY RUBELLA BELINDA HANKS

This column is going to be short on account of nobody much bothered to share any news with me, even though I'm right here in Ruby Bee's Bar & Grill from morning till midnight, fixing everything from grits and redeye gravy to fried chicken and scalloped potatoes. The food's tasty, and the price is right.

Mrs. Twayblade out at the county old folks' home reports the residents spent a real nice afternoon making turkeys out of pine cones and colored paper to decorate their tables on Thanksgiving. Everybody enjoyed themselves except for Petrol Buchanon, who had to be sent to his room after he pinched a nurse's aide on her fanny.

Estelle Oppers is all excited about an inheritance from her Uncle Tooly, who was killed by sheep. It's supposed to arrive sometime this week. She said to tell everybody that she has a big assortment of fingernail polish and lipsticks at bargain prices, and her ten-percent discount on perms will run until December 24.

There's still no date for the grand opening of Smeltner's Pawn Palace, but Kayleen says she should be in business by the end of the year. Progress is just as slow on her remodeling out on County 102 because all the workmen are off deer hunting instead of showing up like they promised.

Arly Hanks, our chief of police, asked me to remind hunters that not wearing bright orange is against the law, just like hunting on property that's been posted. If you're over in Farberville, stop by the sheriff's department to pick up a free pamphlet with tips on gun safety.

Until next time, God bless.

GARLIC CHEESE GRITS

6 cups water
2 teaspoons salt
1 ½ cups grits
2 teaspoons (or more) garlic powder
¼ teaspoon cayenne pepper
1 stick butter
3 eggs, beaten
1 pound grated cheddar cheese

Bring the water to a boil, add the salt, and slowly stir in the grits. Cook according to the directions on the box. Add the rest of the ingredients, stir real well until the butter melts, then pour into a buttered baking dish. Bake 1 hour and 15 minutes, or until the top is puffy and golden.

Chapter 4

"Maybe you should call that Oklahoma lawyer," Ruby Bee said as she tied a scarf on her head and studied the effect in the bathroom mirror. "For all you know, he could be sending some of those killer sheep. You can't just let them run around your living room."

Her only response was a snort from the living room. Estelle had come by to take her to the Sunday morning service at the Assembly Hall, but she'd shown up ten minutes early and was being all persnickety because Ruby Bee hadn't been standing in the parking lot and ready to leap into the station wagon as it rolled by.

Estelle finally relented. "I thought about it, but I don't want to run up my long distance bill. I don't have more than two or three appointments this coming week, one of 'em for nothing but a trim. All I can say is, there are going to be some mighty scruffy folks eating turkey and cranberries this year."

"I suppose it can't hurt to wait," Ruby Bee said as she came into the living room and put on her coat. "There's a lot of that going around. Kayleen's waiting on the plumber, Dahlia and Kevin are waiting on the stork, customers at the SuperSaver are waiting on themselves since all the employees are deer hunting, Antwon Buchanon's waiting on his roof for a chariot to swing low and carry him home, and Arly's waiting for the first casualty on Cotter's Ridge. I'm waiting to find out what the IRS is going to do when they don't get my fourth quarterly payment."

"Is that what's been bothering you?" asked Estelle, pulling on her gloves.

Ruby Bee opened the door, then recoiled as the wind snatched at her scarf. "I reckon so. If business doesn't pick up, I'm not going to have two dimes to rub together on New Year's Day. It's not like Arly can loan me enough to tide me over, either. When I told her that she needed a warmer coat, she just laughed and said something about saving up for mink. One of these days . . ."

"She'll leave?"

Ruby Bee waited to answer until they were settled in Estelle's station wagon and the heater was on. "I'm surprised she's stayed so long. There aren't but a scattering of people her age, and they're married and busy with babies. I can't remember when she last mentioned that nice state trooper, or even hinted that she was seeing somebody on the sly. The light's on in her apartment most every night. It ain't natural."

They drove to the Assembly Hall, but after some discussion about not getting caught in traffic after the service, decided to park across the road in front of the soon-to-be Pawn Palace.

Estelle gestured at the dark interior. "You spoken to her lately?"

"No, I haven't laid eyes on her since she was in the bar and grill the other day when you were talking about Uncle Tooly's will. I guess she's been out at the Wockermann place, trying to do the carpentry work herself. It burns me up how every male in the county that's over the age of ten sees nothing wrong with forgetting about work in order to go deer hunting. It's a good thing doctors don't feel the same way."

"Or lawyers," added Estelle, wondering if Uncle Tooly might have set aside some stocks and bonds in her name because of the homemade cookies she sent every year at Christmas. Blue chips in exchange for chocolate chips, in a manner of speaking.

Ruby Bee pointed at the front of the Assembly Hall. "Well, look who got himself dragged to church this morning. I'd have thought Jim Bob would be up on the ridge in the trailer that he, Roy, and Larry Joe use as a deer camp. You can tell from the way he's walking that he hasn't worn those dress shoes in a good while, and his collar looks tight enough to choke the cud out of a cow. Do you think Mrs. Jim Bob finally put the fear of God in him?"

"Right now she looks like she could put the fear of God in most anybody, including ol' Satan himself," Estelle replied. "Did you ever get a chance to ask her about Brother Verber's mysterious past?"

"There is nothing mysterious about his past, Estelle. We just don't know anything about it. No, I haven't tried to worm the details out of her as of yet. I saw her in the SuperSaver, but she was being so crabby with the checkout girl that I figured it wasn't a good time."

They joined the stream of souls heading into the foyer and found seats toward the back so they could be the first out the door after the closing "Amen." After nodding to Earl and Eileen and a few other folks, Ruby Bee whispered, "There's Kayleen in the second pew. Brother Verber must have nagged her into coming."

"Or sweet-talked her into it," Estelle whispered back, then resumed speculating about her inheritance. Maybe a deed to a piece of acreage she could sell for a tidy sum, or even a set of china or expensive silverware. Uncle Tooly had once owned a fancy antique car; his one-eyed wife might have given him another one as a wedding present. Or a mantel clock, she reminded herself.

Eula Lemoy pounded out the opening hymn, which was kind of hard to recognize and downright impossible to sing along with. Folks coughed and sneezed through the announcements, the passing of the collection plate, and a solo sung by an atonal teenaged girl. Brother Verber presided from his folding chair set to one side, alternately smiling at the congregation and wincing at the sour notes. At one point, Ruby Bee thought he winked, but decided it was more likely a gnat got in his eye.

Eventually, the girl ran out of steam, curtsied, and scurried to her seat. Brother Verber stood up, stuck out what chin he had, and walked to the lectern as if he were leading a processional to the guillotine.

"Brothers and sisters," he said, dragging out the words as he made eye contact with as many folks as he could, "I have in my possession some information that is so startling that you may think it came from a tabloid. Some of you will laugh at what I'm gonna share with you this morning. Some of you will sneer. Some of you, like Earl Buchanon and Lewis Ferncliff, will snooze through the sermon same as you do every Sunday morning. But those of you who listen with an open mind are gonna be shocked. That's right, brothers and sisters—*shocked!*"

Uneasiness rippled through the congregation as they prepared themselves for this electrifying revelation. Earl sat up straight so everybody could see he was wide-awake. Lottie Estes settled her reading glasses on the bridge of her nose, then took a pad and pencil from her purse in case she needed to take notes. Dahlia sighed, wondering if Brother Verber was gonna carry on so long she'd wet her pants. Ruby Bee and Estelle wiggled their eyebrows at each other.

Brother Verber cleared his throat and scanned his notes one last time. "We're gonna begin with a passage from Genesis, chapter twelve, verses one through three: 'Now the Lord had said unto Abraham, Get thee out of thy country, and from thy kindred, and from thy father's house, unto a land that I will shew thee. And I will make of thee a great nation, and I will bless thee, and make thy name great, and thou shalt be a blessing: And I will bless them that bless thee, and curse him that curseth thee: and in thee shall all families of the earth be blessed.' "

He gave them a moment to stew on that, then smiled and shook his head. "That ain't all. Now let's take a gander at chapter twenty-two, verses seventeen and eighteen, where the Lord's still talking to Abraham: 'That in blessing I will bless thee, and in multiplying I will multiply thy seed as the stars of the heaven and as the sand which is upon the sea shore, and thy seed shall possess the gate of his enemies. And in thy seed shall all the nations of the earth be blessed; because thou hast obeyed my voice.' ''

"Sounds like Abraham won't need to buy any seeds at the co-op this spring," Earl said, then grunted as his wife's elbow caught him in the ribcage.

Brother Verber shot Earl a dirty look. "These have to do with producing children, not soybeans, and the multiplying ain't the two-times-two sort of multiplying. What you just now heard is called the Abrahamic Covenant, and it was made some thirty-eight hundred years ago. Yes, the Lord gave Abraham a thirty-eight-hundred-year warranty on his seed because he obeyed the Lord's voice and commandments. You can bet Abraham was pleased as punch, and his children and grandchildren and their children and so forth were, too."

Suddenly, his expression darkened and his hands gripped the sides of the podium. He waited until everybody stopped squirming and sneaking glances at their watches, then dropped his voice to a throaty whisper. "But then the tables turned. Shalmaneser, the king of Assyria, marched his army into Israel, and took prisoners back to places like"—he consulted his notes—"Halah and Medes. Thirteen years later, the Assyrian army came back for more, and that ain't the end of it. In the year five hundred and ninety-six B.C., Nebuchadnezzar, the king of Babylon, attacked Jerusalem and pretty much captured the last of the Israelites. Now where do you think all these seeds of Abraham ended up?"

Nobody offered a guess. Earl's chin was on his chest and he was snoring softly. Dahlia was trying to determine if she could get out of the pew without stepping on too many toes. Beside her, Kevin was tugging at his collar and wondering if Kevin Junior would have Dahlia's eyes. Lottie Estes was agonizing over the correct spelling of Nebuchadnezzar. Mrs. Jim Bob was perplexed, aware that Brother Verber's religious training through the mail-order seminary in Las Vegas had been slanted toward the consequences of sinful behavior rather than obscure biblical history. Beside her, Jim Bob was cursing himself for coming home from the poker game at two in the morning with whiskey on his breath—and discovering his wife sitting in the kitchen.

Brother Verber went in for the kill. "All these seeds ended up in the Caucacus mountains or thereabouts—which is why they became known as Caucasians. Now, they didn't stay there forever, these twelve tribes of Israel. After maybe a hundred years, they packed their bags and migrated toward the west. When they got someplace they liked, they settled down and took names like Celts, Teutones, Gaels, Scots, and Scandinavians. After a time, some of them like the Vikings and Pilgrims sailed across the Atlantic Ocean to a place called North America. Let's have a look at Second Samuel, chapter seven, verse ten, where the Lord says plain as day: 'Moreover I will appoint a place for my people Israel, and will plant them so they may dwell in a place of their own, and move no more; neither shall the children of wickedness afflict them any more, as beforetime.'" He took out a handkerchief and blotted his forehead, stealing a peek at Kayleen. She nodded encouragingly at him, her eyes all dewy with admiration.

"So what this boils down to," he continued, "is two things. One is that we're Caucasians and therefore the true descendants of the twelve tribes of Israel, who were assured by the Lord that they were the chosen people. The second is that we are living in the Promised Land right here and right now!" He thumped the podium for emphasis, then rocked back on his heels and waited while everybody considered what he'd said. Everybody but Earl, of course.

Mrs. Jim Bob stood up. "Are you saying that we're Jewish?" she asked.

"Not for a second," he assured her, hoping he had his facts straight. "I'm saying that the Jews are *not* descended from the twelve tribes of Israel, any more than the Africans or the Ethiopians or the Eskimos—

because they ain't Caucasians. Only the folks from the western Christian nations qualify."

As Mrs. Jim Bob sank down to sort this out, Eula Lemoy fluttered her hand. "And the United States of America is the Promised Land?"

Brother Verber nodded. "Just like the Lord promised in the Abrahamic Covenant. Let's all bow our heads and offer a prayer of thankfulness for this blessing that has been bestowed on us."

Raz Buchanon spat angrily as a gun was fired somewhere higher up on Cotter's Ridge. "These dadburned city folk got no call to come here and start shootin' at anything that moves," he muttered to Marjorie, who'd refused to get out of the truck. "And if Diesel values his worthless hide, he'd better stay away from here. I'd sooner blow off his head as look at him!"

Marjorie blinked as sunlight glinted off the copper tubes and empty Mason jars.

"What's more," Raz went on, "I ain't gonna feel any kindlier toward those soldier fellers if they come snoopin' around here. I'll blast the lot of them to Kingdom Come. You jest see if I don't." He spat again, glared so savagely at a squirrel that it liked to fall off a branch, then replenished his chaw and returned his attention to the fine art of making moonshine. Business was always real good during the holiday season.

Jake Milliford belched as he pushed away from the kitchen table. "Fine dinner," he forced himself to say, not being comfortable throwing out compliments but doing it anyway. Short of stuffing Judy in a gunny sack and putting her in the back of the truck, there wasn't any way he could force her to go to Maggody for four days. He should have been able to just lay down the law 'cause she was his wife, but he knew better than to try it. "I'm gonna go watch the game. When you get finished with the dishes, come into the living room."

"I'm not interested in ballgames," she said as she

carried his plate to the sink. "I told Janine I'd come over this afternoon and help her make curtains for the nursery. She found a real cute gingham print on sale—"

"You don't have to sit there all afternoon. I got something to show you. After that, you can go wherever you please." He left the room before she could start whining, which, as far as he was concerned, was about all she ever did. It wasn't like all he ever did was lie around the house all day or take off two weeks to go deer hunting. No, he worked eight-hour shifts five days a week at the salvage yard just to keep them from having to live in a neighborhood where they'd be surrounded by lazy half-breeds. He didn't go around beating up faggots like some of the fellows did. He took her to church most Sundays, even though he didn't cotton to all the pious shit about lovin' thy neighbor and turnin' the other cheek. The only time he was gonna turn the other cheek was while he was pulling out a gun.

"What do you want?" said Judy, coming to the doorway with her coat over her arm.

He picked up a six-foot aluminum pole. "LaRue gave me this to try. It's called a take-down blowgun, and it's supposed to be accurate up to sixty feet. He said he got himself an eleven-pound turkey."

"So?"

"So I was showing it to you. At halftime, I'm gonna go out back and see if it's as powerful and accurate as LaRue sez. If it is, I'm gonna order one for myself and a shorter one for you."

"What would I do with it? You know I don't like to hunt."

"When the time comes that we have to take to the woods, you may need it for self-defense."

Judy put on her coat. "Well, at least you can't shoot yourself in the foot with it. I'll be back at suppertime. Don't call me over at Janine's. We're going to try to get the curtains done while the baby's napping, and the phone always wakes him up."

"Why would I want to call you?"

"To stop by the store or something. Anyway, don't do it if you want supper on the table tonight. We're determined to finish the curtains in one sitting."

"Okay, okay," he muttered, stroking the polished aluminum of the blowgun. The darts with their colorful plastic tips only cost about ten cents apiece. He might just forget about the game and find out if they were as lethal as LaRue said.

"What's up, Harve?" I asked, having made the tactical error of stopping by the PD for a magazine and feeling obliged to find out who'd left a message on the answering machine. Most of them tend to be from Ruby Bee and therefore on the monotonous side.

"Thought you was gonna have that accident report here yesterday," he said.

"My dog ate it, but I'll write up another one and bring it over tomorrow. It's not exactly the stuff of which bestsellers are made."

He rumbled unhappily. "That ain't the real reason I called, Arly. I need you to do me a favor and go check out a burglary on a county road over past Drippersville. I'm real short-handed on account of all my boys calling in sick. Odd how something always goes around this time of year, ain't it? If I were a suspicious sort—and we both know I'm not—I'd almost wonder if deer season had anything to do with it."

"So what's the deal in Drippersville?"

"It's the fourth damn burglary in the last month. The same MO, too. The houses are in remote areas and the owners are out of town. The perps break a window, collect everything of value, and waltz out the back door and load their vehicles. None of the stolen goods have turned up in the county."

I made the face that Ruby Bee always complains will leave more lines than a road map. "Professionals?"

"Damn straight," Harve said. "They pull out all the trays and serving pieces, then take the silver and leave the cheap stuff on the floor. They don't take jars of pennies or paste jewelry. They didn't bother with a computer that was a couple of years old."

"And nobody's seen them coming or going?"

"Like I said, the houses are in areas without neighbors. The owners are on vacation, and none of them sees anybody lurking nearby when they put suitcases in the trunk. At the third house, the guy'd rigged up a device to make the lights go on at dusk and off at midnight so it'd look like someone was there, but it didn't do a damn bit of good. In fact, the perps hung around long enough to cook a frozen pizza."

I found a notepad and a pencil. "Okay, I'll go out there and look around. Give me directions to the house."

Reed banged down the telephone receiver, then took a couple of deep breaths to steady himself. "The bitch says she's filing for a divorce first thing in the morning," he told Barry. "She already talked to a lawyer, and he told her she can take half my paycheck for the next fifteen years. Fifteen fucking years! Her brother's coming over toward the end of the week to get the rest of her crap." He made a fist and hit the wall with such fury the plaster cracked. "Goddamn it to hell! I'm not putting up with this shit! I've got half a mind to drive over there and beat her until she gets down on her hands and knees and begs to come back."

Barry quite agreed Reed had had half a mind (and not a fraction more). "Then she'll file charges like she did last time, and you'll find yourself doing ninety days at the county jail."

"At least she won't get half of any paychecks," Reed said, examining his knuckles for cuts.

Dylan Gilbert came out of the kitchen, a glass of milk in one hand and a sandwich in the other. "What's going on?"

"Reed was talking to his wife," said Barry. "I would have thought you could hear every word. Are you sure you used to be a college boy?"

"Phi Beta Kappa," he said, then kicked an empty beer can off the couch and sat down. He was wearing jeans and a neatly pressed shirt, and his hair was still damp from the shower. "Sure, I heard, but he calls to yell at her at least three times a day. I was just wondering if there had been any new developments in the drama."

"Hell, no," Reed stomped into the kitchen and returned with a bottle of tequila and a smudged glass. "You know what they call a roomful of lawyers? A target. Maybe we can find out where they hold their annual convention and blow 'em all sky-high."

Barry lifted his eyebrows. "An interesting idea, but a very imprudent one. Let's save our energies and resources for a more significant project. Don't you agree, Dylan?"

"I've never had any use for lawyers, especially the public defenders who want you to plead out so they won't have to waste a day in court. However, I agree that we have better things to do than disrupt a bar association luncheon." He took a bite of the sandwich and washed it down with milk, his eyes never leaving Barry's face. "I've heard Reed's life story, but I don't know much about you."

"And I don't know anything about you," Barry countered.

"There's nothing to know. I grew up in Idaho. When my father lost his ranch to the bloodsuckers at the bank, we moved to a compound where he worked in the machine shop and my mother taught school. I split five years ago, did a couple of years of college, and ended up with the Denver brethren. Now I'm here until something better comes along."

Barry sat back and gave him a bemused look. "Reed said you tried to send a bomb to a federal judge and brought the feds down on you. Did you put a return address on the package or what?"

"Get off it," said Reed. "Nobody's that stupid, fer chrissake." He paused to down a shot of tequila. "Except for that bitch Bobbi Jo and her brother. They've probably been screwing each other since they were in grade school."

Dylan showed small, even teeth. "It seems someone called the FBI and mentioned my name. I don't know what else they had, but they had enough to get the warrant. I didn't stick around to hear the details or to track down the squealer and have a talk with him. One of these days I will, though."

Although Dylan's voice had been unemotional to the point of blandness, Barry felt a twinge of apprehension. Dylan was dangerous, he decided. Reed was too, but in a blustery, see-it-coming sort of way; he was as subtle as a grizzly bear charging through a thicket. Dylan was more of a poisonous snake, silently gliding through the grass, its eyes slitted and its tongue flicking as it approached its prey.

Barry put on his cap and reached for his jacket. "Guess I'm going. I'll see you Friday in Maggody."

Reed ignored him. "Hey, Dylan, you ever rearmed a sixty-six-millimeter light antitank weapon?"

In a much nicer house in a neighborhood populated by white Anglo-Saxon Methodists, Baptists, Presbyterians, and a smattering of Episcopalians, Sterling Pitts sat in his study. The proposal for the group health plan should have occupied his attention, but he was seated in a leather chair, staring sightlessly at the photograph of himself holding up a large, dead fish. An informant in their midst? Members came and went, either voluntarily like Carter Lee or involuntarily like Bradley and Mo. But he, Reed, Barry, and Jake had been involved since they met at a week-long retreat in Missouri. Reed and Barry were fresh out of the army, Reed, in particular, was having a hard time adjusting to civilian life and was ripe to be recruited. Barry had proved himself by setting a fire in a warehouse in Little Rock. Jake was taciturn, but his eyes blazed and he had plenty to say whenever the talk turned to the mongrelization of the white race by civil rights legislation.

Sterling had been unable to recontact his counterpart in Colorado. He'd tried e-mail, but the address had been switched. The only telephone number he knew had been disconnected, which was not surprising since many of those in the movement often moved to ensure their privacy.

He took a pen and wrote down the code names: Silver Fox, Red Rooster, Apocalypse, Blitzer. It was unthinkable that any one of them would betray the cell. Judy Milliford seldom evinced enthusiasm, but she was too mousy to envision in such a role. Kayleen was deeply dedicated; he could hear it in her voice whenever they spoke about the insidiousness of the federal government and the threat posed by the international conspiracy. If she'd not been a woman, she would have easily replaced Mo in the hierarchy.

But Dylan Gilbert swore he'd received the tip from a double agent in Oklahoma. He'd been given no hint about the duration of this despicable infiltration. Sterling looked back down at the code names, imagining faces and recalling fragments of conversation. Had anyone inadvertently slipped up? Had anyone missed a meeting and been unable to supply a satisfactory excuse?

Most important, was there a way to force the informant to expose himself? If so, justice would be served coldly and swiftly. There was no place for mercy if the movement was ultimately to succeed.

Chapter 5

On Sunday afternoon I'd obliged Harve and gone to the scene of the burglary in Drippersville, but it had been a bigger waste of time than trying to teach Diesel to read (Buchanons don't get hooked on phonics). The break-in had been discovered by a neighbor who'd stopped by to put bags over the rose bushes to protect them from frost; the owners were on their way back from Florida to make an inventory of the stolen items. A deputy showed up to take fingerprints, but none of the prints from the earlier burglaries had set off bells and whistles in the FBI files. My report had been written Monday morning in less than ten minutes (I left out my poetic musings about the sense of intrusion that lingered like a bad cold).

By Wednesday morning, I'd written a few more reports, most involving trespassing on private land and one in which a 1982 Pontiac Grand Am was mistaken for Bambi's dear old dad. If Raz had run into any wayward hunters, he'd buried the bodies in shallow graves and kept it to himself. Which was fine with me.

I'd just refilled my coffee mug and settled down to do some serious whittling when Dahlia stormed into the PD.

"You got to look at this," she said, thrusting a much-creased pamphlet at me. "Kevvie tried to hide it underneath his boxers, but I found it anyway. I wanna know what it means."

"How are you feeling?"

She sat down. "I reckon I'm doing fine, excepting I can't sleep for more than fifteen minutes without having to go to the pottie. My finger's a dad-burned pincushion. Kevvie's scared to so much as touch me 'cause he thinks it's not fittin' in front of the baby. I ain't had a Nehi for seven and a half months."

"It'll all be over soon," I said soothingly, "and then you can have a Nehi whenever you want. Have you and Kevin chosen names for the baby?"

"We're gonna name him Kevin Fitzgerald Buchanon, Junior. I think it's kinda long for such a little thing, but Kevvie won't have it any other way. Ma suggested we call him Jerry so's not to confuse the two. I don't know where she came up with that, though."

"Then you're sure it's a boy?" I asked. "Did you have some sort of test at the clinic?"

"I came here 'cause I want you to read that thing and tell me what's going on. There's something about it that stinks like a backed-up septic tank, but I can't rightly put my finger on it."

I picked up the pamphlet. "'Our nation is in terrible danger,'" I read aloud. "No longer can we trust our elected officials to run the country according to the premises laid out by the dedicated and selfless patriots who formulated the Declaration of Independence and the Constitution of the United States. Many of these patriots lost their families, properties, and lives to make this republic free from oppressive governments and dictatorships, a republic with freedom and liberty, a republic guided by the principles of the one true God.'" Frowning, I turned to the second page.

"So whatall does that mean?" demanded Dahlia. "Is it true that Congress and all the big corporations can do whatever they please without paying any attention to the needs of the ordinary folks like Kevvie and me? That the 'Pledge of Allegiance' we always recited in school should have been called 'The Pledge of Alliance with the International Conspiracy'?" She put her hand on her pendulous bosom in case I couldn't follow her. "You know, 'I pledge allegiance to the flag—'"

"I know," I interrupted, continuing to skim the

blurry purple words that had been reproduced on an old-fashioned mimeograph machine. When I was finished, I put it aside and said, "This is crazy stuff, Dahlia. Do you have any idea where Kevin got hold of it?"

"Most likely at the SuperSaver. He don't go anyplace else except there, the Assembly Hall, and his ma and pa's house. He promised to stay real close in case the baby comes early and I got to hightail it to the hospital."

"Was this all you found in the drawer?"

"Oh, I forgot." She dug into a pocket hidden in the folds of her tent dress and pulled out a crumpled slip of paper. "This sez there's a meeting for concerned citizens on Saturday morning at ten o'clock. They can learn how to protect themselves and their families from"—her brow crinkled with exertion as she sounded out the words—"oppression and submission to a foreign army."

I winced. "Does it mention where this is going to be held?"

"It sez to go one mile east on County 102 and look for signs. Shouldn't you be doin' something to stop the country from being invaded by foreigners that want to take away our babies and put us in concentration camps? I don't want someone to snatch my baby right out of my arms, Arly."

"I think we're safe. Maggody's not on the maps, so it's unlikely the foreigners can find us any time soon. May I keep this pamphlet?"

"I 'spose so," she said, sniffing. She wiped her cheeks on her sleeve, then struggled to her feet and trudged out the door. The walls didn't come tumbling down, but the coffee in my mug may have sloshed a couple of times.

I reread the pamphlet more carefully. There were no specifics about the ethnicity of the so-called conspirators, but it wasn't difficult to figure out. A lot of the text was aimed at small farmers, demanding to know why our government ignored their plight in order to bankroll a politically unstable Middle East aggressor state. I doubted the author had North Carolina or Virginia in mind. Affirmative action was another bogeyman under the bed, stealing good jobs from hard-working Christians with families to feed. There were murky references to brainwashing in the public schools, fluoride in the water, and the unlawful imposition of income taxes.

It was one thing for General Pitts and his group to embrace this dogmatic twaddle and act on it by donning olive drab for a weekend. It was another to attempt to recruit locals to their cause. Maggody was hardly a hotbed of resentment leveled at the federal government; the majority of the residents griped more about the weather than they did about taxes. However, we'd had a manifestation of mass hysteria at the end of the summer that rivaled nothing I'd ever seen. Even Estelle and Ruby Bee had been sucked into the madness.

I put the pamphlet in my coat pocket and went out to the car. I'd planned to confront Kayleen, but I decided to grab some lunch first and find out what was on the grapevine. There was a smaller than usual assembly of pickup trucks outside Ruby Bee's, most of them adorned with gun racks and bumper stickers extolling the virtues of the NRA. As I walked across the barroom, I spotted several pamphlets lying beside pitchers and napkin dispensers.

"Where have you been all week, missy?" Ruby Bee asked as I chose a stool near Estelle's roost. "I left three messages on that infernal answering machine on Monday and four yesterday. You better take it to be repaired."

"You're probably right," I said meekly. "Can I have meat loaf and mashed potatoes?"

She folded her arms. "I don't believe you answered my question, and I don't want to hear how you're cooking for yourself in that dingy apartment. There's no way to prepare a well-balanced meal on a stove with only one working burner and an oven that never heats up."

"That's why I'm here for lunch, but if you're not

going to serve me, I'll go across the street to the deli in the SuperSaver and get a ham sandwich. Do dill pickles count as vegetables?"

"Keep your tail in the water," she said, conceding defeat as graciously as always, then went into the kitchen.

I glanced over my shoulder at the customers in the booths, wishing I could eavesdrop to discover their collective reaction to the pamphlets. However, the jukebox drowned out whatever was being said, and everybody appeared more interested in beer than inflammatory rhetoric.

Ruby Bee returned with a plate piled high with meat loaf, et cetera, and I had just picked up my fork when Estelle skidded across the dance floor, her hair tilting at a precarious angle.

"Arly! I been looking everywhere for you! I left my engine running so it'll be faster for you to ride with me!"

Ruby Bee's jaw dropped. "Land sakes, Estelle, you sound like your house is on fire. What's wrong? Did Uncle Tooly's lawyer send those sheep?"

Estelle grabbed my arm, and between gasps, said, "Someone broke into Elsie's house! Let's go!"

"Is he still there?" I said as I reluctantly put down the fork.

"We don't know. Lottie went by to feed the cat, and she noticed right away that a window was broken and the back door was open. She wasn't about to run smackdab into a criminal, so she drove home and called the PD. When nobody answered, she called me to ask me what she should do. I said I had a pretty good idea where to find you."

Catching Harve's professional perps might be more satisfying than meat loaf, I told myself as I slid off the stool. "Can you keep the plate warm in the oven?" I asked Ruby Bee.

"Where's your gun?"

"Where it's supposed to be," I said as Estelle dragged me toward the door. "Calm down, for pity's sake. Why did you come all the way over here instead of calling?"

Instead of answering my question, she dove into the driver's seat and slammed the car into reverse. Before I could close my door, we were halfway across the parking lot.

"Slow down, damn it!" I said as she pulled out in front of a truck.

"If we get there quick enough, we can catch 'em in the act," she said. "You'll be a hero and get a reward from Elsie's insurance company. It seems to me giving you a small sum would be a sight cheaper than replacing Elsie's Hummel collection."

I closed my eyes and reminded myself of the necessity of breathing as she squealed around a corner and headed down an unpaved road. The station wagon was bouncing madly, but the grim driver made no concessions to the specter of bent axles and broken oil pans.

She slammed on the brakes at the foot of Elsie's driveway. "I'll watch the front of the house while you go around back. We don't know how many there are of them or if they're armed, so keep your eyes peeled."

"Wait a minute," I said as she opened her door. "For starters, you're going to stay right here until I make sure there's no one, armed or otherwise, in the house. If you don't see me on the porch within five minutes, drive back to the bar and call the sheriff's office. Have them send a backup to the bar, then lead them here."

Estelle hesitated, one foot on the gravel. "Maybe we ought to go to the PD to get your gun. Ruby Bee'd never forgive me if you got yourself killed."

"Neither would I," I left her twitching indecisively and walked up the driveway, fairly sure the burglars were long gone. There had been no mention of a vehicle by the back door, and even if there'd been one, Lottie's arrival and hasty departure would have sent the burglars on their way.

The back door was ajar, and a window next to it was broken. I eased open the door, listening for an indication someone might be in the house ("fairly sure" is not the same thing as "absolutely certain"), and stepped into the kitchen. When nothing much happened, I veered around a muddy path and continued into the living room, then poked my head into the two bedrooms and bathroom. I was tempted to make sure no one was hiding in a closet or under a bed, but I was worried that Estelle might panic and drive away to summon the sheriff, the state police, and the National Guard. The Mounties, too, if she could find their telephone number.

I went out on the porch. "It's okay, Estelle," I yelled, waving at the station wagon. "Go let Ruby Bee know I didn't get myself shot defending the Hummels."

Her face popped up from the far side. "How do I know there ain't someone behind you sticking a gun in your back?"

This was not your typical crime-scene scenario in which the ranking officer on the scene barks out orders that are promptly and unquestioningly obeyed.

"Suit yourself," I yelled, then went back inside, sat down on a settee, and called the sheriff's office. LaBelle did her best to remind me I'd fallen from grace, but eventually put me through to Harve.

"Another one?" he said after I'd told him where I was. "Goddammit, I feel like I should put bars on all the windows here—the ones that don't already have 'em. Can you tell what was taken?"

I looked around the room. "Probably a TV set, if the cable dangling from the wall is any indication. The Hummel figurines were not deemed worthy. I doubt Elsie had a computer or a silver tea service, but we'll have to wait until she can get back here and determine what's missing. Lottie Estes probably knows how to reach her."

"We've got to put a stop to this, Arly. The election's coming up real soon, and this is making me look bad. If my opponent wasn't dumber than a possum, I'd think he was behind it."

"There has to be a link," I said, feeling slightly

dumber than a possum myself. "The houses are too far apart to have the same carrier, but the owners might have notified the post office to hold their mail. Same thing with the area newspapers, although there's no home delivery in Maggody. Even if she could afford it, Elsie wouldn't have a cleaning service. She didn't leave her cat at a kennel." I plucked at a crocheted doily on the armrest as I racked my mind for other feasible links. "Do you want me to interview all the previous victims and see if I can stumble onto something useful?"

"Yeah, I guess so," Harve said with a drawn-out wheeze. "Your phony soldiers caused any problems as of yet?"

I decided not to mention the pamphlet for the moment. "They won't be here for another two days, which gives me some time to work on the burglaries. It'll be more stimulating than trespassers and drunks."

"I'll send Les out to take fingerprints and photos of whatever footprints you find. He can bring copies of the reports, but they don't say anything that's gonna inspire you. Lemme know if you get anywhere."

I froze as I heard a creak in the kitchen. "Stay on the line," I whispered, then put down the receiver and tiptoed to the doorway. The back door was as I'd left it, and the muddy tracks on the linoleum appeared undisturbed. I took one step, then caught movement in the corner of my eye and leapt back just in time to save myself from being smacked on the head with a broom.

"Estelle, damn it," I said shakily, "what do you think you're doing? You came within an inch of giving me a heart attack."

"Is that what I get for risking life and limb to make sure you weren't being held hostage? If that's all the gratitude you can show, I'll take Elsie's cat and be on my way."

"Good idea." I returned to the telephone to assure Harve I hadn't been beset by burglars. He was in a much better mood when we ended the call.

* * *

"That was a real pretty sermon on Sunday morning, Brother Verber," Kayleen said as she poured a cup of tea. They were in her motel room, but she'd made sure the drapes were pulled back so there'd be no gossip about her entertaining a gentleman. "Would you like lemon and sugar?"

"Yes, and thank you kindly for your compliment. I have to admit I was a little nervous about those unfamiliar names, but I just told myself nobody'd notice if they came out wrong. I must have spent an hour the night before practicing 'Nebuchadnezzar.' It's a sight harder than Matthew, Mark, Luke, or John."

She set the cup and saucer on the table beside his chair, then poured a cup for herself. "You sounded like you'd been saying 'Nebuchadnezzar' since you were in grade school. In fact, I can't think when I've heard it said so melodiously."

He lowered his face to hide its pinkness and tried to keep his hand from shaking as he picked up the dainty porcelain cup. "Mighty fine tea, Sister Kayleen," he said after a tiny slurp. "If I may be so bold, can I ask you why you decided to move to our little community?"

She launched into the story of her ill-fated first marriage, stopping every now and then to wipe her eyes or give him a rueful smile. "So I suppose the reason I'm here is because of that anonymous Good Samaritan. If I could remember his name or where his house was, I'd go over and thank him for bringing me back here."

"I'm sure he was a member of the Voice of the Almighty Lord congregation on account of what a good Christian he was," Brother Verber said, shrewdly doing a little public relations work. "The Methodists down the road are real big on how devout they are, but their teen group had a dance in the basement last spring and they're talking about holding another one before Christmas." He tsked sadly. "Dancing in the basement of the church. I wouldn't be surprised to hear they'll be serving alcoholic beverages to celebrate Baby Jesus' birthday."

"Oh, dear," Kayleen murmured. "I'm confident you'd never allow such a thing in the Assembly Hall. How long have you been a pastor?"

"Long enough to make sure there'll be nothing of a sinful nature taking place in our basement." He finished his tea and stood up. "I'm supposed to go by Sister Barbara's house to finalize plans for the Thanksgiving pageant. Will we be seeing you tonight at the prayer meeting and pot luck supper, Sister Kayleen?"

She thought for a moment, then said, "It's possible, but I'm not promising anything. I'm a little disappointed that you have to leave so soon. I was hoping you might be able to help me find that Samaritan so I can give him a big ol' hug. I'm not familiar with the back roads. Perhaps another time when you're not too busy, you could drive me around. I might recognize the house if I saw it again. It would mean so much to me, Brother Verber, and I'd be real grateful."

He glanced at his watch. It was already past the time he was due at Sister Barbara's house, and he knew he'd have some explaining to do as it was. But Sister Kayleen was watching him with pleading eyes, as if he was the only person who could bring joy into her life. And weren't all Christians admonished to follow in the footsteps of the Good Samaritan by rushing to the aid of their fellow travelers?

"I don't want to interfere with your afternoon. You just run along and get prepared for the pageant. I've met so many nice people here in Maggody, and I'm sure one of them will be willing to help me. A gentleman named Lewis Ferncliff greeted me real warmly after the service on Sunday and said I should call on him if there was any favor at all he could do for me. And a widower named—"

"Oh, I can take you," he said hastily. "I was just thinking how much gas I have in my car."

"Why, we'll take my car, and you can give me directions. You're generous to a fault, Brother Verber. I do believe I'll say a special little prayer for you tonight before I go to bed."

Trying not to allow his gaze to wander toward the bed, he picked up her coat and held it open for her. "It's my Christian duty," he said. "Maybe while we're driving around, I can convince you to become a permanent member of our congregation."

"Aren't you the sly dog," she said with a grin.

"Did you ever think about how the federal government sends money to other countries but won't take care of its own citizens?" Earl Buchanon asked his wife as she wrestled with the balky ironing board.

"Can't say I have," said Eileen, more concerned with not getting her finger pinched. "Did you oil this like I asked you to last week?"

Earl took a cookie off the plate and dunked it in his buttermilk. "What's more, income tax is voluntary, and none of us can be forced to volunteer. There's not a thing in the world those IRS leeches can do if I up and refuse to hand over my money so that the government can send it to countries that'd like to take us over."

"Ow!" She dropped the ironing board and stuck her finger in her mouth. "That blasted thing! If you want your shirts and trousers ironed, you'd better get busy with the oil. Otherwise, you can walk around town looking like a hobo for all I care."

"Do you know how much I paid in taxes last year? Close to two thousand dollars, that's how much. If I had that money now, I could make a down payment on a decent tractor that I don't have to spend half my time tinkering with."

"Or buy me a one-way ticket."

Earl was so surprised that he dropped the cookie. "Where do you want to go?"

"I don't know," she said, looking out the window at the pasture dotted with withered clumps of weeds. "Nowhere, I guess—or at least no time soon. The baby'll be here in a matter of weeks, and Dahlia is gonna need help with housework and the cooking. I'll most likely stay there all day, so you'll have to fend for yourself at lunchtime."

"She doing okay?"

Eileen picked up the ironing board and headed for the hall closet. "If she's having a problem with her blood sugar, she didn't tell me."

"I guess Kevin's all excited," Earl said when she came back into the kitchen.

"That's real insightful of you, Earl, since they come over for supper two or three times a week and that's all Kevin talks about."

He put on his coat and jammed a John Deere cap on his head. "I think I'll go over to the co-op and pick up a bag of layer grit. When I get back, I'll take a look at the ironing board."

"Sure you will," she said as he went out the back door.

Jeremiah McIlhaney came into the dining room, where his wife was chewing on a pencil as she decided who would be honored with Christmas cards and who wouldn't, based mostly on what they'd sent last year. Cousin Queenie had sent a long, rambling, photocopied letter telling how her daughter was a cheerleader and her son won a full scholarship to college and she herself was elected president of the garden club. Millicent drew a line through that name. Eula Lemoy had recycled a card she'd received from somebody else by covering the name with a sticker. Eula was gone with a slash. Aunt Bertha had sent nothing, as usual, but she didn't have any children and was rumored to have a sizable savings account.

Jeremiah hesitated, aware how seriously she took the master list every year. "I was thinking about a sandwich for lunch," he said apologetically, "and a piece of that apple pie we had for supper last night."

Millicent moved to the next name on her list. This was a mite trickier. Cousin Beau's wife had sent a real nice embossed card two years ago, then tried to weasel by this past year with a cheap one. What would she do this year?

Jeremiah licked his lips. "I can see you ain't got time to fix my lunch, so maybe I'll swing by the Dairee

Dee-Lishus and get something there. Are you planning to use the truck Saturday morning?"

She banged down the pencil. "I am trying to concentrate on the list, and every time you interrupt me, I forget what I was thinking. Am I planning to use the truck—when?"

"Saturday morning."

"I told Darla Jean I'd take her shopping in Farberville on Saturday, but we didn't set a time. I suppose we can go after lunch. I wish you'd figure out what's wrong with my car and get it fixed. It was bad enough with Darla Jean borrowing it all the time to get to basketball practice or go riding with Heather. Now that all three of us are dependent on the truck, I just want to scream."

"I told you I'm waiting on a part," he said, retreating toward the living room.

Millicent picked up the pencil and resumed gnawing on it. Cousin Beau's wife was wily enough to send another embossed card this year, which would put her in a position to say something catty at the family reunion if she received a cheap card. Then again . . .

"I cain't work Saturday morning," Kevin said as he stood in the middle of Jim Bob's office. He put a piece of paper on the desk and pointed at it with a trembling finger. "It sez on this schedule that I ain't supposed to come in till three in the afternoon to work the second shift."

Jim Bob ripped the schedule into small pieces and let them flutter to the floor. "What schedule?"

"The schedule you posted in the employees' lounge on Monday," he said, gulping. "That one right there on the floor."

"All I see on the floor are scraps of paper, boy. Next time you're allowed a break, have a look at the schedule in the lounge. See for yourself if you're not supposed to be here at seven o'clock Saturday morning to turn up the thermostat, switch on the lights, and clean the toilets in the restrooms. I'll find out if you're late and take pleasure in firing your skinny ass."

Kevin felt his eyes begin to sting, but he squared his shoulders as best he could and said, "I got something else to do Saturday morning. Besides, it's not fair for you to change the schedule any time you want. Employees got rights, too."

"You got the right to get a job someplace else." Jim Bob lit a fat cigar, then entwined his fingers over his belly and regarded Kevin through a cloud of blue smoke. "I was planning to get in some hunting last weekend, but Mrs. Jim Bob changed my mind. Larry Joe's gonna call in sick first thing Friday morning, then him, Roy, and me are leaving for our camp. But I tell you what, asshole—since you'll be acting assistant manager, I'll pay you an extra dollar an hour till I get back."

Kevin opened and closed his mouth several times, then gave up and left the office. "It ain't fair," he said to a woman studying canned tomatoes. She was still staring at him as he went around the end of the aisle.

Chapter 6

By late Friday morning I was more stumped than a beauty pageant contestant asked to explain the ramifications of global warming. I'd talked to the victims of four of the burglaries (Elsie wasn't back) and come up without a clue. The houses were in different parts of the county and had different post offices, electric cooperatives, and sanitation services. Two of the retired couples frequented the same square dancing club, but one of the couples swore they'd never discussed their vacation plans with anyone there. Only one couple had left pets at a kennel. None of them went to the same church. Three of them had fancy new houses once filled with expensive electronic toys and heirloom silver. The fourth house was similar to Elsie's, modest but clean.

I hadn't talked to Kayleen about the pamphlets, either, since Ruby Bee had informed me that her sole tenant had gone to Malthus for a few days to deal with some legal matters. I could have tracked down Kevin to ask him who'd given the pamphlet to him, but I wasn't masochistic enough to deliberately initiate a conversation with him.

The burglary reports were fanned out in front of me and I was scrutinizing them for some obscure connection when the telephone rang. Hoping that one of the perps was calling to own up, I answered it.

"We got another one," Harve said brusquely, not bothering with pleasantries, "and it's bad."

"How bad is it?"

"About as bad as it gets. This woman and her

daughter over in Mayfly went to visit kin for a week. They'd heard of the rash of burglaries, so they asked one of the daughter's friends to stay in their house while they were gone. They got worried when the house sitter didn't answer the phone for a few days, and called here first thing this morning to request that someone go out to the house and make sure she was okay. The deputy found the girl's body on the living room floor, her head crushed by a blow from a piece of firewood. She was wearing pajamas, so it looks like she heard a noise and got out of bed to see about it."

"Was there a broken window in the back of the house?"

"Yeah," Harve growled, "and the house was set off by itself on a hillside. After killing the girl, the damned clowns went ahead and hauled off two TV sets and a VCR."

"No witnesses spotted a truck or van?" I asked, although it was a perfunctory question at best.

"Hell, no. All we've got is that the coroner estimates she was killed three or four days ago. That fits in with when she stopped answering the phone and showing up for classes at the business college. The mailman noticed the mail was piling up in the box, but he didn't have any reason to go around to the back of the house."

"Did you check him out?"

"He's sixty-three years old and has a heart condition," Harve rumbled for a moment, then added, "I know Mayfly's nowhere near Maggody, but I'm even more short-handed than I was a week ago and the only available deputy started working here two weeks ago. Can you go over and have a look?"

I regretted having offered to tackle the burglaries in the first place, but I'd voluntarily climbed out on that particular limb and I was stuck until it broke—or I fell off it. "Yes, I can leave right now."

"The woman and her daughter should arrive home early this afternoon. I suppose you ought to hang around while they figure out what else is missing and see if they have serial numbers. I don't like the way this is pickin' up so fast, Arly. Folks have homeowner's insurance to replace what's stolen, but that girl wasn't more than twenty years old. Life insurance won't offer much comfort to her family."

I wrote down directions to the house, then calculated my time of arrival and told Harve to warn the deputy at the crime scene. The last thing I needed was to surprise a nervous neophyte with a .38 special in his hand.

Ruby Bee was taking off her apron when Estelle came into the barroom. "I'll be ready to go as soon as I cover the sweet potato pie with aluminum foil," she said. "And remind me to put the 'closed' sign on the door when we leave. Did you hear from that lawyer fellow?"

"No," Estelle said gloomily, "and it's getting harder and harder not to fret about this inheritance. Last night I dreamed I bought a car twice as big and gaudy as Mrs. Jim Bob's convertible. She let on like she didn't care, but everybody knew she was hoppin' mad."

"I saw her coming out of the supermarket this morning, and she looked like she was fit to be tied. It may have been on account of Jim Bob; early this morning I saw him, Roy, and Larry Joe loading up Jim Bob's truck with cases of beer in front of the supermarket. They probably made it all the way to their deer camp before Mrs. Jim Bob found out their plan. Jim Bob might be wise to stay up there till she thaws out in the spring."

She picked up the pie pan and they went out to the parking lot. As they started to get into Estelle's station wagon, a peculiar-looking vehicle almost as wide as a semi drove up. It had a mean-lookin' grill across the front, like it wanted nothing more than to push over a building.

Sterling Pitts rolled down the window. "Good afternoon, ladies. I went out to the property that Kayleen bought, but she's not there. Do you know if she's in her motel room, Mrs. Hanks?"

"Her car wasn't parked out back a few minutes ago when I set out some trash. She told me she was going to Malthus and return sometime today. She's staying in number three, if you want to leave her a note."

Estelle gave him a sugary smile. "Or you can give us a message and we'll be sure and tell her when she gets back. That way you won't have to hunt for paper and pencil, or worry about the note blowing away in the wind."

"It's awful windy," added Ruby Bee. "What's this thing you're driving?"

Pitts caressed the dashboard. "It's more than three tons of America's toughest vehicle. It has one hundred and ninety horsepower and three hundred pounds of torque. With this baby, I can drive through two feet of water, climb sixty-percent grades, and plow through three-foot snowbanks."

"Why would you want to do all that?" asked Estelle.

He rolled up the window and drove out of the lot in the direction from which he'd come. Estelle drove out of the lot in the same direction, although they had a different destination. "I wonder if we should alert Arly that he's in town," she said.

"I don't know where she is. She didn't show up for lunch, and her car's not at the PD or over behind Roy's store. Of course she couldn't go to the trouble of telling her own mother where she was going or when she'd be back. If I didn't know better, I'd think she was raised in a barn."

"Maybe it was an emergency, like chasing down a bank robber or an escaped convict."

"Even so, she should have had the decency to call me so I wouldn't worry," Ruby Bee said irritably, if irrationally. However, she reminded herself of the importance of their current mission and did her best to simmer down.

Minutes later they were at the door of the rectory. Estelle knocked, then stepped back and said, "Brother Verber must have gone somewhere. His car's not out in front."

"Knock again, Estelle, and do it real hard in case he's in the bathroom and didn't hear you the first time. This pie's fresh from the oven."

Estelle did as ordered, but nobody opened the door or even hollered that he was coming as fast as he could. "I guess we'll have to try later."

"He's not here?" said Mrs. Jim Bob as she approached them. She was carrying a covered casserole dish, but her expression was not that of an angel on an errand of mercy. "Where is he? How long's he been gone?"

"We don't know," said Ruby Bee. "We just got here ourselves." There wasn't any way to put her pie behind her back, so she forced herself to smile. "I reckon we're here for the same reason, Mrs. Jim Bob. I heard something about Brother Verber having a touch of the flu and I thought it'd be nice to bring him a special treat."

Mrs. Jim Bob pinched her lips together and stared suspiciously at them. "Did you?" she said at last. "Who would have thought you'd worry about Brother Verber, especially since you're not a member of the congregation. Maybe that has something to do with you selling alcohol."

"To folks like your husband," shot back Ruby Bee.

"My husband has been known to stray at times, but whenever he does, I do my best to get him back on the path of righteousness. I presume you do the same with your daughter, even though it doesn't seem to do a smidgen of good." Ignoring Ruby Bee's gasp, she took a key from under the door mat, unlocked the door, and went inside.

"Well, I never!" said Ruby Bee as the door slammed in her face. "The nerve of her!"

Estelle snorted. "One of these days Mrs. High and Mighty'll get what's coming to her, and I hope I'm there to see it. Come on, Ruby Bee, we might as well go have some sweet potato pie."

Ruby Bee was more in the mood to stomp into the rectory and tell Mrs. Jim Bob what she thought of her, but she followed Estelle back to the station wagon.

*   *   *

Jake saw the Hummer parked at the far edge of the pasture and drove toward it, cursing as his tires spun in the mud. "I hope to hell it don't take a tow truck to get out of here on Monday."

Judy pulled her coat more tightly around her. "Then Sterling can pay for it, since he selected the spot. At least over at Bradley's place, there was a gravel road. This is ridiculous. I never should have agreed to put up with this another year."

He glared at her, then concentrated on getting through the shriveled corn stalks that slapped at the front of the truck. As he parked alongside the Hummer, Pitts came out of the woods and called, "You're early. I wasn't expecting to see you all till six or seven."

Jake climbed out of the truck and pulled down the tailgate. "I took off early so we could get here before dark. My boss thinks I'm over in Farberville having a look at junkers at the auto auction lot. How long you been here, Pitts?"

"We're supposed to use code names on retreats! Unless you wish to risk the possibility of a court martial, Blitzer, address me as Silver Fox."

Jake dragged a canvas tent bag out of the bed, hoisted it onto his shoulder, and said, "Where are we making camp—Silver Fox?"

"I've reconnoitered the area and chosen a clearing with adequate drainage. It's just on the other side of that gully and up about fifty feet. No one can see you from here, but you should be able to see anyone who approaches. I'll show you the way."

Jake looked back at Judy, who was sitting in the cab like she was planted there for all eternity. "Get the sleeping bags and whatever else you can carry," he shouted at her, then slithered down the side of the gully and made his way up the far side.

Sterling waited until Jake reached the top, then turned and continued between thickets of brambles and thin, stunted trees. They arrived at a rocky clearing encircled by scrub pines and more brambles.

Jake dropped the tent. "Where's your crap?"

"I'll set up the communications post in town. I can hardly plug the computer into that tree, can I? I think I hear another vehicle coming across the pasture. I need to make sure it's one of our people instead of some nosy federal agents." He paused to study Jake's face for a telltale flicker of guilt. "I had a communiqué from the outfit over in Oklahoma. It seems they discovered an informant in their midst, a sneaky bastard taking money from the FBI. He'd been in their cell for over two years before they uncovered him."

"Did they hang him by his balls?" Jake asked as he pulled the tent out of the bag and began to unroll it.

"Something like that."

"Sumbitch deserved it."

"My sentiments exactly." Sterling left him to struggle with the tent and returned to the pasture. The truck belonged to Red Rooster. For a moment, he assumed the passenger was Apocalypse, but as the truck got closer, he recognized Dylan Gilbert. It was unfortunate, he told himself as he crossed the gully, that the young man had not drifted elsewhere. Theirs was an enthusiastic group, but hardly as professional as the one in Colorado. Red Rooster had passed along Dylan's remark about the compound in Idaho, too. Sterling knew the brethren there had been ruthless when they'd been under siege by the feds for nearly three weeks. Some of them had been given life; sentences despite the fact they were doing nothing more than protecting their families.

Reed cut off the engine and got out of the truck. "How's it going, Pitts?" he said as he began to unload his camping equipment.

"You're supposed to call me Silver Fox."

"Yeah, okay," said Reed. "How're you doing, Judy? Where's Jake?"

Sterling stomped his boot in the mud. "Refer to him as Blitzer, damn it! This is not a Boy Scout Jamboree. We are here for a purpose—and it's not to roast marshmallows and tell ghost stories. Tell your friend to get his gear, and I'll lead you to the encampment. I myself will be staying at a motel in order to remain in communication with the network."

"What's the matter, Pops?" said Dylan as he lazily emerged from the truck. "Getting too old to rough it with the rest of us?"

"My name is Silver Fox! Can't you morons get that through your thick skulls?"

"Look at this, Silver Fox," Reed said, holding out a blowgun. "Jake—I mean Blitzer—told me to check it out. It's a helluva lot more accurate than a knife. I took down a crow at more than forty feet."

"Interesting," said Sterling.

"You bet it is. I got some paint pellets so I can show everybody how powerful it is. It didn't cost but about thirty dollars." He pointed at a sparrow on a limb across the gully. "Watch this."

He loaded a pellet into the blowgun, leveled it, and took a deep breath. A noise no louder than a mouse's fart accompanied the release of the pellet. The sparrow continued to watch them, its head cocked.

Pitts looked at the orange splotch on the front of his field jacket. "Good work, Red Rooster. I can see how terrified all of our feathered friends will be in the future. Now, would you put that blasted thing away and get your gear?" He looked at Dylan, who was sniggering. "You, too, if you're planning to participate in the retreat. Otherwise, take a hike back to Colorado."

"Yeah, yeah." Dylan balanced a sleeping bag on one shoulder and picked up a duffel bag.

Reed fondled the blowgun. "Hey, I'm real sorry, Sterling. I practiced all day yesterday with this baby, and I was getting to where I could hit something clear across the parking lot behind my apartment. 'Course there were some wild shots while I was learning. This old boy that lives below me liked to have gone crazy when he saw the paint on his car, but I told him next time I'd use a dart and aim for his tires if he didn't stop squawking."

"Just call me Silver Fox," Sterling said in a discouraged voice, then started back across the gully.

"Did you do that on purpose?" asked Judy as Reed walked by.

Reed was torn between not wanting to admit he'd made a bad shot and confessing that he'd purposely assailed their leader, which might amount to treason. "It was one of those things," he muttered. "You aiming to sit there all night?"

"I might."

Dylan joined them. "You're too pretty to spend the next few days wallowing in the mud. Judy, right? I'm Dylan. I think I'm going to like it here more than I thought."

"Hey!" Reed said, thumping Dylan on the back with the blow gun. "You'd better watch that kind of thing. Jake's liable not to like it, and he's one mean fucker when he's riled up. He did six weeks in the county jail for biting off a biker's ear in a brawl."

Judy winked at Dylan, then went back to studying the dusty dashboard. The two men crossed the gully and disappeared into the woods. After a while, Jake emerged and came back to the truck, his eyes hard.

"Thought you was coming to the camp," he said.

"You thought wrong. If Sterling can stay in a motel in town, then I can, too. He can bring me out here to do the cooking and washing up, but there's no reason why I should spend the next three nights in a smelly sleeping bag on the rocks. If you don't like it, I'll find a way to get myself to Emmett in time to baby-sit tomorrow. Take it or leave it, Jake."

"You planning to sleep alone?"

"Heavens, no. I was planning to ask Silver Fox to crawl into bed with me. He may still have a little life in his old pecker. Or maybe that new fellow named Dylan. I could tell from looking at him that he's a real stud. After all, he's got be a good twenty years younger than you."

"Damn it," Jake said, making a fist but keeping it at his side, "you got no call to talk like that. I 'spose you can stay in town as long as Sterling keeps an eye on you. I want you to promise to stay in your motel room and not go wandering around town. From what

I've heard, there are some mighty peculiar folks in Maggody."

Judy decided not to comment about grown men who snuck around the woods with green and brown makeup on their faces and guns that fired paint pellets. Boy, that'd stop the foreign troops in their tracks. They'd be laughing so hard they could be rounded up effortlessly and deposited in makeshift stockades.

"I promise to stay in the motel room," she said.

"Make sure that you do." Jake stared at her, then gathered the rest of his gear and headed for the gully.

"This is more like it," Jim Bob said as he opened a beer and settled his muddy shoes on the crate that served as a coffee table in the trailer. "Hey, Larry Joe, if you're gonna fix yourself a bologna sandwich, make one for me. I skipped breakfast on account of not wanting to disturb Mrs. Jim Bob when I left the house."

"What'd she say when you told her we was going hunting?" asked Larry Joe. "Joyce was mad like she always is, but she said she'd cover for me if the principal at the high school calls to check up on me. It isn't like those little bastards in my shop classes aren't cutting school to go huntin', too. There were so few of them yesterday that I sent them to the library."

"To do what?"

"Hell, I don't know. Study or something," Larry Joe opened a cooler and dug around for the package of bologna. "So what'd she say?"

"Some critter must have died in the outhouse," said Roy Stiver, zipping up his fly as he came into the trailer. "It stinks to high heavens."

Jim Bob slapped his brow. "And us without a can of pine-scented air freshener! I knew we'd forget something essential. Put mustard on my sandwich, Larry Joe—unless we forgot that, too. Cut off the crust while you're at it, and put on the tea kettle."

Roy sat down at the kitchen table and shuffled a deck of cards. "I was just making an observation, for chrissake. You want to play poker or sit there like a boil on a preacher's ass?"

"Deal the cards," Jim Bob said, smugly congratulating himself for changing the subject. Mrs. Jim Bob would have figured out by the middle of the morning where he'd gone, but there wasn't anything she could do about it until he got home. That scene was something he didn't want to think about and spoil his weekend, not when they had plenty of beer, whiskey, bologna, and cards.

"I think we forgot the mustard," Larry Joe said with a sigh.

Instead of going straight back to Maggody, I went to Farberville to report in person to Harve and find out if he'd heard anything from the FBI about the prints. The sheriff's department, which housed the county jail as well as offices, a weight room, and more showers than to be found in all of Maggody, was a complete contrast to my two-room, shabby PD. It always depressed me.

LaBelle glanced up at me over the top of her sequined bifocals, sniffed, and resumed talking on the telephone. From what I could tell, the conversation concerned a young relative with head lice. LaBelle's not a Buchanon, but she should be.

"I need to speak to Harve," I said.

She covered the mouthpiece. "He's busy. You'll have to make an appointment for sometime next week."

"I've just come from a murder scene, and I need to speak to Harve. I cannot wait until next week, or even until you stop offering nit-picking advice to your sister or whoever it is."

"Then go on back to his office," she said with a flip of her hand. "Don't blame me if he bites your head off, though. I warned you."

Harve was seated at his desk, gazing dully at a stack of folders. An ashtray contained a veritable mountain of burned matches, and flakes of gray ash decorated most of the nearby surfaces. The potted plant on his desk appeared discouraged, if not yet dead.

"What'd you find?" he asked.

"Not much." I took out my notebook and flipped it open. "The victim's name was Katherine Avenued, twenty-one, lived alone in an apartment on Thurber Street. Her parents moved to Tucson several years ago. She waited tables at a Mexican restaurant and started taking classes at the business college in August. Her only friend seemed to have been Heidi Coben, the homeowner's daughter. Katherine didn't mention anything out of the ordinary when Heidi last talked to her on Monday. We pulled up a lot of prints, but you know as well as I that if these perps are pros, they wear gloves."

"What else did the Coben women say?"

I tried not to wince as he pulled a splintery cigar butt out of his shirt pocket and reached for a box of matches. "Mrs. Coben received a hefty divorce settlement and could afford nice things. Besides the stuff you already knew about, she's missing a computer, a fax machine, a cordless telephone, a bunch of silver pieces, a pair of antique dueling pistols, a camcorder, and a jewelry box that deserved a spot in Fort Knox. There may be more after she does a thorough search."

Harve fired up the cigar, eyed the overflowing ashtray, and dropped the match on the floor. "They had all that expensive stuff, lived in the middle of nowhere, and *didn't* have a burglar alarm?"

"Heidi said that Katherine set it off by accident when she first moved in. After that, she refused to turn it on because she was afraid she'd do it again. I guess she figured her presence was enough, but she parked her car in the garage and more than likely turned off the lights when she went to bed."

"Damn," Harve drawled, the cigar bobbing. "Did you ask the women all those questions about who could have known they were away?"

"Not a single concurrence," I said as I closed the notebook. "The burglars obviously weren't watching the house, or they would have been aware of Katherine's presence. They weren't worried about the alarm, either."

"Any of the other houses have alarms?"

"No, all the victims have in common is that they chose to live in rural areas. One couple retired here from Chicago, another from someplace in California. One husband's a history professor, one a minister, one a consulting architect. Elsie gets by on Social Security and what I imagine is a modest savings account." I slapped the notebook on his desk. "This is driving me nuts, Harve!"

"You and me both—and you're not up for reelection."

I glowered at him for a moment, wondering what he'd do if I yanked off my badge and stomped out of his office. Probably not much, since my paycheck came from the town council. I calmed myself down and said, "I may as well go by Sterling Pitts's office and try one last time to talk him into rescheduling his so-called maneuvers. You have the address handy?"

He looked it up in the telephone directory, told me how to find it, and was back to staring at the folders when I left. LaBelle ignored me as I went through the reception area, no doubt disappointed that my head was still firmly attached to my neck. She did not instruct me to have a good day.

The Tri-County Patriots' Insurance office was housed in a shabby little building on an unfamiliar street. On one side was a warehouse, and on the other a dry cleaning establishment. There were no vehicles in the parking lot, but through the window I spotted a young woman seated at a desk.

I went inside and said, "Is Mr. Pitts here?"

"Oh, no," she said, popping her gum earnestly. "He won't be back until Tuesday morning. Is there something I can do for you?"

"I guess not," I said. "Did he tell you where he was going?"

"He didn't tell me, but I heard him on the phone with his wife, and he said something about a seminar

in Kansas City. Do you need to file a claim or something? I can give you the forms."

"I just wanted to speak to Pitts," I said, then went
back to my car and headed for Maggody, where I
suspected I'd find him.

Chapter 7

I drove past the old Wockermann place, but I didn't see any vehicles in the driveway or indication anyone was in the house. I considered stopping at Estelle's to ask if she'd noticed any activity, but a UPS truck blocked her driveway. Not wanting to be subjected to a private viewing of the latest batch of fingernail polish, I headed for Ruby Bee's.

She scowled as I took a stool. "I don't suppose it occurred to you to inform me before you took off this morning, did it? After all, I'm only your mother."

"Sorry," I said humbly, in that I'd missed lunch and it was well past suppertime. "The sheriff asked me to investigate a crime over in Mayfly. I just now got back to town, and I sure could use a grilled cheese sandwich and a glass of milk."

"I was so worried about you that I got a bad case of heartburn. I had to suffer through happy hour before I could slip away to my unit to take some medicine." She paused so I could appreciate the immensity of my misdemeanor, then said, "General Pitts and a woman named Judy Milliford checked in about an hour ago. They took separate rooms, so I don't guess he's up to any hanky-panky. I put her between me and Kayleen, and him in the building across the parking lot."

I was not impressed with this minor concession to virtue; the locals refer to the Flamingo Motel as the Stork Club—and not because they're ornithologically challenged. "Have you seen any of the others in this group?"

"I reckon they're camping on Kayleen's property.

She's back in town, by the way. She stopped by to tell me, in case I was worried about her having car trouble on that narrow highway from Malthus. I think that's real considerate of her. Don't you think so?"

"Oh, yes," I said, still hoping for some supper. "About that sandwich and—",

"Ruby Bee!" shrieked Estelle from the doorway. "I don't know what I'm gonna do! I couldn't believe my eyes!"

I spun around, nearly toppling off the stool. "Was your house burglarized?"

"This is a sight worse than that. Get your coat and come with me, Ruby Bee. You got to help me figure out what to do!"

"Does this have anything to do with the militia?" I asked. "Did somebody fire a gun or launch a grenade in your direction?"

This finally got her attention. "No, missy, I haven't seen hide nor hair of them. My inheritance from Uncle Tooly was delivered half an hour ago. The polite young man helped me get the crate into the living room and even pried the top off. Well, I liked to have died when these big ugly birds hissed at me, and the delivery man bolted out the door to his truck and was almost at the stop sign before I got out to the porch."

"What are they?" demanded Ruby Bee.

"How should I know? Are you coming or not? I can't leave them in the living room. I got two appointments tomorrow, and I can't see Eileen having her hair trimmed while she's being hissed at."

"It's Friday night, Estelle, and I usually get a decent crowd. I can't afford to close the bar just because you've got hissy birds in your living room."

I grinned at Ruby Bee. "Don't worry about that. I'll hold down the fort while you go to Estelle's house, as long as you don't mind if I make myself a sandwich."

Estelle acknowledged my generous gesture with a nod, then said, "So are you coming or not, Ruby Bee? If you have some terrible crisis, I'd like to think I'd drop everything and come galloping to your rescue. Remember when you ran out of gas at the flea market and I drove all the way out there, even though it meant canceling an appointment? I seem to recollect it was a good twenty miles each way. And what about the time I went with you to Noow Yark City so you wouldn't—"

"If you'll stop jabbering, I'll get my coat," Ruby Bee said in a wintry voice, clearly not pleased at having certain incidents dredged up. "It seems to me you might should call that lawyer and ask him what you're supposed to do with the birds. He's the one who sent them, after all."

"His office is closed by now. I can call him Monday, but I've got to do something right this minute!"

I waited until they were out the door, then went into the kitchen. I was hunting for the mayo when I heard a voice call, "Hello? Are you open?"

My stomach whimpered as I dutifully returned to the barroom. The voice belonged to a guy approximately my age. He had agreeable features, short brown hair, and a surprised expression as he stared at my badge. To my dismay, he was wearing a camouflage jacket, but he could be nothing more exotic than a hunter stalking a beer instead of a deer. Or so I told myself.

"I'm covering for Ruby Bee while she's out on an errand," I said. "Can I get you something?"

"I stopped for directions. I'm looking for County 102, but I must have missed it in the dark."

I relinquished my hunter conjecture. "Could your destination be Kayleen Smeltner's property?"

"That's right. I guess you heard about us coming, huh? You don't have to concern yourself. We've been doing this for years and never had any problems with the authorities. My name's Barry Kirklin. What's yours?"

"Arly Hanks. The turnoff for County 102 is next to a funny-looking metal structure with a trailer parked in the yard. Kayleen, a woman named Judy something-or-other, and your fearless leader are staying in the motel behind the bar. I don't know which units they're in, but they're the only ones out there."

"Pitts is hardly a contemporary version of Daniel Boone," Barry said with a wry smile. "I'm kind of surprised that Jake would let Judy out of his sight all night, although it's not as if she gives him any reason to distrust her. She's a mousy little housewife, not especially attractive or vivacious. God knows no one would ever accuse her of being sexy."

"The way Kayleen is?" I suggested.

"Kayleen's a potential land mine, but she doesn't seem to realize the impact she has on every man in the room. An interesting mixture of naiveté and sexiness, wouldn't you say?"

Frankly, I didn't think it was the least bit interesting. "Do you want a beer?" I asked him.

"Pitts doesn't permit alcohol on retreats, so I'd better not. I might be in the mood Monday evening—if you'll let me buy you one."

"If you survive the weekend, I'll think about it. As I said, they're out back in the only units liable to have lights on. Surely someone clever enough to unmask an international conspiracy can find them."

"Surely," he said, then turned and left.

Mrs. Jim Bob drove by the rectory, slowing down to peer at the dark windows. Having grilled employees at the SuperSaver, she knew darn well where Jim Bob was, but she had no idea where Brother Verber had been ever since the Wednesday night prayer meeting. She'd been too annoyed to speak to him after the service, due to his failure to appear at her house to discuss the Thanksgiving pageant—which most likely had something to do with a particular person who'd had the nerve to show her painted face again. Maybe he was too kind-hearted to point his finger at the moneylender and order her to slink away in disgrace. Maybe he believed his duty was to welcome sinners into the congregation.

She'd been inside the rectory several times, making sure he hadn't drowned in the bathtub or suffered a stroke in his bed. As a gesture of Christian compassion, she'd even cleaned up his kitchen, run a dust rag over the furniture in the living room, and straightened up the piles of what he assured her was study material (even though it took a lot of willpower to touch the nasty things with names like *Naughty Nipples* and *Whiplash*). Why, she'd gone so far as kneel in the Assembly Hall to pray for the strength to forgive him for his transparently feeble excuse for postponing the pageant meeting.

Surely he'll be grateful, she thought, as she turned around in Lottie's driveway and drove back toward her house on Finger Lane. It wouldn't hurt to keep the rectory more attractive, either. She could have Perkins's eldest clean for him half a day a week, and she herself would bring fresh flowers from her garden in the spring. Although Jim Bob would object, she'd invite Brother Verber to supper several times a week and make a better effort to make him feel appreciated.

Once at home, she sat down at the kitchen table and started on a list of ways the legitimate members of the congregation could keep him occupied in his free time. Lottie might be persuaded to invite him over for coffee, and the Missionary Society could have him attend their weekly meetings to say grace before refreshments. She'd ask him to accompany her to Farberville to select new fabric for the sofa, and afterwards to have lunch at a tea shoppe.

She said a brief prayer of gratitude to the Lord for blessing her with a creative mind, then got back to work.

"I don't see them," Estelle whispered to Ruby Bee, who was standing on her tiptoes next to her while they peeked through the living room window. "They might be in the crate—or they might be running loose in the house. We need to be real careful. They have sharp beaks and beady orange eyes, and they're ornery enough to peck the freckles right off your arm."

"Did you leave the door open when you left?" whispered Ruby Bee, although she wasn't sure why they were worried that the birds might be listening to them.

"You can see for yourself that it's closed. I guess the only thing to do is go inside and find them. If they're in the crate, you put the lid on and I'll get the hammer and nails. First thing Monday morning they'll be on their merry way back to that lawyer in Oklahoma."

"You said Uncle Tooly took to doing experiments. Do you think the birds are freaks that he created in his laboratory? You might be able to sell them to a carnival show, you know. The one at the county fair last September advertised they had a boy that was raised by wolves, a five-legged calf, and a prehistoric fish."

Estelle bit her lip as she tried to recollect exactly what the hissy birds looked like. They were almost as tall as she was, with gangly necks, scruffy brown feathers, and those demonic eyes. "I wouldn't have any idea how to get in touch with a carnival, but I know for a fact I won't get a wink of sleep until they're out of my house. Are you ready?"

"I guess so," said Ruby Bee. "You go first. I'll be close behind you in case I need to jerk you back to safety."

"It'd be better if you went first so you can get the lid on the crate. The hammer's in a drawer in the kitchen, and I'll have to hunt around for nails. I'd feel a sight safer if you were holding down the lid."

Ruby Bee looked at her. "They're *your* birds, not mine, Estelle. If you're too scared to go in there, you can stay at the Flamingo until you can find someone to get 'em in the crate. You could persuade Diesel to come down from the ridge and bite their heads off. General Pitts might agree to attack the house."

"I wonder why Uncle Tooly said in his will that I was to get them. He was a mite odd, but he always seemed fond of me. I had a parakeet when I was in pigtails. He may have assumed that I was a bird fancier on account of that."

"Piss or get off the pot," snapped Ruby Bee. "It's

cold and dark out here. Arly can't handle the Friday night crowd by herself. She went to the police school, but I'll bet they never taught her how to throw a fractious drunk out of a bar. That takes years of practice."

Estelle took a last peek in the window. "I don't see anything. I think I'll go around to the back and look through the kitchen window. You wait here." She disappeared around the corner of the house.

Ruby Bee put her hands in her pockets and tried not to shiver as the wind did its darndest to sneak down her collar. It was crazy to stand here half the night, she thought as she went up on the porch and tried to catch a glimpse of the birds through the glass panes in the door. Surely Estelle was exaggerating. Alfred Hitchcock had made a movie about killer birds, but nobody in real life had ever been attacked like that. Then again, she reminded herself, Uncle Tooly had owned some mighty queer sheep.

A gust of wind liked to push her off the porch. "This is ridiculous," she said, not bothering to whisper. "If you birds are in there, you'd better mind your manners 'cause I'm coming in and I'm not putting up with being hissed at or pecked."

She didn't exactly charge into the house, however, but instead turned the knob and eased open the door a scant inch. Nothing. She tried another inch, then squinted into the room. She was about to throw open the door when something hit her hand. The unexpected burst of pain was so startling that she jumped back, lost her balance, and went tumbling off the porch into a massive forsythia bush.

"Estelle!" she howled, fighting to get free of the brittle branches. One foot was snagged above her head, the other twisted under her in a most undignified position. "Estelle, darn it, get back here!"

"What in tarnation . . . ?" said Estelle as she rounded the corner, not spotting the arms flailing from the middle of the forsythia. "Where are you, Ruby Bee?"

"Here, and I'm stuck, in case you didn't notice. Would you stop gawking and do something?"

"What're you doing?"

"I am trying to get free of this bush. It's got me tangled up like it's got barbed wire for branches." She grunted as she wiggled around to get her hands on the ground.

Estelle pulled back branches as best she could, and after getting swatted in the face and scratched up to her wrists, managed to help Ruby Bee escape. "I still don't understand why you were in the forsythia," she said. "Did you jump in there for a reason?"

"I fell in there," Ruby Bee said, trying to hide her mortification. She went on to relate how she'd opened the front door, then added, "I suppose one of those birds pecked me on the hand. It hurt worse than a pebble from a slingshot. If I hadn't had on gloves, it would have drawn blood."

"I told you they're not the most mannersome critters. You should have—" She broke off with a gurgle of dismay, then grabbed Ruby Bee's arm and hustled her toward the door. "They're over by the station wagon. We'd better get inside before they come after us."

Ruby Bee wasn't inclined to dawdle.

"The public forum is at ten o'clock sharp," Sterling told Barry and Kayleen, who were seated on his bed. The table was burdened with a computer, monitor, and laser printer; a cord slinked from the modem to the telephone across the room. His duffel bag was unpacked and in the closet. A holster hung on the headboard of the bed. On the wall next to a topographical map of the region was a framed picture of wide-eyed kittens in a beribboned basket. Variations of the latter (but not the former) were in all the units.

"I'll put signs along the road first thing in the morning," said Barry. "From what Dylan said when he was out here earlier in the week, we won't get more than a dozen potential recruits. He hit the pool hall, the supermarket, a body shop, and even the launderette, trying to spark some interest in the cause, but he says there's a lot of apathy in this town."

Sterling shook his head. "Apathy is our biggest challenge, and the only way to overcome it is with education and persistence. Kayleen, do you have the printed material to be distributed tomorrow?"

"The boxes are in my trunk," she said. "I gave Dylan all the remaining brochures, so you'd better order some more."

"We don't need to order them now that I have a photocopier at my office. I'll write one up on the computer and run off copies in the evenings when that snoopy secretary of mine isn't there. It seems we're set for the moment, so you"—he gestured at Barry—"can leave. Judy has been ordered to be ready to depart for the encampment at 0600 hours. Kayleen, you can transfer the boxes and ride with us to minimalize visibility."

"In the Hummer?" she said, winking at Barry. "I don't think anybody in this podunk place has ever seen a vehicle like yours. They may ask you to be in the homecoming parade."

Sterling bristled at the implication he had erred in selecting the Hummer. "When the crisis strikes, transportation will play an important role in survival. A tactical withdrawal may be the only solution. Having a proper vehicle may be the difference between being able to escape from a dangerous situation and being stranded and at the mercy of the enemy."

"How much did it cost?" asked Barry.

"None of your damn business. Now get out to the encampment and do whatever it takes to keep Red Rooster from having a hangover in the morning."

Barry gave him a casual salute, smiled at Kayleen, and left the motel room. Instead of continuing to his car out in front of the bar, he pressed his ear against the door.

"—that I haven't received this month's payment," Sterling was saying in a stony voice.

"Moving here left me temporarily short of cash, what with down payments for the two properties and the initial outlay for the remodeling. Give me some time and I'll get caught up."

"I certainly hope so."

"Are you done with me? I spent the last two days rearranging the storage cubicle, and I'd like to take a hot shower and get to bed early."

"Sit down."

Barry headed for his truck.

The telephone rang at the end of the bar. I swallowed a mouthful of cherry cobbler, took a drink of milk, and sauntered down to answer it.

"Is that you, Arly?" said Ruby Bee.

"Arly's locked in the pantry," I said gruffly. "This here's the convict what's holding all the rednecks hostage on account of the SWAT team outside. Let me tell ya, them cops are mean as their hides will hold."

"This ain't the time for childishness, young lady. Estelle and I are experiencing a small problem at her house. Shoo away all the customers and get your smart-aleck self over here this minute."

Resuming my regular voice, I said, "For starters, there's nobody here except yours truly. A foursome from the trailer park came by for coffee and pie, but they're gone. Some college kids came in, looked at my badge, and scurried out the door. Being a highly trained professional, I concluded they were underage. Who else . . .? Oh, a guy asking for directions. That about sums it up. Not a very impressive crowd, I'm sorry to say."

"Then lock up and get out here."

"It's only eight-fifteen, and more people might show up. What if Mrs. Jim Bob comes cruising for truckers and finds the door locked? You wouldn't want to lose her business, would you?" I was being perverse, true, but it had been pretty darn boring for the last hour. I'd not yet sunk to the level of dancing to some nasal ballad on the juke box. I had, however, checked the titles.

"I've about had it with you, Ariel Hanks. You're

not so big that I can't still turn you over my knee and give you a paddling with my hair brush."

"Yes, I am. You may outweigh me, but I'm a good four inches taller than you, and furthermore, I can outrun you. Want to race sometime?" I listened to her sputter incoherently for a moment, then added, "Okay, what's the problem?"

"Well, you know how Estelle's uncle was killed by sheep, and—"

"Sheep?" I said. "You've got to be kidding."

"It was mentioned in my column last week, so I assumed you knew about it."

"You write a column?"

"I told you I'd been asked to do a little column every week for *The Starley City Star Shopper*. I never dreamed you'd make an effort to read what your own mother writes. I'm as sure as I live and breathe that Dear Abby's daughter reads her column, and real faithfully, too."

"You're writing an advice column?" I said, filling a glass with beer. "You're telling people how to manage their marriages and children? Do you honestly think you're qualified to—"

"It's not an advice column. It's more of a friendly letter to let folks know what's going on in Maggody. Now, are you done asking questions? I don't aim to spend the night here at Estelle's. She has so much junk in the guest room that I'd have to sleep on the couch. My back's been acting up lately—if I slept on that lumpy old thing, I wouldn't be able to hobble across the room in the morning."

"What's going on?"

"Just get out here—and bring your gun. You most likely won't need more than two bullets, but it wouldn't hurt to have a spare in case you miss."

For an insane moment, I wondered if I was supposed to shoot her and Estelle. "Does this have something to do with the birds?" I asked. "Are they still in the crate?"

"Not exactly," she said, then hung up, leaving me

to gape at the neon Coors sign on the wall behind the bar.

Reed tossed a piece of wood on the fire, then took a beer from the cooler and sat down on a log. He stared at the flames, imagining what it'd be like if Bobbi Jo was in the tent, all snuggled up in the sleeping bag and waiting for him, her lips moist and her eyes hungry. It was her own damn fault the marriage had gone down the drain, he told himself sourly. He'd offered to drag her along when he went fishing—not every time, but once in a while—but she always stuck up her nose like she thought she was too good to clean a mess of fish. It wasn't like he'd *had* to invite her.

"Hey, good buddy," said Barry as he came into the clearing and dropped his gear. "Where's everybody else?"

"Dylan took my truck to go back to Farberville to get us a couple of pizzas. Jake muttered something about checking on his wife and stalked off. The others are staying in some dumpy motel."

"Yeah, I know. I stopped there before coming up here. You'd better make sure Sterling doesn't smell pepperoni on your breath in the morning. The old fart'll bore you to tears talking about surviving off the land." Barry got himself a beer and squatted across the fire from Reed. "Do you trust Dylan?" he asked.

"No reason not to. Sterling said he talked to one of the brethren in Colorado that confirmed Dylan's story. What's your beef with him?"

"I thought I saw your truck parked behind some abandoned building that sure as hell wasn't a pizza joint. What time did he leave?"

"Maybe six. So what if it's after nine? It's Friday night and the pizza joints are liable to be crowded."

"Not *that* crowded. I'm beginning to wonder if he's who he says he is. What if he's trying to infiltrate our group so he can tip off the feds?"

"Tip 'em off about what?"

Barry shrugged. "Okay, so we haven't done anything illegal as of yet. He doesn't know that. He may believe we're stockpiling assault weapons and building bombs in Sterling's garage. He could even have us confused with that group that used to be over past Harrison. They had a factory in the compound for making hand grenades and another for manufacturing silencers and shit like that to sell at gun shows. Their survival school cost five hundred dollars, and they could pick and choose——" He clamped down on his lower lip, wishing he hadn't mentioned the survival school. Reed had damn near exploded when he'd been rejected. "Anyway, if Dylan's who he says he is, why's your truck in town?"

Jake came into the clearing. "I saw it, too. If we got some bastard in our midst, we're gonna make him real sorry."

From *The Starley City Star Shopper*, November 15:

What's Cooking in Maggody?
BY RUBELLA BELINDA HANKS

I hope all my readers are planning a fine feast for Thanksgiving. If you're not gonna spend the day with kinfolk, come out to Ruby Bee's Bar & Grill. The blue-plate special will feature turkey, stuffing, cranberries, and all the fixin's for a special price of $4.95, including sweet potato pie for dessert. I don't want to brag on myself, but it's been said I make the lightest biscuits west of the Mississippi. Come find out for yourself.

Dahlia is getting along just fine. She and Kevin have settled on a name for the baby: Kevin Fitzgerald Buchanon, Junior. If you want to drop by a little present, I'll see that she gets it.

Dontay Buchanon got out of prison last week, and his wife wants him to know that if he so much as sets foot on their farm he'll end up with a load of buckshot in his behind. If you're reading this, Dontay, you'd better take heed.

The County Extension Homemakers meeting has been changed to the first Tuesday of every month, except for December, when it's the first Monday, and January, when it's the third Thursday.

Elsie McMay got home safely, and she reports that all that was taken in the burglary was her television set.

On Wednesday afternoon Kayleen Smeltner and Brother Verber searched all over this part of the county for the fellow who did her a kindness twenty-three years ago. Give me a call here at Ruby Bee's Bar & Grill if she's talking about you.

Until next time, God bless.

JOAN HESS

RUBY BEE'S SWEET POTATO PIE

¾ cup butter
¾ cup sugar
⅓ cup milk
1 ½ cups grated cooked sweet potatoes
¾ teaspoon ginger
2 tablespoons grated orange rind
1 10-inch pie shell

Cream the butter, adding the sugar as you go, until it's all fluffy and light. Take turns adding the milk and sweet potatoes, then toss in the ginger and orange rind and mix real well. Pour into the pie shell and bake at 300 degrees for maybe 45 minutes, until it's golden brown and set. Serve warm with whipped cream.

Chapter 8

Sterling looked at his watch, which was guaranteed to depths of three hundred feet below sea level and displayed the phases of the moon. "It's 1000 hours. Where is everybody?"

"I forewarned you about the apathy," Barry said, straining to hear the sound of vehicles coming toward the edge of the pasture where they'd set up a card table to distribute information and application forms.

Kayleen was by the table, rearranging booklets with titles like *The Grisly Truth About Fluoridation* and *Is International Drug Trafficking Masterminded by the British Monarchy?* "You'd think there were a few concerned citizens in this town, though. Brother Verber said a couple of folks asked him questions after his sermon last week. I'm not real sure he could answer them, but he said he tried."

"Where's Dylan?" growled Sterling.

Barry pointed at the farmhouse. "I sent him, Red Rooster, and Blitzer to excavate the old root cellar to utilize as a storeroom and bunker. If we lubricate the weapons and wrap them in plastic, we shouldn't have a problem with corrosion. Red Rooster will price cots and water jugs at the army surplus store."

"Good work, Apocalypse," Sterling said, shading his eyes and peering vainly across the pasture. "I realize no one showed up when we tried this at Bradley's place, but I assumed that was because of the remote location. You'd think the citizens of Maggody could— Look! A pickup truck's coming!"

"And someone's walking this way from the direction of the creek," added Barry. "I guess there are a few patriots left."

Kayleen squinted across the corn stalks. "That's Jeremiah McIlhaney in the truck, and he's got Earl Buchanon with him. Neither of them is overly bright, but they're hard workers. They might do just fine."

"Who's the fellow down that way?" asked Sterling.

"I can't rightly say because of the knit cap pulled down so low and those sun glasses and that mustache. I don't think I've seen a mustache like that in Magody, but I may not have met everybody as of yet."

Barry moved to Sterling's side, and in a low voice said, "I don't like this. Could he be a foreign agent?"

"He could be, I suppose. They've been known to infiltrate groups such as ours. We'll have to be real cautious with him until I can determine his background."

"You had any more luck contacting Dylan's old group?"

"No, and it's rather odd. The password worked the first time, but I've tried several times since then to access the message board with no success. The phone's been disconnected."

"Could that be Dylan's doing?"

Sterling stopped staring at the figure on foot and turned to Barry. "Why do—what makes you say this?" he sputtered. "Do you know something that you haven't told me?"

"I just don't trust him, especially after last night."

The truck came to a halt beside the Hummer before Sterling could demand an explanation. "Welcome," he called to the two men as they emerged. "It's heartening to meet patriots like yourselves."

"Hey, Earl, Jeremiah," said Kayleen, giving them her friendliest Betty Crocker smile. "How're you boys this morning? Earl, I hear you're going to be a grandpa in a few weeks. You and Eileen must be real tickled."

"Yeah," said Earl. He stuck his hands in his pocket and studied the mud caked on the sides of the truck. Kayleen winked at Jeremiah. "I saw your daughter the other day at the Dairee Dee-Lishus. She's such a pretty thing. I'll bet the boys hang around her like a litter of lovesick pups.''

Jeremiah felt his ears heating up. ''Thanks, Kayleen,'' he mumbled. He noticed the figure walking toward them and elbowed Earl. ''What's Kevin been doing down at Boone Creek? Don't he know it's too cold for fishing?''

''I dunno,'' said Earl, pulling off his cap to scratch his head. ''I thought Dahlia said he had to work this morning. Maybe the schedule changed or something.''

They stood in silence, watching Kevin as he slipped and slid toward them. When he came around the front of the Hummer, he froze like an ungainly scarecrow and said, ''Uh, Pa, I didn't reckon you'd be here. I was—well, out taking a walk and decided to cut up this way on account of it being a shortcut of sorts, and then I noticed the trucks and—''

''Welcome'', Sterling cut in smoothly. ''You all already know Kayleen. I'm General Pitts and this is Colonel Kirklin. I'd like you to look over our material and take anything that interests you. All of it should—if you're as concerned as we are about the sorry state of the government these days.'' Rather than stepping aside to allow them to get to the card table, however, he launched into a rambling lecture about the erosion of constitutional rights and the perils of an invasion by foreign troops.

Twenty minutes later, after having thoroughly bewildered Earl, Jeremiah, and Kevin (who never had a chance), he gestured dramatically at Cotter's Ridge. ''This may well be your last line of defense, which is why survival training is so vital. You may be forced to take your families up there and live off the land until militias like ours can drive the foreigners into the sea.''

''You'd better drive if you're going to the sea,'' Earl said. ''It's a good⊃six or seven hundred miles to the Gulf of Mexico, and more like two thousand to the Pacific.''

Sterling reminded himself of the necessity of recruiting privates and corporals, who would be expendable in battle. "How astute," he said to Earl, who was grinning at Jeremiah. "Please examine the material, and don't hesitate if you have any questions."

Earl looked at Kevin. "What's that piece of black paper doin' taped on your lip, son?"

"Read 'em and weep," said Jim Bob as he spread his poker hand on the table. "Didn't believe I'd picked up that third cowboy, did ya?"

Roy Stiver folded his cards. "I'm surprised you can count that high, Jim Bob. From what I hear at the barber shop, you have a tough time making change at the SuperSaver. Perkins said you tried to stiff his eldest out of ten dollars."

Jim Bob was casting around for a response that would leave Roy feeling as naked as a picked chicken when Larry Joe came into the trailer, a magazine in his hand.

"Did y'all hear something a minute ago?" he asked.

"I heard Jim Bob guffawing at how lucky he is," said Roy. "I didn't hear you flush the toilet 'cause it ain't but a hole in the ground. If it's the same to you, I'd prefer not to hear exactly which bodily functions you performed out there."

"No, I'm serious, so listen up," Larry Joe said with enough earnestness to get their attention. "Just as I was leaving the outhouse, I heard a strange boom, kind of like a bass drum. I looked in that direction and saw this—this thing behind some bushes. I couldn't make it out real good, but it was more'n five feet tall and it was sizing me up like I might make a tasty meal. I liked to jump out of my skin."

"It was Diesel, you near-sighted dolt," Jim Bob said as he poured bourbon into his glass.

Roy nodded. "Yeah, everybody knows he's living up here. Or maybe it was Raz, making sure we weren't fixing to help ourselves to a couple of jars of shine. That stuff strips paint better than any commercial goop, and your skin along with it if you don't watch what you're doing."

"I don't think it was human," said Larry Joe. "It had eyes like orange marbles and a head no bigger than a baseball."

Jim Bob began to shuffle the cards. "Jesus H. Christ, Larry Joe, the next thing you'll be doing is telling us you saw a flying saucer, too. Are you gonna stand there like a virgin in a roomful of preachers, or are you gonna play poker?"

"They arrived yesterday," I told Harve, who'd called just as I was heading out the door of the PD. His timing was downright uncanny. "Rumor has it that Generalissimo Pitts is driving a Sherman tank, but it may be an exaggeration. Other than that, nobody seems to know or care that they're here. I'm not going to worry about them unless they start firing bazookas at Estelle's Hair Fantasies."

"We'll blow up that bridge when we come to it. I talked to Katherine Avenued's mother this morning about arranging for the body to be shipped to Tucson. McBeen says there's no reason to do more than a perfunctory autopsy since the cause of death's so obvious. He did run a drug screen to make sure she wasn't an addict likely to have unsavory friends. She was clean."

"I told Mrs. Coben and Heidi that I'd go over there this afternoon to get an update on what was stolen. Let's hope Heidi has remembered something Katherine might have mentioned in passing."

"Like the license plate of the truck that followed her all over Farberville the day she was killed?"

"Bingo," I said, unamused.

Harve obviously was, and I had to listen to him snort and snicker for a while before he calmed down and said, "LaBelle said to ask you if Estelle ever got her inheritance."

"She wasn't too thrilled," I said, then went on to describe the previous evening's events. "When I got there, the birds were long gone. From Estelle's hysterical description, I think they're ostriches. Uncle Tooly must have had a twisted sense of humor—or been nursing a grudge against his niece for a long while."

"Maybe so. Anyway, if you find out anything new from the Cobens, lemme know."

"Sure," I said, thinking of the proverbial snowball's chance in hell. Not good, from all accounts.

After I hung up, I took out the reports on the previous burglaries and skimmed them. I had no brilliant insights, however, and I was in the back room turning off the coffee pot when the front door opened. I went to the doorway in time to see Raz slam the door.

"I jest come to tell you," he said, his eyes blazing and saliva dribbling out of the corners of his mouth, "what I'm gonna do if you don't get that goddamn Diesel off the ridge."

"What would that be?"

"He's gonna be right sorry he was ever born, 'cause I'm gonna put so many holes in him that the wind'll whistle 'Dixie' through him."

"Shall I assume you and he had another unpleasant encounter?" I asked as I went behind the desk and sat down. "Do you want to file a complaint?"

"I ain't got no use for no complaint. I reckon a twelve-gauge shotgun is what I need." He stuffed a wad of chewing tobacco in his cheek, apparently forgetting how much I despise the habit. "This morning I went squirrel huntin'. I left Marjorie in the truck, but I put down the window so she could git some fresh air. She must've decided to root for acorns and wandered up the ridge. All of a sudden she started squealing something terrible, so I runned up a ways and found her huddled under a ledge. She was so scared she could hardly poddle back to the truck." He looked around for a place to spit, caught my glare, and swallowed. "I've had it with Diesel. Unless'n you make him take his sorry ass to a place so wild the hoot owls holler in the daytime, I'm gonna git him good."

"How am I supposed to do that, Raz? I don't even know where his cave is. I gather it's near your still, so if you want to tell me where that is, I'll try to find Diesel and talk to him." The last bit was a flagrant lie, of course, but I was curious to see how he would react in such a quandary.

He opted for his standard response. "Ain't got no still."

"Then there's nothing I can do. Give my regards to Marjorie—and stay off the ridge."

After he stalked out the door, I put on lipstick, buffed my badge with my cuff, and headed for Mayfly.

Dahlia went into Jim Bob's SuperSaver and looked around for Kevin. He wasn't in sight, but he could be mopping one of the aisles or stacking oranges in the produce department. Not wanting to have to walk all over the store, she approached the checkout girl.

"Hey, Idalupino. Where's Kevvie?"

"He was here when I started work at nine, but then he got sick and had to go home. I hear tell there's some sort of bug going around that makes you retch your guts out something fierce."

Dahlia chewed on this for a moment. It didn't seem likely that Kevin was at home, since she herself had left less than ten minutes ago. He could have gone to his ma and pa's house, she supposed, on account of not wanting to expose her to his bug. Ever since she'd told him she had a bun in the warmer, he'd fretted like she was a dainty flower. In fact, he was gettin' to be a pain in the butt with all his questions about how she felt and how many times the baby'd kicked and could he fetch anything for her or rub her feet.

"Can I use the phone?" she asked Idalupino, who was flipping through a tabloid.

"It's in the employee lounge. Hey, Dahlia, do you think they really found a statue of Liberace on the back side of the moon?"

"I 'spose they could have," she said, then headed for the lounge to find out if her gallant knight was retching his guts out at his ma and pa's.

Ruby Bee waited until Estelle was settled on her stool and had pulled off her scarf and gloves. "I've been waiting on you for more than an hour," she said in the snippety voice that always irritated Estelle. "You said you'd be here at two so we could go to that garage sale in Hasty. There won't be anything left by now."

"I had something more important to do than look at cracked china and broken fishing rods," Estelle said as she took a piece of paper out of her handbag.

"Another letter from that lawyer?"

She shook her head. "I went over to the high school because I figured Lottie'd be there. Every Saturday she snoops through her students' lockers for incriminating evidence. Once she found a cartoon of her that Darla Jean had drawn—and it wasn't flattering. Another time she found a real steamy note to one of the football players implying the girl—I disremember who—had done some shameless things with him out by Boone Creek."

"So you went to the high school," prompted Ruby Bee, "and Lottie let you inside."

"Yes, and she unlocked the library for me so I could use the encyclopedias. They're on the old side, but I found what I wanted, which was about ostriches. I've got to know what I'm up against if they come back. I still get the heebie-jeebies when I think about 'em."

Ruby Bee caught the hint and poured a glass of sherry. "What all did you find out?"

"It's bad, real bad," she said, checking her notes. "The males can be as tall as eight feet and weigh three hundred and fifty pounds. The females are a mite smaller, but they're nothing to be sneezed at. When they're frightened, they can run forty miles an hour. They can also kick the livin' daylights out of you. What could Uncle Tooly have been thinking to burden me with creatures like that? Why couldn't he have left me tropical fish or a cat?"

"They're gone, Estelle, and I'd be real surprised if you ever see them again." Ruby Bee paused to do some calculating. "They've been gone close to fifteen hours, give or take. If they were going forty miles an hour, that's six hundred miles and they could be in

Mexico or Canada by now, depending, of course, on which way they went."

"Or they could be lurking out behind my garage, ready to attack me. First thing this morning I tried to call that blasted lawyer in Oklahoma on the off chance he was working on a Saturday morning, but all I got was his answering machine saying the office was closed on weekends. I called information, and this sassy girl told me his home number was unlisted. I don't think I slept more than ten minutes all night, imagining them scheming to sneak back in my house."

"I don't blame you," said Ruby Bee. "Tell you what—why don't you stay at the Flamingo until you talk to that lawyer on Monday and he tells you what to do? There's plenty of space, even with Kayleen, General Pitts, and that other woman staying there."

"Oh, I wouldn't want to cause any bother," Estelle said with a self-effacing smile. "You've got all those other folks to deal with. I'll just make sure all my doors and windows are locked tight and sit up all night in the living room with a rolling pin."

Ruby Bee knew darn well she was expected to beg. Normally, she wouldn't, but she'd seen how Estelle's hand shook when she picked up her glass. "You won't cause a bit of bother, so stop being silly. I'll even go back to your house with you and keep an eye out for the birds while you pack an overnight bag."

"The bag's in my station wagon."

"Well, then," Ruby Bee said, taking off her apron, "let's go get you fixed up. I was planning to shampoo carpets in two of the units tomorrow if I can find time. Would you mind staying next to General Pitts?"

"As long as he doesn't practice barking out orders like a drill sergeant. My nerves are too frazzled for that."

They collected Estelle's bag and continued around back to #5. Ruby Bee started to unlock the door, then stopped and frowned.

"That's strange," she murmured. "The door's not locked. I know I locked it last week when I was inspecting all the units to see which carpets needed to be shampooed."

"Maybe it didn't catch," said Estelle.

"It caught." Ruby Bee opened the door, stuck her head in, then went inside. "Somebody was in here recently. I always vacuum after a guest leaves, and you can see that shag has been squashed where a chair was moved. This somebody tried to put it back where it was, but the marks are off by an inch." She sidled around the bed and made sure no one was in the bathroom. "Look at this, Estelle! The toilet seat is up. I always leave it down on account of it looks nicer."

"The lamp's unplugged," called Estelle, who had no desire to evaluate the significance of an upright toilet seat. "Would you have left it that way?"

"Once I had a customer who stole all the light bulbs, including the ones in the ceiling fixture, so I make a point of switching on everything to make sure it works." She emerged from the bathroom to count coat hangers (three) and ashtrays (two). "Nothing's missing, as far as I can tell. It doesn't look like anybody sat on the bed. Whoever it was just raised the toilet seat, unplugged the lamp, and moved the chair out from under the table for a spell."

"Or you could have done those things yourself. You're getting to that age when folks start forgetting things like where they parked their car at the supermarket. The other day I saw Bur Grapper pushing a shopping cart all over the parking lot. He tried to tell me he was looking at the different models—but I didn't just get off the turnip truck."

Ruby Bee put her hands on her hips. "I am nowhere near that age, Estelle Oppers! Bur was old enough to vote by the time I was born. Now are you gonna stay here or not? I need to get some cobblers in the oven."

"I expect I will, but only so that you won't have to worry about me all alone with those hissy birds watching through the windows."

"Don't knock yourself out on my account." Ruby Bee marched out the door, resisting the urge to bang it closed behind her, and headed for the barroom. "Who said I was gonna worry?" she demanded of a starling perched on a garbage can.

"Now whatta we do?" asked Kevin as he squirmed in the muddy leaves, trying to get away from the water dripping off the bluff above him.

Dylan was leaning against a rock at the back of the recess. "Just keep a lookout. We only had a fifteen-minute head start, so the others should be getting close by now. Don't squawk when you see someone coming. Give me a hand signal, okay?"

Kevin clutched the rifle he'd been issued and stared so hard at the line of trees that his eyeballs bulged. It was more exciting than a John Wayne movie, he thought, but scary, too. He and Dylan had been assigned to defend the position while everybody else tried to capture them. His pa and Mr. McIlhaney hadn't looked all that enthusiastic, but they'd accepted weapons and had been listening to General Pitts's orders when he and Dylan had lit out of the campsite. That meant it was seven against two.

"You ever been in a real battle?" he asked Dylan.

"You know, with bullets instead of paint pellets and fellows trying to shoot you?"

"Yes."

"Did you shoot anybody?"

"That's the point, isn't it? It wouldn't be much of a battle if nobody shot anybody else. Shut up a minute. I thought I heard something above us. Keep watching the treeline." He crawled out to the ledge and stood up to peer at the bluff.

Kevin reminded himself that this was a make-believe battle. General Pitts had assured them that the paint pellets might sting but would do no damage. It wasn't like they'd be taken prisoner and subjected to torture. The worst that could happen was they'd lose the game. His pa'd laugh at him, but he did that anyway.

"Owl!" yelped Dylan.

"What's the matter?" demanded Kevin as he scrambled to his feet without thinking, and promptly banged his head so hard he went sprawling back into the leaves. He was about to repeat his question when a gun was fired from the woods. Whimpering, he covered his head and wiggled to the back of the recess.

After a moment, he found the courage to lift his head. Dylan was gone, which was a puzzlement. Had he been taken prisoner without so much as a peep? Or had he abandoned their position? It didn't seem like a comradely thing to do, Kevin thought as he cautiously wiggled back out to the rocky ledge. He couldn't see anybody in the brush on the hillside; he rolled over and looked up, but he didn't see anybody there either.

"This is a fine kettle of fish!" he said peevishly, but softly so's not to tip off the enemy, who had to be around somewhere.

A drop of cold water splashed his nose. He rolled back over and continued wiggling until he reached the edge. Risking life, limb, and a paint pellet to the forehead, he looked down.

Six feet below, Dylan lay flat on the ground, his arms and legs flung out as if he were hanging on to keep from being sucked up by a tornado. On his shoulder was a spreading stain that Kevin realized was not paint. There'd been a gunshot, he reminded himself as he scrambled down to Dylan and poked his arm.

"You okay?" he said, gulping.

Dylan opened his eyes. "Not really, so maybe you'd better get help."

"Yeah, right, that's what I'm gonna do." Kevin took a couple of breaths in case there were more orders. When none were forthcoming, he went galloping downhill. He stopped as he reached the line of trees and waved at Dylan, who was sitting up. "Stay there!" he shouted, then plunged into the brush.

It was slow going. Thorns snagged him with every step, and roots lay in wait to trip him. It hadn't seemed this rough when he and Dylan had come up from the camp, he was thinking as he stepped in the entrance of a burrow and fell on his face.

He was blinking back tears of frustration as he got to his feet, but he was determined to carry on just like the Duke did when he was leading his men through the jungle. Sure, his ankle hurt and his hands were muddy, but he was a soldier. Nothing was gonna prevent him from carrying out the mission. He'd taken one step when the paint pellet hit him in the middle of his chest.

"Bang, you're dead," Reed said cheerfully as he materialized from behind a tree.

Kevin looked down at the orange blotch. "You can't just say 'bang.' You have to fire your gun."

"I used my blowgun." Reed's eyes narrowed and his voice turned ugly. "Did you split and leave Dylan up there by hisself? Are you a deserter?"

"Course not. I was coming——"

"Then you must be a spy, and I caught you behind enemy lines. If this was the real thing, we could hang you without bothering with a trial."

Kevin glanced involuntarily at a nearby branch, then remembered why he was there. "Dylan was shot, and not with a paint pellet. His shoulder's all bloody. He was sitting up when I left him, though, so he ain't dead or anything like that."

"Damn!" said Reed. He took a fat pistol out of his pocket and fired into the air. A flare streaked toward the bluff. "That'll bring everybody. You wait here. When Kayleen shows up, tell her to get the medical kit."

Kevin wasn't sure if he was supposed to salute, but he went ahead and did it. "Yes, sir."

Chapter 9

Mrs. Jim Bob's timing was as uncanny, as Harve's. Thirty seconds after I'd arrived back at the PD after a fruitless trip to Mayfly and was debating whether to do anything about the red light flashing on the answering machine, she burst through the door.

"There you are!" she snapped.

"Well, that's good to know. I've been wondering all week where I was."

Mrs. Jim Bob blinked, then said, "Let's have no more flippant remarks, missy. I want to file a missing person report."

"He's at the deer camp. Ruby Bee saw him loading up cases of beer and supplies yesterday morning."

"I don't believe it," she said as she sank down in the visitor's chair and pursed her lips so tightly veins popped out in her neck. After a long moment of silence, she said, "I don't know why Ruby Bee would say such a thing. She may not have much admiration for him, but she wouldn't stoop so low as to make up a bald-faced lie like that. Doesn't she have any regard for his reputation?"

That was not a topic I wanted to explore. "Why don't you rent a four-wheel-drive and go roam around Cotter's Ridge until you find the deer camp? I'm sure the guys will be delighted to show you around and get some remodeling hints for the outhouse."

"Are you out of your mind?"

I crossed my eyes. "I might be. I certainly must be hearing voices, because I distinctly heard someone imply that Ruby Bee should have regard for Jim Bob's reputation. I hate to break it to you like this, but—"

"Who said anything about Jim Bob?"

"Then who's missing?" I said, surprised.

"Brother Verber. He hasn't been seen since the Wednesday evening prayer service. I want you to fill out a missing person report and issue a countywide alert. It's possible he had an accident and is bleeding to death in a ditch somewhere."

I leaned back in the chair and settled my feet on the corner of the desk. "He's only been gone for three days. Don't you think it's premature to start planning his funeral?"

Mrs. Jim Bob took out a hankie to dab at her nose. "I just know that something terrible has happened to him. How can I live with myself if I don't do everything possible to save him? I realize you don't believe in the power of prayer, being an atheist and all, but I have prayed for his return and begged the Lord to watch over him and keep him out of the arms of the wretched trollop."

"Wretched trollop?" I said.

"That pawn store woman," she said with a shudder. "Brother Verber was riding in her car Wednesday afternoon when he was supposed to be discussing the Thanksgiving pageant. Four hours later he vanished like a puff of smoke. I find that suspicious, and you should, too." She wadded up the hankie in her fist and leaned forward to stare at me. "What if he agreed to go with her after the service, and she took him to an abandoned house where devil worshipers meet and they sacrificed him to Satan?"

"Isn't it more likely that he heard about a sale on plastic poinsettias and dashed off to buy some to decorate the Assembly Hall next month?"

"He would have told me," Mrs. Jim Bob said firmly. "We have a close spiritual bond based on the strength of our faith in the Lord. While we're on the subject, you could use a healthy dose of that, couldn't you? If you'd bother to read the Book of Revelations, you'd be a sight more worried about eternity."

"It feels as if this conversation has been going on for an eternity," I said as I stood up. "If Brother Verber's not back tomorrow for the morning service, I'll ask the sheriff to have his deputies keep an eye out for him. I don't think we can call in the FBI until you get a ransom note."

"Will you question that woman?"

"When I get a chance. Now, if you'll excuse me, I have work to do. You wouldn't want me to get behind on all this fascinating paperwork and disgrace the badge bestowed on me by Hizzoner himself, would you?"

Mrs. Jim Bob tilted her head so she could look down her nose at me. "These days there's little doubt in most folks' minds that this is *not* a suitable job for a woman."

On that note, she swept out the door. I waited a moment in case she reappeared with another parting shot, then hit the button on the answering machine. The first two messages were from Ruby Bee and had something to do with upright toilet seats and shag carpet. The third was from LaBelle.

"Get yourself over to where the make-believe soldiers are camping," she said. "Sheriff Dorfer will meet you there. Ten-four."

Sometimes LaBelle goes through a phase of watching cop shows on television, so I figured she wasn't telling me the time of the message. I put on my coat while I listened to the last message, which again had to do with a toilet seat, then drove out to the old Wockermann place.

As soon as I'd passed the farmhouse, I saw half a dozen vehicles at the far side of the pasture. I followed a path of flattened corn stalks and parked between an ambulance and a monstrosity that could probably drive up a tree. Earl Buchanon and Jeremiah McIlhaney were sitting in one of the pickups, passing a whiskey bottle back and forth. Neither looked particularly pleased when I approached them.

"What's going on?" I asked. "Where's everybody?" Earl pointed a stubby finger at the ridge. "Way the hell up there, but I don't rightly know where. The camp's not too far on the other side of the gully. The sheriff said to tell you a deputy would be waiting there for you."

"What are you and Jeremiah doing, Earl?"

"Drinkin' whiskey so we won't freeze our butts off. The sheriff wants to talk to us after they bring down the body."

"Whose body?" I asked, wishing he was a tad more communicative.

Jeremiah bent forward to look at me. "A young fellow name of Dylan Gilbert. It sounds like he caught a bullet from a hunter."

Earl took a drink of whiskey and wiped his mouth with his hand. "I wish to hell we hadn't showed up in the first place. Eileen ain't gonna like it, especially when she finds out Kevin was here, too."

"Millicent's gonna be hotter than a peppermill that I didn't get the truck back so her and Darla Jean could go shoppin' in Farberville," Jeremiah said. "I'll hear about this till Christmas."

"I'll hear about it till Easter."

"Well, I'll hear about it till the Fourth of July."

I left them to discuss the impending repercussions and went across the gully. Les was leaning against a tree at the campsite, which consisted of four small tents, several coolers and cartons, and the smoldering remains of a campfire. "You made it, huh?" he said.

"It looks like it. What's going on?"

He gave me an abbreviated version of the scenario as we walked uphill. "What I don't understand," he added, "is why a bunch of grown men want to play 'Rambo on the Ridge' when it's the middle of deer season. A couple of years back a woman was shot in her own backyard. She thought she was safe on account of posting her land, but she didn't realize how far a bullet travels. That's likely to be what happened here. Somewhere on the ridge is a guy that's cussing up a storm 'cause he missed a buck. He'll never know what he really hit."

I was too busy battling the brush to respond. Five

minutes later we came into an open area. Harve was puffing on a cigar butt as he watched the paramedics zip up a black body bag. At his feet were strange-looking pistols, each with a tag. Standing in a group were Pitts, Kayleen, the guy who'd introduced himself the previous evening at Ruby Bee's, and two guys I'd never seen before. All of them wore olive drab and boots, although Kayleen still looked quite stylish. Kevin was sitting on a stump, his bony shoulders hunched, his face puckered, and his Adam's apple rippling as if he were trying to swallow a ping pong ball.

"Hey, Harve," I said as I joined him. "Les told me what happened. Are you really satisfied it was an accident?"

"I reckon so. Les and I checked these morons' pistols, and the only thing they can fire are paint pellets. We'll have ballistics check 'em out just to be sure."

The paramedics picked up the stretcher. "We're out of here," one of them said. "You shouldn't hang around, either. It's not the safest place I've been lately."

Harve waited until the paramedics reached the line of trees. "Okay, everybody down to pasture. We've got some talking to do before you pack your gear and get the hell out of here. Those of you who live else-where had better not come back, either."

Sterling harrumped like an ancient bullfrog. "The First Amendment guarantees the right of the people to assemble peaceably. That is precisely what we were doing, and will do so again if we so choose. You are a public servant."

"Don't expect me to wash your windows," Harve said, then stomped on the cigar butt and took off down the hill. Everybody else followed him, except for Kevin, who was surreptitiously wiping his eyes.

"Come on," I said to him. "Like the guy said, this is not the safest place."

"This is all my fault. It was my first mission, and I failed. Dylan told me how we was supposed to watch out for each other. He said that's what they do in a platoon, and we shook hands on it. He even said I was gonna make a real fine WASP."

"As in White Anglo-Saxon Protestant?" I said, confused as usual when trying to follow Kevin's thought process. "That's what you already are."

"No, it stands for White Aryan Superior . . . something or other. Patriot, mebbe. I'd start out as a private, but Dylan said I'd be promoted in no time."

I grabbed his arm and hauled him to his feet. "You can tell me what happened while we walk. Dylan had participated in this kind of thing before, right?"

"Yeah, and he was in a real battle, too. He dint look old enough to have been in Desert Storm. Have there been any wars since then?"

"There've been some military interventions," I said as I ducked under a branch. "Did you see anything at the moment the rifle was fired?"

"Not so's I recollect."

"What exactly do you recollect?"

Kevin stopped and sucked on his lip. "When we first got there, Dylan told me to watch down the hill. If I saw anybody, I was 'sposed to give him a hand signal. He dint say what kind of signal, but I figured I'd kinda wave like this." He flopped his wrist a couple of times. "But I dint see anybody. Then all of a sudden Dylan said he heard something up over us, so he came out and tried to see what it was. That's when he got shot."

"But you never saw anything in the woods?" I asked, shoving him back into motion.

"I saw a li'l squirrel in a tree."

I struggled not to sigh, but I was asking too much of myself. "What's that splotch on your jacket, Kevin?"

"Aw, one of the guys got me with a paint pellet. I told him I dint think it was fair the way he did it, but he just grinned like a mule with a mouthful of thistles."

"Isn't that the point of this nonsense?"

"Real soldiers aren't so dadburned sneaky," he said sullenly.

Rather than examine the goals of guerrilla warfare,

I told him to follow me. We went through the camp-site and crossed the gully. As I came up to the pasture, a raindrop nailed me on the back of my neck.

"I do not understand why we need to give state-ments," Sterling was saying to Harve. Their faces were equally mottled, and their noses were inches apart.

Having seen similar behavior in schoolyards, I hur-ried over to them and said, "Calm down, boys. Harve, why don't you use the PD? It'll be crowded, but no-ticeably warmer and drier."

"You have no more right to detain us," said Ster-ling, "than you do to confiscate our weapons. Aren't you up for re-election soon, Sheriff? If your flagrant disregard for individual rights is made public, you'd best start interviewing for jobs in the private sector. I am a member of the Rotary and Kiwanis clubs, a church deacon, and the vice-president of the county insurance agents' association. Furthermore, I am on a first-name basis with the lieutenant governor—"

"Shuddup," Harve snarled, then looked at me. "Ac-tually, I got a small problem. The county prosecutor's holding a press conference about the burglaries, and he wants me there to field questions. It starts in an hour. Since this was an accident and the statements are nothing more than a formality, I was hoping you'd handle them. Les'll hang around in case you need help. I know I've been asking a lot of favors from you, Arly, and I'll make it up to you after the election."

"How are you planning to do that, Harve? Get me my own team of bloodhounds?"

He thought about it for a moment. "Tell ya what—the next time we have to extradite somebody in New Orleans, I'll assign it to you. If you go a few days early, we can cover expenses and it'll be between the two of us."

"Squandering the taxpayers' money?" inserted Ster-ling with the same supercilious smile I was beginning to know too well.

Kayleen put her hand on his arm. "Honey, you're making things worse. Why don't we go sit in the Hummer?"

I grimaced at Harve. "It shouldn't take long, so I'll do it. As for New Orleans, I'd rather have those bloodhounds."

Ruby Bee used her passkey to let herself into General Pitts's unit. She hung fresh towels in the bathroom, gathered up the damp ones, and went back into the room. Despite the clutter of electronic equipment, everything was tidy and the bed made with surgical precision. She eyed the computer with all its cables, wondering if her electric bill was gonna be sky-high, then ran a feather duster over everything and locked the door behind her.

Estelle opened her door. "Snooping?"

"I'm cleaning the units same as I always do," Ruby Bee said as she headed for Kayleen's unit.

"I'll give you a hand," Estelle said, trotting after her. "Lemme carry those towels."

"I've been doing this by myself for thirty years, and I can manage just fine."

She unlocked the door of #3 and, with Estelle on her heels, went inside. She already knew Kayleen wasn't real orderly, so she wasn't surprised that the bed wasn't made and several articles of clothing were draped over the back of a chair. A small saucepan rested on the hot plate; Kayleen had asked permission, and since she was gonna be there for months, it seemed reasonable. "You can make the bed," she said to Estelle, then went on into the bathroom to exchange towels and clean the sink.

"Kayleen sure does look pretty in this photograph," said Estelle. "This must be her and her husband on their honeymoon at some fancy island resort. I didn't realize he was so much older than her. He reminds me of my grandpappy, who was ninety-seven when he passed away."

"Now who's snooping?" called Ruby Bee as she wiped out the sink.

"I was only making an observation. It's none of my business who she marries. I couldn't care less if she marries Raz Buchanon, although I can't see her sitting beside Marjorie on the sofa."

Ruby Bee came out of the bathroom, mutely made the bed, and went out the door.

Estelle caught up with her as she knocked on Judy Milliford's door. "Isn't she up on the ridge with everybody else?"

"No, I saw her come walking back here less than an hour ago. I invited her to have some coffee in the bar, but she said she needed to take a hot shower and get into some dry clothes. She doesn't sound as gung ho as—" She stopped as the door opened. "I brought you some clean towels."

Judy was dressed in a robe and her face was flushed. "Thanks, Ruby Bee," she said with a small smile. "I was going to take you up on that coffee, but I'm afraid I may have caught a cold. I think I'll just curl up in bed and watch television until I have to go back to the camp and fix supper."

"I thought they were going to live off the land," Ruby Bee said.

Judy's smile faded. "Jake says that's malarkey, that when we take to the mountains, we'll have plenty of supplies with us. If we run low, he can break into the enemy's supply depot and get more. We'll always have fresh fish and game, too."

"That must be a comforting thought," murmured Ruby Bee, "if you have cornmeal, anyway. You go lie down and have a nice nap, Judy. If I can bring you something from the bar, give me a call."

"Thanks," Judy said as she closed the door.

They were walking toward the back door of the bar when Mrs. Jim Bob came into the parking lot in her pink Cadillac. She drove right past them and pulled in beside the brown Mercedes, leapt out of the car, and began pounding on the door of #3.

"I know you're in there!" she shrieked. "I demand to know what you did with him, you wicked, wicked hussy! Don't think you can cower in there until I go away. I'm going to stay right here till you open this door!"

Estelle arched her carefully drawn eyebrows. "Think we should tell her that Kayleen's not there?"

"After what she said to me the other day?" replied Ruby Bee. She watched Mrs. Jim Bob's fist going up and down like a jackhammer for a moment, then went through the back door.

Once we all arrived at the PD, I realized there was no way to cram that many bodies in the back room. Counting myself, we were one shy of a football team— and the preponderance of olive drab made the situation feel even more claustrophobic.

"You two," I said, pointing at Sterling and Kayleen, "can go over to your units at the Flamingo and I'll take your statements there. Jeremiah and Earl, you all go on home and wait for me. Don't tell anybody what happened on the ridge. The last thing I need is a gaggle of sightseers getting themselves shot."

"What about me?" squeaked Kevin.

"You go home, too," I said, already dreading the necessity of taking his statement, even though he was the closest thing we had to an eyewitness. As they left, I heard Earl bawling out Kevin for missing work and Sterling sputtering at Kayleen about his constitutional rights. Now we were down to the size of a basketball team, and the room felt larger (although not the size of a regulation court).

"I reckon I'll go over to the motel," said one of the men I didn't recognize. "My wife's staying there." When I merely looked at him, he added through clenched teeth, "I'm Jake Milliford from Emmett. I didn't see nothing, so you're wasting your time if you think I got anything to say to you."

I could tell from his surly tone that he wasn't accustomed to taking orders from a female. It was tempting to make him squirm, but I flicked a finger at the door. "Stay in her room until I get around to you."

"I'll stay where I damn well please."

I looked at Les. "Would you escort Mr. Milliford to the Flamingo, then remain in the parking lot and keep an eye on all of them? I should be there in an hour or so."

Les escorted his charge out the door, leaving only three of us. Barry smiled at me and said, "Any chance for coffee?"

"If you make it," I said, then sat down behind my desk and pulled out a legal pad. "Name?" I asked the other unfamiliar man.

He didn't look any happier than Jake Milliford, but he sat down and said, "Reed Rondly."

"Rank?" I asked brightly. "Serial number? This is supposed to be a military outfit, isn't it? Or are you all just a bunch of bumbling idiots who like to act out your anal-retentive impulses in the woods?"

Reed licked his lips. "What's your problem, honey? You having your period?"

"Cool it," Barry called from the back room. "Just tell her what you know so we can leave, okay?"

"Okay," he muttered, glaring at me. "We all got here yesterday evening at different times. Dylan rode with me, and Sterling and Jake were at the campsite when we got there at maybe five. Barry showed up later. This morning Sterling, Kayleen, and Judy came just before sunrise, and later on, the three local fellows. Sterling told Dylan to take the kid and pick a position on the bluff. We waited fifteen minutes, then split up so we could come at 'em from different directions. I was trying to figure out what to do about that clear patch when the kid came stumbling by. He told me what happened and I fired a flare to bring everybody. By the time I got to Dylan, Kayleen was giving him mouth-to-mouth, but he died anyway. That's about it."

I finished scribbling all that and said, "Did you hear a shot right before you encountered Kevin?"

"Yeah, but way off from where I was." He leaned back, clearly proud of his recitation. "Bring me some coffee, Barry. Three sugars, no milk."

I sketched a crude map of the area and pushed it toward him. "Make a mark where you were when you heard the shot," I said.

He sneered at my effort, then took the pencil and drew an X indicating he'd been just inside the woods.

"Here, I guess. Hell, I wasn't worried where I was. I was more concerned about where Dylan and the kid were and how I was going to get off a decent shot."

Barry came back into the room, handed a mug to Reed, and put one down on my desk. "You can probably use this, too," he said to me.

"Thanks," I looked over what I'd written, then glanced up at Reed. "And at any time did you have a weapon with live ammo?"

He shrugged. "I got my rifle and some thirty-caliber bullets in the truck in case I decide to do some huntin' after the retreat. I got fired on Thursday, so it ain't like I have anything better to do. Let that dumb-ass process server come find me out here."

"Process server?" I said.

Barry rolled his eyes at me. "Reed's experiencing marital difficulties, and some guy has been chasing him all over Farberville. He stayed away from work because of that, which is why he's currently unemployed."

"Damn that Bobbi Jo," said Reed between noisy slurps of coffee. "It's her own damn fault. If she hadn't bitched at me for coming home drunk, I wouldn't have had to teach her a lesson about who wears the pants and who wears the panties." He leered at me. "What about you, baby? You got black silk panties on that firm little ass of yours?"

I considered getting out my gun, but I didn't want to squander one of my precious bullets on him. "Give me your address and phone number, then get out of here," I said levelly. "Someone at the sheriff's department will type this up and bring it to you to be signed in a couple of days."

He rattled off the information, then added, "I'll be over at that dumpy bar, Barry. I guess we need to find out what Sterling wants to do."

I waited until he left before I dared reach for the mug. After a couple of sips, I said, "Your comrade's a real jerk, isn't he?"

Barry took the vacated chair. "He's under a lot of stress because of the divorce. Usually he's a real sweetheart."

"Sure he is," I said dryly. "You have anything to add to what he said about arrival times?"

"No, as far as I know, that was pretty much it. I had to work Friday, so I was the last one to show up."

I gave him the map. "Where were you when you heard the single shot?"

He studied it for a long while, as if the scattering of lines held some mystical significance. "I guess I was over that way," he said as he drew an X. "I wanted to work my way below the ledge, but I had the same problem Reed did with the open area. I heard the shot, and maybe three or four minutes later, I saw the flare that meant something was wrong."

"You couldn't see the ledge where Dylan was standing when he was shot?" I asked, retrieving my masterpiece to compare Reed's and Barry's marks. One was large and lopsided, the other small and precise.

"No, the bluff juts out and I was coming around from the far side. I couldn't even see the clearing at that point."

"What can you tell me about Dylan? How long has he been a member of your group?"

Barry gave this question as much consideration as he had the map. "He drifted into town about two weeks ago, got a job at the garage, and ended up crashing at Reed's apartment. He claimed he'd been living in Denver."

"Claimed? Did you doubt him?"

"I had some misgivings. I don't know how to say this without making us sound like a gang of desperados. We've never done anything illegal, but groups like ours are often under investigation by certain federal agencies. It's not uncommon for agents to attempt to pose as disciples in order to infiltrate."

My pseudo-professional veneer evaporated. "Are you saying the victim was a federal agent?"

"It occurred to me," he said, shrugging. "It was almost as though he knew ahead of time that Reed was the one to approach, since the rest of us are quite a bit more reticent when discussing . . . our activities."

He put the mug on the floor and held up his hands. "Which are legal, as I said a minute ago. You may not agree with our philosophy, but you have to admit we have the constitutional right to embrace it."

"Which amendments cover racism and paranoia?" I asked sweetly.

"You'll have to ask Sterling. He's our specialist in matters of law." He set the mug on the corner of my desk. "I suppose I won't be buying you a beer on Monday, right?"

"That's very perceptive of you." I stood up so he couldn't look down at me. "I suggest you and your comrades go find some other place to make fools of yourselves. If I have to, I'll declare the entire acreage from the county road to the bluff a crime scene. It'll take a lot of yellow tape to make it off-limits, but I have plenty of free time. That means if you all return, you'll be trespassing, and also that Kayleen can't proceed with the remodeling. I have a feeling that won't sit well with her."

"Probably not. I'll tell Sterling what you said, unless you prefer to tell him yourself."

"Go ahead and tell him whatever you wish. After all, the Constitution guarantees freedom of speech, doesn't it?" I wrote down his address and telephone number, then told him to leave. I still had six more statements to take, but I'd already heard most of Kevin's story and I figured Earl Buchanon and Jeremiah McIlhaney would have little to contribute. For that matter, none of them would if the shooting had been an accident, as Harve believed.

But if Dylan Gilbert had been exposed as a federal agent, it might be a whole 'nuther ballgame, I thought as I reread the notes I'd taken while interviewing Barry. The logical agencies were the FBI and the ATF, but I wasn't at all sure I could call Washington and politely ask them to confirm the identity of an undercover agent.

I gave up worrying about it, and was halfway to my

car when Dahlia came pounding up the road, her massive arms flopping like prehensile wings. "It's Kevvie!" she yelled at me. "He's disappeared!"

"No, he hasn't," I said calmly. "He was out at that gathering on County 102 and then at the PD, but I sent him home half an hour ago."

She huffed and puffed until she caught her breath. "I was over at his parents' house when his pa got there. He told us what happened and said that Kevvie had gone back to the SuperSaver for what was left of his shift. I went right over there to chew him out, but Idalupino said he never showed up. He ain't at home, neither. What if it's time for the baby and I cain't find him? What am I gonna do . . .?"

I didn't have an answer.

Chapter 10

I drove Dahlia back to her in-laws' house. After she'd been settled on the sofa with a quilt and a diet soda, I asked Eileen to drive to Kevin's house and make sure he wasn't hiding under the porch. Then, without enthusiasm, I asked Earl to join me in the kitchen.

"Okay," I began, speaking quietly so Dahlia couldn't overhear us, "what the hell were you, Kevin, and Jeremiah doing out there this morning? Do you honestly believe this country is going to be invaded by a bunch of Swiss paratroopers armed with pocket-knives?"

He hung his head. "Jeremiah and I went because we were curious. There was this pamphlet being handed out all over town that said we didn't have to pay taxes, and I sure could use a new tractor."

"No, Earl, you *don't* have to pay taxes. It's entirely your decision whether to send a check to the IRS or go to prison. Just bear in mind that tax evasion's a federal offense, so you might end up sharing a cell with Raz and having Sunday afternoon visits from Marjorie." I flipped the pad to a clean page and poised my pencil. "Tell me what happened from the time you arrived at the Wockermann place."

"We got there at ten, listened to Pitts carry on about something or other, and then agreed to participate in this military exercise around eleven. I dunno why we said we would, except I used to love to hear my pa talk about being in France during the war. I would've signed on to go to Vietnam, but our troops pulled out before I turned eighteen."

"I get the picture," I said. "Tell me about this morning."

"Fifteen minutes after Dylan and Kevin went up the hill, Pitts told us to scatter on our own. Jeremiah and I weren't sure about that, so we stayed together."

"And?" I said, perhaps a shade impatiently.

"We got to thinking that we should wait near the gully in case they doubled back to sneak behind our line. We were gonna find a place to sit by the tents, but we heard somebody coming, so we went to Jeremiah's truck."

"Where it was dry," I said. "Did you see anybody after that?"

Earl nodded, although it'd be a stretch to say he did so thoughtfully. "Pitts scrambled across the gully and used a phone in that tank of his. I guess he called for an ambulance, 'cause it and the sheriff turned up within half an hour. You came pretty soon after that."

I didn't bother with notes. "Did you and Jeremiah hear any shots?"

This time he shook his head. "We had the windows rolled up and were listening to the radio. Don't go telling Millicent, but Jeremiah has the hots for this little blond-headed country singer with enormous tits, and he wanted me to hear her new song."

Eileen hurried in through the back door. "Kevin's not at home," she said grimly, "and neither is the car. I stopped at the supermarket, and no one's seen hide nor hair of him since nine this morning."

Earl scratched his head. "Jeremiah and me dropped him off in back of the store less than an hour ago. He was mumbling to hisself, but he was almost to the door when we drove away."

"I can't imagine where he is," said Eileen. "He may be a few dips short of a sundae, but he couldn't get lost between the dumpster and the door."

I had reservations about that, but I kept them to myself and said, "He may have decided to go to the Flamingo to beg forgiveness for his self-perceived der-eliction of duty. If I spot him, I'll send him home with his tail between his legs. Is there anything else you should tell me, Earl?"

"Not really," he said, "unless it was that figure I saw come out of the woods way up by the fence at the back of the Assembly Hall. All I caught was a glimpse, and Jeremiah swore I was seeing things."

"Was this before or after Pitts made his call?" I asked.

"Oh, I'd say about fifteen minutes before. I wasn't paying much attention on account of Jeremiah's favorite song coming on. It was something about knockers and knickers, and I told Jeremiah it didn't make a lick of sense, but he said—"

"Let me know if you hear from Kevin," I said. I tiptoed past Dahlia, who was snoring, and let myself out the front door. I suppose I should have been more concerned about Kevin, but he was capable of almost anything, including driving into Farberville to enlist in the army (as if they'd take him).

It was doubtful Jeremiah would have anything to add to Earl's account, so I left him for later, swung by Kevin's house on the off-chance he'd popped up like a fever blister, and then went to the motel behind Ruby Bee's Bar & Grill. Only three more statements, I told myself as I parked, and I'd be rid of the militia once and for all. Kayleen would still be around, but my threat to tie a yellow ribbon around her property was probably adequate to send everybody else away, including the insufferable Reed Rondly. It was kind of a shame about Barry Kirklin, though. I wasn't in the market for a steady beau, much less a husband, but it might have been nice to have a beer and a conversation.

Les got out of his car. "Nobody's so much as poked a toe outside," he reported. "I take that back. Estelle Oppers came out of her room and asked me if I was here because of the toilet seat."

I had a pretty good idea why Estelle was holed up at the Flamingo, although I was getting tired of cryptic messages regarding this nefarious toilet seat. "I don't know what she meant, Les. Maybe plumbers are in such demand these days that they're running around with badges and sidearms. Has Kevin been here?" He shook his head. "Which units are whose?"

Once he'd told me, I decided to give myself a break and start with Kayleen, and then beg a couple of antacid tablets from Ruby Bee before tackling Sterling Pitts and Jake Milliford.

Kayleen must have seen me coming, because she opened the door as I approached. She'd changed into a cashmere sweater and slacks, but her face, devoid of makeup, was sallow. "I know, I know," she said as I went into her room. "You tried to tell me and I wouldn't listen. I've gone deer hunting most every year since I was twelve, and nothing like this ever happened, but—"

"This time it happened." I sat down on the bed and opened my pad. "You didn't go to the campsite until this morning, right?"

"That's right. We got there shortly after six. Judy made breakfast while the rest of us unloaded some things from Sterling's Hummer and prepared for a gathering to share our beliefs with the local citizens. The turnout was disappointing, particularly to Sterling, but he went ahead and gave his talk, then invited them to participate in an exercise."

"Were Dylan and Kevin supposed to be the insidious foreigners or the heroic defenders of truth, justice, and the American way?"

"Oh, I don't think roles were defined," Kayleen said as she sat down on the opposite side of the bed. "We synchronized our watches, waited for fifteen minutes, and then headed out on our own. I thought I'd try to get above their position, but I ended up where it was as steep as the side of a barn."

I handed her my increasingly wrinkled map. "Show me where you were when you heard the first shot."

"Whose marks are these?" she asked.

"Why does it matter?"

She made a vague gesture with her free hand. "It doesn't. Let me see if I can figure out what these lines mean. Is this a tree?"

I pointed out all the relevant landmarks, then watched her as she ran a manicured fingertip up the page.

"I came this way," she murmured. "I spotted Reed ahead of me and shifted over this way. Then I made my way over this way and ended up behind a thicket about here." She drew an X on the opposite side of the map from Barry's. "I guess that's about right, although I wouldn't testify to it in court."

"Did you see anybody besides Reed?"

"Not a soul, and I couldn't see the ledge, either. I didn't know what to think when I heard the first shot, but then I saw the flare and came out from behind the thicket. I reached Dylan's body first, and I could tell he was in big trouble. When Reed got there, I sent him back to camp to get the first aid kit." She made a little noise that was not quite a groan. "Dylan died within minutes. It brought back raw memories of the night Maurice was killed, and I was hunkered there with my arms around my knees when Jake arrived a couple of minutes later."

"Which direction did he come from?"

Kayleen looked down at the map. "I wasn't paying any attention."

"What about Sterling?"

"He said he ran into Reed and learned what had happened. He went to the pasture to use his car phone to call an ambulance, then came back up to the clearing. There was nothing more to do but wait for the paramedics." She went into the bathroom to blow her nose, and returned with a tremulous attempt at a smile. "I feel so silly about getting all upset like this. Here I am, presenting myself as a hardy, self-reliant woman who can take care of herself, and then an accident happens and I go to pieces. I've bought and sold more guns than most folks see in a lifetime, and what's more, I know how violence has pervaded every segment of our society."

"What did you think of Dylan Gilbert?" I asked.

"Nothing, really," she said as she sank back down. "This morning was the first time I met him. We sat together at breakfast on a log down by the gully, and I did my best to be real friendly. He was young, not more than twenty-five, and like most kids that age, full of himself. Not poor Kevin Buchanon, of course. He's about as forceful as a newborn kitten. After the accident, he was mewling like one, too."

"Let's keep talking about Dylan," I said. "Did you have any reason to think there was anything peculiar about him? Was he telling the truth about his past?"

She studied me for a long while, then sighed and said, "You've been listening to Barry, haven't you? I don't know why Barry was making all those dark comments about Dylan, unless it was because he was jealous, like an older child when a baby's brought home from the hospital. Until Dylan came along, Barry was the smart one. After he got out of the army, he found a job at a bookstore and worked his way up to department manager. Dylan had gone to college for a couple of years and studied engineering."

"So you think Barry was jealous?"

"I don't know any other reason why he was whispering behind Dylan's back. I hate to say this, but the federal agencies would hardly bother with the likes of us. There are groups that stockpile weapons and build explosive devices, and some have resorted to violence. We're all hot air and bravado, like I told you when you first objected to the retreat. None of us would ever find the nerve to do something illegal, much less dangerous."

"Dylan found it dangerous," I said, staring at her.

She looked away. "But that was an accident, and it didn't have anything to do with us."

I told her she'd be asked to sign the statement later in the week, then went out into the lot and steeled myself for the final two interviews. Before I'd talked myself into actually knocking on a door, Les emerged from his car.

"Sheriff Dorfer wants you to call him as soon as you can," he said. "It's real important."

"Did he say why?"

"I asked," he admitted, "but that's all LaBelle

would tell me. She's in a real snit these days, isn't she?"

"No kidding," I said as I headed for the PD.

"All I kin say," Kevin said through a mouthful of tamale, "is it ain't fair for whoever shot Dylan to get away with it. Everybody keeps actin' like it was just one of those things. Why, I'd be mighty surprised if Arly bothers with the statements and I sure cain't see the sheriff reading 'em."

His remarks were directed only at the hillside below the ledge. Not even the cute li'l squirrel was anywhere to be seen, having retreated to a leafy nest to escape the cold drizzle.

Kevin finished the tamale he'd had the foresight to pick up at the Dairee Dee-Lishus, crammed the wrapper in his pocket, and discovered that for some crazy reason, he had a cassette in his pocket. Dahlia's relaxation tape, he decided, wondering how he'd ended up with it.

He stood up, this time mindful of his head. "No," he said, continuing to talk out loud because it was kind of creepy out here by his lonesome, "if Arly's gonna sweep this under the carpet, then it's up to Kevin Fitzgerald Buchanon to find the guilty hunter and see that he goes to jail. I owe that much to Dylan."

Over the treetops he could see the roof of the old Wockermann farmhouse, and beyond that the chimney of Estelle's house across the county road. That was about it, but it was comforting to know he wasn't lost. All he needed now, he thought with a sigh, was some sort of plan.

It wasn't likely the hunter had been between the ledge and the campsite, since that was where the make-believe soldiers had been. He shifted his attention to the woods off to his right. They rose steeply, but they didn't look as thick and gnarly, so he decided to go that way and see if maybe he'd find a deer camp.

He climbed down to the spot where Dylan had fallen, although he kept his eyes averted in case there might be bloodstains on the rocks. Robin Buchanon's old shack was somewhere in that direction, and it occurred to him that it might not be bad to get out of the drizzle before he was soaked to the skin. He could even try to scrounge up some dry firewood and build a fire in the rusty pot-bellied stove. Once he was warm, he'd come up with a real good plan that'd have made Dylan proud of him.

The going was easier for the most part, but there were plenty of thorns and treacherous holes covered with leaves. The birds had retreated, too, except for a crow making a racket from an invisible branch. Kevin made his way around the bluff and continued upward, saving his breath for gasping and panting. The mountainside grew rockier as he climbed, and he was obliged to slow his pace on account of patches of mud as slippery as wet linoleum.

Several times he thought he was in spittin' distance of the shack, only to discover outcroppings of slick, silvery limestone or desolate logging trails. The mud was so sticky he had to stop every few minutes and scrape his boots.

Maybe he was confused about the shack, he told himself as he stumbled over a log and came within a hair's breadth of landing on his butt in the soggy leaves. Cotter's Ridge was like one of those mazes where you have to find your way to the middle without crossing any lines. Kevin hadn't had much luck with 'em, even with the ones in the kiddie magazines at the supermarket. Jim Bob had pitched a fit when a customer brought one back claiming it was marked up.

Thinking about Jim Bob made him more forlorn than he already was. There wasn't any way Jim Bob wouldn't find out that his temporary assistant manager had gone AWOL, and on the busiest day of the week, too. But Kevin had figured he owed it to his beloved wife and son to learn how to defend them when the country was overrun with foreign soldiers.

He was close to giving up when he finally caught sight of a sagging roof. He hurried up the road, went up on the porch, and dragged open the door. Inside it was still cold and daylight sliced through cracks and knotholes, but it was better'n outside. Dirt was everywhere, along with twigs, dried leaves, tufts of hair, and droppings that indicated animals had taken refuge over the years.

Hoping he wouldn't run into a bear or a wildcat, Kevin pulled off his cap and eyed the stove. He was trying to remember if he had any matches when a hand clamped down on his shoulder. John Wayne might have whirled around and thrown a punch, but Kevin Fitzgerald Buchanon fainted.

I went into the barroom and looked around for Reed Rondly and Barry Kirklin. They were in the back booth, conversing intently over a pitcher of beer. Before I could reach them, however, Ruby Bee came out of the kitchen and said, "I need to have a word with you, and I need to have it right now."

Reed and Barry glanced up at me. "Stay there," I said to them, then went over to the bar. "What's the matter? Do you need a recipe for ostrich and dumplings?"

Ruby Bee gestured at a good ol' boy slumped at the bar, who appeared to have been crying in his beer for a long while, then moved down to the end and waited for me with a decidedly unfriendly expression. "I have been trying to get in touch with you all day long," she said as I sat on a stool. "You'd better throw that answering machine into the trash and get yourself a new one. What's more, you'd better test it in the store before you pay good money."

I wasn't sure why she'd sidled away from the good ol' boy, then spoken loudly enough to be heard over the roar of the washing machines at the Suds of Fun launderette across the road. "I am not a handyman," I said levelly, "and I don't do toilet seats. If you'll excuse me, I have a sticky situation that requires my professional attention."

"Well, pardon me for daring to interrupt you, Miss Eliot Ness. I'm sure as God made little green apples that someone broke into one of the units out back, but I'll just get in line until you can get around to me. All I can do is pray there's not a rapist hanging around the Flamingo Motel and waiting for his chance to attack me real late at night."

"All right," I said. "Tell me why you think someone broke into a unit."

"The door was unlocked, but that might have been an oversight on my part. However, there's no way getting around the toilet seat, the shag, and the lamp," she said, ticking them off on her fingers. "If there was only one clue, I might wonder if I was imagining things, but the three together prove I'm not."

I tried to keep a straight face. "I can see someone stealing a toilet seat and a lamp, but the carpet? It can't be easy to move the furniture in order to pull out the tacks, roll up the carpet, and carry it out to—"

"Nothing was stolen. The toilet seat was raised, the lamp was unplugged, and the carpet showed signs that the chair had been moved. If that's not evidence of a break-in, then I don't know what is." She put her hands on her hips and waited for me to reel with shock or race out the door to fingerprint the toilet seat.

I opted for a mildly concerned wince. "That's really fine evidence, and I'm sure it'll come in handy at the trial. It may be enough to secure the death penalty. As much as I'd like to drop this other thing and devote all my energy to catching this rapist, I'm afraid it will have to wait. Maybe you and Estelle can train the ostriches to attack on command."

I turned around and went to the back booth. Reed stuck his nose in his stein, but Barry smiled and said, "Change your mind about a beer?"

"No," I said. "I just spoke to the sheriff, who had a call from the county coroner. The coroner said that the gunshot wound did not cause Dylan's death. It probably hurt like hell, but it didn't hit an artery or any organs. It didn't cause any significant internal bleeding, either."

Reed lifted his face. "So what killed him?"

"We won't know until the coroner does a more

thorough autopsy," I said, "and that won't happen for a couple of days."

Barry was no longer smiling. "Could he have had a heart condition? Maybe the trauma of getting shot set off a fatal heart attack. Aneurysms can burst, too. Most people don't know they have one until it's written on the death certificate."

"Wait a minute," Reed said in a strangled voice. "Are you saying anybody could have this—this thing and not know it? Somebody shouts 'Boo!' and you fall over dead?"

Barry snapped his fingers. "Just like that."

I intervened before we lapsed into a medical school seminar. "We won't know until after the autopsy, so there's no point in speculation."

"What about a snake bite?" said Reed.

"After the autopsy," I said, wishing I'd had the words printed on filing cards. "Until then, we're treating Dylan's death as a possible homicide, so I'll have to get more detailed statements from all of you before you leave town. Ruby Bee has three empty units if you want to stay out there tonight."

"I knew a guy once who got stung by a honey bee," continued Reed, who clearly had some vestige of shared ancestry with the Buchanons. "He was deader'n a doornail twenty minutes later. We might should've taken him to the emergency room like he begged, but we thought he was being a sissy."

Barry stood up. "I guess we'll go back to the camp and collect our gear, then stay at the motel. We'll get Jake's and Dylan's gear while we're at it. Come on, Reed."

Reed downed the last inch of beer, belched, and got unsteadily to his feet. "You know, I was kinda curious about Dylan kicking off like that. The kid told me Dylan sat up and was gonna be okay. Five minutes later—"

"Come on," Barry said, clutching Reed's sleeve and aiming him toward the door. "The sooner we go, the sooner we can get back for a hot shower and some decent food. Who knows? Maybe the chief of police will join us at the end of her shift."

"Why don't I line you up with a hot little local number named Marjorie?" I said. "She's on the quiet side, but I've been told she squeals when she's excited."

"Cool," said Reed as he was dragged out the door.

I left before Ruby Bee could delay me with a harangue about my shoddy investigative techniques. Les gave me a thumbs-up sign as I went to Sterling's room. He opened the door within seconds. Unlike Kayleen, he was still wearing fatigues, but his feet were encased in slippers.

"It's about time, Chief Hanks," he said. "I intend to file a civil suit citing you and that boorish sheriff. You have no right to detain us against our wishes. In that I have entered into a contract with the owner of this motel room, I am the legal tenant of record. The Fourth Amendment specifically addresses the right of the people to be secure in their houses against unreasonable searches and seizures. You may not enter this room unless you have a proper warrant."

"You're absolutely right," I said. "Since I don't have a warrant, I'll escort you to the sheriff's department in Farberville. He should be finished with his press conference by the time we get there, but if not, we can join him on the steps. You might even get a chance to share your outrage with the media. They'll go wild over your uniform and those medals you most likely bought at an army surplus store."

He gave me a cold look, then opened the door more widely and gestured at me to enter. "My time is too essential to waste in such a manner. Giving a statement is a waste of time, too, but I will cooperate simply in order to be allowed to leave this festering cold sore of a town."

"And we were thinking about asking you to run for mayor," I said as I opened my pad. "Describe your actions after your band of commandos split up."

"If you've studied military history, you would know that it's rare for a commanding officer to join his men in combat. My responsibility has always been to provide leadership and a careful analysis of the obstacles to our joint success. Therefore, I decided to make myself available at the campsite should anyone require further guidance."

"No one else mentioned this," I said, pretending to be puzzled by my notes. "They all seemed to think you started uphill when they did."

Sterling stepped in front of the mirror above the dresser and regarded his reflection for a long moment. I was on the verge of prompting him when he cleared his throat and said, "Although I am reasonably robust for my age, I am aware of my physical limitations. I felt it was in the best interest of morale that my subordinates have complete confidence in me, so I implied I would participate in the exercise alongside them."

He turned around to give me a self-deprecatory smile. "I didn't want to admit that I lacked the stamina to climb a hill. I'm nearly seventy years old, Chief Hanks. There are many things I can no longer do, and my contributions to the cause must be of a less demanding nature."

He seemed to be fishing for sympathy from me, but the pool was dry. Instead of patting him on the back, I said, "Like sending them out into the woods when it's deer season? Did you lack the stamina—or the courage?"

"I'm not sure," he said, his words almost inaudible. I gave him time to brood while I thought about the earlier statements. "You didn't stay at the campsite, though. Two of your so-called subordinates decided to guard the rear line, and they were there when they heard someone coming. If they heard you, you must have been returning from someplace else."

"When I selected the campsite yesterday afternoon, I noticed a spot partway up the ridge that was protected from the elements by an overhang. Dividing my ascent would allow me to catch my breath, so I went there to wait until I heard some indication that the maneuver was over. You must be feeling a great deal of contempt for me."

"Because you're nothing more than a blustery hypocrite? That would seem to constitute a reason, wouldn't it?" I gave him my map. "Show me where you hid."

His hand was trembling as he pointed to a spot halfway between the campsite and the place where Dylan had been shot. "Somewhere in here, Chief Hanks. If we were to return to the area, I could show you the precise location, but I don't see why it matters. The young man was the victim of a tragic accident."

"That's what the sheriff thought," I said vaguely. "What do you know about Dylan Gilbert's past?"

"Very little," Sterling said, his eyes narrowing as he glanced at the blank computer monitor on a table in the corner. "He said he was born and raised in Idaho, attended college, and lived in Denver before moving here."

I poised my pencil. "Where in Idaho and which college?"

"I don't believe anyone thought to ask him, although he might have said something to Reed."

I lowered the pencil and sighed. "Was he a federal agent?"

"We had no proof, but he may well have been. For one thing, when he first appeared, he gave me some cockamamie story about there being a traitor in our midst. After some consideration, I concluded that he did so in an attempt to divert any suspicion away from himself. When I tried to do a background check on him, I ran into some communication problems. Barry was convinced that Dylan was responsible for them. Then again, my computer may be state of the art, but I myself am not, and I've had difficulties learning how to coerce it into doing what I want. I've certainly seen the 'access denied' message more than once."

"Who did you contact to do this background check?" I asked.

Sterling hesitated, then said, "I don't see why it matters anymore. Dylan said he was a member of a group in Denver that has similar goals. I queried one of them on a private electronic bulletin board and received a response that confirmed this. When I attempted to make further inquiries, the password had been changed."

"What's the name of the contact in Denver?"

"We use code names, and it would be a breach of security if I were to tell you his. If it came out, our group would be forever banished from the movement. We're on probation as it is. Reed and Barry displayed gross incompetence at a retreat in Oklahoma and were ordered to leave. Reed became drunk and insisted on loading his weapon with live ammunition. When Barry tried to wrestle the weapon away from him, it went off and shattered the windshield of a car manned by police officers observing the activities. It was embarrassing for me to have my men behave like that."

"It'll be a helluva lot more embarrassing if it turns out one of your men shot Dylan Gilbert in the back."

He gave me a bewildered look. "But . . . they were using paint pellets."

"Thirty-caliber paint pellets?" I said as I headed for the door.

Chapter 11

Jake and Judy Milliford were occupying #2. As I approached, I could hear angry voices from inside, but I couldn't make out the words. I knocked and moved to a prudent distance in case whoever opened the door was foaming at the mouth. I've always hated saliva on my shirt.

Jake yanked open the door. He wasn't foaming, but he was far from a genial host. "Whatta ya want?"

"I want to wake up and discover this was all a bad dream," I said truthfully. "However, until that lovely moment arrives, I'm obliged to maintain the pretense by taking your statement. I'll need to speak to your wife, too."

"She don't know nuthin' about this," he said, blocking the doorway like a brawny nightclub bouncer.

"We can do this now, or we can do it later at the sheriff's department. The interrogation rooms are not luxurious, but they have a certain charm. I'm thinking about redoing my apartment in the same pea green and puke color scheme."

"Let her in," said a woman's voice.

Jake moved out of the doorway. "Get on with it," he growled.

Judy was seated on the bed. We sized each other up for a moment, then she said, "Why don't you take the chair, Chief Hanks? That way you'll have the table to write on."

"Thanks," I said as I sat down and pulled out the map. Thus far I had six Xs, four drawn by the parties and the two I'd drawn to indicate Kevin and Dylan. I offered the map to Jake. "Show me where you were when you heard the first shot."

He kept his thumbs hooked over his belt. "What difference does it make where I was?"

"Probably none," I admitted, "but this is an official investigation. If you refuse to cooperate, you should get a lawyer as soon as possible. In fact, you'd better use the phone on the nightstand."

Judy's eyes widened. "But Jake told me it was an accident . . ."

"We're still obliged to investigate," I said.

Jake snatched the map out of my hand and scowled at it. "This ain't nothing but a bunch of scratches. How the hell am I supposed to make any sense out of it?" He studied it for a minute, his forehead creased, and finally tapped it with a greasy finger. "I was over this way."

"Did you see Barry?"

He dropped the map on the rumpled bed and crossed his arms. "All I saw was that kid's goofy face peeking over the ledge. Then Dylan stood up and turned around like he thought there was somebody above them. For some fool reason, the kid jumped up like a snake had bit him on his ass, and then went back down. A shot was fired, and Dylan fell off the ledge. I was climbing down the rocks to see what the hell was going on when I saw the flare. It took me another four or five minutes to get there."

"And Kayleen was already there?"

"Yeah," he muttered, "and she said he was dead. After that, we just sat there, her sniveling and me worrying about a bullet in *my* back."

I drew an X over the trace of grease he'd left. "You should have been able to see Barry, or at least hear him in the brush."

"Well, I didn't, and he didn't hear me, neither. I was being real quiet on account of the kid. I dunno if he could've got me, but I had a feeling Dylan was a damn good shot."

"What did you think about the rumor that he was a federal agent?" I asked.

"I didn't have any trouble buying it after what happened last night." He took a can of tobacco out of his pocket and stuck a wad in his cheek. "Damn sumbitch shouldn't have come spying on us. If I'd had my rifle, I'd have shot him myself. As it was, Reed, Barry, and me decided to have ourselves a little interrogation session after everybody else left for the night. I learned a thing or two from the gooks in 'Nam."

"Jake!" said Judy. "Are you really stupid enough to say things like that in front of a police officer who's investigating a death?"

He gave her a puzzled look. "It ain't like we had a chance to go through with it. He's dead, ain't he?"

"That doesn't mean you're not stupid," she said sharply.

I held up my hand. "Why don't you discuss this later? Jake, you said something took place last night that made you suspect Dylan. What was it?"

He went into the bathroom to spit in the sink (and wouldn't Ruby Bee love that?), then came back out and said, "We were running low on beer, so Dylan offered to go get some, and a couple of pizzas while he was at it. He borrowed Reed's truck and left around six. When he finally showed up four hours later, he said the truck broke down halfway to Farberville and he spent the whole time messin' with it. Thing is, Barry and me both saw the truck parked on a side road here in town."

"Did you tell him that?" I asked.

"It was gonna be discussed tonight. Damn, I was really looking forward to that."

I did not allow myself to imagine what might have happened. "Where exactly was the truck parked?"

"On some road," he said, shrugging.

"Could he have been in it?"

"Not unless he was lying down on the seat. I'd have seen him if he was sitting up."

I made a note to myself to have a word with Barry

and Reed about their recalcitrance. "What were you doing in town?"

Jake tugged at his collar while stealing a peek at his wife. He might have gotten away with it if she and I both hadn't been staring at him. "I was thinking to go by the supermarket and get an extra can of Red-man. When I was almost there, I remembered I'd left my wallet at the camp. I drove on out to the edge of town, turned around, and took my time on the way back."

And I'd been named after a Shakespearean sprite instead of a photograph of Ruby Bee's Bar & Grill taken from an airplane. "What time did you get back?" I asked.

"Ten-thirty or so, about the time Barry showed up." He suddenly found the need to retreat to the bathroom, this time closing the door and running water in the sink.

I wanted to ask Judy if he had a legitimate reason to spy on her, but her back was rigid and her expression laden with warning. "Tell me what you did today," I said.

"I went to the camp with Sterling and Kayleen to cook breakfast. Afterwards, I hauled the skillet and dishes down to the creek and washed them, and checked my supplies to make sure I had what I needed for supper. I sat in Jake's tent for a good while, listening to their nonsense, and when it got to be too much for me, I walked back here."

"What time would that have been?"

"I don't know for sure, but Sterling was telling everybody what to do like he always does. I waited until they all left, then came here to take a shower, get into dry clothes, and work on a needlepoint sampler for my grandchild's bedroom. I don't believe in this international conspiracy or any of their other wild ideas. Jake wasn't like this when we got married. He was . . . normal back then."

"And now?" I asked gently.

"He's so full of hate sometimes I think he's going to explode. When we're in the truck, he points out people on the street—ordinary people going about their business—and says how they're responsible for all the problems in this country. He gets things in the mail that make me sick. Most of the time I put them in the trash without even telling him."

The water was still running in the sink, but I knew we only had a few minutes to talk before Mr. Congeniality came out of the bathroom. "Did you have any conversations with Dylan Gilbert that led you to believe he was an agent?"

"We didn't say much to each other. Jake stuck to me like a thistle seed whenever Dylan came near me, and I didn't want to make it worse for Dylan by being friendly to him. I wanted to ask him if Colorado is as pretty as people say, but I never got a chance."

I heard the toilet flush. I leaned forward and said, "Do you have any idea why Jake was in town last night?"

She shook her head.

I collected my pad and map, nodded at her, and left the room. I waved at Les, then headed for the PD to make some long distance calls that would send the town council into paroxysms of outrage when they got the bill. Did I care?

Larry Joe wiped the window with a damp paper towel, but the grime was invincible. "I don't see him, but he's still out there. I can feel him watching me."

"You'd better lay off the whiskey," Jim Bob said, sniggering. "I went outside this morning and I sure as hell didn't see anything. Maybe this alien of yours has a crush on you, Larry Joe. Could make for some interesting sex, huh?"

"You ain't as funny as you think," Larry Joe said, his nose pressed against the windowpane.

Roy came into the trailer. "I went down to where you said you saw something. There were odd marks in the mud, but that doesn't mean much. They could be black bear tracks that some other animal has trampled on."

Larry Joe looked at Jim Bob, who was cleaning his

fingernails with a fork. "I told you there was something there last night. If you're so all-fired sure there wasn't, why don't you go have a look for yourself?"

"Why should I get wet just because you and Roy are crazier than Jekel Buchanon? 'Member how he used to parade around town in high heels and his ma's flannel nightgown, farting so much everybody in the barbershop liked to pass out?"

"I saw something," insisted Larry Joe, "and it wasn't any bear, black or pink or green with yellow polkadots. You know what I think, Jim Bob? I think you're too much of a coward to go out there."

Jim Bob banged down the fork. "Don't go calling me a coward. I ain't afraid of anything—including you and your goddamn alien!"

"Then prove it. Go down to where Roy found the tracks and see for yourself."

"I'll point out the place," volunteered Roy.

Jim Bob shook a cigar out of the package and slowly pulled off the cellophane, then stuck it in the corner of his mouth and grinned at Larry Joe. "I thought we came here to drink whiskey and play poker. Let's not waste time bickering over what you thought you saw. You want me to make some sandwiches before we start?"

"We should have waited until dark," Estelle grumbled as she and Ruby Bee strolled toward the rectory. Both of them were doing their level best to look nonchalant instead of bent on committing a crime. "What if somebody sees us?"

"Since when is there something suspicious about paying a neighborly call?" said Ruby Bee. She stopped to smile and wave as Lottie Estes chugged by in her boxy little car. "See? Nobody's paying us any mind. Besides, if we wait until it's dark, we won't be able to see anything unless we turn on the lights."

They arrived at the door without further debate. Ruby Bee, having appointed herself master criminal, knocked loudly and called, "Brother Verber? Are you in there?" She did this a couple more times, then dropped her purse on the mat and bent over to pick it up, adroitly collecting the key in the process. Estelle shielded her as she unlocked the door, eased it open, and replaced the key.

"Yoohoo, Brother Verber," she said. "It's Ruby Bee and Estelle. Are you home?"

Estelle shoved her inside. "We can't stand here all afternoon. Sooner or later someone like Mrs. Jim Bob'll drive by, and we'll end up in the poky. You know how bad-tempered Arly can be about this sort of thing."

"Then stop yakking and start searching," Ruby Bee said absently as she eyed the spic-and-span kitchenette and the perfectly aligned magazines on the coffee table. It was most likely Mrs. Jim Bob's doing, she thought as she tried to decide where to find Brother Verber's personal effects. "Come on, Estelle, it's already four o'clock and I need to be back at the bar before five. Let's try the bedroom."

Even though they were assuming no one else was in the trailer, they tiptoed down the short hallway, stopping to peer into the bathroom before arriving in the bedroom. It was as orderly as the living room and kitchenette, with no clothes or shoes scattered on the floor. Ruby Bee was a little surprised at the number of cologne and hair tonic bottles on the dresser, having always believed preachers disdained that sort of vanity. Maybe it had to do with him courting Kayleen, she thought with a tiny smirk.

"You take the dresser drawers and I'll take the closet," she told Estelle. "Remember, we're looking for photographs, letters—"

"I know what we're looking for," said Estelle, who wasn't overly fond of being bossed around. However, Ruby Bee had come to her aid when Uncle Tooly's bequest had arrived, and she'd flatout refused to take money for the motel room. Not that the rate was much, Estelle reminded herself, or that the room wasn't empty anyway.

Ruby Bee opened the closet door. "It looks like a tornado came through here. Mrs. Jim Bob must have gathered up all the dirty clothes and just thrown 'em in here. There are some boxes on the shelf, but I can't reach them. See if you can, Estelle."

Estelle was about to get hold of a promising shoe box when the door opened in the living room. "Someone's here," she whispered. "Now what do we do?"

Ruby Bee felt her blood run cold. "Don't panic," she whispered back. "We can come up with a way to explain this to him."

"Brother Verber?" cooed Mrs. Jim Bob. "I just came by to see how you're doing."

"Get in here," Ruby Bee said, thoroughly panicked. She and Estelle jammed themselves into the closet and managed to pull the door closed just as they heard footsteps in the hallway. The air was stuffy and reeked of sweat and stale cologne. Shirts and coats hanging above their heads brushed like ghostly caresses. The only light came from underneath the door.

"I don't understand," Mrs. Jim Bob said in a thin, quivery voice. "How could you disappear like this without telling me? I am the guiding beacon of the congregation, as well as the president of the Missionary Society. Don't I invite you over for supper every week?" She continued in that vein, her voice fading but still audible as she left the bedroom.

"Who's she talking to?" whispered Estelle.

"Herself, I suppose." Ruby Bee wiggled around, trying to avoid something sharp poking her in the fanny. "Lordy, it's hard to breathe. It seems to me she might have laundered these clothes before putting them in here. What's more, Brother Verber could use a stronger deodorant. Whatever he—"

"I don't understand," wailed Mrs. Jim Bob from the living room. "What about all those times we knelt to pray in the Assembly Hall or on this very sofa? You said you could hear the Good Lord admiring us for our humility and trust. I thought I could trust you . . ."

"Do you have any more bright ideas?" said Estelle.

Ruby Bee crossed her fingers. "She'll leave before too long, and then we can, too. How long can she sit in there and talk to herself?"

The response came not from Estelle, but from the living room. "I am going to stay right here," Mrs. Jim Bob vowed, "until you come back. It may take all night, but I will be here when you walk through the door—and you'd better have a good explanation for tormenting me like this. What's more, after you've begged my forgiveness, you're gonna get down on your knees and do some serious apologizing to the Lord."

Ruby Bee and Estelle did what they could to get comfortable on the closet floor.

When I finally replaced the receiver, I'd learned several things about the FBI and the ATF. One was that their offices were open during the weekends, which was good to know if Swiss paratroopers came marching down the road. Another, however, was that they were boorish and uncooperative when it came to discussing their undercover agents. I'd explained the situation, blithely assuming they'd take a deep interest in the possible homicide of one of their own. I might as well have tried to convince them that Jimmy Hoffa was eating supper at Ruby Bee's Bar & Grill.

I decided I'd better make sure he wasn't, and perhaps have a piece of pie while I was at it. When I got there, I was startled to find a dozen or so guys standing around in the parking lot. "What's wrong?" I asked as I got out of the car. "Is Ruby Bee holding a fire drill?"

"It's closed," said a red-faced man in a denim jacket. "It's nigh on to happy hour, but Ruby Bee ain't nowhere to be found. Ollie and me was going to have us a beer."

I frowned at the "closed" sign on the door. "The bar was open earlier this afternoon. Do any of you know how long the sign's been there?"

A few of them admitted they didn't, while the rest scuffed their feet and bobbled their heads like a flock of lethargic turkeys. I suggested they find another bar, then got back in my car and tried to think where Ruby Bee would have gone at such a crucial time. As far as

I knew, Dylan Gilbert's death had not been broadcast around town, so she couldn't have appointed herself my deputy, as she and Estelle had done so often in the past, and gone charging off to crack the case.

I remembered her dour remarks about the possibility of someone lurking in one of the units. Les wasn't renowned for taking the initiative, but surely he would have informed me if a rapist had accosted her in the parking lot and carried her off on his shoulder.

I went around back and found him sitting in his car. "Any more messages from LaBelle?" I asked him.

"Nothing since the first one. Hey, could you take over for a few minutes? It's been a long time since I answered a call of nature."

"Sure," I said, "but let me ask you something. Did Ruby Bee come back here this afternoon?"

"I didn't see her, and Estelle hasn't returned." His ears turned pink as he gave me a strained smile.

"About that break?"

"Go on, Les. When you get back, contact LaBelle and tell her we're going to need someone here the rest of the night. I'm going to have to take more detailed statements from all these people, but I've got some other things to do first."

He babbled his thanks and peeled out of the parking lot, pelting me with gravel. I noticed that Ruby Bee's car was parked in front of #1, but Estelle's station wagon was gone, indicating that they were off together. Telling myself they were probably on an ostrich hunt, I sat down on the hood of my car and glumly watched a formation of geese fly by on their way to a more congenial climate. The best I could do was get back in my car and turn on the heater. Florida, it was not.

I took out my pad and studied the various statements. Earl had said something that began to puzzle me as I tried to get everything straight in my admittedly muddled mind. Judy had said she left the campsite shortly after the troops had dispersed at 11:15 or so. Earl and Jeremiah had backtracked minutes later, then retreated to the pickup when they heard someone coming. Sterling had claimed to have taken refuge under an overhang; Barry, Reed, Jake, and Kayleen had embraced the exercise and gone creeping up the hill.

So whom had Earl and Jeremiah heard? And whom had Earl seen shortly before Sterling called for an ambulance?

The clouds did not part to allow a ray of sunlight to enlighten me. I could come up with no reason for Brother Verber to be on the ridge, unless he'd heard rumors of naked devil worshipers and gone to check it out. But according to Mrs. Jim Bob, he'd disappeared by Thursday morning. Even his obsession with writhing female bodies would not have kept him in the woods for more than forty-eight hours.

My three least favorite stooges, Jim Bob, Larry Joe, and Roy, were up there somewhere, but their version of deer hunting involved playing poker and staying drunk. Deer could graze beside the trailer in perfect safety. Raz was too wily to risk being spotted, and Diesel would hardly seek out camaraderie.

I wrote myself a note to call Mrs. Twayblade at the county home and find out if she was missing any of her white-haired charges. She'd misplaced a couple of them in the past, but she'd tightened up security since then.

Whoever it was had not approached the campsite from the gully. It was possible Earl and Jeremiah had heard Judy as she was leaving. I had no idea when they'd begun passing the bottle back and forth; they certainly could have been smashed enough to misinterpret the sounds. I drew a box around Jeremiah's name to remind myself to ask him.

Even if my theory was right, it did nothing to explain who'd cut across the back of the Assembly Hall lawn. It could have been an uninvolved person, such as a kid buying hooch from Raz or a ditzy birdwatcher.

I'd gotten nowhere when Reed drove into the lot. I climbed out of my car and said, "Where's Barry?"

"He's coming." He took a backpack and a cooler

out of the back of the truck, which was littered with tools, beer cans, greasy blankets, and unidentifiable auto parts. "Which room is mine?"

I gestured at #6. "You and Barry can share that one, but you'll have to get the key from Ruby Bee when she reopens the bar."

"When's that gonna be?"

"Beats me," I said. "Why didn't you tell me that you, Jake, and Barry were convinced Dylan was an undercover agent?"

"We weren't, that's why. We decided to have a serious talk with him later this evening. I guess it's a little late for that." He, like Jake, sounded disappointed at the lost opportunity to engage in brutality.

"But you suspected he was," I prompted.

"Barry and Jake said so, but they didn't know him as well as I did. He sounded okay to me."

"He was staying at your apartment, wasn't he?"

"Till he found someplace he could afford. Look, lady, I don't aim to stand here all night. Why don't you trot your sweet ass into the bar and get the room key?"

"Why don't you hand over your apartment key so I can go through Dylan's things? Then you can trot your sweet ass to someone else's room until Ruby Bee gets back and has you sign the register."

"You got a search warrant?"

I waited a beat, then said, "I can hold you as a material witness until I get one. As investigating officer, I have the right to examine the victim's personal possessions in order to locate his next of kin, as well as any incriminatory items that may suggest a motive for his murder." Or I thought I did, anyway.

He dug a key out of his pocket and slapped it in my outstretched palm. "Don't go grubbing through my stuff, or you'll be real sorry. One of the amendments, I think the third, protects against illegal search and seizure."

"The fourth," I said, then told him which was Sterling's room. He was already inside when Les returned, his demeanor a good deal calmer. I told him what to tell Barry when he arrived, then drove out of the motel parking lot. The "closed" sign still hung on the bar's door, to the consternation of two good ol' boys who seemed to be struggling with the concept. I glanced at the PD's three parking spaces, and then at the empty area in front of the soon-to-be pawnshop. Mrs. Jim Bob's Cadillac was parked in front of the Assembly Hall, and lights were on in Brother Verber's trailer. At least one stray was back in the fold, I told myself as I drove down County 102 to see if Estelle's station wagon was there. It wasn't, so I went on to Farberville to see what I could learn about Dylan Gilbert.

The Airport Arms was cleverly situated across from the airport. In the unpaved parking lot were a Harley-Davidson, a battered white car with Missouri plates, another with no plates, and an overflowing Dumpster. It was likely to be the most disreputable apartment building in Farberville, if not Stump County.

Reed's apartment was on the second floor, with a view of the runway across the highway. The staircase creaked and shifted as I went up it, and the railing was too splintery to touch. I let myself inside the apartment. My stomach lurched as the odor of beer and decaying food hit me, but I turned on a light and ordered myself to pick my way through pizza boxes, catalogs, unopened bills, and several crusty car batteries. It was definitely not *Playboy* magazine's prototype of a bachelor pad.

The bedroom floor was covered with mildewed towels, discarded underwear and jeans, and plates coated with blue and gray fuzz. I tried to open a window, but it was either nailed closed or impossibly warped. I saw a duffel bag in one corner beside a limp, dingy pillow and a blanket. Assuming this was Dylan's allotted area, I knelt down and dumped out the contents of the bag. I wasn't anticipating anything more illuminating than socks and boxers, so I was surprised when I found a small spiral-bound notebook.

My elation faded as I flipped through it, finding one blank page after another. I was about to toss it in the bag when I came upon a notation that read: "Ingram MAC 10, #7826⁴." After pondering this for a moment, I checked to see if there was anything else in the notebook, and then set it aside.

I made sure the duffel bag was empty, then sat back and once again read the cryptic notation. I was still in what Ruby Bee would condemn as an undignified posture when I heard the front door open.

I hate it when that happens.

Chapter 12

Before I could scramble to my feet, a man appeared in the doorway. Technically, I'd have to say he *loomed*, since he was husky enough to fill the space, but he wasn't snarling or even frowning. He wore a navy blue suit, a white dress shirt, a serious tie, and shiny black shoes. I continued my inventory: dark eyes, mahogany complexion, straight nose, slightly weak chin, and when he smiled, white teeth with a boyish gap in the front. I doubted he was one of Reed's neighbors.

"What are you doing?" he asked.

I began stuffing socks and shirts back into the duffel bag. "Packing," I said. "How about you?"

"I was in the neighborhood, so I thought I'd stop by."

"Give me a break, buddy. Nobody stops by the Airport Arms Apartments unless his arm is twisted so tightly behind his back that he can pat himself on the top of his head." I stopped, my hand in midair, and stared up at him. "You're the process server, aren't you? Reed Rondly's not here, but I can tell you where he is if you'd like to slap him with a summons. It may not make his day, but it'll certainly make mine."

"Where would that be?"

"In Maggody, a little town about twenty miles east of here. Reed's at the Flamingo Motel. Watch for a sign with a mottled pink bird on the verge of blinking its last." I put the rest of Dylan's clothes in the duffel bag, then stood up and brushed cracker crumbs off my knees. "Good luck catching up with him."

He pointed at the notebook on the floor. "You missed something."

"So I did." I scooped up the notebook and tucked it in my pocket. "I didn't see you when I got here. Were you watching the apartment?"

He nodded. "Before I took my present job, I worked in a private investigator's office, mostly doing surveillance work."

I picked up the duffel bag. "I guess I'm ready to go. If you decide to drop by the motel and surprise Reed, be prepared to duck. He's a racist pig with the temperament to match."

The man stepped back to allow me to go past him. "I'll keep that in mind."

He followed me into the living room. I'd planned to do a quick search of the kitchen and bathroom, but I couldn't come up with a credible explanation. We continued out to the balcony, and he waited while I locked the door. As we walked down the staircase, I said, "Are you heading for Maggody?"

"Not just yet," he said, "but you'll most likely see me again, Chief Hanks."

"How do you know my name?" I said, almost dropping the duffel bag.

"You're wearing a badge." On that note, he went around the corner of the apartment building.

I stood by the car for a moment, wondering if I'd just interacted with a spy from a John LeCarré novel. He'd told me virtually nothing except that he'd once worked for a private investigator. My badge identified me as the chief of police, but I'd refused from day one of the "unsuitable job" to wear a name tag. If he'd gotten his information from something in my car, he would have addressed me as "Chief Taco Bell."

I gave up worrying about him and drove to the sheriff's department. LaBelle was on the phone, this time talking about her bladder infection. She eyed me coldly, then pointed toward Harve's office and resumed reciting her symptoms. She sounded especially proud of her urinary tract.

"Any update from McBeen?" I asked Harve as I came through the doorway.

"Not yet." He held up a plastic bag. "This here's the slug from the boy's shoulder. It could have been fired from any hunting rifle from here to the North Pole." He slumped back and sighed. "McBeen said he'd have a better chance at finding the cause of death if he had the boy's medical records. We went through his wallet, but all we found was two hundred and thirty-seven dollars. That plastic doohickey where most folks keep their driver's license and credit cards was empty."

"He worked at the same garage as Reed. Aren't they supposed to have his Social Security number?"

"Supposed to, yeah. The guy that owns the place said the kid kept stalling, and then quit on Thursday. They settled up out of the cash register."

I told Harve what little I'd learned about Dylan, most of it based on the befuddled speculation of the militia. "Frankly," I admitted, "I'm not sure if any of it's true, including the truck being parked in town. It is peculiar that he didn't have any identification with him, though. You'd think the FBI or the ATF could have produced fake documents for an undercover agent." I took the notebook out of my pocket, opened it to the single entry, and tossed it on the desk. "I found this in Dylan's bag. See what you make of it."

Harve whistled softly. "An Ingram MAC ten is a right serious automatic pistol, and the rest of it looks like the serial number. I'll follow up on it."

"I wish you'd follow up on getting information from the feds," I muttered. "There's an FBI office here, but all I got was a recorded message telling me to call during regular business hours. A guy at the Little Rock office gave me a number in DC. The guy there was as helpful as a chunk of asphalt. I had the same reaction from the ATF. It's possible you or the county prosecutor can get something out of them."

"I know ol' Tinker Tonnato, the local FBI agent. I guess he figures the terrorists are gonna have to twiddle their thumbs while he gets in some weekend hunting. I'll call him first thing Monday morning."

"Even if Dylan had a medical condition, whoever fired the rifle is still looking at a charge of first degree murder." I picked up the plastic bag and studied the misshapen lump of steel. "You sure you and Les got all their weapons?"

"Yeah," Harve said as he reached for a cigar. "All the fellows staying at the camp had handguns and the Rondly boy had a rifle, but they kept them locked in their vehicles. Earl Buchanon told me that Pitts was the only one to come back to the pasture, and that was to use the phone in that ridiculous-looking tank of his. The only other weapon any of them had in their possession was the flare gun that Rondly used to signal there was an emergency."

Noxious smoke was drifting toward me, so I put down the plastic bag and stood up. "How did the press conference go? Did you win any votes?"

"I told 'em we're doing everything we can short of assigning a deputy to every house set off by itself. A couple of the reporters had the same idea you did. At least I could tell them we'd already eliminated anything the homeowners might have had in common. My best guess is the perps are watching the houses somehow."

"From the woods?" I said dryly. "They sit in trees and train binoculars on the back door on the chance the owners are going to come out carrying luggage? What are the odds they'd get lucky six times in the last month? And think about Mayfly, Harve. They waited two or three days before they broke in, which means they were pretty damn confident that Mrs. Coben and her daughter would be gone for more than a day."

"Did either of them tell anybody?"

"Mrs. Coben said she mentioned their trip to a couple of people who live out that way. Heidi had broken up with her boyfriend a couple of weeks earlier, and she was holed up at home, sulking and refusing to talk to anybody. Katherine Avenued may have told people, but Heidi described her as being so shy she rarely smiled or spoke to anybody. Katherine's neighbors at the apartment house had never done more than say hello to her on the sidewalk, and her classmates and co-workers said the same thing. Besides, Mayfly is at least twenty miles away from the other houses that were burglarized."

"I know," Harve said, "but there has to be something, damn it! We can't blame it on a full moon, since that doesn't happen six times a month."

I told Harve I'd keep him posted, then drove back to Maggody, hoping I'd be in time to see Reed Rondly's reaction when the process server knocked on the door.

Not much had changed in my absence. Mrs. Jim Bob's Cadillac was still parked in front of the Assembly Hall, and Ruby Bee's Bar & Grill was still closed. Les had been relieved by an unfamiliar deputy who introduced himself as Corporal Batson and assured me that although there'd been some movement between units, no one had left the motel parking lot. A car, presumably Barry Kirklin's, was parked next to Reed's truck. Estelle's station wagon was still gone. I was warning Batson about the process server when Sterling came out of #5.

"I have been waiting for you for more than two hours," he said. "That lame-brained deputy refuses to allow us to do something about dinner. Kayleen called the barroom, but no one answered. Prisoners of war are treated better than this, Chief Hanks. The Fifth Amendment clearly prohibits the deprivation of liberty without due process of law."

"Are you suggesting that I arrest you? It's okay with me."

"On Monday morning I shall place a call to the lieutenant governor to make a formal complaint. Now, what do you propose to do in order that we receive a decent meal?"

"I'll send the lame-brained deputy over to the supermarket to get some roots and berries. If you all promise to behave, you can have a picnic out here in your tank. Half the town could probably squeeze into the back seat. How much did this thing cost?"

"That's none of your business," he said, then closed his door.

I asked Batson to go across the road to purchase sandwiches and soft drinks, then sat on the hood of my car and tried to envision what had taken place on Cotter's Ridge earlier in the day. None of the current residents of the Flamingo seemed to have an adequate motive to take a shot at Dylan. Sterling, Barry, and Jake suspected Dylan had been a federal agent, but they weren't firmly convinced. Reed and Kayleen were skeptical, at best. And none of them had been carrying a rifle.

Perhaps Harve's first assessment was right, I told myself, and the incident had been nothing more than a coincidence of cosmic dimensions. The burglaries could be that, too, although it was hard to ignore the parallels in all six of them. My eyes drifted to the window of #3 as I remembered what Kayleen had said about Maurice's murder. They'd been awakened by the sound of breaking glass.

I slid off the hood and walked across the lot to knock on her door. When she opened it, I said, "May I come in? I need to ask you something."

Barry and Reed had taken refuge in her room until they could get into their unit. Reed was stretched out on the bed, muddy boots and all, with a beer balanced on his belly. Barry was seated by a table, where it looked as though he and Kayleen were in the midst of a card game.

"Did you find out what killed Dylan?" asked Kayleen. "Was it a heart attack?"

"We don't know yet," I said, "and most likely won't for a day or two. I realize this is a sensitive subject, but I want to ask you about the night Maurice was killed."

"Poor old Mo," drawled Reed, lifting his head to take a gulp of beer.

Kayleen sat down at the table. "Why, Arly? It couldn't possibly have anything to do with what happened today."

Barry leaned forward to squeeze her hand. "I don't see how it could, but it won't hurt to answer a few questions."

"I suppose not," she said unhappily.

Feeling a bit like an employee of the Spanish Inquisition, I said, "I'm sure you're aware that Elsie Buchanon's house was burglarized last week. There have been some other burglaries, too, and I'm trying to find a link."

"Like what?"

"For starters, were you and Maurice supposed to have been away on a trip when the break-in took place?"

She thought for a long moment. "Maurice had suggested going to a gun show somewhere—Kansas City, I think—but we didn't like the looks of the weather." She swallowed several times and her eyes filled with tears. "If we'd decided to go, Maurice would still be alive, wouldn't he? It was my doing, since I was the one who was afraid the roads might turn icy."

Reed belched. "That don't mean Mo'd be around these days. He was old as the hills, and so gimpy he could barely get around. Every meeting we had, all he'd do is complain about his damn prostrate or whatever it was."

"Shut up!" snapped Barry.

I touched Kayleen's shoulder. "Did you or your husband tell anyone that you were going to Kansas City? A neighbor, maybe, or a storekeeper?"

"I didn't," she said, "and I don't think Maurice did, although I can't be sure. He did a lot of business over the telephone. If someone had wanted to make an appointment, he might have mentioned the possibility of a trip. Do you think the burglars broke in because they believed the house was empty?"

I nodded. "That's the only thing we've come up with thus far. I guess I'd better call the sheriff's department over in Chowden County. We might be able to exchange some information and figure out if the same perps simply moved their operation to Stump County."

Barry began to gather up the cards. "Any idea when we can get in our room?"

"Did any of your training include a course in picking locks?" I asked. "Or were you too busy learning how to survive on pizza and beer?"

He gave me a level look. "Anyone with a credit card could get past these locks. Want me to demonstrate?"

Before I could answer, there was a knock on the door. I admitted Corporal Batson, who was carrying several sacks from the SuperSaver.

"Hope ham 'n cheese is okay with everybody," he said apologetically. He handed me a bill. "I said you'd drop by and settle up. You can probably get the sheriff to reimburse you. It may take a while, though. Our budget's so tight we can't afford to fix the microwave in the break room."

I told Barry that he and Reed could move into #6, and Kayleen was distributing sandwiches to her guests as the deputy and I left the room. In #5, I could see Sterling hunched in front of a computer screen, his expression indicative that he wasn't having much luck in his endeavor. Wondering if he was trying to make contact with the Colorado group, I took a sandwich and soda out of one of the sacks and went back across the lot.

He jerked open the door before I could knock. "It's about time, Chief Hanks. I'm beginning to feel lightheaded from lack of food. Proper nutrition is vital to maintaining mental acuity."

"Is that protected by the Constitution, too?" I said as I handed him the sandwich. "Does one of the amendments guarantee three square meals a day?"

"The Constitution should be treated with reverence, not derision. It's our only defense against the federal government and its illegitimate manipulation of individual rights."

I fluttered my eyelashes. "Hope ham 'n cheese is okay, General Pitts."

"Yeah, yeah, I heard it," Jim Bob said, flipping over his cards and pushing back his chair. "More than likely

Diesel's playin' Injun and taken to beating a tom-tom, or maybe those screwy militia boys are firing cannons at the low-water bridge."

Larry Joe peeked at his hole card to see if it had transformed itself into an ace, then gestured at Roy to rake the pot. "That don't explain what I saw—and I know I saw something straight out of one of Brother Verber's hell-and-damnation sermons. It was evil."

"I heard it, too," inserted Roy as he arranged the chips into tidy stacks.

"So what?" said Jim Bob. "That doesn't prove it's a friggin' demon here to punish us for taking a few days off to relax. Now if I was at the delectable Cherri Lucinda's love nest, I might be worried that Mrs. Jim Bob had struck a deal with Satan. I wouldn't put it past her to sell my soul for a new Cadillac. In fact, I can see her writing up the contract, with Brother Verber there at her side to notarize it."

Larry Joe went to the window to peer out at the utter darkness. "This ain't anything to joke about, Jim Bob. Roy saw the tracks in the mud, and you yourself heard that noise."

Jim Bob grunted. "I heard a noise, not a demonic screech. I reckon I need to make a trip to the outhouse. Will my rifle be enough protection, or should I take a submachine gun and a bible?"

He grabbed a flashlight and went out the door, mumbling to himself about nervous Nellies. The weeds had been trampled into a serviceable path that led around the corner of the trailer and fifty feet down the hillside to an outhouse fashioned of irregular scraps of plywood and a warped sheet of siding. The corrugated tin roof provided minimal protection from rain and gusts of wind.

After he'd finished his business, he came back out and pointed the flashlight at the tangle of vines that Larry Joe kept harping about. He saw exactly what he expected to see, which was nothing more than whatever Mother Nature had planted. Larry Joe had been teaching school too long, Jim Bob decided as he let the beam of the flashlight bobble on the runty trees. Maybe being surrounded by all those hormones had addled his mind.

Jim Bob decided to have himself a little fun. He positioned himself behind the rusty carcass of an old truck, switched off the flashlight, and threw a pebble at the kitchen window. The resulting clink was sharp and loud. Within seconds, Larry Joe's face appeared in the window, and Roy's just behind him. Their expressions were so bumfuzzled that it was all Jim Bob could do not to start laughing.

Eventually they moved away from the window. Jim Bob gave them a couple of minutes to persuade each other that a bird had crashed into the window, then threw another pebble. This time Roy reached the window first, with Larry Joe a close second. Their jaws were wagging something fierce, and Jim Bob could see the whites of their eyes.

He found a third pebble and was leaning back to scare the holy shit out of them when he heard a crackle directly behind him. He spun around. What he saw was enough to make him drop the flashlight and bolt for the trailer.

Despite her in-laws' objections, Dahlia had insisted on being taken home so she could be there if Kevvie turned up. Now she kinda wished she hadn't, what with the wind rattling the loose shingles and rustling the leaves alongside the house.

She turned on the television for company, and was heading for the kitchen when another of those dad-burned contractions stopped her in her tracks. The doctor had called them by some fancy name and told her she'd be getting them as the due date got closer, but that wasn't much comfort when her innards were being squeezed like someone was wringing out wet laundry. To top it off, Kevin Junior kicked so hard that a warm dribble ran down her leg.

Once the contraction eased, she went on into the kitchen for a diet soda and a handful of carrot sticks, then sat down across from the television. The silly sitcom did nothing to keep her from brooding. Kevvie had no business going off like this, she thought as she chomped away like a leaf shredder. Here she was, within weeks of havin' the baby, and she was all alone, tormented by the contractions, poking her finger all the time, visiting the potty every ten minutes, and reduced to carrot and celery sticks whenever her stomach rumbled.

"I hope you don't turn out like your pa," she said to Kevin Junior. "He's about as useless as a one-horned cow. What's more, he's liable to git his sorry self fired on account of missing work. Jim Bob's kin, but he ain't gonna be thinking of that when he kicks your pa out the door. We'll all end up at one of those homeless shelters."

The very idea set her lower lip to quivering, and tears to sliding down her cheeks. Her granny had grown up during the Depression, and her stories about scrimping for food were scarier than any tales told around the campfire during church camp—shoes with cardboard soles, clothes from charity stores, watery soup and stale bread.

Dahlia was reduced to snuffling when the telephone rang. She lunged for the receiver. "Kevvie?"

"No, this is Idalupino down at the SuperSaver. Listen, I just heard something peculiar. My second cousin Canon Buchanon was just here, and he said he saw Kevin's car parked by the low-water bridge. Nobody was in the car. He didn't see a body floating in the creek or lying on the gravel bar, but it was right dark and he was leery of going into the woods after what happened this morning. Anyways, I thought you'd want to know about the car."

"Thanks," Dahlia said numbly. She replaced the receiver and slumped back, doing her best to come up with some sort of explanation for what she'd heard. It had to do with that militia game, she figured, since Kevvie's pa had told them about all those grown folks pretending to be soldiers. Eileen had been real scornful, but Dahlia had been a little proud that Kevvie had been chosen for such an important role. She wasn't clear about why they were told they were gorillas, unless they were pretending that Cotter's Ridge was a jungle.

A contraction interrupted her laborious thought process. She grimaced and moaned her way through it, then went into the bedroom and searched the dresser drawers for another pamphlet that might tell about an evening meeting. Finding nothing of significance, she checked under his pillow and on his shelf in the medicine cabinet in the bathroom.

She trudged back into the living room and dialed her in-laws' number. The line was busy. What if, she asked herself, Kevvie was lost on Cotter's Ridge, all cold and scared and hungry? Or even worse, if he'd been shot like that other fellow and was bleeding like a stuck pig while she sat at home eating carrot sticks?

The line was busy at the PD, and nobody answered at Ruby Bee's Bar & Grill. Canon Buchanon was living in his car these days, so there wasn't any way to call him to find out if he'd heard any gunshots while he was down by the low-water bridge. She tried her in-laws' again, but Eileen was still on the line, probably talking to Millicent McIlhaney.

Frustrated, Dahlia ate the last carrot stick and finished the soda. On the television screen, a man with big teeth was begging her to buy a contraption that cut potatoes into fancy slices, but she couldn't bear to listen while Kevvie was in terrible danger. She turned off the set, put on her coat and gloves, went outside, and started down the road. It was a good two miles to the low-water bridge, even if she cut through the schoolyard and the pasture behind the old Emporium. It would take nearly an hour, she realized, and when she got there, all she could do was holler Kevvie's name and pray he answered.

She slowed down as she approached Raz's shack. A light was on in the front room and smoke curled out of the chimney. More important, his truck was parked in the yard. She reminded herself that even though he was an ornery cuss, he was a neighbor and a Buchanon just like Kevvie.

Still, it took her a few minutes to find the courage

to go up to his porch and knock on the door. "Raz?" she called. "Lemme in before I turn blue."

The door opened far enough for him to glare at her through the crack. "I don't much cotton to uninvited company. Whatta ya want?"

Dahlia glared right back, hoping her knees weren't knockin' so loud he could hear them. "I want you to drive me to the low-water bridge and help me find Kevvie up on the ridge."

"Cain't do it. Me and Marjorie are watching a movie about a talking mule. It's the first one all week that's caught her fancy."

"You listen to me, Raz Buchanon, and you listen good. I haft to go find Kevvie, and I don't have time to walk all that way. If you won't help me, I'll break down your door and wring your neck. Then I'll git the key to the truck and drive myself." She held up a ham-sized fist. "I don't aim to raise a child on my own. What's it gonna be, Raz?"

He scratched his chin. "Tell ya what, we'll take you there, but we ain't about to go up on the ridge. Marjorie's still crumpy from the last time we wuz there."

"Leave her here," Dahlia said coldly.

"By herself? Why, I couldn't do that. She's a pedigreed sow, ye know, and has a delicate nature."

"All right, then git her and let's go. I gotta rescue Kevvie before the end of the month when I have the baby."

Within minutes, Raz, Marjorie, and Dahlia were headed for County 102. Raz was making his displeasure known by hitting every pothole. Marjorie sat in the middle, her eyes closed. On the passenger's side, Dahlia stared out the window, battling nausea from the stench in the truck, wishing she'd used the potty before she left the house, and wondering what she was gonna do when Raz left her at the bridge and drove away. The first thing would be to find a bush and relieve herself, of course, but after that . . . she just didn't have a clue.

Chapter 13

A very bored dispatcher informed me that the Chowden County sheriff would be in his office first thing in the morning, and no one else knew anything about the case. I replaced the receiver and rocked back, trying to sort out the profusion of problems that had popped up like crab grass in the last week. They came in all sizes and degrees of magnitude, from the brutal murder in Mayfly to the disappearances of local residents. At the moment Kevin, Ruby Bee, and Estelle were out of pocket, as well as two unnamed ostriches. At least Brother Verber had reappeared from his unauthorized outing.

There wasn't anything I could do about Dylan's death until the autopsy was final, nor could I make any progress with the burglaries until I talked to the sheriff. I could clear up one minor issue, however, so I locked the PD and drove to the rectory to ask Brother Verber if he was the person whom Earl had seen coming down from the ridge at noon.

Mrs. Jim Bob's Cadillac hadn't moved. I was reluctant to question Brother Verber in front of her, but I didn't want to put it off until the following afternoon after church. As I walked up the gravel path, the door swung open.

"It's high time, I must say!" Mrs. Jim Bob began, then stopped and took a harder look at me. "I thought you were somebody else."

"There are days I wish I was."

"Have you finally decided to do the job you were hired to do?"

"I saw the lights and assumed Brother Verber was back," I said as I went into the trailer. "What are you doing here, looking for photographs to paste on milk cartons?"

She appeared rather unkempt, even by my admittedly lackadaisical standards. Her hair was mussed, and her skirt and blouse were so wrinkled she might have slept in them. To add to the overall effect, one of her pumps was blue, the other brown. She stared at me, most likely trying to come up with a withering response, then abruptly sat down on the edge of the sofa.

"I'm worried about him," she said in a low voice.

"He's not as worldly as some would have you think. No matter how hard I've tried to convince him otherwise, he thinks drinking is fine as long as it's sacramental wine. The Good Lord may think differently, and so may the state police." She looked up at me with a piteous expression. "Would you have heard if he was arrested?"

"I'm sure I would have," I said. I was dangerously close to offering sympathy when I saw Ruby Bee at the end of the hallway, a finger pressed to her lips. Gulping, I made myself look at Mrs. Jim Bob. "How long have you been here?"

"I don't know. A couple of hours, maybe. I got to where I couldn't stand wandering around my house. He *has* to come back soon so he can prepare tomorrow's sermon. I want to see for myself that he's safe and sound."

"I, ah, don't think you should stay here," I said lamely.

"Why not?" Mrs. Jim Bob countered, regaining a bit of her more typical vinegary spirit. "It's not like I broke down the door to come inside. Brother Verber himself mentioned that he keeps a key under the mat. He wouldn't have done that if he minded me using it. Besides, this place was a real mess, and I took it upon myself to clean it up and stock the refrigerator with a few casseroles and a pot of chicken soup. I'm sure he'll be thrilled to find me here."

I caught a glimpse of Estelle behind Ruby Bee, both of them frantically signaling me not to acknowledge their presence. "Well, sure he would be, but . . . but I think I ought to call in a missing person report to the sheriff's department so they can start searching for him."

"I made that clear this morning."

"I've changed my mind. Why don't you come with me to the PD so you can answer any questions that may arise?"

Mrs. Jim Bob crossed her arms. "I've already told you everything I know. He was seen in the hussy's car Wednesday afternoon, and he had the audacity to wink at her several times during the prayer meeting that same evening. He sat next to her at the potluck, smirking like a dead hog in the sunshine, and she was so syrupy that I kept expecting her to crawl into his lap. She's nothing but a common tramp who's set her sights on him. What if she talked him into eloping?"

"And forgot to go along?" I opened the door and gestured at her to stand up. "Why don't you come with me so you can tell your theories to Sheriff Dorfer? He'll be fascinated."

She switched off the light as she went out the door, but I figured Ruby Bee and Estelle could find their way in the dark. When we arrived at our respective cars, Mrs. Jim Bob said, "You can tell Sheriff Dorfer to call me at home if he wants to. All this worrying has taken its toll on me. I need to lie down."

After she'd driven away, I leaned against my car and waited for the miscreants to come out of the rectory. They could probably see me in the diffused glow from the streetlight, but I doubted they had the nerve to linger inside the rectory until I left. Mrs. Jim Bob was more than capable of returning to continue her vigil.

Eventually the door opened and two shadowy figures scurried toward the old hardware store. I caught up with them at the edge of the road and said, "Would you care to explain what you were doing?"

Ruby Bee put her hands on her hips. "We weren't doing anything that concerns you, missy."

"That's right," added Estelle.

"I want an explanation," I said in a stony voice Ruby Bee had used when I'd missed my curfew in high school.

"Well," Ruby Bee began, "we thought it'd be nice to take Brother Verber a plate of supper so when he got back, he'd have something filling to eat. I had pot roast left over from lunch, along with carrots, potatoes, black-eyed peas, and a piece of apple pie."

"And a clover-leaf roll," said Estelle. "It was cold, of course, but all he had to do was heat it in the oven for—"

"Stop it," I interrupted. "If that's all you were doing—and don't think for a minute that I believe you—then why were you cowering in the hallway? Couldn't you have told Mrs. Jim Bob this same story?"

Ruby Bee moistened her lips. "She's been acting right peculiar these last few weeks, and I'm not one to spit in the devil's teeth. It seemed better to wait until she left. We had no way of knowing she was gonna plunk herself down and start mouthing off. She sounded so crazy we were too scared to come out of the bedroom. For all we knew, she'd taken a knife out of a drawer or brought one of Jim Bob's shotguns with her."

"And if Brother Verber returned?" I asked.

Estelle took over. "We figured she'd grab his ear and haul him over to the Assembly Hall to pray for forgiveness. That was one of the things she kept saying over and over again. The rest of it doesn't bear repeating, although I must say some of it didn't sound very charitable coming from someone who goes around telling everybody what a good Christian she is."

"I should say not," said Ruby Bee. "I'd better get back to the bar in case some customers show up. Come on, Estelle."

They went behind the building, where I presumed

Estelle's station wagon was parked. I had no idea what they'd been up to, but I wasn't sure I wanted to know.

I went back to my car and drove to the PD. The red light was blinking on the answering machine. Ruby Bee hadn't dawdled in Brother Verber's trailer long enough to call me before they emerged, and Mrs. Jim Bob couldn't have made it home yet. I hit the button and heard McBeen's raspy voice:

"I got some preliminary results for you. The boy died of respiratory failure, probably after a few convulsions. Could have been he was allergic to bee venom and was stung, but we haven't found any welts. Nothing in his stomach indicates oral ingestion of anything more lethal than eggs and biscuits. All I can do is overnight some blood and tissue samples to the state lab in Little Rock, where they're equipped to run sophisticated tox screens. I'll try to bully them into getting back to me tomorrow afternoon."

The second message was even more perplexing. It was from Harve, who'd received an amazingly quick response to his query about the Ingram MAC 10. It seemed the weapon had been seized in a raid on a compound in central Missouri and was implicated in the cold-blooded killing of a local radio personality who'd been both revered and reviled for scoffing at the militia movement. A month before the shooting, the weapon had been reported stolen from a dealer in Arkansas. The dealer's name was Maurice W. Smeltner.

Harve hadn't caught the significance of the name, but I did. It now seemed likely that Dylan had been a federal agent who'd infiltrated this particular militia not because he thought they were capable of violence, but because he was tracing the Ingram MAC 10 back to its original source. Since Maurice was no longer available, he'd ended up with Kayleen.

I had an urge to leap to my feet and in a single bound be pounding on the door of #3 and demanding answers. However, I didn't have any questions, and it had been a grueling day. Sunday's agenda was beginning to swell up faster than Boone Creek in the spring.

I suppose I should have gone to Ruby Bee's to insist that she and Estelle tell me the truth, or called Dahlia to find out if Kevin had returned, or filed a missing person report concerning Brother Verber, or finger-printed the toilet seat in #4.

Maybe I *should* have done at least one of those, but I locked up the PD and went across the road to my apartment for a can of chicken noodle soup and an undemanding late-night movie. Considering the way things were going, the only thing on was apt to be *Village of the Damned.*

It's never been one of my favorites.

"You won't believe your ears," Ruby Bee said to Estelle, who'd arrived at the barroom for breakfast the next morning. "I found out what that tight-lipped deputy was doing parked in the lot all night long. You'd have thought that since I own the motel I deserved an explanation right then and there. Anyway, a while ago I took trays to everybody, and Kayleen explained why all the militia folks are staying out back. One of them, a boy from Colorado, was shot while they were playing their war game on Cotter's Ridge."

"Shouldn't he be staying in a hospital?" said Estelle as she poured herself a cup of coffee.

"He's in the morgue—and nobody knows what killed him."

"You just said he was shot. Can I have some cream for this? It's strong enough to bubble the paint off aluminum siding."

Ruby Bee didn't much care for the aspersion, but she slid the ceramic pitcher down the bar before she got back to the more important affair of repeating gossip. "At first, Arly and the sheriff agreed it was an ordinary hunting accident, but then they found out the bullet wound wasn't all that serious." She leaned forward and lowered her voice. "What's more, Earl and Kevin were there, as well as Jeremiah McIlhaney. I'd liked to have been a fly on the wall when those three told their wives."

Estelle wasn't ready for conversation, so she busied herself calculating the precise amount of cream needed to make the coffee palatable. Ruby Bee went into the kitchen to check on the ham in the oven, then returned just as Eileen came into the barroom and said, "Where's Arly?"

Ruby Bee shrugged. "She hasn't been here this morning."

"She's not at the police department or her apartment. It's real important that I talk to her!"

Estelle patted the stool beside her. "You'd better sit down, Eileen. You're white as a slab of cream cheese. Ruby Bee, why don't you get Eileen a cup of coffee?"

"I've got to find Arly!" said Eileen, remaining where she was. "Yesterday Kevin went off somewhere, and now Dahlia's gone, too. I called their house this morning, then went over there. Nobody was home. I thought maybe Kevin had rushed her to the hospital, but according to the reception desk, they're not there. The clinic hasn't heard from them either, and they were supposed to call before they left for the hospital."

Ruby Bee went ahead and filled a cup with coffee. "Could they have gone to a different hospital?"

"I don't see why they would. The clinic gave them instructions to go to the one in Farberville, and they've already filled out the admission forms and made sure they know which door to go in. Kevin came close to passing out when he heard how much the delivery will cost, but the hospital agreed to monthly payments." Eileen took a swallow of coffee, grimaced, and put down the cup. "I'm beside myself with worry. Earl thinks Kevin came home real late, and by way of apology, took Dahlia for a drive this morning. He says Dahlia forgot her promise to call us when he showed up."

"He could be right," said Estelle.

It was obvious that Eileen was on the verge of bawling, so Ruby Bee hurried around the bar and gave her a hug. "It's gonna turn out fine," she said, "but when Arly shows up, I'll have her call you just to be on the safe side." She waited until Eileen trudged out of the bar, then looked at Estelle. "I don't know what Arly can do, though. The way folks are coming and going these days, you'd think there was a revolving door at both ends of town. It's a dad-burned shame those militia folks pushed their way through it."

"The fellow that got shot would be the first to agree with you. I think I'm gonna go out to my house later this morning to collect yesterday's mail and make sure Elsie's burglars didn't drop by."

"What about the birds?"

"It's broad daylight and there's no way they could be inside," Estelle said coolly, ignoring the sudden flutters in her stomach. "Anyway, all we have to fear is fear itself."

"I don't recollect Winston Churchill being pecked so hard he fell off a porch."

"He didn't say it. It was Franklin Delano Roosevelt."

Ruby Bee gaped at her. "It most certainly was not. It was Churchill trying to calm everybody down when the Nazis started bombing England."

"I beg your pardon. I distinctly remember from my high school history class that it was President Roosevelt."

"Are you sure you didn't *hear* him say it?" Ruby Bee said sweetly. "I've always wondered how much gray hair you're covering up."

Estelle clamped down on her magenta-colored lip until she could trust herself. "I learned about it in school, and my memory's a sight better than yours, Mrs. Walking Amnesia. Why don't we just settle this by calling Lottie? She's a teacher, so she might know."

Ruby Bee was already regretting taking such a firm stance, but she wasn't about to let it show. She opened the cash register, took out a dime, and slapped it down on the bar. "Go right ahead and call anybody you like."

"We'll just see, won't we?" Estelle marched down to the pay phone and dialed Lottie's number. As soon as she heard Lottie's voice, she posed the question and waited for a response. Rather than chortling with self-congratulation, her eyes grew round as silver dollars and her jaw began to waggle. Minutes later, she staggered back to her stool.

"Well?" said Ruby Bee. "Which one was it?"

"I don't think Lottie ever said, because she was hellbent on telling me something else. After I left the high school library, she remembered having flipped through a magazine—*Farmer's Digest*, I think she said—that had ostriches on the cover. She hunted it up and read an article about how breeding them is big business these days. The eggs are worth a thousand dollars, chicks about three thousand, and a mature pair is"—she put her hand on her mouth to hold back the makings of a whimper, but it came out anyway—"between forty-five and sixty thousand dollars. Those hissy birds that Uncle Tooly gave me are worth a fortune, and you let them run off into the woods like nothing more valuable than scruffy little guinea hens."

Ruby Bee didn't recollect letting them do anything except come close to scaring her to death. However, there was no point in saying as much—or mentioning that Estelle had been the one too cowardly to open the door. "Maybe we can get them back. For all we know, they're in your yard. If they're not, they're likely to be on the ridge. We'd have heard if they were wandering around town, alarming folks."

"What'll we do if we find 'em? Ask 'em real politely to follow us back to the house and climb into the crate?"

This was indeed a problem. After tossing back and forth suggestions that ranged from the ludicrous, like roping them cowboy style, to the outright insane, like jumping on their backs, they came up with a plan of sorts that involved being able to get close enough to throw bed sheets over their heads. Estelle finished her coffee while Ruby Bee collected sheets from #1, then they climbed into the station wagon and headed for Cotter's Ridge.

I arrived in Malthus at eight, found the sheriff's department, identified myself, and was ushered into his office one minute later (his version of LaBelle was a nervous youngster with acne and a stammer).

Sheriff Flatchett was almost a carbon copy of Harve in terms of bulk and age, but there was something unsavory about him, something that implied he might be persuaded to look the other way in exchange for an envelope stuffed with money. Rumor has it there are no chickens in the chicken houses of Chowden County, but instead grow lights and irrigation systems. Rumor also has it that Sheriff Flatchett spends his vacations in Europe.

"I've heard of you," he said, not bothering to stand up or feign a smile. "Over in Maggody, right?"

"That's right," I said. I waited a moment to be invited to sit down, then did it anyway. "I'm here because of a string of burglaries in Stump County. One of them included a homicide."

"Is that so?" he said without interest.

I reminded myself that I needed his cooperation, if not his undying devotion. "Yes, and I understand you had one here about a year ago. Maurice Smeltner was the victim."

"Yeah, ol' Mo took three slugs to his abdomen and was dead as a lizard before we got there. They lived way the hell out at the end of an unpaved road. Decent house, though, with one of those above-ground pools. According to his widow, swimming was about the only exercise Mo could handle after hip-replacement surgery. He met her while he was recuperating in a nursing home, and I guess he figured he could get looked after for free if he married her. Mo preferred to keep his wallet in his pocket. Odds are he never had a Girl Scout cookie in his life."

"Kayleen Smeltner told me that they were awakened by the sound of breaking glass, and her husband went down to investigate. When she heard shots, she called for help and reached the top of the stairs just as three men ran out the door."

Flatchett nodded. "To the best of my recollection, that's what she said. She didn't hear an engine start up, so we assumed they parked someplace else and came on foot. We rounded up the usual suspects, as they say in Hollywood. Nobody admitted participating in it, and none of our snitches heard anything in the bars and poolrooms."

All the cases in Stump County had involved a vehicle, but I wasn't ready to give up. "Did they get away with any of Smeltner's weapons?"

"Yeah, I seem to think they did. Hold on and I'll pull the file. You want some coffee?"

"Yes, please," I said, then waited impatiently as he left the office, bellowed at the dispatcher to fetch two cups of coffee, and eventually returned with a stained manila folder.

He read in silence until the youngster brought the coffee and darted away. "By the time Mo got downstairs, they'd pried open the case in his office. They took a thirty-thirty rifle, a forty-four Magnum, and an Ingram MAC ten. I reckon once they shot him, they decided it might be wise to leave with what they already had."

I took out my notebook and read off the serial number I'd discovered in Dylan's duffel bag. "That match?"

"Sure does," said Flatchett, closing the folder and giving me a sharp look. "The FBI asked me that very same question a while back. You think that this case, the cases over in your county, and that murder in Missouri are all the responsibility of one group?"

"I don't know what I think," I said morosely.

"Were there other burglaries around the same time?"

"Some tools were taken from a shed not too far from the Smeltner place. A widow reported a peeping Tom, but over the years she's reported everything from a caravan of drunken gypsies to a platoon of Nazis in the woods behind her house." He reopened the folder and scanned the pages. "Oh, and another guy on the same road claimed that someone had left footprints in his wife's flowerbed alongside the house. I guess all of them out that way were a might edgy. After the murder, most of them moved into town."

"What about burglaries elsewhere in Chowden County?"

Flatchett began to doodle on the folder. "Nothing out of the ordinary. It used to be you were safe living in a small town, where your neighbors could keep an eye on things while you were gone. Nowadays, we got crime just like the city folks. I've enjoyed talking to you, but the reason I'm not hunting this weekend is that I'm supposed to attend a prayer breakfast over at the Methodist church—and elections are coming up soon."

I wasn't sure if he'd been as candid as possible, but I doubted he was going to toss out anything more.

"Thanks for your time, Sheriff Flatchett. Harve Dorfer and I'd appreciate it if you could let us have copies of the reports from those burglaries."

"I'll fax 'em to his office tomorrow or the next day," he said, pulling back his cuff to look at his watch. "You might want to talk to Mo's daughter. Miss Lila's a spinster and lives here in Malthus. I don't know her address right off hand, but she's in the directory."

I thanked him more profusely and left to find Miss Lila Smeltner.

Dahlia had found out in no time flat that Kevvie'd had enough sense to lock the car before going off into the wilderness. She'd walked back up County 102, planning to stop at Estelle's and call Eileen, but the house was dark and locked up tighter than a tick. Walking all the way home would have been impossible, what with the contractions so strong she had to sit down at the edge of the road and ride 'em out.

Having decided it was too darn cold to spend the night crouched in ditches, she'd found an unlocked door at the old Wockermann place and spent the night under a tarp, shivering, groaning, and making trips outside to squat on the remains of the patio and pray some critter didn't nip her on the butt. At dawn, she'd explored the house and found a half-full bottle of soda pop, and somewhat later, a lunch box with some stale crusts of bread and a withered apple that bore a remarkable resemblance to her granny.

Now, the contractions had stopped for the most part. She felt a little light-headed, which is what the doctor had said would happen if she didn't eat properly. The soda pop would fix that, she told herself as she went into the front room to look at Estelle's house.

The station wagon wasn't there, and it didn't look like any lights were on inside. She went through the kitchen and out to the patio to study the ridge. Kevvie had been the only eyewitness to the shooting, she thought as she sucked on her cheeks, and it was possible he'd seen something real important that he'd forgotten to tell anyone. Or maybe he had to investigate it for hisself, because it might put her and Kevin Junior in danger.

Dahlia realized she was feeling more perky than she had in the last three months. The soda pop must have given her a sugar buzz, she decided with a contented smile, just like before she got in the family way and could eat a whole package of vanilla sandwich cookies at one time. She patted her belly. "I sure do hope you have a sweet tooth, too," she said to Kevin Junior as she set off across the pasture, following tire tracks and humming the theme song from *Gilligan's Island*.

Jim Bob looked around real carefully as he opened the door of the trailer and pissed on the concrete block that served as a step.

"See anything?" asked Larry Joe.

"Yeah," he said as he closed the door. "I saw trees and wet leaves and a squirrel on a stump next to my four-wheel. I'm shakin'. I'm shakin'," like a molded salad."

"You were shaking last night when you came stumbling inside, slobbering something awful. It made me think of Durasell Buchanon after he accidentally flushed his dentures down the toilet. I never could figure out why he went around telling everybody about it."

Jim Bob took a beer out of the cooler. "Where's Roy?"

"He got up early and went outside to look for more tracks in the mud. That was more than an hour ago. I've been watching out the window for him, but I haven't seen so much as a branch twitch. Do you think we should go search for him?"

"Fuck that," said Jim Bob. "If he wants to be that goddamn stupid, he can take care of himself. Want to play some gin, dollar a point?"

Larry Joe stayed by the window. "Joyce liked to skin me alive that last time I played gin with you and lost thirty-eight dollars. What's more, I had to babysit all weekend while she visited her sister in Paris."

"Jesus H. Christ, Larry Joe! You let her go all the way to Paris over thirty-eight dollars? You're stupider than Roy. Where would you have let her go if you'd lost a hundred dollars—the moon?"

"It ain't all that far," protested Larry Joe.

"Of course it's all that far, you pinhead. I don't know how you ever got certified to teach, unless you paid someone to go in your place—or you were such a pain in the ass that they gave you the certificate just to get rid of you." Jim Bob banged down the beer can so hard that foam splashed onto the table. "Jesus H. Christ!"

"There ain't no reason to say those things, Jim Bob. I got my certificate because I passed all the required classes. I may not have been class valedictorian, but I do know that Paris is only about seventy-five miles from here down in Logan County. You got a problem with that?"

"Oh, I was just yanking your cord. If you want, we can play for a dime a point," Jim Bob said, picking up the cards.

Lila Smeltner was dressed in church clothes when she opened the door, but her gray hair was wrapped so tightly around pink foam rollers that my scalp tingled. She was at least sixty years old, which made me wonder how she'd felt about having a stepmother who was twenty years younger, twenty pounds heavier, and a foot taller.

"Yes?" she said suspiciously. "If you're one of those missionaries, you can turn right around and go find someone else to pester. I've been a member of the First Baptist Church since I was baptized fifty-one years ago. If the Lord won't take me as I am, I'll negotiate with Satan for long-term accommodations."

I opened my coat to show her my badge. "I'm Arly Hanks from Maggody, Miss Lila. Sheriff Flatchett gave me your name. If I'm not catching you at a bad time, I'd like to ask you a few questions."

"About what?"

"Your father's murder," I said. "There's been a similar case in Stump County, and I'm trying to determine if it was committed by the same men."

Miss Lila hesitated for a long moment, then opened the screen door. "You can ask your questions, but I don't know anything more than what Kayleen and the sheriff told me. When Papa got remarried, I bought this little house. There's a crowd, you know, and Kayleen appeared to be taking good care of him. Besides, we couldn't get cable out there."

The living room was sparsely furnished but meticulously clean. The only thing on the white walls was a photograph of a sour-looking couple dressed in somber clothing. I moved aside a throw pillow and sat down on a love seat that must have been purchased in a fit of girlish optimism. "So you and Kayleen got along okay?"

"Why wouldn't we? Papa could be very demanding and impossible to please, and I wasn't looking forward to his arrival back home after his hip surgery. To be blunt, Miss Hanks, he was a crotchety old coot. Until I retired from the county clerk's office, I'd have to get up at five every morning to fix breakfast, spend all day bent over ledgers, and then go home to fix supper, clean house, do laundry, make sure he'd remembered to take all his pills, and answer his correspondence. Many a time I regretted not running off with Snicker Dobson on the night we graduated from high school.

He enlisted in the army the next day and was sent to Korea."

"Was he killed?" I asked gently.

"Hell no," she said. "He came back four years later and married Marigold Murt. Everybody knew there was so much incest in her family that half a dozen of them made for a full-blown family reunion."

I managed a smile of sorts. "So you were more than willing to step aside and allow Kayleen to take care of your father. Were you concerned about the disparity in their ages?"

"What difference did it make to me?"

I tried to choose my words carefully. "Well, if you thought perhaps Kayleen married your father for reasons other than . . ."

"You mean did I think she was a gold digger? That vein wore out years ago. Papa owned the house outright, but I couldn't even get fifteen thousand dollars for it when I sold it last spring. Medical bills ate up what little savings he had, and he was having to sell his gun collection to stay out of the county nursing home. Kayleen knew all that before she married him. She may have been crazy, but she wasn't a gold digger."

"I guess not," I said, thinking over what she'd said. "You inherited the family home and she got the gun collection—right?"

"What remained of it," said Miss Lila. "Once a month or so she'd get him to hobble out to the car and they'd go to a gun show to sell what they could. At one time the collection had been insured for twenty thousand dollars, but I'd be surprised if he had a quarter of it when he was killed by those burglars."

She was keeping an eye on a clock on the mantel, which warned me that my allotted time was about up. "I have one last question," I said. "Can you tell me anything about a militia group that your father and Kayleen might have joined?"

"I don't know much about it, mostly because I thought it was ridiculous and told Papa so right to his face. A few years back he met some fellow at a gun show, and came home all excited because he thought he'd found a way to avoid paying taxes. It wasn't like he was paying more than a pittance, but he would have walked into town to save gas if it hadn't been so far. I never had a store-bought dress until I got my job at the county clerk's office. Anyway, Papa started going to meetings and writing letters to the IRS, and it took me six months to make him understand that he could lose his property and be sent to prison if he didn't pay taxes."

"I'll let you get ready for church," I said as I stood up. "You've been very helpful, Miss Lila."

"No, I haven't," she said, "but that's your problem, not mine. Am I right in thinking Kayleen's living in your town?"

I nodded. "She's planning to open a pawnshop."

"I'm not surprised. I always thought she was more interested in Papa's collection than he was, but of course he was having all those health problems toward the end. Give her my regards when you see her."

"I'll be sure and do that. May I ask one more question?"

She went to the door and opened it. "One more, Miss Hanks. My Sunday school class is composed of teenagers. The last time I was late I found two of them grappling behind the piano."

"The man who encouraged your father not to pay taxes—was his name Sterling Pitts?"

"I believe so," she said as she closed the door.

I swung by a fast-food joint for a sausage biscuit and orange juice, then drove back toward Maggody at a leisurely speed. My mind, on the other hand, was going a hundred miles an hour—or more.

Chapter 14

Dahlia was making turtlish headway up the ridge since she had to sit and catch her breath every few minutes. It didn't help that the contractions had started up again, or that black clouds were rolling into the valley, accompanied by fierce wind and the murmur of thunder in the distance.

She could kinda make out where folks had stomped around and left footprints in the mud, and after a spell she arrived at a clearing that fit with what Kevvie's pa had said about the shooting the previous day. Not that he'd been there, of course, since he and Mr. McIlhaney had been too yellow-bellied to try to sneak up on Kevvie and the other fellow.

Kevvie hadn't been afraid, though. He'd been as brave as a real soldier like Rambo. Dahlia sat down on a log and marveled at his courage while she ate the last crust. After a few minutes, she started feeling restless again, so she heaved herself to her feet.

She was trying to guess which way to go when she spotted a wad of paper under a bush. Her heart pounded as she unfolded it, but it proved to be nothing but a greasy wrapper from the Dairee Dee-Lishus. Still, it was a clue, so she put it in her pocket and began to climb once more.

She'd given up wearing a wristwatch when it became impossible to find one that didn't cut into her flesh. Now was the first time she wished she had one, since it felt like the contractions were coming more and more quickly and the doctor had said how important it was to time 'em. 'Course she was supposed to call, which was a might difficult at the moment.

"Kevvie!" she bellowed into the woods. When she didn't get an answer, she found a log and sat down to figure out what to do. It was a long way back to County 102, and then a longer way back to town if Estelle hadn't come home so Dahlia could use the telephone. On the other hand, Kevvie could be most anywhere on Cotter's Ridge.

She took out the wrapper and stared at it as if it might change itself into something helpful—like a map. It wasn't all bedraggled like it'd be if it'd been under the bush for years, she decided. It was wet, but not real muddy or faded. The militia fellows that'd camped out were supposed to find their food in the woods, so they wouldn't have been eating something from the Dairee Dee-Lishus. Kevvie would have, though, and nobody seemed to know where he went after he'd been let out at the SuperSaver.

This meant she was going in the right direction. She panted through a contraction, then resumed pushing her way through the brush. Pretty soon she fell into a regular routine of panting, peeing, and plaintively calling Kevvie's name. It worked out real good.

Estelle stopped the station wagon and uncurled her bloodless fingers from the steering wheel. "I'm surprised we've made it this far," she said, nervously eyeing the thick, dark woods on either side of the narrow road. "Every time we go around a bend I expect to run into a tree trunk or bog down in a patch of mud."

"So turn around," said Ruby Bee. "We're chasing after your inheritance, not mine. It makes no matter to me if you want to give up and go back to town. Being closed all those hours yesterday evening didn't exactly remedy my money problems, you know."

Estelle pressed down on the gas pedal. The back tires spun for a heart-stopping moment, then caught and the station wagon lurched forward. "That was your idea, and it didn't have anything to do with fetching the ostriches. You just wanted to poke through

Brother Verber's shoe boxes. Instead, we got to sit on his boxers for more than three hours, listening to Mrs. Jim Bob carry on about him having lust in his heart for Kayleen. I don't think it's fitting for a married woman to concern herself with anybody else's lust but her husband's. Surely Jim Bob's got enough of that to keep her occupied."

"Hush!" said Ruby Bee. "I heard something."

"You heard the muffler scraping on a rock."

"No, it was something else." Ruby Bee rolled down the window and stared at the impenetrable growth. After a minute, she rolled up the window and shook her head. "I don't know what I heard, on account of you jabbering like a magpie, but it wasn't like anything I've ever heard before."

Estelle wrenched the steering wheel to avoid a fallen branch. She kept her teeth clenched until she got the station wagon back on course, then said, "I been thinking what I'll do if we actually catch them ostriches, so I can sell them. I might just try advertising in the *Shopper* and some of the other small town papers like that. First I'll go to all the local beauty shops and find out how much they charge, then—"

"Hush!" said Ruby Bee, this time a mite shrilly.

"What?"

"I smell something burning. Unless there's a troop of scouts near by, I'd say your engine's overheating."

"Me, too," said Estelle as she looked at the bright red light on the dashboard. "I must have busted the oil pan going over that stump a ways back. Now what are we gonna do?"

The militia was holding a meeting in Sterling's room. It was crowded, even without Kayleen, who'd opted to go to church, and Judy Milliford, who'd flat-out refused to go anywhere but home. Barry was seated on the only chair. Jake was leaning against the door, his thumbs hooked over his belt. Reed and Sterling were both attempting to pace, which made for some moves that might have come from a Saturday morning cartoon show.

"Watch where you're going!" snapped Sterling as Reed bumped into him. "It's impossible for me to concentrate with you stumbling around like this. What's more, you stink like a brewery. How many times have I stressed the need to be clear-headed and alert? You wouldn't be able to see the enemy if he walked out of the bathroom and aimed an automatic at your head."

"Sure I would," Reed said as he tripped over the corner of the bed and floundered into the closet, nearly garrotting himself on a wire hanger before he hit the wall and slithered to the floor.

Sterling took a deep breath and let it out slowly. "Here's where we stand—or at least those of us who are not in the closet. I remain unable to access the electronic board. Normally, when the password is changed, I receive a coded message that allows me to determine the new password. This time I received nothing. I do not think it's a coincidence that access was denied the day after Dylan joined us on a probationary basis. Comments?"

Jake spat into a paper cup. "How do we know he was ever in Colorado or Idaho? We got no proof of that."

"Yeah, we do," Reed said as he crawled out of the closet and unsteadily got to his feet. "Remember what all he told us, Barry?"

"He told us next to nothing," said Barry.

Sterling considered reminding them to use code names, but he decided it wasn't worth the effort. "Keep in mind that the communications officer did confirm that Dylan had been in their outfit."

Barry shrugged. "He confirmed that someone named Dylan Gilbert had been a member. I never saw any identification."

"Fer chrissake," said Reed, "I've never seen your fuckin' driver's license, either. Does that make you an FBI agent?"

Barry stood up and pulled out his wallet. "You want to see it now? Hey, how about my library card? You want to see that too?"

"I don't give a shit about your library card!" shouted Reed, raising a fist. "How about we step outside and I'll put your goddamn library card in a place where the sun don't shine!"

The door opened, squashing Jake against the wall, and Kayleen entered the room. "What on earth is going on? There's a deputy in a car parked less than twenty feet from here. Don't you think we have enough problems without you getting arrested for disturbing the peace?"

They all thought this over for a moment, then Barry sat back down and Reed fell across the bed. Jake rubbed his nose in silence.

"Thank you," said Sterling. "We certainly do not wish to prolong our involuntary confinement in this flop house."

"Or stay locked up here," Reed muttered.

Kayleen rewarded them with a warm smile. "The best way to get out of here is to get our story straight and stick to it. We really have no choice but to cooperate with the authorities in this situation. Do you all agree?"

"I ain't talkin' to that woman cop," said Jake as he went into the bathroom to see if his nose was bleeding.

She waited until he returned, then said, "I think we've already been asked about yesterday morning on the ridge. What went on Friday night up there?"

"Pizza," said Reed. "Dylan offered to go get some. He took my truck and didn't come back for almost four hours on account of the truck breaking down. Made sense to me, but then Barry and Jake got all hot and bothered because they thought they saw the truck in town."

"What time was that?" Kayleen asked Barry.

"Around eight-fifteen, after we finalized plans for the maneuvers," he said.

Reed sat up and stared at him. "You didn't show up at the camp till way later than that. What time did you get back, Jake?"

Jake was staring at Barry too. "Close to nine-thirty."

What were you doing all that while, watching the stop-light change colors?"

"I hung around the bar, hoping I could convince some of the patrons to go to the meeting the next morning. Yeah, I realize I could have spent some quality time listening to Reed complain about his wife, but I didn't have the intestinal stamina for it."

Kayleen looked at Jake. "What time did you see the truck?"

"On my way back to the camp. I thought you wanted to go to church. You'd better get going or you'll miss the chance to get your weekly bellyful of piety."

"In a minute," she said, examining them as if they were steaks in the supermarket meat department. It was hard to tell from her expression if she was finding them overly marbled with fat, but it was likely. "Let me see if I've got this right. Sterling and I remained in this room until shortly before ten, discussing recruitment tactics. The rest of you, as well as Dylan and Judy, were on your own between eight and nine-thirty."

Barry frowned at her. "So what? Dylan was shot yesterday morning, not Friday night. I've already told you where I was. Since Reed didn't have his truck, he was stuck at the camp. I don't know what Jake was doing, but I don't understand why it matters to you."

"Nor do I," said Sterling, trying to regain control of his meeting. "As long as we're forced to remain here, I think we should take the opportunity to evaluate our three potential recruits. I've made some observations about each one. Let's begin with the boy."

Kayleen fluttered her fingers and left. The deputy, who was a real sweetie, told her he thought it'd be just fine for her to go to church. He went so far as to offer her a ride, but she politely declined and left in her Mercedes.

I wanted to hash over my ideas with Harve, but I needed some more information before I could get it all straight. Or at least not quite so crooked, anyway.

As soon as I got back to Maggody, I drove to Kevin and Dahlia's house. The lights were on in the living room, but no one came to the door in response to my repeated knocks. I was on my way around to the back door when Eileen drove into the yard and slammed on the brakes.

"Are they back?" she said as she scrambled out of the car.

"No one answered the door," I said.

"I don't know what to do. As far as I can tell, Kevin never came home and now Dahlia's disappeared too. I've been driving all over town, praying I'd see their car. They're good-hearted kids, but they're not the smartest folks to come down the pike. You yourself know all the messes they've gotten into over the years."

"I certainly do," I said. "Do you have a house key?"

Eileen took a key out of her pocket and handed it to me. We went inside, made sure no one was there, and went back to the porch.

"Could the baby have decided to come early?" I asked her. "I haven't had any experience in that department, but I understand it's not uncommon."

"The hospital keeps insisting she hasn't checked in, and the clinic says the same thing. Her overnight bag's by the front door. I opened it in case there might be some sort of clue, but all that's in it is her nightgown, a magazine, toiletries, her relaxation tape, and a dozen chocolate bars. She must have decided that the instant the baby's here, her diabetes will be cured. She has some pretty peculiar ideas these days."

I patted her arm. "They'll turn up before too long. You probably should go home in case they call."

"I suppose you're right," she said discouragedly.

I waited until she left, then drove to the PD, noting as I passed that Ruby Bee's Bar & Grill was once again closed. Mrs. Jim Bob's Cadillac was not parked in front of the rectory, however, so if Ruby Bee and Estelle had gone back there for some convoluted reason, they were free to leave. What was more disturbing was that Brother Verber's car wasn't there, either. It was almost time for the Sunday morning service, and it looked as if he was cutting it close.

After all, timeliness is next to godliness (or something like that).

Larry Joe put on his coat and gloves, then picked up his rifle and said, "I'm gonna look for Roy. Are you coming or not?"

Jim Bob let him wait for an answer while he lit a cigar and took a couple of puffs. "Well, Larry Joe, it's like this. I'd like to go with you. I can't think of anything I'd rather do than do-si-do around the woods, getting wetter and colder till I'm shivering like a hound dog in a blizzard. If we get real lucky, we can be standing under a tree when it gets hit by lightning. I've been told your hair stands on end, but I've always had a hankering to see for myself."

"You're scared to go outside, aren't you?"

Jim Bob's eyes narrowed. "Don't start up with that shit again. If Roy wants to get hisself lost out there, it's his business. If you want to do the same, it's yours. What I want to do is get myself a beer and spend the morning looking through a couple of magazines that feature buck-naked girls with big tits."

Larry Joe hesitated, then jammed on his cap and left the trailer. Jim Bob waited for several minutes in case Larry Joe changed his mind. When it seemed safe, he went to the kitchen window in time to see Larry Joe's back as he plunged into the woods.

Once he'd settled down with a sandwich, a beer, and a dog-eared magazine, he ordered himself not to think about the terrifying creature he'd seen, but the image kept blotting out the simpery blonde on the page. A clap of thunder caused him to jerk so violently that he bit his tongue and spilled the beer across the cushion.

"Goddammit," he said, getting up to hunt for one of Larry Joe's undershirts to clean up the mess. "Roy and Larry Joe are out of their friggin' minds, because no one with the sense God gave a goose would—"

He froze as he realized two unblinking orange eyes were regarding him through the kitchen window. He finally persuaded himself to drop to the floor and crawl into the bedroom, where he could huddle in the corner. Sweat flowed into his eyes and dripped off the tip of his nose. He wasn't exactly moaning, but he knew the strange noises he heard were coming from his own throat.

As he sat there with his arms wrapped around his knees, he realized there was only one thing to do— and that was get out to the four-wheel and get his ass off Cotter's Ridge. It wasn't easy to persuade himself to get up, but he did. After he'd peeked around the corner to make sure the creature was gone, he grabbed his coat, stuck the packet of cigars in his pocket, and pushed the button on the doorknob to make sure there was no way the creature could get inside the trailer.

He was halfway there when he remembered he'd tossed the keys to Larry Joe at some point and told him to fetch another case of beer. Had Larry Joe given them back? He slapped his coat pockets as if they were smoldering. He made it to the four-wheel and ascertained that not only were the keys not in the ignition, but that Larry Joe had locked all the doors, including the tailgate.

He hurried back to the trailer and tried to open a window, any window. Not one of them budged. He rattled the doorknob, then threw himself against the door till it felt like he'd busted his arm. A flicker of lightning was followed almost immediately by thunder.

"Shit!" he said, looking over his shoulder in case something was sneaking up on him. "This is your fault, Roy Stiver, and you're gonna pay for it. You too, Larry Joe Lambertino. I'm the mayor and I can kick you all off the town council quicker than a snake going through a hollow log. What have you got to say to that?"

If he'd had a response, he most likely would have dived under the trailer. As it was, he turned up his collar, tried one last time to beat the door down, and headed along the path to see if he could catch up with Larry Joe.

"What now?" I asked Raz as he barged into the PD.

"I've had it with that goddamn Diesel! I jest came to give you warning that I'm goin' after him like he was a rabid polecat. This here time he's gone too far and I ain't gonna stand for it no longer."

"Calm down," I said. "It's your fault, too. How many times have I told you to stay off the ridge?"

"I reckon it's a free country and I kin go wherever I damn well please. As soon as I go by my house and git a box of shotgun shells, I'm fixin' to go right back up there and teach Diesel a lesson he won't fergit till his dyin' day. That'd be today, come to think of it."

"Raz," I said, letting my irritation show, "if you shoot Diesel, you'll end up in jail. I can't see you being anybody's new boyfriend, but things may be rougher down at the prison than I think. Marjorie will end up being served with eggs and grits. I'll have a minimum of seven years to find your still. I'm sorry that Diesel continues to frighten Marjorie, but—"

"He shot her."

My hand instinctively went to my mouth. "Oh, Raz—why didn't you say so in the first place? Is she . . .?"

He cackled at my horrified expression. "Dead? 'Course she ain't dead. I wouldn't have gone to the bother of coming here if she was dead. I'd have wrung Diesel's neck with my bare hands. Come out to the truck."

I trailed after him. Marjorie was sitting in the cab, her ears drooping and her eyes downcast. If I were into anthropomorphism, I would have inferred that she was embarrassed.

"See fer yourself," Raz said as he pointed at her side, which was covered with an orange blot. Not covered completely, mind you; Marjorie weighs upwards of four hundred pounds and it would take a gallon of Sherwin-Williams's finest to do the job.

"He shot her with a paint pellet?" I said.

"He shore did," Raz muttered, "and he's gonna pay 'for it. Marjorie's making out like it don't matter, but I kin tell she's so riled up she don't know if she's comin' or goin'. Jest look at her, Arly. Ain't she a helluva sorry sight?"

I nodded with great solemnity. "She sure is. Why don't you go on home and clean her up? Maybe she can be persuaded to have a little soup and watch one of those televised church services. After listening to a couple of hymns, she'll snap right out of it. Pedigreed sows are amazingly resilient, despite their delicate natures."

"Mebbe so," he said, opening the door on the driver's side.

I'd taken a step toward the PD when I realized there was something amiss with the story. "Raz," I said, "did you actually see Diesel shoot Marjorie?"

"Nope," he said, "but he done it jest the same."

"When did this happen?"

"Bout an hour ago."

"But where would he have gotten hold of the pellet and the pistol? He hasn't been in town in almost a year, and even if he has, these things aren't available at the SuperSaver. The yahoos in the militia had their pistols confiscated before we went to the PD."

"I know he done it," Raz said mulishly. "Marjorie's taken a strong dislike to him, and I kin tell when she's seen him."

I returned to the passenger's side of the truck, but I didn't quite have the nerve to put my hand inside. "Is the paint still wet?"

"It was purty near dry when she came squealing into the clearing. Some of it was sticky, like molasses, but it was dry by the time we got to pavement. What are you gittin' at?"

I wished I knew. "I was thinking that if the paint takes a long time to dry, she might have brushed up against a tree or rock that had been shot yesterday during the lethal retreat. But if you're telling the truth, then this must have happened this morning. Did you hear the shot?"

He took the opportunity to stuff a wad of tobacco in his cheek while he thought. "I don't recollect hearin', much of anything," he said in a creaky, puzzled voice. "I tend to keep my ears peeled when I'm up there."

"Then why did you assume she'd been shot?"

He spat out the window. "'Cause I don't live under a bridge, that's why. I heard tell about those military folks and how they was gonna use paint instead of bullets. Marjorie sure as hell wouldn't have let herself get near enough to Diesel that he could slap her with a paint brush."

I told him to go home and went back inside the PD. My stomach was gurgling more loudly than the coffee maker; my brain, in contrast, was anesthetized with confusion. The one thing I was sure of was that Diesel had not been recruited by the militia group. Those who prefer to live in caves are not what you'd describe as sociable. What's more, Diesel had been mistaken for Bigfoot in the past; by now he most likely resembled an ambulatory hairball.

I tried to call Harve, but LaBelle tartly informed me that he was attending various churches in order to drum up votes. This morning he was scheduled for an early service with the Episcopalians and a second with the Unitarians, who, in LaBelle's opinion, were nothing but a bunch of human secularists.

I thanked her for the insight into comparative religion and hung up, but I couldn't decide what to do. It was highly unlikely that I could find Diesel's cave, much less interrogate him. McBeen had promised to do what he could to expedite the tox screen at the state lab, but he and I both knew from experience that it could be days before we had a report. No cause of death—no confirmation of a homicide. No Ruby Bee—no chicken-fried steak, mashed potatoes, and turnip greens.

This last realization brought me to my senses, so I went to my apartment to eat a bowl of cornflakes. As I sat by the window and crunched like a brontosaurus, I saw Mrs. Jim Bob drive by, presumably on her way to church. I reminded myself that I'd promised her an official missing person report if Brother Verber wasn't back in time to terrorize the congregation with descriptions of Satan's fiery furnace. Maybe I'd throw in Ruby Bee, Estelle, Kevin, Dahlia, and the two ostriches for good measure.

Or better yet, report myself missing and make a run for the nearest border.

Chapter 15

"Wonder where he went?" said Larry Joe as he scratched his head, releasing a flurry of dandruff flakes that vanished almost immediately in the wind. "He's not in the trailer or the outhouse. Do you think he went to organize a search party?"

Roy grunted scornfully. "Because he cares more about his friends than he does about his own hide? Yeah, Larry Joe, he's probably at the airport renting a helicopter so he can rescue us. When he gets here, we can give him a medal."

"Well, where is he?"

"Skedaddling down the ridge. If you hadn't had the keys in your coat pocket, we wouldn't be standing by his four-wheel, either. I don't see any point in staying up here any longer. What say we grab our stuff and go back to town?"

Larry Joe shrugged. "We might as well. I was beginning to get sick of bologna and beer, and Joyce usually fixes a roast for Sunday dinner."

He and Roy went back into the trailer, threw their dirty clothes into bags, and made sure the trailer was locked securely before they got into the four-wheel and started for Maggody.

After I finished the cereal, I decided to return to the Flamingo Motel to check on the guests and see if I could find out when and how Diesel obtained the pistol.

Ruby Bee's Bar & Grill remained closed. I couldn't remember her mentioning a flea market of particular interest, but she and Estelle were always enthusiastic about the prospect of buying a chipped teacup for a quarter or a battered egg beater for a dime. This may explain some of my more whimsical birthday presents (and I'm sure there'll come a day when my only chance of survival depends on a bicycle pump, a muffin tin, and a 1984 world almanac).

Les was back on duty. He'd brought a book with him this time, and as I approached, gave me a guilty look as he stuck it under the seat. "Morning," he said. "I just got here, but Batson said everything's been quiet. Ruby Bee brought them breakfast trays. Right now most of them are holed up in the middle unit over there"—he pointed at #5—"having a talk, I guess. Kayleen asked for permission to go to church, and Batson didn't see any reason not to let her."

I knocked on the door of #5, and when Sterling opened it, said, "Will you please step outside? I have a question for you."

"Ask your question right here, Chief Hanks," he said. "I prefer to have witnesses. I may need them to testify in court about your abridgment of my constitutional rights."

"Fine," I said, exceedingly tired of his pet phrase. "Did each of you bring your own pistol to Cotter's Ridge yesterday?"

"'A well-regulated militia being necessary to the security of a free state, the right of the people to keep and bear arms shall not be infringed.' In case you didn't recognize that, it's the Second Amendment to the Constitution of the United States."

"And a most inspiring amendment it is," I said. "Would you like me to repeat my question?"

Sterling gave me an exasperated look. "I keep all the pistols in a storage box, including several extras for anyone who wants to participate. We currently have an inventory of twelve. Before an exercise begins, I distribute them. Afterwards, I return them to the box, secure it, and leave the box in a closet at my office."

I did a mental tally. "That means you passed out nine of them yesterday. Where are the rest of them?"

"In the trunk of my Hummer. Is that a crime?"

I gave him an equally exasperated look. "No, it is not a crime. Will you show them to me?"

I guess he couldn't come up with an amendment that gave him the constitutional right not to let me count his pistols, because he pushed past me and went out to the back end of the Hummer. He unlocked the trunk, pulled out a wooden box, and set it on the ground. His idea of security was a cheap little padlock that I could have unlocked with a bobby pin. However, I let him tackle it with a key.

He opened the lid and gave me a smug smile. "The sheriff confiscated nine. There are three in the box, which means all twelve are accounted for. Are you satisfied, Chief Hanks?"

I picked up one of the odd-looking things, which fell somewhere between a Colt .45 and a child's water gun. Above the barrel was a two-inch-high triangular container. "Is this where the paint pellets are loaded?" I asked.

"You want to try it?" Barry said from the doorway.

"Go ahead, Sterling—let her have a pellet."

Sterling didn't look pleased as he took a pellet from the box and dropped it in the container. "Since you are a trained police officer, I assume you can figure out how to pump it and squeeze the trigger."

I aimed the weapon at Ruby Bee's unit and fired. The resultant bang might not have sent Raz dropping to the ground, but it was certainly loud enough to have caught his attention. The jagged orange splotch on the door was bleeding sluggishly, confirming Raz's comment about the viscosity of the paint. "That's all for now," I said brightly.

"Good shot," Les called as I walked back to my car, but I was thinking too hard to respond.

When I got to the PD, I called LaBelle and said, "I want you to go to the evidence room and ask to see the pistols that Harve brought in after the shooting on the ridge. Count them very carefully, then come back and tell me how many there are."

"When were you elected sheriff of Stump County?"

"Please do it," I said, scowling like a gargoyle but keeping a civil tone. "Sheriff Dorfer assigned me to this case, and he would want you to cooperate."

I heard the receiver hit the desk and the sound of footsteps as she left the office. I spread out all the statements and notes I had, reading each one and sprinkling the margins with question marks. The one statement I really needed was Kevin's, but I'd have to wait until he came back under his own steam—or was escorted back to Maggody by a couple of grim MPs, with Dahlia wringing her hands in their wake.

"I'm back," announced LaBelle as if her mission was completed and it was time for applause.

I sighed and said, "How many pistols?"

"I don't know why you care. Paint didn't kill that boy."

"I realize the paint pellets are not deadly. However, shooting one at a person without his or her consent could qualify as assault, and I've got an innocent by-stander who is distraught enough to file charges. I'm trying to determine the location of the weapon that was used."

"Nine," she said, then hung up.

Even in Maggody, where math does not reign su-preme, nine and three made twelve. None of the obvi-ous suspects at the Flamingo Motel could have taken a pistol out of the Hummer and left under the benevo-lent gaze of the deputy assigned to watch them.

The door opened. I steeled myself for another mal-odorous encounter with Raz, and therefore was sur-prised (okay, delighted) when the process server came into the PD. He was dressed as he had been the previ-ous day, which meant he could attend the Voice of the Almighty Lord service on his way back to Farber-ville. If he wanted to, that is; I never recommend it for recreational purposes.

"Looking for the Flamingo Motel?" I asked. "It's down that way, behind Ruby Bee's Bar and Grill. There's a sheriff's deputy in the lot, so this might be a good time to serve the papers."

"I'm not a process server," he said as he sat down across from me and put a briefcase on the floor.

"You're not?"

"That was your idea, not mine. It seemed easier not to contradict you."

"Then who the hell are you?" I demanded, rising out of my chair.

"My name is Tonnato, and I'm in charge of the FBI office in Farberville. Your calls to the Little Rock office and to the bureau headquarters in Washington created quite a stir. I was ordered to cut short a visit to my daughter's house and come back to Farberville."

I stared at him for a moment, then swallowed and said, "Let me see some identification, please."

He took a leather wallet from his pocket and tossed it on the desk. I gingerly opened it, as if it might explode, and found myself looking at a shiny badge and an ID card with Tonnato's somber face.

"Okay," I said, "you're an FBI agent. Does this so-called stir I created have to do with Dylan Gilbert? Was he an agent?"

"No, but we were aware of his activities and to some extent, cooperated with him."

"Well, you sure didn't cooperate with me," I said testily. "If he wasn't an agent, who was he and why did he have the serial number of a weapon used in a homicide?"

"The young man, whose name was not Dylan Gilbert, was the son of the radio talk show host who was killed by a member of a Missouri-based militia. We were indirectly involved, since we monitor these groups in the hope we can catch them in a federal offense and come down hard on them. The killer was apprehended, but the victim's son was convinced there was a conspiracy that stretched into Arkansas. We suggested he assume the identity of Dylan Gilbert, a sociopath who'd blown off several of his fingers making pipe bombs in his basement and then decided to squeal on his buddies from the sanctuary of the witness protection program."

"You can do that?" I asked.

"Oh, Chief Hanks, we can do all sorts of things. We're the FBI, not the DAR. The real Dylan Gilbert has been providing us with a great deal of useful information, including how to access the top-secret electronic boards. We allowed Sterling Pitts to get a limited confirmation of Dylan's participation in the Colorado militia, then intercepted all his messages."

I thought all this over for a minute. "Are you saying that the group in the motel is a part of this conspiracy? They don't really seem"—I struggled for a word—"*capable* of anything more sophisticated than shooting paint pellets at each other."

Tonnato shook his head. "I agree with you, Chief Hanks. I've been keeping an eye on them for several years. They share the same beliefs as other extremist groups, but they appear to be ineffective. This morning they were bickering among themselves with such fervor that two of them were on the verge of a fistfight. I was disappointed when it failed to take place."

"Wait a minute," I said, frowning at him. "How do you know what they were doing this morning? I would have known if you were skulking around the motel units."

"I don't skulk," he said primly, as if I'd compared him to a coyote. "I merely listened in on the conversation that took place in unit Number Five. Would you like to hear a tape of it?"

"How did you get into the room to plant a bug?" I asked, thoroughly stunned by now and in danger of falling out of my chair.

"I had no need to get into the room, Chief Hanks. Over twenty years ago the technology existed to overhear any conversation held in the proximity of a particular telephone. All you had to do was dial the number and sit back. It was called an 'Infinity Transmitter' and was available to the public for less than a thousand dollars. Just imagine what government agents have these days."

"But . . how did you get the number?"

"I have resources," said Tonnato as he took a

midget-sized cassette and recorder out of his briefcase. "Since this was obtained without a warrant, it's not admissible in court. I am not involved in your investigation and, even under oath, will deny the agency's relationship with the victim's son. Once you've listened to the tape, I'll need to take it with me."

His tone was affable and his smile back in place, but I had a prickly feeling that his eyes were warning me: "Don't mess with the feds."

"Okay," I said meekly. "Let me listen to it."

Ruby Bee carried the sheets as she and Estelle walked up the muddy logging trail. Lightning flickered every few minutes, and the thunder followed within a matter of seconds. Although it was late morning, the clouds were heavy enough to block out most of the light, giving the woods an eerie feeling of twilight.

"I'm beginning to regret this," Estelle said as she picked her way through a puddle. "The hissy birds could be in Mexico, like you said, or in the bottom of a ravine with their necks broke. Diesel could have caught 'em and be roasting them over a campfire. How in heaven's name are we gonna find them?"

"I don't know," said Ruby Bee, "but I don't aim to be in your station wagon when the creekbed floods and washes it down the mountain. We'll sit out the storm in Robin Buchanon's shack. After that, we can see if your engine will start."

"How far is it?"

"I don't know," Ruby Bee repeated, this time with an edge to her voice. "I'm pretty sure we're headed in the right direction, but—" She broke off and cupped a hand to her ear.

Estelle glanced at her. "But what?"

"I heard it again. It wasn't a gun being fired, but more of a hollow sound. If I didn't know those militia folks were at the Flamingo, I'd have thought they might be firing some kind of artillery weapon. Step lively, Estelle!"

They stepped as lively as they could up the road, saving their breath, and exchanged pinched smiles when they saw the lopsided roof beyond some trees. It wasn't much in the way of shelter, not by a long shot, but they scurried inside and closed the door.

Estelle was about to ask about the mysterious noise when they heard the floor creak in what had once been Robin's bedroom. "Oh dear," she mouthed, jabbing her finger at the closed door.

"A bear?" whispered Ruby Bee.

Clutching each other, they inched backward toward the front door. A second creak was accompanied by a groan, and a third by a string of pants.

Estelle stopped. "That's no bear. I'll bet it's an escaped convict that holed up here."

"Why would he do that?"

"I've never been an escaped convict, so I really couldn't say. I do know bears don't pant, though."

Ruby Bee looked at her. "Why not? Remember when we went to the zoo in Little Rock in August and that polar bear was lying on the concrete, his tongue hanging out?"

"Are you saying you think there's a polar bear in there?" said Estelle. "That's the most ridiculous thing I've ever heard."

The door opened and Dahlia came into the front room. "You got to help me," she said in a matter-of-fact voice. "Kevin Junior is coming."

Ruby Bee's jaw fell. "What are you doing here, Dahlia?"

"I *was* lookin' for Kevvie, but now I'm having a baby. I jest don't know how to do it. The doctor said to time the contractions, so I've been counting one-Mississippi, two-Mississippi. As far as I can tell, they're around two hundred and fifty Mississippis apart."

After a moment of silence, Estelle said, "Maybe four minutes. What'll we do, Ruby Bee?"

Ruby Bee stared at her. "How should I know? When I had Arly, I was in a hospital with nurses milling around like hens. When the pain got real bad, they gave me a shot, and when I woke up, they gave me a baby in a pink blanket. I think it'd be best to take Dahlia back to town."

Dahlia's face crumpled like a wet washrag. "I don't reckon I've got time to walk all that way to the county road. Besides, I ain't about to give birth under a bush in the middle of a storm."

"Then I guess we're going to find out what happened after they gave me the shot," said Ruby Bee as she set the sheets on a crudely hewn table. "Is there a bed in the back, Dahlia?"

"Yeah," Dahlia said, "but the rope rotted and the mattress is on the floor and pretty much gnawed up."

Ruby Bee thought for a moment. "Estelle, let's drag the mattress in here and cover it with the sheets. It won't be real comfortable, but it's bound to be better than the floor. Once Dahlia's settled, we can try to find some dry wood and get a fire going in the stove so we can boil water."

"And do what with it?" asked Estelle. "Have a cup of tea?"

"That's what they say to do," Ruby Bee said grimly as she headed for the back room.

I scanned the notes I'd taken while listening to the tape. Agent Tonnato, who didn't seem tremendously interested, was finishing a cup of coffee and tapping his foot as if waiting for an overdue train. I'd heard the tape three times, but the sound of my own voice asking Sterling to step outside startled me each time. It was just as well I'd been in the parking lot during the taping and missed Reed's crude remarks about my anatomy.

Tonnato set down the mug. "I need to go to the office and call in a report, Chief Hanks. I don't know if anything said has relevance to your investigation, but I hope it did. I doubt we can make the homicide into a federal crime, so you're on your own." He put the tape player into his briefcase and stood up. "If you come across anything that might concern us, don't hesitate to call." He handed me a business card. "This has my home number."

I got to the door before he could leave. "The homicide of someone you encouraged to infiltrate a militia doesn't concern you?"

"Not especially," he said, "and we didn't encourage him. Once he made it clear that he wanted to do it, we assisted him in a limited manner—just as I've assisted you."

"And he died," I said bluntly.

"Yes, he did. I took the liberty of requesting that the state lab expedite the tox screen. Your county coroner should hear something by mid-afternoon."

I held my position. "About this surveillance, Tonnato. Are you saying you can hear anything that's said in this room from the comfort of your office? You can tape the conversation without a warrant?"

"It's a very handy device," he said, assessing his chances of leaving without being obliged to resort to karate or whatever it was FBI agents utilized to knock people senseless.

"Do you eavesdrop for personal amusement?" I persisted. "Do you listen to couples in bed?"

"I monitor the conversations of potentially dangerous people. You would agree that preventing the placement of a bomb in a building is more important than a warrant, wouldn't you?"

"Do you keep files on everybody in this country?"

Tonnato gave me a disappointed look. "You've been reading their material. A lot of it appeals to the very people who have sworn to uphold and defend the laws of the land. Good luck with your investigation, Chief Hanks."

He made it past me and went out to a nondescript car. I was still stinging from his comment as I watched him drive away, but since brooding does not become me, I made myself go back to my desk and reread my notes.

One discrepancy was impossible to miss: Barry Kirklin had told his cohorts that he was at the bar until almost 9:30 on Friday night. I'd closed the bar at 8:30 and gone to rescue Ruby Bee and Estelle from the two ostriches. Ergo, he'd lied.

A reason came to mind. I winced as thunder rattled the PD as if it were a cardboard box, then went outside and drove to the motel to talk to him. Les acknowledged my arrival with a nod, then resumed reading.

I knocked on the door of #6. Barry opened the door, started to smile, and then caught my expression. "Is something wrong?" he asked.

"Yes, it is," I said. "Are you alone?"

"Reed's over drinking beer with Jake. Do you want to come in?"

I went into the room and sat in a chair. The telephone, once an innocuous modern convenience, was on the bedside table, but I didn't care if J. Edgar Hoover was eavesdropping from his grave. "On Friday night," I began coldly, "you arrived in Maggody and then went to Sterling's room. Once you'd been dismissed, you went to Judy's room, didn't you? You and she fooled around for about an hour before you went to the campsite."

He blinked at me. "Why do you think that?"

"Because it explains a lot of things. Jake had legitimate cause to suspect she was having an affair, which is why he was in town. Why didn't he see you go into her room?"

"I drove away, parked behind a school, and returned on foot across the field out back. She let me in through the bathroom window in case Kayleen or Sterling was watching. I wouldn't have risked it if I'd known Jake was spying on her, but we both thought he was at the camp. I lied about being in the bar, but I had to come up with something when . . ." His voice trailed off as he realized the implications of my questions.

"Don't bother to ask," I said, no doubt escalating his paranoia to heretofore unseen heights. "You found out later that night that Jake had been in town. Yesterday morning you managed to tell Judy to wait for you after the game started, and then retraced your way back to the campsite. You and she discussed this until the flare went off. At that point, she split it for the motel room and you did the same for the bluff. That's why you were so vague about your location when the rifle was fired."

"Aren't you clever," he said flatly.

"You probably should admit it, Barry. It's not going to get you a slap on the back from Jake, but it does mean you and Judy have an alibi for the shooting."

"I didn't know I needed one," he said in a voice that was oddly belligerent for someone who'd just confessed to adultery—and, if I ended up with a case of homicide, impeding the investigation.

"It can't hurt to have one, can it?" I said as I left. I could sense his presence at the window as I paused to collect my thoughts, but I ignored him. I now knew where Barry had been Friday evening, and had a pretty good idea where Jake had been. I tended to believe their story about Reed's truck having been parked in town, which meant Dylan (who wasn't Dylan, but Tonnato had never mentioned his real name) had been in town, too.

I turned slowly and stared at #4. Perhaps Ruby Bee's would-be rapist had been someone who was more interested in listening to conversations than assaulting fiftyish women. This someone might have been equipped with the same sort of device Tonnato had used. In that there weren't phones on the ridge, an empty motel room had been appropriated.

Willing myself not to think about Ruby Bee's reaction when she saw the paint on her door, I used the key she kept under a flowerpot to let myself into her unit, and took the pass key off a hook in the bedroom. I wasn't sure I'd find anything in #4 to confirm my suspicion, but I walked across the lot and went inside.

Estelle's overnight bag was on the floor. Various items of clothing were scattered around the room and half a dozen bottles of fingernail polish were lined up on the top of the dresser. According to Ruby Bee, a chair had been moved, a lamp unplugged, and—horror of horrors—the toilet seat raised. I did not have to overly tax my deductive skills to conclude that a male had plugged in some sort of electronic apparatus, sat at the table, and at some point responded to a call of nature. If he'd been present while the meeting was taking place in the next room, he couldn't have risked even a tiny penlight and instead had relied on a tape recorder. And was aware that batteries have a knack of going dead at the crucial moment.

Dylan wouldn't have taken the tape recorder and eavesdropping device back to the camp, where they might have been discovered in his gear. The bed of Reed's truck was cluttered with junk, but stashing them there was dangerous, too. Kayleen had mentioned in the illegally recorded conversation that she and Sterling had continued to talk until ten o'clock. Dylan had returned to the camp shortly thereafter.

I lifted up one side of the mattress, but the cover of the box springs showed no evidence of being slit. I wormed my way under the bed and examined the bottom of the cover, then emerged and tried the shelf in the closet. Nothing was hidden in the medicine cabinet in the bathroom. Growing frustrated, I removed drawers, felt behind the radiator, and crawled under the table to make sure nothing was taped there. Dylan would not have disposed of his equipment on the first night of the retreat, and he had no way of knowing it would be his last night.

"Where is it?" I said, beginning to wonder if I was chasing the whiffle-bird, which is a first cousin of a wild goose. He hadn't attempted the old purloined-letter ploy, in that the Flamingo Motel doesn't bother to provide newfangled amenities like clock radios.

Discouraged, I restored everything to its proper place, checked to see that all the drawers were closed, and smoothed the bedspread. Although I hadn't disturbed the insipid print of fluffy kitties, I conscientiously straightened it so Estelle wouldn't worry that one leg was getting shorter in her old age.

As I stepped back to make sure the print was perfect, it struck me how difficult it would have been to align it in the dark. I removed it, found a recess in the wall, and removed a tape recorder and a small metal gizmo that resembled a circuit board. My ebullience faded as I opened the lid of the tape recorder and saw that the spools were empty. I reexamined the recess, but found no cassette.

Dylan must have taken it with him, I thought as I replaced the electronic toys and hung the print on the wall. If by some fluke one of the militia had found the recorder, at least there would have been no proof that someone had been bugging the room next door. Harve hadn't discovered a cassette in any of Dylan's pockets or with his camping gear. In a more cosmopolitan setting, Dylan might have tucked it in an envelope and dropped it in a public mailbox, but the town council has yet to replace the one that the local teenagers shot full of holes.

I locked the door and was heading for #1 to return the passkey when Les got out of his car. "I just finished talking to LaBelle," he said. "She said to tell you that McBeen heard from the state lab. The victim died of nicotine poisoning. It's supposed to be one of the most toxic drugs around."

I decided the passkey could stay in my pocket for the time being. "I'm going back to the PD to call McBeen. Don't let any of these wackos leave, and when Kayleen comes back from church, tell her to stay here. Got that?"

"Yes, ma'am," he said, saluting me.

It was turning into one weird day.

Chapter 16

Ruby Bee had busted up a chair to start a fire, but they hadn't boiled water because they couldn't find a pan that wasn't rusty and caked with grime, and they'd never quite figured out what they'd do with the water anyway. Estelle was kneeling next to Dahlia, who was panting and hooing through another contraction.

When Dahlia's heavy breathing dropped back to normal, Estelle forced herself to smile reassuringly and say, "That wasn't so bad, was it? You did real fine."

"You sure did," said Ruby Bee.

Dahlia's nostrils flared, but she didn't say anything and turned her face toward the wall. Over the last hour she'd become downright surly, glaring like she'd bite any hand that came into range. Ruby Bee was beginning to wish there'd been a polar bear in the back room after all.

Estelle got up and tiptoed across the room to where Ruby Bee was peering out the window like she thought a midwife might drive up any second. "The labor pains are coming every three minutes," she said in a low voice. "It's gonna happen whether or not any of us, including Dahlia, has the foggiest idea what to do. I always closed my eyes when it happened in a movie so I wouldn't pass out cold like my second cousin Zelda did. She hit her head and had to have seventeen stitches. They had to shave off her hair, and she walked around for four months looking like a hedgehog."

"Was she Uncle Tooly's daughter?" Ruby Bee said

in a crabby voice, since this whole mess was his fault. And Estelle's as well, since she should have had the sense not to accept anything from a person killed by sheep.

"No, she was not." Estelle looked back to make sure Dahlia was doing all right, then said, "Why don't you rip that other sheet into pieces we can use for towels?"

"I bought those sheets at Sears not more than a year ago. If I'd realized that when I took them out of the closet, I would have found some old ones."

"I don't imagine you'll be using them after this," said Estelle.

"I want something to drink," Dahlia suddenly said.

"My lips are cracking and I cain't hardly talk."

Ruby Bee dropped the sheet. "I'll go back to the station wagon and look for a cup or something. You stay here, Estelle."

"Well, thank you, Dr. Spock," said Estelle.

Ruby Bee thought about responding in a suitable fashion, but the idea of getting away from the cabin, if only for a few minutes, was so appealing that she darted out the front door like a preacher leaving a whorehouse. Once out in the wind, she regretted her spontaneous offer, but there wasn't much else to do but trudge down to the station wagon.

She came close to screaming when she saw someone coming up the road. However, she managed to get her heart out of her throat as she recognized Kayleen. "What are you doing here?" she asked.

"I heard Kevin Buchanon disappeared, and I was afraid he came up this way on account of feeling responsible for Dylan's death. It was a terrible tragedy, but he should be at Dahlia's side during her last few weeks of pregnancy when she needs him the most."

"She needs him right this minute," Ruby Bee said without hesitation. "She's in labor, but not for long. Don't you have some medical training?"

Kayleen quickened her pace. "I'm trained as a nurse's aide, but mostly I worked in nursing homes." "The contractions are three minutes apart, and

Dahlia's holding up real well. She swears all her puffing and panting is what she learned on some tape and is what the doctor wants her to do. Have you delivered a baby?"

"No, but I watched several deliveries while I was a student. Did you boil water?"

"Why?"

"I don't know," Kayleen said as she fell into step with Ruby Bee.

Mrs. Jim Bob sat alone on the front pew in the Assembly Hall. Brother Verber had not miraculously appeared and proclaimed himself born again, or plain born, or anything else. Lottie Estes had played a couple of hymns, but she'd run out of steam and everybody'd left to take advantage of this unexpected free time.

She'd lost them both, she thought, her thin lips quivering. Her source of spiritual fortitude had cast his lot with the strumpet, and her source of income had taken it upon himself to spend a weekend playing poker and drinking Satan's poison. Where could she find comfort in her bereavement? Not here, in the cavernous room where the last notes of Lottie's laborious renditions lingered like a chest cold. The Methodist preacher wore blue jeans and rode a bicycle, and the Baptist preacher in Emmett was known to chase fast women.

Even the Lord had not seen fit to answer her prayers. She got down on her knees and gave it one more shot, but Brother Verber did not emerge from the storage room, nor did Jim Bob crawl down the aisle on his belly like the viper he was.

Mrs. Jim Bob stood up and smoothed her skirt, gazed sadly at the unoccupied pulpit, and went out to the porch. She was standing there, trying to decide if she should go home or sit for a spell in the rectory, when she spotted Jim Bob's four-wheel coming down the road.

Her despondency was replaced with blind, mindless rage. Without hesitating, she ran across the lawn and into the street, waving her arms above her head and shrieking for him to pull over. The four-wheel squealed to a stop at the side of the road and Roy stuck out his head.

"Are you okay?" he asked.

She lowered her arms but not her voice. "Where's that low-down, lying, adulterous scoundrel?"

Roy figured she wasn't referring to Larry Joe. "The last I saw him he was still at the deer camp. Larry Joe and me decided to come on back to town."

"That doesn't make a whit of sense, Roy Stiver, and you know it. Is Jim Bob off with one of his women?"

Red-faced, Roy told her the whole story, although he omitted the number of bottles of whiskey and cases of beer they'd gone through in the last forty-eight hours. Once he'd finished, he realized how outright stupid it sounded, but he couldn't help it.

"I don't believe you," said Mrs. Jim Bob. "Three grown men running around the woods like chickens with their heads cut off because they thought they saw a monster? Of course their eyes were so blood-shot from indulging in whiskey that it's a wonder they didn't see the Mormon Tabernacle Choir up there too—or maybe you did and forgot to tell me. Did they sing for you?"

"It's the honest-to-God truth," Roy said, squirming in the seat as she glowered at him. "I dropped Larry Joe off at his place not five minutes ago. You can call him if you don't believe me. Are you sure Jim Bob's not at home right now?"

"Don't you think I know who's in my own house? No, there's a woman involved. I can smell her cheap perfume as I stand here. I can see her painted face and tight dress. Jim Bob arranged for her to meet him at the deer camp, didn't he? You'd better come clean if you know what's good for you, Roy Stiver."

"Look, Mrs. Jim Bob, I told you what happened. If Jim Bob was responsible for that creature, then he fooled Larry Joe and me."

She came to a decision. "Get out of the car."

"I was thinking I'd dump my stuff at the store and then drive it out to your house."

"Get out of the car!" she said, spitting out each word as if it was a watermelon seed.

Roy obliged. "What are you aiming to do?"

"I am going to the deer camp to catch him in the act of fornication." She climbed into the four-wheel and shook a finger at him. "Fornication is a sin, and so is bearing false witness. You might step inside the Voice of the Almighty Assembly Hall and beg for forgiveness."

"Good idea," said Roy. He watched her drive away, then walked down the road toward his antiques store, thinking maybe it was time to take up deep-sea fishing.

"I got your message," I said to McBeen as soon as he answered the phone. I'd considered driving into Farberville to talk to him at the morgue, but it seemed like things were heating up rapidly here in my own stompin' ground. "Nicotine poisoning, right?"

"I wouldn't have said so if it wasn't," I said.

"Then tell me about it," I said.

"Nicotine has a rating of six on the toxicity scale, which is the top. That's a frightening statistic, since it's a legal pesticide and readily available at any garden store. There was a case awhile back when a man soaked some cigarettes in a jug of water, strained it, and used it to make iced tea for his bedridden wife. She died in a matter of days. Absorption through the skin or eye doesn't take near that long. Based on the witnesses' accounts, the victim in this case was sitting up one minute and dead ten minutes later."

"That's what they all claimed," I said. "Could there have been nicotine on the bullet?"

"The state lab says not. I've got the body on the table, and we'll go over every inch of it for evidence of penetration. You might ought to have another talk with the other boy who was there."

"He's not available at the moment." I listened to him snorting impatiently while I thought. "Here's something that may help, McBeen," I added. "The victim was facing the bluff when he got shot in the shoulder. I can't see Kevin being implicated in the poisoning, so you probably should roll the body over and take a look at the backside."

After I'd hung up, I found the notes I'd taken while interviewing Jake Milliford, the only one of the witnesses who'd said he could see Dylan. He'd claimed Dylan stood up and turned around; then Kevin jumped up seconds *before* the rifle was fired. It seemed likely Kevin had reacted to something more significant than a squirrel breaking into chatter, but since he wasn't around to discuss it, I'd have to settle for the less-than-lovable Jake.

The telephone rang before I could make it out the door. I doubted McBeen had discovered anything in a scant minute, but I crossed my fingers for luck and picked up the receiver.

"Arly!" said Eileen, her voice jolting my eardrum.

"I'm over at Kevin and Dahlia's house."

So the old cross-the-fingers business does work, I thought smugly. "So they're back?"

"No, but I found out where Dahlia is. I stopped at Raz's shack to ask him if he'd noticed anything out of the ordinary," She took a shuddery breath. "Dahlia showed up on his porch last night and insisted that he drive her to the low-water bridge. She wanted him to help her search for Kevin up on the ridge, but he dropped her out there and left."

"Oh, boy," I said as Eileen began to cry. "Calm down, okay? I'll go out there right now and see what's going on. She may be doing nothing more than sitting on Estelle's porch."

"It's nearly noon. If she hasn't had anything to eat since last night, her blood sugar must be way out of control by now. What if she's lying in the woods in a diabetic coma?"

"I'm on my way out the door," I said. "As soon as I find her, I'll take her to the hospital so they can make sure she's okay. Stay there and I'll call you the minute I get the chance."

I banged down the receiver and ran out to my car, but as I started to pull out onto the road, I realized there was no way I could drive very far up onto Cotter's Ridge without tearing off the bottom of the car.

I sure as hell couldn't park at the low-water bridge, go on foot to find her, and then carry all three hundred plus pounds of her back down.

"Shit!" I said, shaking the steering wheel as I tried to think. It would take at least an hour to borrow a Jeep from the sheriff's department compound, and with Harve out of pocket, possibly the rest of the day. Jim Bob had taken his four-wheel to the deer camp, so I couldn't appropriate it (it would have been fun, though).

I was grinding my teeth, when a lightbulb went on between my ears. I turned toward the Flamingo Motel, and slammed down the accelerator. When I squealed into the lot, Les came tumbling out of his car, his hand on the holster of his weapon and his expression that of someone expecting the arrival of Bonnie and Clyde. I waved him off and pounded on the door of #5.

"What now, Chief Hanks?" said Sterling as he opened the door.

"I need to borrow your Hummer," I said.

"Don't be absurd. You have brazenly trampled all over my constitutional rights, but this time you've gone too far. The Fourth Amendment specifically prohibits illegal search and seizure. I insist on a warrant."

I forced myself to calm down and gave him a somewhat garbled explanation of the crisis, mentioning several times that he and the other members of the militia were directly responsible for the chain of events. I tossed in some malarkey about his personal liability should anything dire happen to Kevin, Dahlia, or their unborn baby.

When he glanced over my shoulder, I turned around and saw Jake, Judy, and Barry in the doorway of #3, and Reed out on the walkway.

"All of you will be sued," I shouted as if I knew what I was talking about. "You'll lose your houses, vehicles, machine guns, bazookas, torpedo launchers—and your goddamn paint pistols! What's more, you could face charges of—of criminal negligence!"

I really must go to law school one of these days.

"All right," said Sterling, "but I'll drive. Let me get my coat and the key."

Having used up my allotment of adrenaline, I

slumped against the wall. Barry came over and said, "Do you know for a fact that this woman is up there?"

"No," I admitted, making a face as I thought about the vast labyrinth of logging trails throughout the hundreds of acres comprising Cotter's Ridge. "She should have been able to find the place where Dylan was shot, though, and she can't have gone too far past it."

"Do you want me to come along?"

"Maybe you should," I said. "Sterling and I might not be able to lift her into the Hummer. Can you get some blankets and pillows out of your room?"

Sterling came outside and unlocked the Hummer. As soon as Barry reappeared with a blanket and a pillow, the three of us managed to climb into the monstrosity. Don't assume I'm a wimp; the first step was a good two feet above the ground.

"Where precisely are we going?" asked Sterling as he drove out to the road.

I rubbed my temples. "We need to stop at Kayleen's and Estelle's houses in case she's there. If she's not . . ." I studied the dashboard, which was pretty mundane for a tank. "Can you drive this thing to the spot where Dylan was shot?"

"I can climb a sixty-percent grade," Sterling said gruffly. "The sides of the gully, however, are much steeper than that. We could attempt to use the winch, but it might take several hours."

I'd forgotten about the damn gully. "There are some logging trails around there. We can drive up the one west of the area and fan out from there."

"You should have had Jake and Reed come along," Barry said from the backseat.

"To do that," I said, choosing my words, "I'd have been compelled to bring my gun and two of my bullets, because at some point I would be unable to stop myself from shooting them. This means I'd have only one bullet left. Maggody may be a one-horse town, but plenty of jackasses come through."

"I resent that," said Sterling.

"It's good to know you're paying attention," I said, then pointed out Estelle's Hair Fantasies on the right.

The house was locked and the garage empty. We went back to the old Wockermann place, where we found some muddy tracks that were still damp, but no sign of Dahlia. I told Sterling how to get to the logging road, then rolled down the window and called Dahlia's name as we crunched up the mountainside.

"This thing's like a tyrannosaurus," I yelled above the grinding and groaning of the engine. "The sheriff ought to get one for his marijuana busts."

Sterling glanced at me out of the corner of his eye. "He'd better stick to generic four-wheel drives. The taxpayers might object to the fifty-five-thousand-dollar price tag."

I was calculating our location when I saw Estelle's station wagon. I gestured to Sterling to go around it and continue up the hill to a painfully familiar Stump County landmark—Robin Buchanon's shack. It ranks right up there with the Washington Monument in Maggodian folklore, from fairly recent events all the way back to the beginning of the century, when Robin's great-grandpappy shot a revenuer and disappeared onto the ridge with his common-law wife and twelve feral children.

Barry tapped me on the shoulder. "We've gone too far. The bluff's back that way."

"No, we haven't," I said with a grimace. "I just didn't realize how close we were. I may not know *what's* going on, but I know exactly *where* it's going on."

Neither he nor Sterling looked particularly convinced by my remark, but we bounced up the road and into the expanse of weeds in front of the shack. Ruby Bee came out the door before I could drop to the ground.

"Thank goodness you found us," she said. "The pains are coming every two minutes, and Dahlia snarls something awful when any of us gets too close. Kayleen offered to examine her, but—"

"Kayleen's here?" I said.

"Yes, and Estelle. We were chasing after the ostriches, but—"

"Ostriches?" said Sterling.

Ruby Bee shrugged. "Sixty thousand dollars is sixty thousand dollars, even when it hisses, but——"

"When it hisses at you?" said Barry, having politely waited to take his turn.

I held up my hand. "Why don't we sort through this later? Can Dahlia hang on for another forty minutes?" I asked Ruby Bee.

"How should I know? I suppose you'd better ask her, or Kayleen, anyway. She knows more about birthing than the rest of us."

We all went into the cabin and formed a huddle by the door. Kayleen, who'd been sitting on the floor at a prudent distance from Dahlia, scrabbled to her feet and clutched my arm. "There's something wrong, but I don't know what. We've got to get her to a hospital."

"I ain't going nowhere without Kevvie!" Dahlia howled, then moaned and began to make peculiar noises, as if her lungs had been punctured.

"Forty minutes, minimum," I said to Kayleen.

"Then let's go."

I knelt next to Dahlia, whose face was thick with sweat and alarmingly white. "Kevin's waiting for you at the hospital, along with Earl and Eileen. Can you walk, or do we need to carry you?"

"I reckon I can walk."

Kayleen and I hung onto Dahlia's massive arms as we all moved outside. Ruby Bee and Estelle brought the remains of the corncob-filled mattress and spread it out in the back of the Hummer. Halfway across the yard, Dahlia stopped and went through the "ha-ha-ha-hoo!" pattern, but eventually announced she was ready to go on—as long as Kevvie was waitin' for her.

I mumbled something, and while she was being settled in the back of the Hummer, asked Sterling for his car phone.

He stuck out his jaw. "Will I be reimbursed for the cost of the call?"

"Absolutely," I said, then called Eileen, told her what was happening, and suggested she and Earl meet us at the hospital. In response to her question, I conceded that no one had seen Kevin.

"Leave a note for him," I added. "He's liable to show up at any moment."

"Do you really think so?" Eileen said.

By this time I would have lied to Mother Teresa, so I didn't have any problem assuring her that as sure as God made little green apples, he would. I replaced the phone, did a nose count to make sure everybody was in the Hummer, and gestured imperiously to its driver.

We careened down the logging road like a boulder in an avalanche and took off for Farberville. Sterling must have been worried about the effect a birth might have on the back floor of the Hummer, because he passed everything on the road, including a state police car.

This had an impact on the decibel level, which already was high. Dahlia alternated between panting and demanding to know where Kevin had been all this time. Ruby Bee and Estelle squealed every time Sterling swung into the oncoming traffic lane. Kayleen was forced to shout her encouragement to be heard. The addition of the siren and flashing lights added to the excitement.

I leaned toward Sterling and said, "Pull over and I'll tell the trooper what's going on."

"Nonsense," he replied, honking the horn until a chicken truck edged toward the shoulder. "There's no time to waste. I'm not admitting any culpability should the delivery have been jeopardized, but people have been sued for the most idiotic things. One of my policy owners threatened to sue me because he thought his policy protected him from getting in an accident, so therefore it was safe for him to disregard the speed limit."

Somehow or other, we arrived at the emergency room entrance without running over any pedestrians or Japanese imports. The state trooper was out of his car before I could get inside to find a nurse.

"Emergency!" I shouted at him, then pushed through the glass door, grabbed the first person I saw in a white uniform, and explained the situation.

"Two minutes apart?" she said. "That doesn't necessarily mean the baby's coming any second. Can the expectant mother walk?"

"She might need a wheelchair," I said, then went back outside as Earl and Eileen drove up. The tailgate had been opened. Dahlia was still lying on the remains of the mattress, her lips pumping away. A crowd was gathering, either in response to the flashing lights and sirens, or to the massive bulk of the Hummer.

The state trooper had pretty much figured out what was going on, but he wasn't happy. "Why didn't you pull over?" he asked me. "You could have gotten yourselves and a lot of innocent bystanders killed."

"I suggested it, but the driver was caught up in the melodrama of the moment."

The trooper shrugged. "Yeah, it happens. What the hell is this thing?"

I aimed him at Sterling, watched a pair of orderlies load Dahlia into a wheelchair, and joined Earl and Eileen. "She and the baby will be fine," I said. "The doctor will have her blood sugar tested and get it up to where it needs to be. The rest just sort of happens, so I've been told."

Eileen had Dahlia's overnight bag in one hand. She looked down at it and sighed. "I hope so."

"What about Kevin?" asked Earl.

Dahlia smacked at the orderlies until they backed away from the wheelchair, then looked up at me. "Kevvie ain't really here, is he?"

"I'll do everything possible to find him and get him here before the baby comes," she said.

"I found a clue while I was in the woods," she said, digging around in her pocket. She thrust a wadded piece of paper at me. "This proves Kevvie was there."

I took her offering. "We didn't really have a chance to search for him. I'll go back and comb the ridge all night, if necessary."

"I'm comin' with you," said Earl. "The women can keep Eileen company in the waiting room."

I went over to Sterling, who was explaining all the features of the Hummer to a large group composed of orderlies, bloodied and battered people waiting to be attended to in the emergency room, and the trooper. "Are you up for a real-life paramilitary exercise?"

Chapter 17

I was thinking how best to organize my very own Maggody militia when Kevin crashed into the rear end of the Hummer in his 1970s vintage car. None of us quite knew what to say, so what ensued might best be described as a stunned silence.

Dahlia rallied first. "Kevvie!" she screamed. "Where have you been? Doncha know I'm having the baby?"

He staggered out of the car, wiped a trickle of blood off his forehead, smiled at her, and collapsed on the pavement. It was not a pretty sight.

There was a great to-do as a gurney was brought out and Kevin and Dahlia were wheeled away. Eileen and Earl were as agitated as fleas on a poodle, but followed the orderlies inside. The crowd, having gotten more than its collective money's worth, drifted away to treat or be treated, depending on their roles in the overall scheme of the emergency room. Ruby Bee and Estelle had scurried after Eileen, which left me with Sterling, Barry, and Kayleen.

"You might as well go on back to the motel," I told them. "Thanks for what you did today."

Sterling squared his shoulders as if awaiting presentation of the Congressional Medal of Honor. "It was the least we could do, Chief Hanks. We do not despise the government, but merely resent the perverted direction it has taken since its original founders took it upon themselves to—"

"Can it," I said, "and market it as chicken noodle shit."

This, for obvious reasons, was not well received and

the three climbed into the Hummer and drove away. I went into the emergency room, where Earl, Eileen, Estelle, and Ruby Bee were standing in a corner, conversing in low voices.

"What's going on?" I asked.

Eileen stepped forward and said, "Dahlia's been admitted to the maternity ward, and Kevin's being seen to down here. I'm sure he'll be allowed to join her once his cut has been stitched up. I think he just banged his head when he hit the Hummer."

I took in the paleness of their faces. "You all go to the cafeteria and get some coffee, then go up to the waiting room on the maternity floor. I'll make sure Kevin gets to Dahlia's bedside."

Once they'd departed in the elevator, I went through another set of doors and down a corridor, poking my head into curtained cubicles in search of my quarry.

He was sitting on the gurney, wan but gaining color and holding a gauze pad to his forehead. He waved at me as I came around the corner, and said, "How's Dahlia doing?"

"She's okay now—no thanks to you. Last night she went to Cotter's Ridge to find you, and ended up at Robin's cabin. If Ruby Bee, Estelle, and Kayleen hadn't shown up, she might have given birth alone and terrified. Where the hell have you been?"

"I went back there on account of doing the right thing. Dylan was like my best buddy, exceptin' I'd only met him, and I dint think you cared about who shot him. I went into Robin's cabin to dry off, but then I got real scared and . . . well, fainted. The next thing I knew, I woke up and there was the murder weapon staring me in the face."

"And?" I said, wondering if he'd had a concussion.

"As sure as I'm sitting here," he said grandly, "Diesel done it."

"Diesel done—I mean, *did* it?"

"Well, it must have been him. I mean, who else is livin' in a cave on the ridge? It was fixed up real nice, considering, with some oddments of furniture and a whole shelf of books. A lot of them was poetry. I dint know what to make of that."

"I can imagine you didn't," I said. "You saw a rifle?"

"Bigger'n life, and one of them blowguns, too. Kin I go to Dahlia now? I'm what they call her coach, and I haft to pant with her and give her her ice chips and massages and things."

I climbed up on the other end of the gurney. "In a minute, Kevin. I truly am trying to find out what happened to Dylan, and you're the best witness I have. Yesterday you gave me an abbreviated version. I need a few specifics." I immediately regretted the polysyllabic words, but he grinned at me, so I forged ahead. "What happened right before Dylan was shot in the shoulder?"

Kevin gnawed on his lip for a moment. "He yelped. I was so bumfuzzled that I jumped up, but I hit my head and fell down. The next thing, he was gone and I crawled out and saw him on the ground."

"He yelped?" I echoed.

"Like he got stung by a yellow jacket, I 'spose," Kevin said, his hand drifting to the back of his neck. "It must have hurt something awful."

"Did he touch his neck?"

"I disremember exactly," he said apologetically. "I'd really like to be with Dahlia. She's gonna need her tape, and I got it in my pocket here. It's this smarmy woman saying how to breathe so the pain won't be so bad. I don't rightly know why makin' funny noises is gonna help, but the folks at the clinic——"

"You don't have that cassette," I said, coming out of a trance. "It's in the overnight bag that your mother brought to the hospital."

"It is?" he asked as if I'd pulled something worthy of Houdini. "I don't know how it got there, but I had it in my pocket yesterday." He rooted around for a moment, then gave me an abashed look. "Mebbe not."

"Let's move on so you can go upstairs. You went

back to the site of the shooting, took refuge in Robin's shack, and ended up in Diesel's cave, where you saw a rifle. Then what happened?"

He cleared his throat as if preparing to offer a narrative rife with complexity and profundity, although in my experience, such a thing was well beyond his repertoire. "I figured out right away that Diesel wasn't there, so I took off like a bat outta hell on account of being sure he was a cold-blooded murderer. I went for the longest while, praying I'd find a road, and then, jest when I was so tuckered out I was about to drop, I saw Mrs. Jim Bob."

I don't know what I was expecting, but this was not among the possibilities. "Mrs. Jim Bob?"

"She was driving Jim Bob's four-wheel and acting mighty peculiar. I dunno why she thought I knew the whereabouts of Brother Verber, or Jim Bob, for that matter, but I swore up and down I dint, and she finally took me back to my car by the low-water bridge. I drove home to make amends to Dahlia, found a note from my ma, and came here as fast as I could." He wiped his face with the gauze pad, leaving streaks of blood that resembled war paint. "I got to be with her, Arly. Dahlia, that is—not my ma."

"One last question," I said, "and then I'll help you find the right floor. You told me that when you were shot with the paint pellet, it wasn't fair. Why not?"

"Because he used a dadburned blowgun. What's the point of packing pistols if you don't use them? Kin I go now?"

The nurses we passed voiced objections, but I propelled Kevin back to the waiting room, held onto his arm as we took the elevator to the maternity floor, and then steered him down the hall to the sacred hallows of the delivery wing. Earl, Eileen, Ruby Bee, and Estelle were seated on benches in the hall, but we breezed by them and I found a dewy-faced nursing student who promised to patch up Kevin and escort him to Dahlia's room.

"Everything's under control," I said mendaciously as I rejoined the group. "Dahlia's in the care of doctors and has her devoted husband at her side. I, however, need to get back to Maggody and I don't have transportation." I held out my hand to Earl, who looked as if he'd rather be most anyplace else, including a dungeon, and added, "Key to your truck, please?"

He wasn't especially delighted, but he forked it over and I left them for the duration.

As I drove into Maggody, I looked up at Cotter's Ridge, speculating about my chances of finding Diesel's cave. Kevin might have been wrong about the rifle he'd seen, or even hallucinating. The cassette he'd discovered in his pocket was intriguing. Dylan certainly could have stashed it there; he'd only just met Kevin and would not necessarily have realized he was dealing with a congenital bumbler.

I reminded myself of the number of times I'd unsuccessfully tried to locate Raz's still. An idea, albeit iffy, came to mind. I drove to Raz's shack, took a deep breath, and knocked on his door.

As soon as he appeared, I said, "I ought to cuff you this minute and take you to the county jail."

"Now what'd I do?" he whined.

"You failed to tell me that you drove Dahlia to the low-water bridge last night."

"Ye didn't ask me. Listen, I got Marjorie in a washtub so's I can scrub off the paint, and I need to git back to her."

"I don't care," I said. "She'll be a whole lot less happy if I drag you out to the car and she spends the next seventy-two hours shriveling up like a great white prune. Are you going to cooperate or not?"

Raz stared at me. "It ain't against the law to fergit something, particularly seeing as I was frettin' about Marjorie. If you'd asked me, I'd have told you."

"Well, you didn't. You endangered Dahlia and impeded my investigation. I may not be able to make the charges stick, but you'll be seriously inconvenienced if you don't agree to do something for me."

"I ain't got a still and I ain't gonna tell you where it is," he said, wiping spittle off his lips.

Sensing victory, I allowed myself a wry smile. "I'm not going to bother. I want you to go to Diesel's cave, ask him where he found the rifle, and also if he's found a cassette. Bring them both back here to your place and wait for me."

Raz looked at me as if I'd suggested he enroll in college. "Diesel ain't about to let me git within spittin' distance of him. Iff'n he hears the truck, he'll be in the next county afore I turn off the engine. That, or he'll blow my brains out."

"If he's there, it's time for you two to kiss and make up. If not, look around for the cassette and the rifle. If he blows your brains out, then your chances of a Nobel prize are diminished, but you can always try. I'll expect to see you in one hour."

"Marjorie ain't a-gonna like this."

"One hour," I said flatly. "Otherwise, seventy-two hours in the county jail."

I hurried back to Earl's truck and drove away before permitting myself to smirk. My next destination was the motel, where I found Les in his cop car and all the militia vehicles in a tidy row. Les was so engrossed in his book that he failed to notice my arrival.

"What're you reading?" I asked.

He flung the book into the back seat. "Nothing much. Everybody came back half an hour ago and went into their rooms. Kayleen said you all had found Dahlia and got her to the hospital. Is she having the baby?"

"I guess so," I said, taking a look at the book on the back seat. *"Constructing Homemade Grenade Launchers: The Ultimate Hobby?* Geez, Les, why are you reading crap like that?"

He hunched his shoulders. "General Pitts said I looked bored and loaned it to me. I don't suppose Sheriff Dorfer would be real happy about me reading on duty."

"I'll never breathe a word," I said solemnly, then went to Kayleen's room and knocked on the door.

She gave me a startled look as she opened the door. "Is Dahlia doing okay?"

"She was when I left," I said, continuing into the room. "What can you tell me about blowguns?"

"Blowguns?" She sat down on the bed and thought for a moment. "Well, they're a fad, partly because they're so new there are no restrictions. Some folks fool around with them, and others have taken to hunting with them. You can get one for less than thirty dollars. They come in lengths from eighteen inches to six feet."

"Do you sell them?"

"I've special-ordered a few of them in the last few months. Reed asked me to get him one, then proceeded to shoot Sterling with a paint pellet on Friday afternoon. From what I heard, I kind of wish I'd been there."

"Who else has one?" I said.

"I don't really know," she said slowly. "Jake said something about having a couple of them. I didn't notice one in Dylan's gear, but that doesn't mean much. Same with Barry. I guess you'll have to ask them."

Wishing I had my handy-dandy notebook, I did the best I could to keep all this straight. "What about you? Do you have one?"

She shook her head. "Like I said, I ordered them as a favor. Down the road I may decide to stock them, but there's not much profit selling a thirty-dollar item."

"Let me ask you something else," I said ever so adroitly. "What was said in Sterling's room Friday night when you, Barry, and he were there?"

"The same old things, I'm afraid. How to recruit new members, who was in charge of distributing literature, and so on. I'm beginning to think I might just drop out of the group and get on with my life. This isn't to say I'm not concerned about the possibility of a massive social upheaval, but at the same time, I don't want to miss out on what might be the best years of my life. I'm not too old to remarry and feather another nest."

I share a certain number of genes with my mother, alas. "With Brother Verber?"

Kayleen stood up and crossed to the mirror above the dresser to examine herself. "I don't see why not," she said with a trace of defiance. "He's got a Christian heart and a gentle, trusting nature, and he seems to enjoy my companionship. That's all I ask of a relationship."

"Does he remind you of Maurice?" I asked dryly.

"I met his daughter this morning, and she gave him a less than glowing testimonial. I believe she used the phrase 'crotchety old coot' to describe him. She said to give you her regards, by the way."

"Lila resented her father because she believed he was responsible for her never getting married. Whatever took place was long before my time, so I don't have any idea what really happened. Maurice was difficult, but a lot of his persnickety manner came from pain. He could also be real affectionate, and he loved to travel and meet young people. Every gun show we went to was like another honeymoon."

I managed not to make any puns, although it wasn't easy. "From what Miss Lila said, he was pretty frail."

"He could get around with his walker, and he did a few laps in the pool every day. The doctor assured me that Maurice was recovering from the surgery and was as healthy as a horse. No heart trouble, no problems with cholesterol or high blood pressure, no nothing." Her eyes began to water, and she brushed away a tear. "I honestly believed we'd have a lot of years together."

"I have a question about that night," I said. "If Maurice was all that infirm, how did he even get downstairs? I'd think the burglars could have looted the ground floor long before he reached the bottom step."

Kayleen blushed and looked away. "I don't like to talk about this, but Maurice and I weren't sharing a bedroom. He slept on a rollaway bed in his office and used the guest bathroom. I stayed upstairs in one of the bedrooms. I know it's wrong for a husband and wife not to . . . be together once they've taken their vows and been blessed by the Lord, and I was praying that Maurice might get strong enough to handle the stairs before too long."

"Sheriff Flatchett didn't mention that," I said.

"I didn't see any need to tell him about our private arrangement. I folded up the bed and put it in the closet in the hall. I feel so silly getting all upset in front of you, Arly, but I can't help it. Maurice didn't want anybody to know how feeble he was. I had no choice but to respect his wishes."

"I understand," I said softly, then gave her a minute to regain her composure. I did so not out of any great compassion, mind you, but out of a genuine distaste for emotional scenes. Divorce can do that to you. "You mentioned that Maurice left you enough to get by on and even buy property here in Maggody. Lila seemed to think all you received was the depleted gun collection, in her opinion worth no more than five thousand dollars. Did she lie about that out of spite, too?"

"There was some life insurance money," Kayleen said as she vanished into the bathroom.

I nearly keeled over as it came together like mashed potatoes and gravy. I made it to the chair and sank down, listening in awe as pieces of the puzzle slammed into each other in much the same fashion as Kevin's car had slammed into the Hummer outside the emergency room. Although I hadn't listened to the cassette, I would have crossed my heart and sworn to die that I knew what the conversation had been about.

Furthermore, I was in the wrong room.

Before I could rectify this, Kayleen emerged. Her freshly applied lipstick was a bit crooked, but her gaze was level. She went to the window and pulled back the drape, then said, "I'm thinking about going back to the hospital. All I can do is hold Eileen's hand, but that's better than sitting here, worrying about the baby. Is it okay with you, Arly?"

"Is the deputy still out there?"

"Why, yes," she said, frowning at what she must have felt was a stupid question.

I produced another one. "How much life insurance money was there, Kayleen? There's no point in lying about it. One of Big Brother's favorite offspring, the IRS, has the figures. It may not be legal for them to divulge it, but they can be coaxed, as can the insurance company that held the policy. Not the individual agent, though. He's liable to invoke his Fifth Amendment rights. God, I'm getting sick of that."

"What are you talking about?" she said.

"Sterling won't want to discuss how he can afford a fifty-five-thousand-dollar tank and a computer and other expensive equipment. If he owned a large agency with a lot of employees to drum up business, I might buy it. His agency probably doesn't generate enough income to fill the Hummer's gas tank every week." I went to the window and made sure she hadn't lied about Les's presence twenty feet from the door. He may have had the book in his lap, but he was making a show of scanning the units as if they were cells on death row.

Kayleen sat down on the bed. "Sterling and I have never talked about his personal finances. As for the insurance money, the policy was for half a million dollars. I guess when Maurice took it out, he thought he was going to get rich."

I waved at Les, then turned around. "His daughter and the sheriff both said he was a tightwad. Tightwads don't spend a ton of money on life insurance premiums so their heirs can squander it. Did he even know you and Sterling arranged for the policy?"

"I knew I would outlive Maurice, and the last thing I wanted to do was be forced to go back to work. Is there something wrong with making sure I had security in my old age?"

"Darn right you knew you were going to outlive Maurice," I said coldly, "especially since you chose the night to kill him. It was a really good scheme, by the way. You set the stage by prowling around your neighbors' houses so everybody'd believe your story about masked men in your house. You had plenty of time to take a few weapons and hide them to give the nonexistent burglars a motive. Then you shot your husband, broke a window and the gun case, and called for help. You would have gotten away with it if you hadn't sold the Ingram MAC ten."

"You're out of your mind, Arly. I consider Ruby Bee and Estelle to be my dearest friends. They're not going to like it when they hear you said all these terrible things about me. When I say my prayers tonight, I'll ask God to help you come to your senses."

"Thanks," I said with a facetiously bright smile.

"And I was wrong a minute ago. I said you would have gotten away with it, but you wouldn't have if Dylan hadn't been killed. You already know he died of nicotine poisoning. The rifle might have done the trick, but I guess you had to be sure."

She gaped at me, then stood up and edged over to the dresser. "I'm beginning to think you're plumb crazy. Why in heaven's name would I want to kill that boy? I hardly knew him, and I didn't believe all the accusations about him being a government agent."

I once again checked to make sure Les was attentive enough to gallop across the lot if I needed him (there wasn't a moment for him to make a grenade launcher). "He wasn't a government agent," I said, glancing at the telephone and wondering if Agent Tonnato was on the other end of the line. "Dylan was actually the son of the man who was murdered with the Ingram you let slip out of your hands. Friday night he got into the room next to Sterling's and taped everything that was said between seven and ten. After Barry left, you and Sterling discussed new recruits—but you weren't referring to your militia roster. Had you decided what to do once you and Brother Verber came up the aisle? A long boat ride, or maybe a sprinkle of this or that in his spaghetti sauce?"

"I'm just heartbroken to hear you say those things, Arly. I've had a hard life, losing two husbands and having to work night shifts, but I swear I had nothing to do with any of this."

"Ruby Bee managed to support herself and bring up a child without resorting to murdering lonely old men. I won't be surprised if it turns out you've gone through more than two husbands." I went to the door. "Get your coat, Kayleen. I'll have the deputy take you to the sheriff's office."

"I'm not going anywhere," she said in a thin voice.

"All you've done is make wild accusations. You can't prove any of it. Sheriff Flatchett did a thorough investigation, and he was satisfied that I was telling the truth. Why can't you do the same? I deserve the chance to live out my life with a loving husband and caring friends. Maggody's a clean town without the kind of people who pollute the air just by breathing it."

She was damn good. Her eyes glittered with tears and her lips quivered, and she looked willing to fall to her knees and clasp her hands like a malnourished orphan. Then again, black widow spiders have a decorative red mark on their backs and no doubt find each other attractive.

I shook my head. "I don't have much proof yet, but I've sent someone to get the rifle that you hid on the ridge. The person who found it has the blowgun, too. The dart you dipped in nicotine and took out of Dylan's neck as soon as you reached his body may never be found, since you could have put it in your pocket and disposed of it."

"But I didn't," Kayleen said as she took a three-inch needle with a plastic tip out of her pocket. "It took me a long time to soak loose tobacco and then boil it down to a sticky goo. You can see some near the tip, so I assume it's still . . . serviceable, in a manner of speaking."

Did I mention I was in the wrong room? What's more, it was all my stupid, semi-arrogant fault for not leaving when I first realized she was a murderer. I could have called a cheery good-bye, gone outside, and used Les's radio to summon Harve and whomever else he could round up. Harve could have held his own press conference, impressed the electorate, and started tracking down a pair of bloodhounds.

As it was, I was obliged to settle for the trite, "You'll never get away with it, so put that thing down before you make it worse."

"Does that queer hermit I've heard about have the rifle?" she said, brandishing the dart.

I pressed my back against the wall. "Maybe."

"That's what I figured. I saw him on the top of the ridge, watching the maneuver. He ducked out of sight as soon as I fired the shot, but he may have lingered long enough to see me stash the rifle and blowgun. I was following what I hoped were his tracks when I ran into Ruby Bee." She came close enough to me that I could see the dark brown residue on the dart. "Do you know where his cave is?"

"Sure," I said quickly. "It's not too far from Raz's still."

"Ruby Bee said you've been looking for the still for several years—but you haven't found it."

It was odd the way my mother could interfere even when she was twenty miles away in a hospital waiting room.

"Earlier this week Raz broke down and told me," I said, struggling not to allow my voice to crack. I'm much better at lying when I'm not being threatened with an untimely demise. "You want me to draw you a map?"

"I don't want to hurt your feelings, but your maps are kind of hard to read. You'd better take me there. I'm sure I can reason with the hermit, or give him a few dollars in exchange for the rifle. He's one witness I won't have to worry about, isn't he?"

She actually laughed, but I wasn't in the mood to share the merriment. She kept right on smiling as she put on her coat, careful to keep the dart within jabbing distance, and then said, "We're going to walk outside and get into your car. I'll be behind you, and the dart will easily penetrate your clothes should it be necessary."

"And I'll have five minutes to tell the deputy what happened before I lose consciousness."

"Which means I'll go to prison. You'll be dead."

There was that. I shrugged and opened the door, painfully aware of her breath on the back of my neck as we went out into the parking lot. I was weighing my chances of escaping somewhere on the ridge versus running toward Les's car when the door of #5 opened.

"Kayleen! Good news," boomed Sterling, practically pounding on his chest like a silverback. "I've just spoken to the lieutenant governor, and he's going to take care of this in the next hour. Chief Hanks, it may be time for you to start practicing the phrase, 'Do you want fries with that?'"

Kayleen hesitated. In that I really, really didn't want to go back to Cotter's Ridge, I spun around and punched her in the nose hard enough to put her on the gravel. I picked up the dart by its plastic tip and started yelling at Les to get his boss on the radio. Doors opened and the entire militia came stumbling out, drunk, sober, half-dressed, clad in camouflage—the whole gamut. The only thing they seemed to have in common was outrage, but for once their paranoia had a basis in fact: cops can be brutal.

Chapter 18

Once Kayleen had been safely stashed in the back of Les's car, I went into the kitchen of the bar and found an empty jar with a lid for the dart. It was more than mildly tempting to pour myself a beer and sit in solitude, contemplating my near-death experience, but the neon Coors sign wasn't the light I was supposed to have seen.

Sterling was shouting at Les as I came back out. He was pretty much incoherent, although the word "amendment" was coming through on a regular basis, along with the tried-and-true "constitutional rights."

I poked Sterling in the back. "Look, buddy, you may not have pulled any triggers, but you conspired with Kayleen to murder Maurice Smeltner—and it stinks of premeditation."

"You have no proof."

"A mere technicality. When the insurance company that paid out half a million dollars to the grieving widow takes a harder look at the application, I suspect they'll find a whole slew of forged signatures, like Mo's and that of a physician who purportedly did a physical examination."

That stopped him cold. "What do you know about that?"

"And even if Kayleen takes the rap for that," I continued, "the IRS is going to want to have a long talk about unreported income, tax evasion, and fraud."

"I had to fund our group," he said, looking imploringly at Barry, Reed, and Jake. "No one but dedicated patriots such as ourselves will be prepared to defend the country in the face of the invasion that will lead to Armageddon. You know it's coming, don't you? Women and the inferior races have the vote, the despots in Washington burdened us with an illegal tax levy to fuel the international conspiracy, and the banks are controlled by the Federal Reserve." He swung around and gripped Les's shoulder. "Haven't you seen the secret codes on the backs of highway signs? They exist to aid the enemy's armies when they arrive to round up able-bodied men and execute them like dogs. Any of us who's been in the armed services or even in a hospital has a device in his buttocks that can be monitored via satellite."

Les stepped back. "Don't go talking about my buttocks unless you want to ride to Farberville in the trunk."

Reed scowled at Sterling. "Did Kayleen really kill Mo? He wasn't what I'd call a party animal, but he wasn't hurting anybody. I mean, we all got to get old some day, don't we? Doesn't mean we ought to be shot in the gut."

"Sacrifices had to be made," Sterling whimpered.

I told Les to put the general in the backseat with Kayleen. When they were gone, I faced the remaining members of the militia. "Get on home. You'll be hearing from the sheriff's department, and possibly the FBI. I don't think you'll have much free time to play in the woods, since there'll be lots and lots of interrogations. Grand juries can be demanding."

Reed was whining to Barry as they went into #6. Jake spat on the ground and went into #2. They'd be gone by mid-afternoon, and the sheriff would have the Hummer and the Mercedes impounded by morning. The Flamingo Motel would regain its ghost town ambiance, and only Ruby Bee would be criss-crossing the parking lot to dust or squirt air freshener in the bathrooms.

"I cain't believe it," Raz said, nearly choking on his chaw as he surveyed the ruins of his still. "I reckon

I'm gonna take this rifle back to Diesel's cave, and when he comes in, I'm gonna nail him between the eyes like the sorry sumbitch deserves. Why would he go and do this, Marjorie? I know fer a fact he takes a jar of hooch ever now and then."

Marjorie blinked, then went back to chewing on a plastic case she'd found. A strip of thin black cellophane tape dangled out of her mouth, ticklin' her chin.

"Wait jest a dadburn minute! Iff'n it's Diesel, he's dead meat."

Raz crept closer, his mouth screwed up, and carefully pulled back a branch. "Well, look at these critters," he said. "I ain't never seen nuthin like this in all my born days—and I can smell my hooch on 'em. You know what I think, Marjorie? These giant chickens are drunk as Cooter Brown."

It took him a long time to get the thievin' birds in the back of his truck, and he was sweating something awful. He wiped his forehead with the back of his hand, then got turned around and headed home. He wasn't real sure what to do with the birds, but he figgered they could stay out in his barn till he came up with something.

He was gonna ask Marjorie what she thought, but she was lookin' kind of green, so he fiddled with the radio until he found one of her favorite songs.

I swung by Raz's, but his truck was gone. I went on to the PD to make a pot of coffee before I headed for Harve's office. On a whim, I took out Agent Tonnato's business card, called the office and got the answering machine, then called the home number.

"Tonnato," he said.

I identified myself, then said, "Did you overhear the conversation in Kayleen Smeltner's motel room half an hour ago?"

"The only thing I've overheard today was my wife telling her sister what a sloppy paint job I'm doing on the deck. Why don't you go home and check under your bed for communists, Chief Hanks?"

He banged down the receiver, so I did, too. I poured a cup of coffee, settled my feet on the corner of the desk, and mentally reviewed my spontaneous construction of my case against Kayleen. It seemed to make as much sense as most of the things that took place in and around Maggody, and I was gathering up my notes when the telephone rang.

"Arly," chirped LaBelle, "I know you're on the way, but this couldn't wait. Are you missing any of your local residents?"

I thought for a minute. "Not as many as I was a couple of hours ago. What are you—the census taker?"

"Well, we just got a call from the Pulaski County sheriff's office. Three days ago they raided a place outside the Little Rock city limits and found one of yours. Ruby Bee's not gonna have any trouble writing her column this week, lemme tell you."

"So tell me."

"There are certain words I don't use, but the place is called Madam Caressa's Social Club. The employees are all women, and the customers are men, if you get my drift. Most of the men were allowed to put up bail and leave, but yours was so inebriated and incoherent that they took him to the hospital for a seventy-two-hour psychiatric evaluation."

I sat down and rested my forehead on my fist. "Brother Verber, right? Hey, LaBelle, why don't you call Mrs. Jim Bob and tell her the news? She's been worried sick, so this will make her feel a whole lot better. It's real possible that she'll want to drive down there to pick him up herself."

LaBelle happily agreed, and I made it out the door before she realized what she was getting herself into and called me back.

I could tell from the look she gave me when I arrived at the sheriff's department that Mrs. Jim Bob hadn't gurgled in gratitude and thanked LaBelle for sharing the information. I hurried by her desk and into Harve's office, where he and the county prosecutor were waiting.

It took me most of an hour to cover everything. I was unable to explain how the Ingram MAC 10 had ended up in Missouri, but suggested that an argument could be made that taking a stolen weapon across state lines for use in a felony might be racketeering, and thus a way to involve the FBI. The prosecutor was ambivalent, but Harve was so delighted at passing the buck that he offered to send a deputy back to Raz's shack for the rifle.

He also volunteered to walk me out to my car. "Good work, Arly. I'm so distracted these days that I'd probably have let it go as a hunting accident."

"Another burglary?" I asked.

"No, but the newspapers are carrying on like there's a serial killer systematically exterminating the population. Now that this militia business is done, think you'll have time to get back on the burglaries?"

"I'll reread the files," I said, then left for the hospital.

I went to the maternity waiting room. Ruby Bee and Estelle were reading magazines, while Earl snored in a corner and Eileen stood by the door, twisting a tissue into shreds.

"No progress?" I asked.

"No," Eileen said glumly. "They let me go to her room for a minute, but she was bawling because the nurse wanted to put on a fetal monitor. I don't know where she got this crazy idea that any kind of test is going to hurt the baby."

"Oh, I know where she got it," Estelle said as she opened her two-gallon handbag and pulled out a folded newspaper. "There's an ad almost every week in *The Starley City Star Shopper* that says all the tests are potentially harmful to the baby. If you send nineteen ninety-five to the address in the ad, they send you a kit to determine the sex of your baby."

"Let me see that," I said.

"The ad's right under my column," said Ruby Bee. "I must say I'm getting a lot of compliments these days from folks that enjoy knowing about their neighbors. The folks that write the Emmett and Hasty columns must be as dull as June Bug Buchanon. She'd talk your ear off, and afterwards you couldn't recall a thing she'd said."

I read the ad. "This should have been in a tabloid between stories about coconut trees at the South Pole and man-eating rabbits." Aware that Ruby Bee was watching me, I scanned her column. "Glad to know that Petrol hasn't lost his zest. I don't remember asking you to remind anybody about hunter orange, but that's okay." I thought about telling them that Kayleen wouldn't be opening her pawnshop anytime in the foreseeable future, but it could wait.

"Here's the first column," said Ruby Bee, handing me a carefully folded piece of newsprint.

I obediently read her maiden foray into journalism. "Wow, I didn't know the Four-H club was doing so well . . . and a baby shower for Dahlia with punch and cake. Maggody was certainly on the go that week, what with Edwina in Branson, the Bidens planning their trip, and Elsie . . ."

"What?" said Ruby Bee, poised to snatch back the column if I snickered.

"I need to make a call from the lobby," I said. I rode the elevator back down, found a dime, and called Harve. "Do you ever look at those small town weekly newspapers?"

"Not in an election year," he said. "I'd like to talk, but we're kinda busy over here. Both of the suspects have lawyers falling all over themselves, and for some fool reason, LaBelle said she was going home to get drunk. Les keeps trying to tell me about a goddamn grenade launcher we can use to blow up marijuana patches, and—"

"This has to do with the burglaries, Harve, although I can't deny that I'd find ways to enjoy a grenade launcher. The newspaper I'm looking at is packed with columns written by amateur correspondents. Most of what's in them is tedious, but there seems to be a common trend—and that's to announce who's away visiting relatives or planning a trip. The burglars had all the time in the world to empty the suitable residences."

"Can we catch 'em?"

I may have been a bit cocky, but it felt good. "Have someone round up all these papers and we'll see about staking out the most likely candidates. It may take a week or two, but—"

"A week would be better, on account of the election, but just the same, nailing those bastards would make a lot of people sleep better at night."

"If you wanted to sell stolen property, Harve, where would you start?"

"Pawn store," he said promptly. "but nothing's turned up. We've got some of the serial numbers and fairly good descriptions of jewelry and that sort of thing."

"What if," I said, regretting my failure to keep track of who was where and when, "you were a fence, and had connections with fences in other states? You wouldn't have to risk selling stolen goods that were on the hot sheet, would you? You could put the stolen property in a storage facility and wait until you could move it out of state. No rush, especially if you had reciprocal agreements across the country."

Harve wasn't puffing on a cigar anymore. "What are you getting at, Arly?"

"Malthus," I said. "It's in Chowden County. You might ask Sheriff Flatchett about rental storage space. He may know all sorts of things."

"You know," Harve said, sighing, "sometimes I think about dropping out of the race and retiring to someplace like Florida."

"Hurricanes and theme parks."

"Then maybe southern California."

"Mudslides, floods, earthquakes, sinkholes, brush fires, and theme parks."

Harve harrumphed. "I'm sure as hell not retiring to Maggody. You may not have any of those things you listed, but you not only attract the strangest bunch of folks I ever met, you grow them out that way, too."

I hung up the phone.

* * *

When Jake and Judy got back to Emmet, Jake announced he was going to find LaRue. He dumped all the camping gear in the yard, told her to put it away, and drove off.

Judy went inside and called Janine to make sure the baby was fine. Afterwards, she crammed as much of her clothes as she could in a suitcase, put the money she'd been setting aside into her purse, and walked down the road to the café where the Greyhound buses stopped.

After she'd had a cup of coffee, she took a dime from her purse and used the pay phone to call the Stump County sheriff's department.

"About those burglaries," she said without identifying herself. "You might want to ask Jake Milliford out in Emmett how he and his buddy LaRue can afford all their fancy guns."

When Reed got back to the Airport Arms, he sat in the truck and tried to come up with a way to sell Dylan's car. He was thinking he should have asked Jake about the salvage yard when a guy on a damn-fine Harley drove up.

The guy pulled up the visor of his helmet and said, "You Reed Rondly?"

"Yeah, but why's it your business?"

The guy threw a fat envelope into the truck. "Just doin' my job, which is serving court orders. Have a good day."

The motorcycle was long gone before Reed got his mouth closed.

When Barry got back to his apartment, he found a message on his answering machine from an unfamiliar woman, warning him that her husband LaRue and Jake were on the way "to kick the shit out of you—and believe you me, they can do it, no matter how tough you are."

Barry decided it was time to find another group of brethren in some place like Wyoming.

When Jim Bob got back to the deer camp after six hours of being lost in the rain, blundering up and down the ridge, not seeing Roy or Larry Joe or any other living thing, he felt darn sorry for himself. To top it off, his four-wheel was gone and the trailer was still locked and by now he was so hungry he would have eaten some of that greenish bologna Larry Joe had thrown out in the grass—except something had already gotten it.

He sat on the concrete block, wiping his chin and trying to find the strength to get up and follow the logging road off the ridge, when he saw something staring at him through a bush.

It was back, he thought wildly. It looked different somehow—hairier and heftier and more like an ape—but he didn't hang around to think about the differences and instead ran down to the outhouse, scrambled inside, and banged down the latch.

He peered through a knothole and saw movement, but not enough to figure out what was going on. His heart was pounding like it was about to burst out of his chest, and his eyes were clouded with blotches of red.

He sat down to wait. It wasn't likely that Larry Joe and Roy would come back, but he wasn't about to go outside until they did.

When I got back to the waiting room, everybody was beaming except for Earl, who looked a little groggy.

"It's a boy!" said Ruby Bee, clapping her hands.

"Kevin just came out and told us," said Eileen. "Dahlia's fine, and as soon as they take her to her room, Earl and I can poke our heads in for a minute. Once the baby's been cleaned up, they'll roll him out in the nursery so we can see him. I'm just as pleased as punch!"

"Aren't we all!" said Estelle.

Eileen had to elbow Earl before he agreed, but he grunted something and we were all smiling mindlessly (there wasn't much else to do) when Kevin came to the door.

"It's a girl," he croaked, swaying like a top-heavy stalk of corn.

I caught his arm, shoved him down in the nearest chair, and held his head between his knees until he began to protest.

Earl was wide awake. "What do you mean, it's a girl? You just came in here and said it was a boy. Which is it?"

"Both," Kevin said numbly.

"Twins?" Eileen said, doing some swaying herself.

Two more Buchanons, I thought as we crowded around Kevin and began to congratulate him. Just what I needed.

If you loved
THE MAGGODY MILITIA,
you won't want to miss
these other tales of murder,
mystery, and mayhem
in Maggody by Joan Hess. . . .

MALICE IN MAGGODY

Arly Hanks returns to her hometown of Maggody, Arkansas (pop. 755), after her marriage goes sour in the Big Apple. She figures taking the local sheriff's job will give her some much needed R&R. What she gets is M&M—murder and malice. First Raz Buchanon's favorite hunting dog is snatched, then an EPA official (who okayed dumping sewage in the town's favorite fishing hole) disappears . . . and then a pretty barmaid turns up dead at the Flamingo Motel from real unnatural causes. Now Arly's in danger of landing up the creek without a paddle—where the quiet of the Ozarks may be shattered by the sounds of death.

"Funny and fast-moving . . . I almost split a gusset."—Charlotte MacLeod

MISCHIEF IN MAGGODY

Arly Hanks took the job of chief of police after her big-city marriage went on the rocks. She needed to be in a quiet place like Maggody, where nothing exciting ever happened. Especially murder. But hard-cussin', hard-drinkin' Robin Buchanon, local moonshiner, just turned up deader than a skunk flattened by a big rig. What she left behind was a cabin full of kids, a booby-trapped patch of marijuana, and a town waiting for the next body to drop.

"I love Maggody!"—Barbara Michaels

MUCH ADO IN MAGGODY

There's trouble in Maggody again, and Arly Hanks has her hands full. The trouble's name is Brandon Bernswallow, the local bank president's playboy son, who became the new head teller and bumped longtime employee Johnna Mae Nookim right down to minimum wage. The fighting-mad women of Maggody are planning a scheme to give the male chauvinists their comeuppance. But they are just as appalled as the menfolk when the bank—and Bernswallow—go up in flames. Arly is determined to sift through the ashes. . . and discover who cooked up this case of down-home murder.

"Jolly, raunchy, more than entertaining."
—*Chicago Sun-Times*

MADNESS IN MAGGODY

No doubt about it, local gossips had finally gotten something right: a maniac was loose in Maggody. So Arly Hanks is back in action. Someone sabotaged the grand opening of Jim Bob's SuperSaver Buy 4 Less with tainted tamale sauce and straight pins in the cupcakes. Now Arly's got 23 cases of food poisoning and a whole passel of suspects who want Jim Bob's store to go belly up, including her very own mother, Ruby Bee. What Arly doesn't have is an inkling of the other high crimes and misdemeanors about to be perpetrated in a Magoddy gone bonkers: sex scandals, scams . . . and very sudden death.

"Brash, bawdy . . . fun!"—*Kirkus Reviews*

MORTAL REMAINS IN MAGGODY

Ordinarily Arly Hanks is known for saying nothing ever happens in Maggody, but lately that's all changed: Word is buzzing all the way from Ruby Bee's Bar & Grill to Estelle's Hair Fantasies that Hollywood (or at least Burbank) is coming to this tiny Ozarks town to shoot on location. Everyone is starstruck. Then things really heat up. First the actors are peeling off their clothes, and if that weren't enough, they're suddenly turning up missing—or dead. Before the director can yell "action," the credits are rolling on a moonshine-style mystery....

"Inspired!"—*Chicago Tribune*

MAGGODY IN MANHATTAN

Arly Hanks can't even look at a postcard of Manhattan's skyline without feeling dizzy and nauseated. But when Ruby Bee wins an all-expenses-paid trip to New York as a finalist in the KoKo-Nut Cooking Contest and is arrested for attempted murder, it looks like Arly to the rescue. Checking into the Chadwick Hotel, Arly finds herself sharing recipes with the good-looking, single Durmond Pilverman. She also begins to suspect that too many chefs are spoiling the broth when a dead body turns up in the hotel dumpster. And the .38 she finds hidden in Durmond's dresser has her wondering if she's been sleeping with the enemy....

"A delectable dish!"
—*New York Times Book Review*

O LITTLE TOWN OF MAGGODY

Arly Hanks is still hiding out in her hometown of Maggody, Arkansas, the land of moonshine, Ruby Bee's Bar & Grill, Nashville on the radio, cheatin' hearts and, well, maybe murder. Matt Montana, country music's superstar, has come home to Maggody for the holidays. For a town in the grip of a recession, the news means Christmas is bringing a savior. Only one thing is missing: Matt Montana's Aunt Adele, who has mysteriously disappeared. Of course, it's left to smart and spunky Arly to save Christmas for the wacky, delightful community of Maggody, where anything can happen—and usually does.

"All the ingredients of a good yuletide murder mystery."—*Denver Post*

MARTIANS IN MAGGODY

For Arly Hanks, Maggody is a sleepy little town where nothing ever happens—until the day UFOs, Martians, Bigfoot, *and* tabloid reporters descend on Maggody . . . and bring along a case of murder. What starts out as a headache and begins to look like a panic turns serious when a dead body is found out at Boone Creek. Now Arly's got a very down-to-earth puzzle on her hands, and she suspects it's directly connected to an extraterrestrial hoax.

"A rollicking tour de force."—*Boston magazine*

MIRACLES IN MAGGODY

Arly Hanks usually handles all the crime that comes her way in Maggody with the ease that Ruby Bee at Ruby Bee's Bar & Grill gets out her blue-plate specials. But that's before tele-vangelist Malachi Hope rolls into town and sets up a tent revival that promises to put Maggody on the map . . . and Arly in the hot seat. Before Arly can say "Amen," she's got two murders on her hands, and unless she pulls off a few miracles of her own, she might not get out of this crisis alive. . . .

"Another outrageously funny episode in a stellar series." —*Booklist*

the wait

a novel by

FRANK TURNER HOLLON

OTHER BOOKS BY FRANK TURNER HOLLON

The Pains of April

The God File

A Thin Difference

Life is a Strange Place (Barry Munday)

The Point of Fracture

Glitter Girl and the Crazy Cheese

blood and circumstance

the wait

a novel by

FRANK TURNER HOLLON

MacAdam/Cage
155 Sansome Street, Suite 550
San Francisco, CA 94104
www.macadamcage.com

Library of Congress Cataloging-in-Publication Data

Hollon, Frank Turner, 1963-
  The wait : a novel / by Frank Turner Hollon.
    p. cm.
  ISBN 978-1-59692-291-4
  1. Life—Fiction. I. Title.
PS3608.O494W35 2008
813'.6—dc22

2007050807

Paperback edition: May 2008
ISBN 978-1-59692-293-8

Manufactured in the United States of America

10 9 8 7 6 5 4 3 2 1

Book design by Dorothy Carico Smith.

Between the wish and the thing, life lies waiting.

—Unknown

PART I

in the beginning

My father almost never got drunk. When he did, it was usually a happy, goofy drunk. But one night when I was nine years old, after a Christmas party, for reasons still unknown, he told me the story of my conception. This is how I remember it.

Bobby Winters stared out the motel window. From behind he could hear his little brother in the bathroom. It was a day like any other day, except Bobby knew something bad would happen soon. He could always tell when his brother was about to do something stupid. It was just a matter of trying to keep the damage to a minimum.

Mark came out from the bathroom completely naked with a pistol in his left hand.

"We're gonna rob this motel," is what he said.

Bobby just kept staring out the window. He knew better than to argue. Everything had already been said before.

Mark continued, "We ain't got no money left. After it gets dark, I'll go into the lobby alone when it's clear. You keep the car runnin'. We'll haul ass outta here. Maybe go to Texas or somewhere."

Even though they were only nineteen and twenty years old, it seemed to Bobby he'd been keeping Mark alive for centuries.

Bobby turned around and said slowly, careful to control his voice, "Don't hurt anybody, Mark."

Mark smiled. "You worry too fuckin' much. Like somebody's grandmother or somethin'?"

When the sun was gone and the lobby empty, Mark pushed open the glass door and walked quickly to the man behind the counter. The man was standing alone, bent at the waist, reading a magazine open on the counter. Before he could raise his face from the page, Mark placed the barrel of the pistol against the crown of the man's head and pulled the trigger.

Bobby heard the shot. "Jesus," he whispered, and then began to count out loud quietly for no particular purpose. "One. Two. Three. Four. Five. Six. Seven. Eight. Nine. Ten. Eleven. Twelve. Thirteen. Fourteen. Fifteen. Sixteen."

The car door slammed. Bobby spun the tires on the gravel and yanked the steering wheel to the right. Mark counted the cash. Twenties in one pile, tens in another. The odd bills were stacked to the side.

"Two hundred forty dollars. Shit, that's pretty good. It'll get us to Texas. That's for damn sure."

The siren ended the sentence. Bobby saw the police car in the rearview mirror.

"Where'd that son-of-a-bitch come from?" Mark asked, like he couldn't believe it. Like he couldn't believe a police car might actually be there.

Bobby ran through a yellow light and tapped the gas. His chest pounded.

"What did you do back there, Mark?" he asked, looking in the rearview mirror.

"It don't matter," Mark answered.

"I need to know," Bobby said.

Mark turned around to see another police car joining the chase.

"It don't matter," Mark repeated.

Bobby raised his voice, "I need to know what I'm runnin' from, Goddamnit."

Both men were aware, on different levels, and for different reasons, who held the pistol and who didn't. Mark felt himself squeeze the handle.

"Put it this way, they ain't takin' me. I ain't goin', so you better haul ass."

Bobby took a slow, deep breath. A promise was a promise, he thought. Blood is blood, and you can't turn your back. Whatever happens, that's just the way it is. You gotta ride it out.

So he pushed down on the gas and the car topped one hundred miles an hour. In the darkness, down the country road, the bushes and trees passed so fast they were only shadows. The blue lights of the police car spun around, reminding Bobby of a toy he had as a little boy. It would shine with colors in the sunlight, and for a moment he wondered where it had gone.

Bobby passed a truck on the two-lane road and then another truck. He could see houses and lights up ahead in the distance. The two police cars got stuck behind the second truck, unable to pass because oncoming cars couldn't pull over in a construction area. Space grew between the chaser and the chased.

Bobby pushed the accelerator against the floorboard. He looked in the rearview mirror. Sweat eased slowly down the skin underneath his arms to the waistband of his underwear. His heart still pounded.

"Those stupid motherfuckers," Mark said, looking back over the seat, laughing like a crazy man.

The hill came so fast. The road was flat, and suddenly there was a hill. No time to slow down. No time to know until the car was in the air, the road curving to the left, and the car flew into the field, landing hard, flipping over and over, slinging mud and grass and bits of plastic until it slammed sideways into a cow and finally twisted to a hissing stop, quiet on the downslope of the hill, outside of sight from the road.

The police cars barreled past, slowing down for the hill the drivers knew would come and then turning left around the curve, the drivers looking ahead into the distance for red taillights.

Bobby's first thought was nothing. Then he knew something bad had happened, like he was sure it would.

"Mark," he said.

It was dark in the field. One of the headlights of the

car shined out away from the road and Bobby could see a cow on its side.

"Mark."

Bobby crawled out the busted window. He could feel burning on the side of his face, and his right arm hung limp. Bobby walked around to the far side of the car, and in the darkness, like a mannequin in the grass, he saw his brother's body. The shirt was yanked up over his face and his pants pulled to his knees. Dirt and grass covered a portion of his underwear and stuck to the blood from the peeled back flesh.

In the distance, Bobby could hear the sirens.

"Mark," he said, bending over his little brother.

But Mark was dead, and the promise had been broken, no matter who was to blame. It was over, just like he knew it would end, sooner or later.

Bobby felt a strange relief. A heaviness lifted from his body. Something he could not define or admit, a lonely freedom.

Bobby Winters stood and looked out across the field. He could see lights through the woods, far off, flickering as the tree limbs moved gently in the evening breeze. He began to walk toward the lights and away from the car, and his brother, and the cows. As he walked he didn't think of much, only walking. Beyond the lights he didn't wonder where he might go, or what would happen, because it didn't matter. He was alive, and Mark wasn't, and there was a reason, whether he understood it or not.

At the edge of the field, Bobby turned back for one last look. He could see the blue lights circling down the long road. He could see the one headlight from the upside-down car, and the cows, and a bump on the ground he knew was his brother. He turned and walked into the woods and kept walking until he reached a house. It was a small house, with a front porch and rocking chairs. Bobby saw a light in a back window and followed the light. He looked inside and saw a woman lying naked on a bed. Before he could decide what to think of her, a man, wearing only socks, the lady's husband, came to the bed. He stood looking down at his wife in a way Bobby had never seen before.

The man touched his wife on her leg with the back of his hand and then ran his hand slowly up to the edge of her hip. And she let him touch her, but not in a way Bobby had ever had a woman let him touch her before, but instead, in a way he couldn't possibly describe.

He knew it was wrong to watch, but it wasn't a choice. The man leaned down and they kissed. His hand slid to his wife's breast, and he squeezed gently and released, leaving his hand resting on the breast. Bobby could see her breathe. The air pulled in, the chest expanded, and the air pushed out. The man opened his wife's legs and positioned himself in between, rising above her like he was floating, careful not to touch until she guided him inside.

Bobby watched as they moved, the man floating above, the husband and wife only touching where he entered her, slowly back and forth, where she accepted him, the two looking only at each other like there was nothing else in the world worth seeing. And rising, and building, deeper, and a tiny bit deeper, until the man closed his eyes and pushed one last time while Bobby Winters watched at the window and witnessed the acts leading to the conception of James Early Winwood.

There was a sound behind him, but he didn't turn around. He didn't stop watching until the gunshot opened the night, and the bullet tore through the neck of Bobby Winters, shattering the skin and slicing through the cord, bringing Bobby to his knees, his cheek skidding down the brick wall until he was in the dirt, face down under the window. And his heart stopped.

The gunshot spewed blood all over the window. The man inside dismounted like he had taken the bullet himself and fell to the carpet in complete nakedness, leaving his spread-eagled wife afraid to move a muscle until she saw the outline of the police officer's head at the window. She jumped upright, covering her nipples with the palms of her sweaty hands.

My father told the story like he was the man at the window, knowing things he couldn't possibly know. My mind has filled so many gaps through the years it's not possible to reconstruct what my father actually told me that night after the Christmas party. We never spoke of it again.

Perhaps the single most important moment in each of our lives is the moment of conception. Thank God most of us are spared the nasty little sexual details of our parents churning away on one another. Although I'm fascinated by my father's story, I wish he'd never told me. I already had some vague feeling of oddness surrounding my creation before I knew about the Winters brothers, but now the oddness has taken form. I'm left with a trap door of anarchy shaped unfairly by events beyond my control. The fact it happened before my birth makes it no more or less unfair.

Certain cultures believe the soul of the person who dies travels to the nearest new life and takes up residence. It's a curious belief, perhaps predicated by our desire to continue, or at least exist day-to-day with the hope of unlimited life. But let's be honest, how much of Bobby Winters do you think drifted through the cracks around the window, floated invisibly into my mother's vaginal canal, and affixed to the embryo, invading like a bad smell caught in the fabric of a boy's underwear? Probably not much, but the way my dad told the story, who the hell could say what's not possible.

When I was in high school, a group of us drove to the beach for a party one Saturday night. There was this girl there, the younger sister of a friend. I'd seen her before, but she was two years younger, and two years is a lot when you're eighteen. I tried not to look at her, but there was something beyond my control happening. I was attracted to her like a mayfly pulled to a yellow dock light.

I went outside just to break away from the tension. She came outside behind me, took my hand in the shadows, and led me away without a word between us. She started to run, pulling me behind, and my heart beat like a bank robber's. We veered between two houses and ended up in the backyard next to a pool. It was so dark I couldn't see her face.

"The Prestons are in Mexico on vacation," she whispered.

I heard the snap of her blue jeans, and the sounds of undress. I tried to equalize my breathing so she couldn't possibly hear the wheeze of my asthma, so she couldn't possibly tell I was on the verge of hyperventilating, maybe fainting, and cracking my stupid head on the patio cement.

She giggled. "Take off your clothes."

My eyes began to adjust to the moonlight and there she stood, as naked and pure as anybody had ever stood, anywhere, in the history of mankind. And I felt this feeling I'd never felt before, maybe like my father felt about my mother on the night Bobby Winters watched. I don't know.

I took off all my clothes, and we walked down the steps into the coolness of the black water. I kissed her, and touched her body like a starving man. We held on to each other, and then she stopped me from doing what we had no business doing, what I couldn't stop myself from doing, and it was the last time I ever saw the girl. Even now, this many years later, when I'm alone in my bed I can think about her and touch the feeling again. Like I'm there, in the dark waters of the Prestons' pool, in the summer moonlight.

People are born with ranges of potential. One man may be born with athletic potential and, if left unfulfilled due to worldly circumstances or laziness, it may be wasted. On the other hand, the man may reach levels unreached before, taking advantage of the possibilities. I cannot hit a baseball out of Yankee Stadium. I cannot get my bat around on a ninety-five-mile-per-hour fastball. My individual potential lies in awareness. As a young child I remember sitting in new surroundings, watching. There is so much to notice if you know what to look for. So much to be aware of around you.

My mother said when she took me to a new place I wouldn't speak for at least an hour. Just looking around at movements, listening for inflection, establishing the walls of the fish tank. I wonder if my range of potential awareness has anything to do with the strange circumstances of my conception? I wonder if the feeling caused by my friend's sister was a result of the blinding darkness of the night, the quickness of the situation, or the finality of our contact? I don't know, but I'd love to see her naked in the darkness again, if only for a minute.

The first moment which I am aware of being alive is the flash of a memory. I am looking up from the confines of a crib at the face of a man with a black mustache. I can see him clearly, but I don't know who he is. The man is wearing a white button-down shirt. His hair is medium-length black. He's neither smiling nor frowning, just leaning over me like a stranger.

I've never figured out who the man could be, but surely there must be a reason the moment remains my first memory, as opposed to the moment before, or the moment after. We are forged by a handful of events from conception to death. These events, together, form the sound that life makes.

And so I was born nine and a half months from the date Bobby Winters was shot to death watching my parents on the other side of the window. Born unto this world, another soul amongst many. A tiny, cold, wet-skinned child, filled with the fear of this life and the outcry of potential. But I can't remember anything until the mustached man appeared over my crib rail. I imagine my father was both amazed and overwhelmed at the miracle of my birth. I imagine my mother was absolutely sure she would never have another child, for any reason, ever, and I was blessed at such an early age with the inability of being aware of anything whatsoever. Instead, my lungs concentrated on drawing the next breath, the simplest possible act of living, and in this simple act, set in motion the rest of my life.

two

It would be best if we could tell the intelligence of a person instantly by the size of their heads. A big-headed man has more brains and therefore more intelligence. A little-headed guy is obviously stupid and will be treated accordingly.

My mother called me Early. My father apparently tried to stick with James, but it became obvious fairly soon that James didn't fit. Oddly, neither did Early, but my mother won the battle anyway. She had a secret weapon in such battles. The weapon of indifference. Impossible to counter. Virtually invisible, but nonetheless lethal, like a small daily dose of poison. It'll wear you down until quitting seems right.

My mother was unnatural, removed, artistic, and dramatic. We looked at her a lot and sometimes she looked back, usually extraordinarily busy with some project or another. She would paint entire rooms and then paint them again, a different color, the next day.

My father would come home from work and ask, "Christine, wasn't the dining room blue yesterday?"

Usually, my mother wouldn't answer such questions. I think she believed she was truly a special person born in the wrong time and place. I called her Christine because she said it was her name, and it only seemed weird when I turned four or five years old and none of the other kids called their mothers by their first name. Around other people I would say "Mom" in a very low voice at the beginning of my sentences.

"Mom, can I have a popsicle?"

"What?"

"Mom, can I have a popsicle?

Outside I would say, "My mom likes to give me popsicles," emphasizing "mom."

My father was the opposite. I remember him as warmth, a smile. He was very human, but of course, in retrospect, I know my father's memory enjoys the benefits of death. He died in a car accident when I was eleven years old, leaving me and my mother alone like two strangers connected and disconnected from my father.

It changed me, as you can imagine, forever. One day he was there before I left for school, and then he never came back to us. I couldn't possibly forgive him. I understand it wasn't his fault. I understand he didn't drive away and live somewhere in California.

My father was hit by a train. One of those cross-cutting

events. We watch TV while somebody down the block miscarries. We eat a piece of pie while a man dies across town in a pool of his own blood. But sometimes, the events cut across our lives like the time the train killed my father while he sat in his car listening to the radio, drumming his hands on the steering wheel, with a big black train bearing down.

If he did it on purpose, it was an inefficient way to die, but brilliant. It leaves everybody thinking, would a man kill himself with a train when he could take a handful of pills, or blow a hole through his head? If he wanted it to look like an accident, he might.

I can barely read my own handwriting. After my Dad died I wrote down imaginary conversations we probably never had.

Dad: When you're having a bad dream, Early, just remind yourself it's only a dream.

Me: I don't know how.

Dad: You're smart. Just say, 'Hey, it's only a dream. I can do whatever I want because I know I'll wake up in the morning.' And then punch the monster in the nose, or light the bad man's hair on fire, or stand on the train tracks and watch the engine run right through you.

Me: Somebody told me, if you die in your dream, you die in real life.

Dad: And how do you suppose the person who told you that could know? They couldn't ask anybody who ever did it, right? Because they're all dead. You're a smart boy. Be in charge of your own dreams, real and unreal.

The story of the Winters brothers is another example

of one of those cross-cutting events. The boy could have gone to another house, another window, but he didn't. He could have died at the wreck scene, or shown up two minutes later, but he didn't. His life-ending event coincided, collided, with my life-beginning event, and nobody planned it that way.

My mother made a big deal out of Thanksgiving. It was really weird. Birthdays were uneventful. Christmas, Fourth of July, Easter, just another reason to be out of school. Most of the time she was too busy to pay any attention to us at all, but when Thanksgiving rolled around, it was a different story. We had to have all the excess, the biggest turkey in town, three kinds of cranberry sauce, mincemeat pies. It was some sort of trade-off I never really understood and still don't. But who says I'm supposed to understand everything anyway? And who says I need to figure it all out?

If I breathe deeply, eyes closed, for three full minutes, it suddenly doesn't seem so important anymore. Nothing can endear one person to another like allowing oneself to be saved. Or demanding it. Or requiring it. Vulnerable, spread-eagle emotionally, like my mother, I've remained detached and efficient the majority of my life. And like my father, I've allowed the world at times to be too much with me and prayed for the train to come. This balance, or imbalance, is the essence of my person.

Eddie Miller was my best friend from ages five to seven. He was one year younger and soft, like a chubby marshmallow. Eddie would do anything I said, follow me anywhere I went. He was getting hurt all the time, once falling off his bike in the road carrying a Coke bottle. The bottle busted and Eddie ripped a gash in his chin. Of course, he was getting the Coke for me. I was three blocks away in a tree fort, waiting impatiently for my cold Coke that never arrived.

Mrs. Miller asked me to step outside one day.

"Why did you tell Eddie there's no such thing as Santa Claus?"

I played dumb.

"Answer me," she said, louder.

I said, unapologetically, "I thought he should know it's a big lie."

The scowl on Mrs. Miller's face left a deep impression. "Well, Mr. Know-it-all, we've got one or two good Christmases left. If you ruin it, I'll whip your bottom red. I don't care who your parents are."

At the time, I didn't pay much attention to the last sentence. I immediately went back to Eddie in his room.

"Eddie, that stuff I said about Santa Claus wasn't true. He's alive, and he'll probably come see you for two more Christmases. After that, you're on your own."

Eddie didn't listen. He just stood up and peed in his toy box like he always did. He told me I could pee in the toy box, too, if I wanted, but it never seemed right so I didn't do it.

My other best friend was Jake Crane. He was a year older and the complete opposite of Eddie Miller. Jake's mom was wild as hell and good-looking. I knew she was good-looking even before I knew the difference, mostly by the way my dad acted around her.

Miss Crane was black-headed and wore tight pants with high-heeled shoes. She laughed and smacked her red lips. There were rumors she took a shower with Andy Bradshaw's brother who was in college, but who knows if that was true.

Jake's grandmother lived in his house. She was the meanest woman I've ever known. The first time she back-handed Jake's little brother I froze in fear. The kid was lifted from the floor and rolled across the room, his nose bleeding, like a boxer. And for nothing. Just changing the television station. That's how they lived, in between the sexual energy of their mother and the violence of an old woman.

Jake stole cigarettes from his mom. He taught me how to cup the cherry so nobody could see it at night. One time we were in the dark outside his mom's bedroom window smoking one of those long, skinny cigarettes when she came into the bedroom. Neither of us said any-thing to each other as she took off her shirt, reached around to unhook her bra, and stood before us naked from the waist up. I had never seen such a thing, and truthfully it scared the shit out of me, but I didn't turn away. Thank God she went in the bathroom to take off the rest of her clothes or I might have passed out in front of Jake Crane.

People wanted to be near Jake in elementary school. There was a power about him. A loose energy field. But it was the best he'd ever be. At sixteen, all of his good days were mostly behind him, his loose energy dissipated into the air of the world. It's like an airplane. It has to reach a certain speed to lift from the ground and take flight. That was the reason no one before the Wright Brothers could invent the airplane. Such speeds weren't possible. Once they were possible, gliding in the sky was a given. For Jake Crane, he never quite reached the speed of lift.

three

At around age four, I started having dreams of a scary circle on the floor. I know it sounds ridiculous, but I'd awake from those dreams in terror. The circle was black and a few feet across. In the middle of a perfectly good dream, the circle would appear on the floor. I never knew if it was a hole or what. I only knew the monster was the fear itself.

Other people running around in the dream couldn't see the circle. I'd yell. I'd warn them. One time I pulled a kid away from the hole. Nobody ever stepped inside. Besides being weird, there were no signs the circle was evil or dangerous, but I knew what it meant. I knew what the black circle held.

My grandfather was a very patient man. He was from a time before the world became too busy to enjoy, and we went fishing sometimes in a pond out in the country. I was maybe five or six. Paw-Paw would spend hours gathering together two cane fishing poles, red-and-white plastic corks, crickets, cheese sandwiches, and a little cooler with two grape sodas. The ritual was part of the event, as satisfying to him as the fishing itself, and I would watch him thread the thin, clear fishing line through the tiny hole in the hook, the knot just right, imagining the tug of the fish swallowing the kicking cricket.

The pond had lots of turtles. Paw-Paw let me push the boat away from the pier and the little motor would take us to parts of the pond my grandfather was sure the fish would bite. I learned catching a fish wasn't really important. For Paw-Paw, the importance seemed to lie in the silence. Watching a turtle sunning on the bank. Staring at the red-and-white plastic cork floating on top of the coffee-colored water. The beauty, for my grandfather, was in the wait. For me, the wait was agonizing. It would always be. It was hard to understand anything except the joy of seeing the cork bob, and the line pull tight, and the unfortunate little fish dangling from the hook through his lip.

It must be frightening for the bream. His wet google-eye scanning for something familiar, but instead seeing big round faces, and grape soda cans, and the hand that wraps around the body and holds tight while the other hand unhooks the hook from the lip.

My grandmother was very different from Paw-Paw. Nanny was small and quick. She laughed hard and found certain things funny I didn't find funny at all. She cooked and sang little songs in the kitchen, laughing sometimes at herself, and finding a rhythm in the work. Paw-Paw took her fishing with him once, and afterwards they both agreed never to do it again. Apparently, she talked incessantly about turtles, and ripples in the water, and all the other things in which my grandfather found such solace. However, there was no solace to be found in the discussion of these things, only in the things themselves, and besides, Nanny told me, "One stick of dynamite in that stupid pond, and we could eat fish for a year. What's the point in trying to trick the silly things into biting a cricket on a hook?"

My grandfather heard her make that particular statement as we sat at the kitchen table eating biscuits and honey for breakfast. The old man rolled his eyes at me and sipped his coffee from the saucer. After his cup was empty, he had a habit of lifting the saucer to his mouth and drinking all the coffee he'd spilled from the cup. The low slurping sound sticks in my memory and makes me wish I could see my grandfather one more time.

When I was seven years old, I had my worst asthma attack. I was with my grandfather just after we pulled the boat from the pond. It was springtime, and all the weeds were in bloom. For some reason I decided to run around the other side of the pond to see a bullfrog I'd seen from the boat. I couldn't find the bullfrog, but when I arrived, there was a wheezing in my chest. It wasn't until I ran back to my grandfather that the tightness began. It was like the devil had wrapped his big red hand around my heart and started to squeeze, and squeeze, until there was no room for the air to go inside.

My grandfather saw the look on my face. He dropped the cane poles where he stood and carried me to the car to get my inhaler. The car was parked under a shade tree, and he put me on the backseat. I'd had asthma attacks before, but the one at the pond was the worst. I was afraid I'd die, and as my grandfather got down on one knee next to me at the car door, he started to pray.

"God, hear me pray now. Today we need you to put your hand on Early in the backseat of this car here. And loosen the grip on his lungs so he can breathe your air freely. And if you feel the need, take me with you in return, but I'll stay here if you want, and I promise to never sneak another sip of scotch whiskey."

He spoke the words so slowly it was like the world had fallen into slow motion. I watched the leaves on the trees up above swaying gently in the breeze, and I started to feel the panic subside, and with the panic gone I felt my chest loosen. I could breathe again.

On the ride home, Paw-Paw kept looking at me in the rearview mirror, afraid to take his eyes away from either me or the road for too long. It was probably the day I began to struggle with the idea of God. Had He truly put his hands upon me, as my grandfather prayed, and loosened the grip, or instead, was my grandfather's prayer itself soothing and calming, allowing me to escape the panic and provide time for my body to return to normal? And what kind of God would care to trade my life for my grandfather's secret whiskey sips? It just seemed enormously confusing, and my abilities of perception—usually so helpful in crawling inside the minds of other people—actually seemed to complicate the idea of God.

Nothing in my young life really compared to the day my father died. Up until then, things were moving along fairly well. Besides Eddie's mom yelling at me about Santa Claus, the occasional asthma attack, and the lingering questions concerning my conception, life was pretty good. By age ten, I'd already made a conscious decision to be average. It seemed much easier than the alternative. The truly gifted, original, unique people in society must be prepared to suffer and fail as miserably as the ungifted, lazy, and idiotic. We like to pretend our culture embraces originality, but in truth we embrace repetition, familiarity. We only appreciate originality in hindsight, when it's no longer original.

It's much easier to decide to be average. The expectation level is mild. Disappointments are infrequent. I imagine the suffering of unacceptance is highly overrated. How easy can it be for a person to know they're better, but endure ridicule from a lesser man, a lesser man defending lesser men? Don't get me wrong. I'm not some self-suppressed genius. I'm probably average anyway. I just cut short the discovery process. I was unable to figure out how God could take my father away and leave me with my mother. It didn't make any sense at all, from any direction, so I figured hiding amongst the average was the safest place to be. I wish I could say I had a cold shiver up my eleven-year-old spine the moment the train killed my dad. I was at school, probably chasing somebody around in the dusty schoolyard during P.E. class, or picking my nose in the back of Mrs. Eubanks' room, or thinking about something stupid when it happened.

When the principal came to the door of the classroom I thought I was in trouble for pushing Missy Jesup earlier during a softball game. It wasn't much of a push, but I was afraid she'd told on me and the principal, Mr. Walker, might be at the door on Missy's behalf. I was afraid I was in trouble. Instead, my father was dead.

My mom stood beside me in the principal's office with her hand stiff on my shoulder.

Mr. Walker said, "Early, I need to tell you something."

The door was closed and the window shades were shut.

"Missy Jesup exaggerates," I said.

Mr. Walker got down on one knee. He was a tall man, and on his knee we nearly looked eye to eye. I remember he wore a white button-down shirt. The sleeves were rolled up, and his tie was loosened a little at the neck. The skin around the collar was red and bumpy, like chicken skin.

I don't know why my mother didn't tell me. I don't know why she just stood there and made Mr. Walker say the words.

"It's not about Missy Jesup, Early. It's about your father."

That's when I felt the world turn a little bit.

We looked at each other hard for a few seconds, and I could see the redness in his eyes.

"No," I said, "it's not about my father. It's about Missy Jesup. I pushed her."

Mr. Walker looked up at my mother. The hand on my

shoulder didn't twitch. It was like a deadweight, a sock full of brown sand.

"There's been an accident, Early. Your father passed away."

I remember thinking, "Passed away? What a strange way to put it. Like he vanished into thin air."

I managed to say, "I don't understand."

I didn't look up at my mother when she said directly, "Your father died today. He got hit by a train."

Mr. Walker and I were still face to face. Like some sort of interpreter, he nodded his head and said softly, "It's true."

My father was dead. I'd seen him that morning before I went to school. And the next time I saw him he was dead in a coffin, propped up like he'd fallen asleep watching baseball on television. I wanted to touch his shoulder, wake him up, remind him it was time to throw the football in the yard. But he didn't wake up, and they buried him in the ground.

A few days after the funeral I went into my mother's room. She was sitting up in bed reading a book. We looked at each other for a long few seconds.

I finally said, in a flat voice, "I just don't understand. Why would God, the same God who made us, kill Daddy with a train?"

My mother didn't answer. She just looked at me.

I said, "When I get older, will I understand it better?"

My mother continued to hold her book open on her lap like she hoped the conversation would be short.

"Probably not," she said.

The words seemed to pass slowly from my mother's mouth to my ears and then inside me. They were very final, but I couldn't leave it.

"So when kids grow up, they don't figure all this out, about God and dying and that kind of stuff?"

"No, Early, they don't. I guess we just become more comfortable with the mystery."

My eyes wandered down to the floor. My father's shoes were next to the bed. Mom leaned over to look down at the shoes herself. There was a space between us. It had always been there, but before, when my father was there, he and I shared the space my mother required. It didn't seem so big back then.

"I wish that day never happened," I said.

Mom said, in a slightly different voice, "Save your wishes, Early. You'll need 'em later. Life is for doing, not undoing, and wishes are for the future, not the past. Your father loved you."

Did you ever see a kid drawing a picture? And it looked so easy? The face of a clown, or maybe the wings of a bird, and you thought, "I can do that. It's like riding a bike, or eating. Anybody can do it."

And then you tried. The wings didn't look like wings at all, but more like brown walls. The clown looked like nobody.

And then it occurred to you. That kid can draw. That kid can do something I can't. That kid can draw.

four

After the death of my father, I fell into a moral tail-spin, grasping at right and wrong, ultimately choosing the rebellion of invisibility. But before I settled on invisible and average, I managed to break a few laws.

We used to take our bicycles to school. Eddie's mother wouldn't allow him to ride to school with Jake, and Jake considered Eddie to be just this side of retarded. So I alternated between the two. Eddie and I stopped at the drugstore most mornings. I stole candy.

I didn't just steal the candy haphazard and random. I spent entire days drawing diagrams of the store. Locating mirrors, cameras, the viewpoint of the pharmacist in the back and the fat lady at the front on the register. I made Eddie repeat the plan over and over.

"I stand by the candy bars and keep my eyes on the

door."

"And how long do you stand in that spot?"

Eddie squeezed up his face.

"I forget."

"Five, Eddie, five. Count slowly. Five Mississippis. By then I've got the property in my pocket. If you stand there too long staring into space they'll get suspicious."

Eddie said, "Why don't we just pay for the candy bar? I've got a dollar."

I would say, very condescendingly, "You just don't get it, do you? It's the plan, Eddie. It's the point. Remember? We agreed. Everything should belong to everybody."

Eddie thought a moment. "Does that mean somebody could just take our bikes outside and ride away?"

I didn't have an answer for his question.

The next day, at the drugstore, we put the plan into action. It had already worked twice before, but on this particular day I decided we'd go for the mother lode, two Snickers bars.

We walked around the store very awkward and stiff. Looking at mirrors, pretending to size up hairbrushes or some other such thing. The adrenaline rushed through my veins like a raging river. The only thing that kept me from vomiting was the requirement to look composed in front of Eddie. He picked up a tube of shampoo, and his hands shook wildly.

Eddie whispered, "I don't really want a Snickers."

"Don't back out on me now. We've come this far."

I took Eddie by the elbow and led him toward the candy. The janitor, a black man older than my mother, was mopping something off the floor near the front door. He glanced in our direction and went back to mopping.

I positioned Eddie according to the diagram. One by one I checked each point of interest. With my eyes directly on the eyes of the fat lady stocking the shelf behind the counter, my hand reached out and fumbled for the candy bars. I shoved them quickly into my pocket. It felt like my heart would explode.

From behind, seemingly out of nowhere, I heard the black man whisper, "It ain't worth it."

I turned and saw the janitor mopping the floor only a few feet behind me and Eddie. His eyes were looking downward. I couldn't speak. I thought of running but my legs wouldn't move me, so I just stood there. Eddie's mouth was actually open. He was white as cotton.

With his eyes still looking downward, the man whispered, "Put 'em back."

I'd never been so afraid in all my life. All he had to do was raise his voice, or look up at the fat lady, and we'd be caught. Maybe go to jail in a police car. Who knows?

I slowly slipped the candy bars out of my pocket. Keeping my eyes on the black man, I put the candy back on the shelf and waited to see what would happen next.

The janitor pushed the mop a few extra times across the linoleum floor and turned away. He left us standing there. Eddie was the first to move and I followed him outside, never to return to that drugstore again in my life.

I've often thought about that day. If my plan had been successful again, and maybe again after that, would I have lost the fear of being caught? Would I have slipped over the edge and learned to steal for a living? Probably not, but who really knows? The small daily twists and turns through the maps of our lives are sometimes just as important as the big dramatic forks in the road.

Years later I read in the newspaper about kids making elaborate plans to kill people at school. They drew up diagrams, considered evacuation routes, and planned it all down to the detail. One kid was the leader, and one kid was the follower. They couldn't have been more nervous than me that morning standing by the candy with Eddie Miller, but at the end of their day those boys murdered twelve kids and then stuck guns in their own mouths. Somewhere along the way they must have gotten extremely lost.

The first completely naked woman I saw was in a magazine. Jake Crane stole two dirty magazines from Mr. Henderson's garage. We'd been in the garage a few days before to help the old man move a worktable. In the corner was a stack of *Playboys* and *Penthouses*. After my encounter at the drugstore I was hesitant to plan a theft, but this was different. They were just stacked up in the garage. It's not like they were worth much on the open market, but to two twelve year olds, the value was high. Curiosity and hormones drove the scheme, and Jake took the wheel.

The old man didn't leave home much. We staked out the place after school for three days in a row. Documented his comings and goings. Finally, on the third day, the old man drove away and left the garage door wide open. Jake waited for the car to turn the corner and took off like a shot. There was nothing subtle or sly. Snatch and grab, run like hell to the spot in the woods, and stare at vaginas.

We both acted like we knew a lot about the damn things. This many years later, from experience, I don't think anybody knows a lot about the damn things. Not even women. And yet our mothers have 'em, and babies come from 'em, and God knows what else goes on in there. But that day in the woods, turning the pages of Mr. Henderson's dirty magazines, I was transfixed, and so was Jake.

It didn't make a lot of sense, but I knew we had to see a real one. The opportunity presented itself when Jake's cousins came to visit. Two sisters, Mona and Janine, seventeen and eighteen years old.

It was nighttime. The cousins, their mom, and Jake's mom were all talking in the living room. We waited until the right moment and slipped outside. Jake and I climbed on his roof and positioned ourselves directly above the bathroom window. The window was small but strategically located above the shower.

Mona was the first to enter the bathroom. We laid our bodies at a downward angle, faces peeking over the roof edge, just a few feet from the small rectangular window. We counted on the darkness outside, and the bright light in the bathroom, to make us virtually invisible.

Mona messed with her hair and looked in the mirror very intently at a bump on her chin. She pulled off her t-shirt and dropped it to the floor at her bare feet. In an instant the white bra was on the floor next to the shirt. I could feel a slow rise in my jeans and a dryness in my mouth. No words passed between me and Jake.

Mona walked from the mirror to the tub, her smallish, taut breasts barely moving as she walked. She turned the shower on and looked upward at the window, but didn't flinch. We held our positions, the edge of the black shingle shoved up against the bridge of my nose.

And then she dropped her pants to the floor. And before we could wish for more, the cream-colored panties were down. The brown patch was there to be seen for an instant, and then Mona stepped into the shower.

We watched her wash herself and I remember being amazed at how little time she spent touching the good parts. It almost seemed she didn't understand their importance, or certainly there would have been more attention to the details. The part where she dried herself with the white towel, as I recall, was the best. Mona squatted down a bit to reach far places and ran the towel through the crack of her ass. The pressure in my pants reached new levels, like an unscratchable itch deep below the surface in some primal region of my loins. I closed my eyes for a few seconds and hoped Jake didn't notice.

I'm not sure of the exact moment, but at some point I became uncomfortable watching the girl. She went back to the mirror and spent more time examining the bump on her chin. She stepped away and looked at her body in the mirror, clearly unhappy with her hips. It became apparent that Mona wasn't just perky tits and a patch of brown. She was a person. A person in the bathroom, believing she was alone, looking at herself in a time of privacy, and I wondered if anyone had ever spied on me in such a time.

Mona left the bathroom. The window had fogged up slightly, so we moved our heads to find clear spots and waited for the next girl. Jake's mother came through the bathroom door. There was no protocol for such a situation. I waited for Jake to speak, and secretly wished he wouldn't. Since seeing Miss Crane topless that fateful day, my imagination had painted vivid pictures in my mind.

Miss Crane flipped off her shoes. She unsnapped the button on her pants. Jake lifted himself up, and I immediately followed suit. We sat that way for a while.

"Let's steal a beer from the cooler."

"Okay," I said.

And we did. A Budweiser. I tried not to let my face show the nasty taste, swallowing the cold liquid quickly and handing the beer back to Jake. After just a few sips my head felt light. We brushed our teeth with our fingers to get rid of the smell and sat down in the living room with the women. I couldn't look at Mona. She wore a yellow t-shirt with no bra underneath, and a pair of shorts. Just minutes earlier I'd watched while she washed and dried herself. Knowing she was so close, with no window between us, no contrast in darkness to hide my face, I felt an odd mix of dirty and good. Unable to look at Mona, but at the same time surrounded by her presence.

Twenty years later, in the grocery store, I ran into Mona in the cereal aisle. She was fingering a box of Captain Crunch. I barely recognized her. She was at least a hundred pounds heavier, and those perfect little breasts, three children later, hung like dog teats from her chest.

I continued to smoke cigarettes off and on, separate from any physical addiction, but learning to like the idea of smoking alone. I'm sure my mother knew, just like I'm sure she knew about the beer, and the dirty magazines hidden in my closet, and sneaking out my window at night to terrorize the neighborhood, ringing doorbells and lighting things on fire. But she never said a word. She never started the first conversation about any of it. At the time it seemed purposeful, cold, like she'd be damned before she paid me the least ounce of attention. It wasn't until many years later I figured out she simply wasn't capable.

I entered high school in this state of misidentification. I didn't fit any of the standard categories, and I wasn't strong enough to start my own. It seemed everybody else had a better idea of the world than I did, and on the first day, the very first day of high school, I was tested. After weaving through the lunch line in the unfamiliar cafeteria, I found an empty table. A goofy-looking freshman named Peter Jankins sat next to me. Although I secretly longed to belong to a group, Pete Jankins wasn't exactly what I had in mind. He was even goofier than me, acne between his eyes, big shoes.

A few minutes into our delicious meal, two guys sat down across from us. Seniors. Big sons-of-bitches. One of them wore a football letter jacket. The other just smiled at us, reminding me of the time I watched the neighbor's cat push around a lizard until the lizard gave up all hope.

After a few minutes of me feeling like the lizard, the guy with the smile on his face turned up his chocolate milkshake and filled his mouth. He rose slowly from the chair, leaned over my tray of lunch, opened his mouth, and spit a stream of milkshake down upon my Salisbury steak and brown gravy.

The guy leaned back and sat down in his chair, content to watch the lizard. I looked at Pete, his mouth agape, and then looked at the guy across the table. If I did nothing, just let it happen, it would continue to happen my whole life, in one form or another.

Time seemed to slow down, but there was really no time to think. I just shoved my tray as hard as possible across the table, stood, turned my back, and walked away at a crisp pace. As I walked away, I expected to feel a large hand on my shoulder. Maybe a fist against the back of my head. But I didn't look back. I just walked outside, turned the corner, and wore a baseball cap to school the rest of the year, hoping I'd never see the smiling guy again, and if I did he wouldn't recognize me. I stayed out of the cafeteria, and on at least two occasions had the opportunity to hear Pete Jankins tell the story like I was David and the milkshake guy was Goliath and I killed the giant, when really all I did was push away my lunch tray as a minimal display of defiance and flee the scene.

Although I was pleased to have taken such action on my own behalf, spending the rest of the year in hiding helped contribute to my desire to become invisible and my decision to remain average. I started to seek people to save, because in retrospect, after the death of my father, I was never really able to build strong friendships, and everybody knows, if you're unsteady, become a savior.

ho am I?

The universal question, for the high school student in particular. Repeated like a mantra in the teenage subconscious, a low hum below the surface, everpresent, annoying yet elusive. I loved baseball, but I wasn't good enough to play in high school, so I didn't fit with the baseball players. My grades were average (fittingly), and therefore the National Honor Society skipped me. For a while I tried to pass as a drughead, or whatever the hell they call themselves, but I didn't care much for drugs. I remember actually putting pepper in my eyes one morning before school so I'd look stoned.

Monica Houston said, "What's wrong with your eyes?"

I smiled stupidly and mumbled, "What do you think?"

She squinted to see. "It looks like bits of black pepper."

I panicked and defended myself too lucidly. "It's not pepper. That's stupid. I smoked a big joint on the way to school."

"With who?" She asked.

I hesitated an amazingly long time. "Nobody."

Monica Houston said, "Let me make sure I understand. You smoked a big joint on the way to school by yourself and somehow ended up with black pepper in your eyes."

It was too much work to be a drughead, especially since I didn't like drugs, so I fell into a sort of no man's land. The high school abyss. But all that changed the day I met Kate. She became my focus. At first from a distance, and then later with no distance between us at all.

There was a graveyard down Dugger Road, tucked away under big oak trees with Spanish moss hanging from the limbs like long gray beards. During the day the sunlight would cut through in sharp spears to the ground below, succeeding only briefly, allowing the earth to stay moist and the gravestones to turn a dark shade of green. But at night it was the scariest and darkest place in all the world.

Who knows where or when the legend of Onionhead began? He was described as a large man, some sort of caretaker of the cemetery, with a bald head and huge black boots. Some said he was grotesquely deformed, one eye lower than the other, with six fingers on his right hand. The image and description was formed through years of eyewitness accounts and outright lies, but if you were sixteen years old and taking your first midnight ride down the long twisting road to the cemetery, almost anything was believable.

I'd heard about Onionhead since grammar school. He didn't become real until we were able to drive. Going out to the cemetery on a Saturday night with a carload of teenagers was one of the things to do. At the time we had no idea why we did it. It was an early challenge of manhood, I suppose. Facing fear to impress each other, or more importantly, to impress a girl. I can remember my first visit to that cemetery like it was yesterday.

Jake somehow got permission to use his parents' van. At the time, I was working as a stock boy at a local grocery store. My shift ended at nine o'clock on Friday nights, when the store closed. I saw the gold van sitting out in the parking lot. There was no plan to go look for Onionhead. The plan was to drink peppermint schnapps and smoke cigars. Beer had long since lost its luster for us. We'd moved to a level of importance in the world worthy of peppermint schnapps and Swisher Sweets. The van smelled like a barroom.

Joey Shannon sat in the passenger's seat. His nickname was Bluto. He was round and unshaven, with a unique ability to shotgun a fourteen-ounce Old Milwaukee like it was nothing. He was the arm wrestling champion of the western world and often took on challengers at strange times.

The other guy in the gold van was Toad. I never knew his real name. His nickname was such a perfect fit it never crossed my mind he might have another name. He was the guy who always sat in the corner. One night he rode home in the trunk of a girl's car because there wasn't enough room inside. Toad didn't seem to mind.

We all drank from the same bottle and tried not to make a face when the warm schnapps burned our throats. We inhaled cigar smoke and blew smoke rings when the van wasn't moving. As lost as I was in the world, it felt good to be young. There is a beauty in youth that exists all alone. A freedom that can never be recaptured.

And then Bluto said, "Let's go out to Onionhead."

The suggestion may have lingered and died, covered up by a new idea, but Jake immediately followed with, "Hell yeah, let's go out to Onionhead."

We made a U-turn on Front Street and headed toward Dugger Road.

"I've seen that big bastard," Jake said. He was the best cusser amongst us. Jake's cuss words seemed to fit in his sentences like they belonged. He took a drag from his cigar and held his arm out the window for the ash to blow away.

We went further and further out of town. There were no streetlights and the houses were set back from the road, offering just a twinkle of light through the woods as we sped past. Jake turned down the radio when we pulled off on the dirt road. The van moved slowly and then we turned down another skinny dirt road. Jake switched off the headlights. I couldn't see anything except the cherry ends of the cigars, like little Christmas lights inside the van.

And then we stopped. I wondered if anyone else could hear my heartbeat. There was total silence. Bluto opened the passenger door and the dome light covered us in a dull yellow. We piled out of the van and closed the doors gently. My eyes adjusted to the darkness enough to see we were standing in a circle in front of the vehicle. We were only a few yards from the entrance gate to the graveyard.

Jake whispered, "Follow me. And be quiet. Don't talk until we get where we're going."

Toad asked, "Where we going?"

"You'll know when we get there," Jake said.

In a line we walked through the gate. I could see the shapes and shadows of gravestones. There were no lights in any direction, just the moon. I was third in line, behind Bluto, who was behind Jake. I followed the big white t-shirt in front maybe fifty yards, until Bluto stopped. Toad bumped into me from the back.

I heard Bluto whisper, "Jake? Jake?"

He turned to me and said, "Where the hell's Jake?"

Nobody wanted to be the first to run.

"Listen," Toad said.

We listened. There was a distant rustling of leaves. And then silence again. I was more afraid than the time in the drugstore, but not so afraid to be the first to run. The first person to run would hear about it the rest of their lives. They'd hear the story told over and over in class, at the football game, forever, about the time they ran.

The silence was broken. The horn on the van blasted. I felt Bluto brush past me as he took off. I ran. There was the sound of footsteps all around. The horn continued to blare in the night. I expected to feel a hand grab my shoulder, a six-fingered hand, and pull me back to the cemetery. I expected to die.

I passed Bluto and arrived at the van ahead of the others. The first thing I saw was Jake standing at the driver's door, his arm inside the van on the horn, holding the bottle of schnapps with his other hand, laughing. I stopped and then felt the force of Toad's body hit me from behind, knocking me to the ground face-first. He fell over the top of me, and the dome light in the van came on, shining a yellow light on Jake's laughing face.

It was quiet again.

"Y'all are a bunch of titty-babies," Jake said. "There ain't no Onionhead. It's all made up. My cousin made it up."

"How do you know?" Toad asked from the ground beside me.

"There ain't no tooth fairy either, Toad, or Santy Claus," Jake explained.

I stood up. Jake handed me the bottle of schnapps, and I took a swig. It was the first time I noticed I no longer held my cigar. I looked back the way we'd come to see if I could see the little red dot of light on the ground. There was nothing to see.

We laughed. Knowing there was no Onionhead was almost disappointing. Bluto opened the other bottle of schnapps, and we lit up a new round of cigars.

Overcoming the myth, rising above Onionhead, made me feel a little more like a man. It was a separation from all those kids at school who still talked about it like it was real. Those kids who lied about ever going to the cemetery in the first place.

"I've got an idea," Jake said.

Even though I felt more like a man, and even though I was glad to shatter the Onionhead myth, I was ready to leave that place and go back to town.

Jake continued, "Let's go back and get Lori and her

two friends. One of us will stay out here and hide. We'll get the girls to walk out to the middle of the graveyard, and the guy can jump out of his hiding place and scare the holy crap outta the girls. It'll be classic."

Jake liked Lori. I'd never met her two friends before. Jake said, "One of the girls is a year older, seventeen. She's good lookin'. I don't know about the other one. I think she's a Fatty O'Patty."

Bluto asked the question, "Who's gonna stay?"

Jake answered, "I'd stay, but I've gotta drive the van. The rest of you can draw straws."

It was hard to argue with drawing straws. We each had a sixty-six percent chance of not having to stay. The odds were good I'd be sitting in the comfortable van for the ride back to town. Jake picked up little sticks and turned his back to measure two sticks the same size and one smaller. When he turned back around he held in his hand the tops of three sticks. "Who goes first?"

Bluto grabbed one and held it up. "You're safe," Jake said.

There was just me and Toad. It seemed right that Toad should be the one to stay. He was the runt of the litter.

"You pick," Toad said to me.

I took a deep breath. It appeared fate would be on my side. Toad seemed destined to lose and stay in the graveyard.

I pulled the stick on the right and held it up. It was short. Too short.

Jake held up the third stick. He looked at me and said, "You're short, big boy."

He handed me a bottle of schnapps and said, "Follow the same path y'all walked before. About twenty yards ahead of that spot, where you stopped last time, you'll find a big headstone. It's the biggest one out there. You can't miss it. Sit behind it. We'll be back in thirty minutes. When you see my lights flash, you'll know we're comin'. Wait until we get the girls all the way there before you jump out. And then scream."

Toad said, "This'll be great. I bet Lori pees her pants."

I was slightly in shock. Somehow I'd forgotten Onionhead didn't exist. I'd forgotten my newfound manhood. I just stood there while they piled in the van. The headlights kicked on and illuminated the cemetery. Far in the back I caught a glimpse of a big headstone. The van backed out, turned around, and left me alone in a graveyard. I stood still and listened to the van until I couldn't hear the engine. I began to walk slowly in the direction of the big headstone, quiet with my steps, holding the bottle by the neck to use as a weapon if necessary. Every ten yards or so I'd stop and listen. I tried to imagine where the van might be. How close to town? How many more minutes until the headlights would be back at the gate?

My heart pounded. I took deep breaths and held my eyes as open as they would go. I listened for any sound. Finally I could see the big headstone. It was as tall as my chest. Instead of getting behind it, I decided to sit down in front. I figured I'd have time to hide when the lights showed up down the dirt road.

I squatted with my back against the stone. I could feel the coolness through my shirt. I set the bottle down next to me and wondered again where the van might be in the journey. What if they couldn't find the girls? Maybe it was a joke. Maybe they weren't coming back. My mind shot in quick circles, trying to decide what to do if they didn't come back. Where to go? I sat there for what felt like a long time.

And then I heard a sound. It was just sound. A noise where there had been none before. It could have been a bird on the ground, or a rabbit in the leaves. And then I heard it again. It was louder the second time. A footstep, and then another, off to my left. There was nothing to see. I looked down at my shirt and thanked God it was dark blue and not white, like Bluto's t-shirt. The sound stopped. It stopped long enough for me to believe I had never really heard it in the first place. And then I heard it again. A step, and then another step. Someone else was in the graveyard. Someone was walking in my direction.

My hand reached out and took hold of the neck of the bottle. I could run, I thought, but where would I run to? And what if I fell? I might run right into a gravestone, or a tree, or the fence.

There was another step, and then another. To my left, moving closer, maybe thirty yards away, three first downs on a football field. I looked toward the front gate. How long had it been? My hand tightened on the neck of the bottle, still half-full. I lowered my head so my white face wouldn't show in the darkness, my chin against my chest, eyes cutting hard to the left.

Slowly, a figure appeared. At first it was nothing but a movement in the black dark. And then it was an outline.

Ten yards to my left I saw a person appear. A very large person. Dark clothing with a white head. A large, bald, white head. He was looking toward the back of the graveyard, his profile etched in the black background. It was Onionhead. It was no myth. It was no concoction of teenage lies. It was a very large man with a very large head. A head like a big onion.

To this day I can see the figure, the arms down at his sides, the milky-white hands at the ends of the sleeves, the enormous head resting like a glow-in-the dark ball on his broad shoulders.

His head began to turn very slowly toward me. He seemed to be scanning the cemetery for anything out of place, anything disturbed. As he turned further, I could see something wasn't right with him. Something was off-center, distorted. I was sure he could hear me breathing, or smell the cigar on my clothes or the peppermint from the bottle. If his face made a full turn, if his eyes met mine, I decided I would run. I would run toward the gates. Whatever happened would be better than feeling the hands of Onionhead upon my clothes. If he took one more step in my direction, I would go.

The lights. Through the woods I saw the headlights of the van. Onionhead turned to the lights, and then turned to me. It was only two seconds, maybe three, that we looked at each other, but God knows it felt like eternity. I ran. I left the bottle and ran toward the gate like an arrow shot from a bow. I didn't look back.

The van turned the corner of the dirt road and stopped at the gate, the headlights like spotlights shining and showing the way. I didn't care if anyone laughed. I didn't care if the girls whispered at school about my blind run through the cemetery. I had seen Onionhead. I had come face-to-face with the legend of Onionhead and lived to remember it all. At least that's how I felt as I ran in the direction of the gold van. But as I got closer I saw Jake, and Toad, and Bluto, and three girls climb out and stand next to the van. And the next thing I knew I was there with them. I recognized Lori, and the fat girl, but the other one, the seventeen-year-old, she was something else. She was different.

And that's how Kate first saw me. Running like a wild man out of the blackness of a midnight cemetery with my face contorted in pure fear. I turned around. There was nothing behind me. No gigantic white-headed man. No murderous Onionhead.

"What the hell, man?" Jake said. "You were supposed to wait until we got 'em back there. Are you stupid?"

To this day I can recall the feeling of not being able to take my eyes from Kate's face. I just stared at her. There was something besides beauty. Something you had to look for. It took me years to figure it out. A brokenness underneath.

and walked three or four blocks. I kept my car far behind until she turned down a driveway. I couldn't see the house as I drove by. It was set back far in the woods. The dirt driveway and the section of town made me think it wasn't the fanciest house. An old, short-haired dog stood guard at the entrance of the property near the end of the road. One of his ears was chewed clean off and the other stuck up to the sky.

My sophomore year ended, and I spent the summer working construction. The alarm clock woke me up every morning at four-thirty. I had to be at Huey's house by five. He was the foreman. I rode in the back of his brown pickup truck almost an hour to the job site. I'd lie with my back against the truckbed and watch the sky turn from black to gold. It was my first construction job. No place for the hardworking. Most guys exerted themselves as little as possible trying to maintain the appearance of working. I never really figured it out, I guess. I busted my ass in the summer sun from the moment I arrived until I climbed in the back of Huey's truck at the end of the day. Even Huey told me once to slow down before I killed myself, but like I said, I never really figured it out. It seemed to me there wasn't much point in working if you weren't working hard. And it didn't matter what anybody thought, including Huey. I didn't compare myself to the other men. How hard I worked had nothing to do with them at all. Mostly they watched me and talked about how fast their cars would go or the size of their dicks.

I worked construction off and on for years after that summer. I learned two things. I learned I worked harder than most people, and I sure as hell didn't want to spend my life listening to some lazy hungover bastard talk about his pecker, or his car, or both. Huey and the boys did more to motivate me to go to college than anything else.

It was harder to find opportunities to see Kate during the summer. On weekends I'd ride around in Jake's van, inspired by the possibility of seeing her outside McDonald's or in the car next to us at a red light. As the months passed, time began to lift Kate onto a pedestal, approaching mythical status, without a flaw. I'd see her, and she'd smile, and I'd wonder if she knew we'd end up together. And then I'd wonder if such a thing was possible. She seemed so far above me, but at the same time she seemed so vulnerable, and the vulnerability slowly took on the appearance of something else. Something romantic, exciting, even sexual.

At the end of the summer, just a few weeks before school was set to start, I got my chance. A kid had a party. His parents were out of town. Jake knew the guy, sort of, and we showed up on Saturday night after a bottle of cinnamon schnapps and a pack of Jake's mom's cigarettes. We got there late, and the place was already out of control. Jake's girlfriend, Lori, was there, and I hoped Kate had come with her.

Lori was sitting on the swing. After a few minutes of conversation, I casually asked, "Is Kate here?"

Lori smiled a drunken smile. "You like Kate, dontcha?" she asked.

I took a swig of the warm schnapps and tried to think of an answer. Nothing came to me, so I just sat there like no question had been asked.

Lori kissed Jake on his sweaty neck. She smiled again.

"Kate's in the car. She drank too much and got sick. We put her in the backseat."

I'd noticed Lori's car parked out by the road. Now it was just a matter of separating without being noticed, slipping away and walking alone down the long driveway.

A few minutes passed.

I said convincingly, "I left the cigarettes in the damn van."

"You don't even smoke," Lori said.

"I smoke when I feel like it, and I don't smoke when I don't feel like it. It's not the cigarette's decision."

Nobody said anything.

"I'll be back in a minute," and I moved off slowly like a cow from the herd, easing down the path.

The driveway was dark. I slowly passed Lori's car, trying to see if Kate was sitting up in the backseat. From behind the car I lined up the back window with the front window and the lights in the house to catch a silhouette of her head. There was no silhouette, so I put my face to the window and tried to see. The outline of the shape of Kate's body resting on the backseat slowly formed. I tapped lightly on the window, a bold move for me, but clouded in the warmth of the schnapps and Kate's state of intoxication.

There was no response. I tried the driver's door and it was unlocked. The dome light came on, revealing Kate lying on the backseat, face up, eyes closed, asleep. Or at least she looked asleep. She very well could have been dead. Her hand rested on her stomach. Her fingers were small, with the nails chewed to the quick. I'd never noticed before. It struck me as strange. What would a person like Kate worry about?

She was wearing shorts. The way one leg was lifted and the other was down on the floorboard, I could see the edge of her panties between her legs, white in the light from inside the car. I'd never looked at a girl so closely in all my life. The lines on her face. The tiny hairs where a mustache would be. The rise of her breasts beneath the thin red shirt, and the smooth skin of her belly between the edge of the bottom of the shirt and the top of the short pants.

It was a glorious experience, and in the glory of the moment it occurred to me we were alone, and drunk, and she was so near. I closed the car door gently and caused the darkness.

I waited a long time until my eyes readjusted. From my place in the front seat I looked down upon this girl who occupied nearly every minute of my mind. My hand was so close to her body. Just a move away from touching skin, or resting on the fabric of her shirt, or God knows, sliding my finger through the space left open to the warm panties underneath.

I took a big breath. The air inside the car was hot and stagnant. For some reason I thought of the morning I stood next to Eddie in the drugstore, stolen candy bars in my pocket, waiting. Kate's breathing was deep and consistent. I closed my eyes and tried to smell her. The clean, perfumed smell of a girl, even in a hot car, passed out drunk, rising above all else.

"Kate," I whispered, hoping she would answer, but there was nothing.

I looked back toward the house in the distance. There was no movement along the driveway. The sounds of laughter were far off, nowhere near the car, or me, or Kate, or my hand reaching between the front seat and the back and descending so slowly downward until the fingertips touched the softness of the skin, and moved gently, and it is wrong, and I know it's wrong, and I cannot pull my hand away, and there's a sound outside the car, and I jerk my body around to face forward, and close my eyes like I'm asleep, and when the car door flies open I act confused, blinded by the light.

"Get your asses up," Jake said, and a few minutes later, when no one was looking, I put my hand to my face and it smelled like Kate, and I wondered again how anyone like her could chew her fingernails to the quick.

With Lori's help, Kate woke up and lifted herself to a seated position. I climbed in the backseat beside her for the ride to take her home.

"My head hurts," she said.

Jake turned up the radio, and I wished he'd turn it down again.

"Turn off the radio, please," Kate said, and I looked at her. She saw me looking. "I look like shit," she said.

"No, you don't."

She was seventeen. I was sixteen. She would be a senior in a few weeks, and I'd be a junior. Jake slowed down and then gunned it through a stop sign. We were almost to Kate's street. I waited for Lori and Jake to start a conversation in the front seat between themselves.

"Why do you bite your fingernails?" I asked quietly.

She looked at me, straight into my eyes, the street-lights passing outside. It was a look I hadn't seen from her before. Like I'd gotten a glimpse at something I wasn't supposed to see. Like she was surprised I'd noticed any-thing about her fingers. But there was no answer. Just a stare, and then Kate noticed where we were.

"Stop here," she said.

"What?" Lori asked.

Kate raised her voice, "Stop here."

"Stop," Lori told Jake. "She wants to get out here."

Jake slowed down. "But her house is up the—"

Lori pushed Jake on the shoulder like he was being inconsiderate.

"What?" he asked, not catching on to the signals of a woman.

Lori raised her eyebrows. "Stop here, please."

The car rolled to a stop. Kate got out with no words and closed the car door.

"Go," Lori said.

Jake asked, "You want me to leave her on the side of the road?"

Lori whispered, "Just go, Jake. I'll tell you why."

And the car rolled away, leaving Kate Shepherd on the side of the road. I looked back through the rear window. She stood, bent over slightly, looking at the ground near her feet. She was under a streetlight, and the shadow thrown by her body spread out on the pavement like a tall ghost. When we were far enough away, Kate started to walk.

Lori explained, "She doesn't like people to go to her house."

"Why not?" I asked.

"She just doesn't. I don't know why. I always pick her up at different places. I think something's the matter with her father. Robin says he's crazy or something, and the house is like a shack, all rotten, with dogs everywhere."

I looked back through the rear window, but we'd already turned down another street.

"What about her mother?" I asked.

Lori stuck her head in the backseat. "You do like her, dontcha?"

I was weak. The night had taken its toll. "Maybe," I said.

"What about her mother?"

"She never talks about her mother. I don't know."

"Does she have any sisters or brothers?"

"I don't think so. I think she moved here from Oklahoma."

After that night my focus became even stronger. Kate filled all the empty places in me. She rounded the rough edges and gave me purpose. She didn't know it yet, but Kate was my girlfriend, and I had plans. Detailed, elaborate plans, considering every possibility, I could save her from all that was bad and protect her from the world. And who I was, who I would become, would have a starting point, a structure, a method of measurement. The difference between me and Kate would narrow into nothing.

seven

People who make bad grades in school sometimes like to say they're bored, or it wasn't challenging. The implication is clear. They made poor grades because they were smarter than everyone else, including the teachers.

I don't know how my smartness compared with other people, but I know my grades weren't too good. Of course, I spent a large percentage of my junior year in high school creating vivid sexual fantasies and searching for shortcuts. I'm not sure why there was such a contrast in my drive to work hard on a construction site and my quest for shortcuts in the classroom, but the contrast existed and I didn't do anything to figure it out, despite the motivation for a college education caused by moronic co-workers.

Mr. Lee taught Biology. He was a small Asian man.

Back then we thought all small Asian men were Chinese. We called him China Lee. I think he was from Vietnam, or Korea maybe, I'm not sure. His accent was strong and his fingers were thin like pencils, holding up things in front of his special safety goggles.

"Okay, cass. Weed pwoblem numbar fwee."

It took Jody Gardner two weeks to understand Mr. Lee well enough to respond to his name at roll call. He was marked absent every day.

The first two tests didn't go well. I needed to make a B on the semester exam to pass the class, so I decided to cheat. On a piece of paper about the size of a business card, I wrote, in super-tiny letters, the answers to every question in the damn book. I messed up once and had to do it again, but finally, in super-tiny writing, I had everything I needed to know.

I taped the piece of paper lightly to the backside of my thigh, just above the hem of my khaki shorts. The idea was to position the paper under my leg in the chair so I could simply move my leg to the side an inch and see the cheat sheet as needed during the exam.

Mr. Lee was like a prison guard. He roamed around the room watching with those beady eyes. Every time I looked up he was watching me, waiting, somehow knowing my plan, like he'd gotten inside my house and watched me write the tiny cheat sheet, twice.

Out of sheer frustration I started reading the questions on the test. To my amazement I knew almost all the answers. Answers I surely hadn't learned in class in between sexual gymnastics and inappropriate thoughts.

But there they were, coming out of my pen all over the page. Fill-in-the-blank. Multiple choice. Bing, bing, bing.

In my plan to cheat I'd learned I didn't need to. Finding the answers in the book, identifying them as somehow important, and writing them down in such a focused and concentrated fashion burned the answers in my mind. They were there to stay, and more importantly, I learned a study method that served me well throughout my higher education. Prepare to cheat, and then don't.

I was left with a peculiar dilemma. Beneath my leg was proof of my immoral intentions, but I never looked down. Under Mr. Lee's burning eyes, how was I to get up and walk away? I'd managed, by fidgeting and sweating, to disconnect the cheat sheet from my leg. The tape was folded over and the evidence was left between my bare leg and the wooden seat.

People began to stand and walk to the front of the class, but Mr. Lee's eyes stayed on me. I'd finished the test. There were only two questions I couldn't answer. I'd never looked down, but who would believe me? Who would believe I could make an A on the final exam after making F's on the other tests without cheating? I'd created a sticky quandary.

Everyone was gone but me.

"Meester Weenwood, au yuu feeneshed?"

We looked at each other. I wondered what was running around in that crafty mind of his. Had he seen me sneak my hand down to adjust the paper under the leg? Had he noticed the glistening of sweat on my upper lip in anticipation of the misdeed? The room seemed overly warm. I felt a touch of asthma and moved my hand to feel the bulge of the inhaler in my front pocket.

I held the exam in my hand and reached it out in the direction of Mr. Lee, who stood to my right, twenty feet away. I held it there, waiting for him to move, or not move, or whatever came next. I half-expected police officers to arrive and take me into custody, but instead, Mr. Lee walked over to my desk and took the exam from my hand.

He studied the papers, looking occasionally at me over the top of the page. When he finished, Mr. Lee lowered the exam from his face. I held his stare.

"I didn't cheat," I said.

Mr. Lee's mouth tightened. His chin seemed to rise slightly. There was not the tiniest hint of a smile.

"I know," he said.

We were only a few feet apart. There was no way to snatch the cheat sheet and shove it in my pocket, or eat it, or anything else. I was left in the shaky hands of fate, with my eyes still locked upon the eyes of China Lee. I stood slowly from my chair, prepared for a small piece of paper to fall at my feet, taking the eyes of Mr. Lee with it to the floor.

But there was no such feeling. And his eyes stayed with mine. And I turned and walked, hands in pockets, out the door into the crowded hallway. Around the corner I reached my hand and felt the back of my leg. And there, hidden beneath the edge of my shorts, stuck to my sweaty leg, was the cheat sheet. When I'd sat down, the pants leg edge had pulled naturally further up the thigh. And when I'd stood, the edge naturally hung down lower, covering the evidence of my evil scheme. Fate had rewarded me and I made a D+ in biology. Maybe I was just bored.

I had a job as a waiter that year in a nice restaurant downtown. I found it difficult. Instead of being able to lower my head and work my ass off like I'd done in previous construction jobs, suddenly I had to talk to people. What's more, I had to pretend like they were interesting and important, and I cared whether they wanted regular or low-fat ranch dressing on their stupid little salads.

The balance was difficult. It kept my mind off Kate, but not for long. She looked tired sometimes. I'd watch her across the baseball field sitting in the aluminum bleachers doing her homework. She'd look out across the green field at nothing for long stretches. Sometimes she'd shut her eyes and take a deep breath.

Everything she did was very mysterious. I'd never been around women much, except my mother, and I don't think my mother was typical of women in general. I wasn't comfortable asking my mother questions about anything at all, much less sex, or menstrual cycles, or the hopes and fears of teenage girls.

Instead I mostly watched Kate and tried to learn things. I practiced conversations with myself. I tried to imagine situations we might find ourselves in. I took notes on small pieces of paper, like my cheat sheet, in case I ever got up the nerve to call her on the telephone. Notes of things to say to fill the ungodly dead spots in a hypothetical conversation. As the year drug on, my obsession with Kate became familiar, like a favorite shirt. It wore well and aged one day at a time.

I continued, along with everybody else, to struggle with identity. I embraced the role of savior but slowly came to recognize a savior must have someone to save, or you're really just a stalker. It's hard to tell what Kate knew or didn't know of my obsession. The sight of a certain face, Kate's face, made me feel physically different. I didn't need to actually see her. I could think about her and the chemicals would squirt out and leave me drunk. It was hard to understand why it didn't happen to everybody else who saw Kate. People seemed to pass all around, even speak with her in the hallway, or sit next to her in the classroom, and then walk away unfazed.

In the middle of my junior year there was a school dance. I generally stayed away from any school-related functions, social clubs, or any other organized activity for that matter. I might have been average, but there's a big difference between being average and being a conformist. A conformist is an average guy sitting around the room with a bunch of other average guys. I was average alone.

I went to the dance because I knew Kate would be there. She was on a date with a guy named Jeff Temple. I'd seen him around her before. Jeff was a senior, played on the baseball team, and had no appreciation whatsoever of the value of Kate Shepherd. I could tell by the way he walked with her, and the way he smiled at all the right times. He just didn't know.

I wasn't really mad at him. How could I be? I was more frustrated than anything else. Frustrated that neither one of them could recognize the obvious when they walked into the dance together. I sat over in the corner with Jake and Lori, hidden in the dark recesses of the high school fringe. Kate seemed to be having fun, but I knew she wasn't. She acted like she liked Jeff Temple, but I knew better. It wasn't possible at the time to understand the woman I believed I knew so well didn't really exist. I'd created my own person. Built, like the bride of Frankenstein, to be exactly who I wanted her to be. That's the problem with love. The chemicals make you drunk. People in love shouldn't be allowed to operate heavy machinery.

He left her alone for awhile to stand next to his buddies. I wanted her to see me. I stood and walked out of the dark corner into a patch of light.

"You don't belong here," I wanted to tell her. "Let's leave. You and me. Go drive around. Go sit together at night in the aluminum baseball bleachers and talk about nothing. Just hold hands in the dark, and you can tell me what I already know," I wanted to say.

But we never say things like that in the real world, only in the movies. And in the real world, the boyfriend comes back before Kate sees me, and they walk off together, and I go home and masturbate.

It all came down to one night. The night of Kate's graduation. I'd squandered the entire year, never gathering the nerve to ask her on a single date, or call her on the telephone. The fear had extended beyond the natural boy/girl fear into a category of being afraid the real Kate Shepherd couldn't measure up to the Kate Shepherd inside my mind, the one that caused the release of all those chemicals. But I'd decided I couldn't just do nothing. I couldn't let her graduate, and maybe slide out of my life without something. Anything. I wasn't even sure what it would be.

It ended up being one of those nights we remember our entire lives. There was a party at David Ansley's house after the graduation ceremony. Kate was laughing and drinking. I'd heard stories of her drinking too much and worse.

From the other side of this party I watched Kate go from happy and laughing to alone and stoic, and eventually to drunk and angry. It was the talk of the party. She cussed out Jeff Temple by the pool and he broke up with her in front of the world.

For everyone else, it was high school drama at its best. For me, it was painful. Through the past year I'd melted into Kate Shepherd, and as I said before, the difference between me and Kate narrowed to nothing. I could see the brokenness. It wasn't just a random act. It was the night of her graduation. It was everything coming together. It was Jeff going to college when she wasn't. It was being dropped off a block from her home. It was the knowing and not knowing.

I followed her out to the road in front of David Ansley's big house, but lost her in the darkness. I called out her name but didn't get an answer, and wondered if she recognized my voice, or if she was passed out in the woods somewhere.

Back at the party Jeff Temple didn't seem to have a care in the world. He drank a cold beer and laughed with his buddies. I watched him grab a girl on the ass with a cigar hanging from his mouth.

I wanted to beat the shit out of him. I wanted to make him stand before the crowd, blood trickling from his nose, tears in his blue eyes, and say, "I'm sorry, Kate. I was wrong. You're too good for me."

But of course I didn't do it. Of course I just watched him from across the party as long as I could stand it, and then left alone to find Kate. There was still no answer on the street. I figured she might have gotten a ride home. One of her friends must have cared enough to get her safely to her bed.

I drove across town in the direction of Kate's house. It was midnight, and I had no real plan. Of all the situations I'd envisioned, this wasn't one.

I parked out by the road, near the mailbox. The dirt driveway snaked through the center of the wooded lot. Far back in the lot I could see a single yellow light. There were a few houses on the street, but everything was quiet. I got out of my car and closed the door gently. This was it. The moment I'd waited for. She needed me. I could tell her why. Everything would come together for both of us. She needed saving, and I could explain the reasons, and then I could proceed with the plan.

I put my hands in my blue jean pockets and started down the driveway. I could barely see the road at my feet as I twisted around one curve and then another. The yellow light came from the porch of a small wooden house. It hadn't been painted in twenty years. A scruffy white dog crawled from beneath the porch. Her teats were engorged and hung below a fat belly. I could hear the whimpering of puppies. I stopped to wait for the dog's decision to bark or not to bark. She wagged her tail and smelled my shoe.

I stepped up on the porch. The boards creaked under my feet. There was a dull glow from the single yellow bulb. It wasn't until I reached the door that I realized it was only a screen door. Inside was dark like a cave. I pressed my face against the screen and tried to see anything at all. The outline of a piece of furniture, a couch, anything.

In a low voice, almost to myself, I said, "Kate?"

There was no answer. No sound of any kind inside. I put my hand on the handle of the screen door and pulled gently to test whether it was locked. The door opened a few inches, the hinges making a rusty squeaking sound.

In the silence my ears were raw for sound, listening for any noise. From below, on the other side of the door, came a deep gutteral groan, low and long. I froze with my hand on the handle of the door.

The noise stopped and I waited. It came again, the prelude to something violent.

From inside the room I heard a man's voice, "He won't bite."

I couldn't see anything in the direction the voice had come. With the light outside, I knew the man and the beast at my feet could see me clearly, the outline of a stranger testing the door at midnight.

A lamp flicked on inside. In an instant I could see what I could only imagine the second before. At the base of the screen door, sitting on a dirty welcome mat, was a stout, red-faced pit bull with a brown leather collar. In a reclining chair in the corner of the room sat a man with one leg elevated. He wore a short-sleeved gray shirt and a pair of old dark pants, unbuttoned at the waist. We looked at each other.

The man repeated, "He won't bite," but the tone of the statement was neither friendly nor unfriendly. The words were tired, spoken out of habit.

"Is Kate here?" I asked, my hand still holding the door between me and the world inside the room.

The man's foot was swollen and black. I could see crust on the top of the foot, the big toe white against the darker colors. The man's other foot rested on the floor next to a bottle of clear liquid. It looked like a liquor bottle without a label.

The smell from inside was hard. Old cigarette smoke, dog hair, and sour milk, maybe. There was no ceiling fan or air conditioner running. The wall of hot air started where my nose touched the screen. The man looked to be maybe fifty years old. He'd been sitting in the dark waiting for God knows what. I couldn't imagine Kate in such a place. I just couldn't see her walking through that room, passing the man in the chair, stopping to open the screen door, stepping around the pit bull, smelling the smell.

The man kept his stare on me. "Kate ain't here. She left," he said, in the same flat voice as before.

"Where'd she go?" I asked, and noticed his eyes drift slowly away to a place on the wall, just an empty place on the wall, no framed picture or even a stain to look at.

"Where does anybody go?" he said.

The man moved slightly in the chair and winced in pain. I looked down at the dog at my feet and when our eyes connected he made his favorite sound again. A deep, slow growl from a place inside his thick chest.

The man took both hands, placed them on either side of his knee, and lifted up the foot high enough to move it a few inches. He settled back in the old chair.

I asked him, "What happened to your foot?"

"I shot a hole in it," is what he said.

His answer begged more questions, but suddenly I didn't care. I came for Kate. The old man, whoever he was, didn't matter. If he wanted to die in that chair in the dark it was his business, not mine, and not Kate's anymore either.

"When's she comin' back?" I asked.

The man reached for the bottle next to his chair. He lifted it to his lips and took a swig. There was no reaction to the clear liquid rolling down his throat, and just by the way he swallowed I knew the man had taken so many swigs like that in his lifetime he couldn't tell you anymore if it burned or not. He was a dead man, kept alive by inertia and the gravitational pull of millions of years of evolution. He was less alive than dead.

"She ain't comin' back, boy. Not this time. She's gone for good." From his voice I could tell he believed it was true.

"How do you know?" I asked.

The man smiled, or at least it looked like a smile, mostly on one side of his face, and he said, "You must not know Kate too good, do ya?"

If the dog hadn't been there I'd've flung the screen door open and stood above that old man. I'd've told him he didn't know what I knew, and he never would, and whatever he thought he knew about Kate was bullshit, and he'd never see her again because she'd be with me, and I wouldn't allow it. But there was a pit bull at the door, and a wall of hot air, and the feeling that if I ever went inside that room I wouldn't be able to leave. I'd be like the old man in the chair, staring at a place on the wall and hoping to die before the sun came up.

eight

Nobody saw her all summer. I drove past the house late at night, but eventually even the yellow porch light through the trees burned out. Lori heard Kate moved back to her mom's house in Oklahoma. Jeff Temple told people she always talked about going to California. He also told people Kate gave him a blow job behind the concession stand between innings of the high school baseball playoffs. After I heard him say it, the picture in my mind was like a snapshot. Jeff in his baseball uniform behind the brick wall encircling the air-conditioning unit. He's peeking over the edge of the wall with his hat backwards and baseball pants to his knees. Kate's bent over at the waist, her mouth around him, a buzz in her head from the two mixed drinks she had earlier in the car. I have to remind myself I wasn't there.

I've got very little recollection of my entire senior year of high school. Blurred images of classrooms, waiting tables in the evening, skinny dipping with the wonderful sixteen-year-old girl that night on the coast and feeling guilty about it the next day like I'd cheated on Kate, even though Kate had gone away.

I stayed to myself, mostly. My mother and I passed each other in the house. I wondered why she didn't date. Christine wasn't the type of person to mourn her husband's untimely death by remaining a widow, but outwardly she seemed to have no interest in men, or anyone else for that matter. She was a complicated person. Creative and driven, yet off to the side, lonely for a particular unseen reason.

I thought about my father often. Right after he died I found a photograph of him in a bottom drawer. As my memory of my father slowly eroded, the photograph took the place of real memories. It was the way I'd remember him my entire life. Smiling, his head turned a bit to the side like he was considering something mischievous, wearing a t-shirt, extremely alive. When I thought of him, I thought of him this way, and it always made me feel good.

"What happened to that girl?" my mother asked. I was sitting at the kitchen table in my underwear, eating a bowl of cereal. It was the first time my mother ever asked about Kate or any other girl.

"What girl?" I asked, looking down into the bowl.

"Wasn't her name Kate?" Christine asked.

I turned and looked at my mother where she stood by the refrigerator. It was the first time I'd looked at her, really looked at her, in an awfully long time. She seemed older.

"You wouldn't like her," I said.

My mother answered, "It doesn't matter whether I'd like her. It only matters whether you like her. That's kinda the point, isn't it?"

It seemed like a very profound thing to say. I was a week away from driving off to college and my mother decided to say something profound in the kitchen.

"Aren't you worried I'll fail out of college?" I asked.

"No," she said.

Between words, the kitchen was quiet. There were no bellowing televisions or radios in the house. No sounds of traffic in the neighborhood.

"Aren't you worried I'll piss away my money on beer and road trips?"

"No," my mother said.

"I mean, I'm eighteen years old. I'm driving away to college in a few days. Into the den of temptation. Aren't you worried I'll do something stupid?"

"Not really," Christine said. "Why would you start now? You're a smart kid, good with your money, you'll find your way around."

She was standing, leaning against the refrigerator, her arms crossed over a long faded blue night shirt, no bra.

"Do you ever think of Dad?" I asked.

She seemed to study me, and then smiled just a little bit. It was almost like she didn't want to do it. Didn't want the smile to get the best of her, and when it did she waited for it to come and go, her mouth slowly melting back to the way it was until there was no smile left.

"Sometimes," she said, and I knew it was true. I knew he slipped around the corners of her mind like he did with me, and I wondered what he looked like to her. What pictures she held in her memory of my father.

"Dad told me a story once," I said. "A story about two brothers robbing a motel, and one of them gets shot outside our bedroom window."

Christine didn't answer. I could see her mind had drifted free to someplace I couldn't go, a place only she and my father were allowed to go, and now it was her place alone.

I interrupted, "What are you gonna do here by yourself when I leave?"

"Same things I do now," she said.

A week later I loaded up the car to go to college. Christine left earlier that morning for some important appointment, probably scheduled just to avoid saying goodbye, and so I sat in the car in the driveway alone. I backed out, looking at the house where I grew up. Looking at my bedroom window.

In just a few minutes the car was on the highway. I rolled down the windows, turned up the radio, and started to get a certain feeling. It was the entrance into my time of selfishness, a time of free flight, between the dependence of childhood and the responsibility of age. At the moment, I didn't have the understanding to describe the feeling in words. Like so many things in this life, freedom can't be appreciated until later, after it's gone.

I found a niche in college. The stupid high school categories didn't exist. There were people from all over the world, and they seemed self-contained, more interested in standing out than fitting in. The lines between independence, fear of the future, and loneliness faded slowly, until I began to see myself in the mix.

My grades improved. In the evenings I worked at a barbeque restaurant. My clothes smelled like hickory smoke and sauce. I had a roommate who failed out after the first semester, and then another roommate who just disappeared one morning. He was there in the bed when I went to class, but when I got back he was gone. He left behind a can of Pork N Beans and one sky-blue sock. I never saw the guy again. I threw the sock in the trash and waited two weeks to eat the beans, in case he came back. His name was Barrett, Barrett Kinard I think, or something like that. I remember he wore a pair of strange rubber booties in the shower and over explained a toe fungus problem he'd had since childhood.

After the first few weeks of newness, I felt like I belonged in college. The library was vast and quiet. Between the circle of buildings, long sidewalks cut through patches of bright green grass, girls sat cross-legged on wooden benches, and towering oak trees spread shade. It was really a beautiful place to be, and I stayed there my freshman summer and into my sophomore year.

When I went home, Christine seemed happy to see me, but after a day it usually wore away and then it was like I'd never left. My room was exactly the same, which seemed strange to me. I'd changed, but my room, the place I'd fallen asleep so many nights, had the same posters on the walls, the same baseball pillowcases, and the same smell. I wondered if my mom ever sat on the edge of my bed and thought about me. Probably so, but we couldn't talk about it, and who'd want to anyway.

Eddie Miller was a year younger. At the beginning of my sophomore year, Eddie became my new roommate. He was lazy and funny and mostly unfocused. When I went to work, he went to the library. When I went to sleep, he went to the bar down the street.

"You're gonna fail, Eddie."

"Naw," he said, and smiled, lying on the couch in the middle of the day watching a soap opera. He wore shorts and a pair of white socks.

"Hey, remember that girl you used to like in high school?" he said, out of nowhere.

I still carried her with me. I hadn't seen Kate for almost two years, since the night of the party. I hadn't heard her voice. Sometimes, when I walked across campus, I'd see a girl up ahead and I'd think it was Kate Shepherd, and I'd follow her and it wouldn't be. It would be another girl instead, a girl who didn't even really look like Kate, but it would get me thinking about her and wondering where she might be.

I pretended not to remember who he was talking about. "Who?"

"That girl, Kate, the one who got drunk at David Ansley's party and disappeared."

Sitting at the old, beat-up dining room table, I flicked a piece of french fry across the wooden tabletop. It spun to the far edge and came to a stop hanging on the cliff, half-on, half-off.

"What about her?" I asked.

"I saw her last night," Eddie said, his mouth covered by the brown square couch pillow.

"What?" I asked.

"I saw her last night at the bar next door to Nicky's, up the street. She was fucked up. Could barely walk. Whatever happened to her anyway?"

I teetered on the edge. To ask another question would pull me into the reality of finding Kate Shepherd, maybe saving Kate Shepherd. Or I could just let it go. Go to work. Spend a few hours at the library. Get up tomorrow and make it to class on time as always.

"I think she had a black eye," Eddie said, watching TV as he spoke.

I had always wanted to touch her face. To hold it in my hands.

"A black eye," I repeated.

"Yeah. She looked pretty bad. Whatever happened to her anyway?" he asked again, not really expecting an answer.

I thought about it for a little while. "I don't know," I said. "I don't know what happened to her."

Eddie's eyes slowly shut like cat's eyes, and then opened up again as he floated between sleep. The show he was watching had something to do with rich people living in a very exclusive town, and a serial killer who stalked only women with red dresses.

"How can you watch that stupid shit?" I asked.

Eddie mumbled something I couldn't understand.

Somewhere in the world, in a foxhole, a soldier was glad Eddie Miller wasn't watching his back. He was a good-hearted guy, but fourteen hours of sleep a day is just too much for anyone.

It was dark outside. I threw the book bag over my shoulder and headed in the direction of the library. I knew I wouldn't stop there. I walked past the library steps, turned left down the side street, and ended up at the front door of the bar next to Nicky's. It was just a hole-in-the-wall. A long wooden bar with fifteen or twenty stools. There were two pool tables in the back and a side area with tables and chairs. The smoke from a million cigarettes soaked into the walls. Beer and urine, perfume and onion rings. It was a college bar, the early crowd already in their seats. I found a small table in the far corner and sat with my back against the wall.

At the bar sat a guy and his girlfriend. They talked about people they knew and drank beer out of big, cold mugs. He didn't look at her as she spoke, but she almost always looked at him, like he might get away if she didn't pay enough attention. As she drank down the beer in front of her and ordered another, the girl's voice got progressively louder and louder and the guy joined the conversation less and less. He stared off into the distance.

Two big white guys and one skinny black man shot pool to my left. The black man was older, maybe fifty, and leaned over the table to line up his shot, a cigarette hanging from the side of his mouth. The smoke caused his eyes to narrow until it looked like he was closing his eyes on purpose to shoot a blind shot. He wasn't as good as the white guys thought he was, but I sat in my chair and watched him win game after game anyway. Money changed hands.

I recognized a few people in the bar. Just enough to nod my head. Whenever a figure would appear at the door, my head would swing around to look. But Kate wasn't there. Maybe Eddie was wrong. Maybe it was somebody who looked like Kate. What would she be doing there anyway?

It was dark outside. I'd had all I could stand of the drunk girl at the bar telling a story about the day she almost drowned at the beach. By the end of the story I wished she had drowned. Maybe her boyfriend could find some peace. I grabbed up my book bag off the table and left the barroom.

Outside the door, to my right, were a few restaurants and other bars. It was fairly well lit, with people roaming around outside. To the left, the street headed into a more residential area. I went left and planned to cut across the railroad tracks back to campus and then to my apartment on the other side.

A police car passed and the red-headed officer eyed me. I walked down the sidewalk, cracked and broken with roots pushing up from underneath, and thought about the old saying, "Step on a crack, break your mama's back." What a terrible thing to tell a child.

Up ahead I saw the dark figure of a person sitting on the curb of the street. She was huddled over, her arms wrapped around her bent knees, her face turned to the side, resting cheek-down on the top of one knee.

It was a girl, or a woman, with dark hair and some kind of dark, flowing dress. As I got closer I could hear her humming, more like a lyric mumble, and she rocked her body forward and back slowly.

I got behind her, only a few yards away, and stopped. Was it Kate? It looked like her from the back. But I couldn't see her face and I couldn't make out the words she hummed. Next to her was a small bottle, and next to the bottle, in the light from a passing car, I saw a glass pipe.

She said in a low voice, "It's the only color I know."

Was it Kate's voice? It sounded like it. I moved closer and leaned my body over hers. A car passed, and I could see part of her cheek and the edge of her chin. The rest was covered by brown hair hanging down.

There was a part of me that wanted badly to walk away and not know. The part that never missed a class, and showed up early at work, and knew Eddie would fail. The part that balanced my checkbook, and looked forward to my time in the library, and secretly liked the way my boyhood room never changed. But Kate had been with me all along, and I couldn't make myself walk away without knowing.

She said, "He held it in his hand. I saw it." And it sounded less like Kate because she said it drawn-out and slurred. I wasn't sure how to feel about wishing it was Kate, or wishing it wasn't, or hoping it was someone else lost in this big world. And I wasn't sure if I was still a savior, but I remembered the man in Kate's house that night, sitting in the darkness, his foot propped up and rotten, waiting for something to happen. He was probably dead by now.

"Kate?" I whispered, the same as I had the time she was passed out in the back of Lori's car.

"Is that you?" I said.

She didn't respond, just kept rocking. Kept humming.

So I reached my hand down to pull back the brown hair. I touched it, and pushed it back off her face. I held it that way until another car passed, and in the few seconds of light from the headlights I saw it was Kate Shepherd, the girl I'd thought about for so long. Alone, her eye black, sitting on a street curb talking to no one, a crack pipe by her side.

There wasn't much thinking to do. I'd been through it a million times in my mind. I knelt down, put my arm under her knees, the other arm on her back, and lifted the girl off the ground, my book bag on my back. She didn't flinch. She just put her face into my shoulder, and I could feel the low hum against my skin under the fabric of my shirt.

nine

It's the nature of this round world, spinning around and around in circles, eventually everything comes back to you if you only wait. Kate came back to me, and I carried her across the campus that night. Her bones were light, but even so, by the time I reached my apartment the muscles in my arms were burning.

I put her down on my bed. Eddie was out for the night and his bedroom was dark. I sat down in the chair across the room from her and stretched out my arms on each side, feeling the burn slowly dissipate. It was dark in the room, and quiet, with the only light coming from the kitchen. Kate's breathing was low and the mumbling had stopped. She was asleep like a child, completely, with no cares and no idea where she slept and who watched.

In my mind, like I said before, I'd rehearsed a million

times the moment like the one on the street when I picked up Kate and took her away, but after that moment of gallantry I hadn't really considered what would happen next. Now she was here, in my bed. The moment of gallantry was over. My arms didn't burn anymore. This girl, a girl I really barely knew, would wake up in my room. She might not even remember my name. Should I take off her dress and put on a t-shirt and a pair of my shorts? Where should I be sitting when she opens her eyes?

I sat in the chair and just let my mind spin like the world. It was done. She was still pretty, thinner than I remembered, but with the same gentle face and presence. It didn't matter where she'd gone the night of David Ansley's party until I saw her sitting on the curb. We were together like I knew we'd be.

I heard the front door open and close around two-thirty in the morning. Eddie was home. I hadn't slept all night. No part of me wanted to sleep. I saw him walk past my bedroom door on the way to the bathroom. He sounded like a racehorse pissing on a cookie sheet. It went on and on until I couldn't believe any man's bladder could hold so much beer. On the way back down the hall Eddie stopped at my open door. He craned his neck inside to see me sitting in the chair. He turned his head a click to see Kate in my bed. I could smell the burnt smell of cigarettes and spilled beer from ten feet away.

Eddie entered the room quietly. We still hadn't spoken. He stood by the bed between me and Kate, looking down at her. I rose from the chair and stood next to him.

"She's beautiful," I whispered.

Eddie didn't say anything. He looked at me, and I could see in his face he didn't agree. I could tell he was confused about the situation, the girl in my bed, and the fact I'd gone and found Kate at the bar next to Nicky's. He didn't see her the way I did. Maybe nobody would. But for the first time, the very first time, it was clear to me I saw Kate Shepherd physically different than other people saw her.

Eddie went to his room and closed his door too hard, the way drunk people sometimes do. I sat back down in the chair. When I woke up and opened my eyes, Kate was looking at me from her place on the pillow. The morning light from the window was a deep yellow. Her eyes were brown like I remembered. A rich brown, the darkness of chocolate. We looked at each other for a few seconds, and then a few seconds longer. It lasted so long I wondered if one of us might be dead, but I was afraid to move. Afraid of what she might say, the first words that might come from her mouth. Finally, finally, she smiled. It wasn't much, just a tiny upturn of the mouth, but it was a smile. No doubt about it.

And then she said in a voice I could barely hear, "Early Winwood."

She remembered my name. To hear her speak it was the best possibility. It allowed the moment to float forward, the potential to remain unlimited. Maybe it was better than I'd imagined. Maybe she came looking for me. Maybe it was no natural coincidence her world crossed mine outside a bar on that certain night.

"What are you doing here?" she whispered, childlike.

"You're in my apartment. You're in my bed. I carried you here."

The expression on her face didn't change, and we were staring at each other again for impossible periods of time. But as the minutes passed, the discomfort of the silence left the room, steadily, until there was no discomfort at all. We just looked at each other, and I stopped trying to figure out what she was thinking, or what she might say next.

"Where are your parents?" she asked.

"My mom's at home. My father is a writer in New York City," I said.

For the life of me I don't know why I lied. I'd never said such a thing to anyone before. As soon as it left my mouth I wished it was never said, but there didn't seem to be a way to take it back or explain it. The lie hung between us. It occurred to me she thought we were at my house back home. She didn't even know what town she was in.

"Where do you live now?" I asked.

Kate's face on the pillow didn't move. Her words were certain.

"Here," she said.

More time passed. Maybe five minutes. Maybe more. I can't be sure.

"Where's your stuff?"

"I don't know," she said.

I reminded Kate where I'd found her the night before. Her eyes drifted from me to the window and then back to me like she was searching for a memory, found it, and brought the memory to her lips to speak it.

"There's a house down the block from there, a yellow house. My suitcase is upstairs."

I stood from the chair and left the room. The yellow house was where she said it would be. A girl from my business class passed me on the sidewalk. It would be the first class I'd missed all semester.

I knocked on the front door. There was no answer. I knocked again. Still nothing.

I tried the doorknob. It was unlocked. The house was a wreck inside. A rolled up carpet rested upright against the far wall. Ratty clothes, towels, and trash were strewn across the floor. It wasn't the remnants of a party the night before. It was old trash, the smell of neglect and decay. A house uncared for.

I didn't call out. I turned up the stairs and walked slowly, listening for any sound. I stopped at the top of the staircase. Still no noise inside the house. The air was musty and stale, like an attic. I moved slowly into the first bedroom to the left. In the corner, on a thin, stained mattress, was a body. The body of a man asleep on his back, bare chested. He was unshaven, one sock on and one sock off. Next to the mattress was a bent aluminum can with the tell-tale black residue on top and a pack of open restaurant matches.

The room stunk of human odor. Clothes were scattered on the floor. There was a hole the size of a fist through the sheetrock near the man's head and a splattered stain on the ceiling. I was disgusted at the idea of Kate inside a place such as that. Anywhere in the house. Anywhere near the man asleep on the piss-stained mattress.

"Where's Kate's stuff?" I said.

He didn't move. He didn't even twitch. He didn't jump up, startled the way a normal person would be startled by a stranger standing in their bedroom. The man's mouth was open, and I could hear his body sucking air inside him, despite everything.

I raised my voice, surprised by the angry edge, "Where's Kate's stuff?"

The man began to open his eyes, struggling against the glare from the window. He lifted his hand to his face to shield the light and finally focused on me standing near the doorway.

All he said was, "Fuck you." That's all he had to say. That's all that came out of his mouth, and it's all it took for me to lose control of myself like I'd never done in my entire life.

The reaction was instant. There was no internal discussion. No weighing the options. The anger was overwhelming. I was over him, the first kick landing squarely in his rib cage. My fist came down against the side of his face with a force I'd never felt, bones crushed underneath. The second punch, and then the third, and I could feel spit flying against my face, his and mine. And I swear to God I wanted to kill the man. There was blood on the wall around the hole in the sheetrock, blood on my hands. It was violence I'd never imagined could come from me. Extreme and beyond control, with my fist down again against his teeth, caving inside, and I wanted to bite him, rip a piece of his flesh away in my mouth before I fell backwards from the force of my own rage and stood again over the man I'd brutally beaten in his bed, his face in his hands, curled into a fetal position, soundless and wet.

I said, "Where's Kate's stuff?"

One of his hands left his face, slowly and then upwards until the index finger separated from the ball of blood and pointed down the hall.

I left the man and went to the next room. There was a big blue suitcase open on the floor with clothes out and around. In the corner of the room was a pile of burnt things, looked like a newspaper and a child's doll, with black streaks and soot up the wall nearly to the ceiling. I put the loose clothes in the suitcase, zipped the sides, and carried it down the stairs like it was a normal day in a normal house, a normal man carrying a suitcase, with blood beginning to dry on my right hand, beginning to feel stiff over the skin.

When I got back to the apartment Eddie was sitting at the old wooden dining room table, eating a bowl of cereal. He watched me carry the suitcase into my bedroom. Kate wasn't in the bed, and I thought she'd gone. I thought he'd let her walk out the door. But then there was a sound from the bathroom. The sound of vomiting, retching.

I opened the bathroom door. Kate was on the floor, her head resting on the toilet seat. I wiped her mouth with a towel. Her eyes still closed, and I wondered if she knew it was me, or maybe thought it was the man in the yellow house. But when she opened her eyes there was no look of surprise.

"I got your things from the house," I said.

She looked up at me, and again I was struck by the

way she stared. I thought of Jeff Temple's story of the time behind the concession stand during the baseball game, and I knew it couldn't be true. I imagined the man on the mattress in the yellow house was Jeff Temple, his baseball cap on backwards, pants down to his knees, a smile on his bloody face.

"I'm pregnant," she said.

In hindsight, these many years later, it was the moment I could have let myself off the hook. It was the fork in the road. I probably should have been rattling off questions like, who's the father? How can you get drunk and use drugs with a baby inside you? Did you plan to bring your child home to the room in the yellow house with the burnt doll and rancid smell and the man sleeping on a piss-stained mattress?

But those questions never entered my mind. Instead, I could see her clothes hanging in my closet, making room for her underwear in the chest of drawers, asking my boss for a few days off of work to get Kate settled, finding a doctor, being with her during the first days her body craved the drug, wiping the vomit from the side of her mouth.

And then, with the same uncharacteristic lack of thought I displayed in the violent attack earlier, I said out loud, "We can get married."

For a moment I wasn't actually sure I said the words loud enough to be heard. Kate's face was unchanged. There was no reaction at all, and for some reason I thought of my father, and his hand in mine when we walked together one morning on a beach a long time ago, when I was maybe four or five years old.

"What do you want to be when you grow up?" he asked. And I said, "I want to be with you."

He squeezed my hand a little tighter and looked down at me as we walked. When he looked back up across the water there was a smile on his face not meant for anyone but him. A pride in me, his son, he never found anywhere else. And I wondered what he would think of me as I lowered the towel and wiped the glistening saliva from Kate's chin where it rested on the toilet seat.

ten

We talked all day. I fixed Kate a sandwich for lunch. She told me about leaving the party that night, and getting a ride home, packing a bag and leaving her father sitting in the living room where I found him later.

"I went to Oklahoma to stay with my mother and her boyfriend, but she just had a new baby. It didn't work out."

"Where'd you go from there?"

Kate answered my questions with a tired indifference. She was worn out, surviving for the sake of survival when there was nothing else better to do.

"A boy in the trailer park, his name was Darren, offered me a ride to California. I had a friend who lived in Sacramento. We mostly slept in the car…"

Her eyes drifted past me again, and she seemed to remember something she'd forgotten.

"Let's talk about something else," she said. "Let's talk about you."

I told her about my job, and taking business classes. I told her about Eddie, and the time we got caught stealing. And then I told her about going to her house that night and talking to her father.

"He was sitting in the dark. There was a dog at the door. When's the last time you talked to him?" I asked.

"That night."

"You haven't talked to your father since then?"

She didn't answer right away. She didn't even seem to hear my question. I waited.

Kate said, "Why did you go to my house that night?"

It was the question I knew would come eventually. The dilemma I expected to face. Should I tell her about my infatuation? Would she consider my dedication honorable or creepy?

Through the years, in anticipation of such a conversation, I'd changed my mind back and forth. Eventually, I'd settled on a middle ground, waiting to size up Kate's reaction, waiting to actually get to know her before gauging her possibilities.

"I was just worried about you."

I thought about Jeff Temple, the cigar in one hand and beer in the other, standing by the pool, laughing. I thought about the man on the mattress in the yellow house.

"Do you have a boyfriend?" I asked.

She smiled, and even though I'd seen her smile earlier, I'd forgotten what it did to me.

"No," she said, like she'd never been asked before.

I called in sick to work. Kate took a shower and we ordered pizza. My mind was a whirlwind of ideas and plans. In the mirror, accidentally, I caught a glimpse of Kate in her bra and panties. It was only a glimpse, maybe lasted one second, and I turned away, but it was a remarkable one second. I can still see her closely in my mind, wet hair, bent over slightly looking for something in the drawer, white panties, freckles on her back. She seemed not to recognize the value of her body, just moving around like nothing at all.

It was nighttime again. The whole day had passed and we'd never left the apartment, barely stepping foot outside my room. We sat down on the bed together. Kate smelled clean. I held a notepad and pen in my lap.

"Do you want to make your life better?" I asked sincerely.

Kate smiled. "Yeah," she said.

"I mean really? Do you seriously want to make your life better? Because we can do it. We can sit here and list out every part of your life, and under each part list out how to solve the problems, how to make each part better."

She seemed not to understand, so I moved forward.

"See, on this first page we'll break down the sections of your life: education, employment, finances."

I wrote as I spoke, making sure to pick the most general categories first.

She was hesitant. "Okay," she finally said, and then asked, "What else?"

"Well, family relationships. Maybe substance abuse issues. The baby."

Kate touched her hand to her belly, reminding herself it was real. My categories had become more specific. She could see I'd thought about what I was saying. She seemed to be impressed I'd taken the time to break her life into identifiable pieces, something she'd never considered.

"What else?" she asked curiously.

"Maybe, spirituality. I don't know. And long-term goals, like marriage, maybe."

We both looked down at the list I'd made, top to bottom, in a column like a grocery list. Like we could go to the store and pick out each of the items and mark them off one by one.

"Now what?" she asked.

"Well, we turn over to the next page, and we write the first thing on the list at the top of the next page in big letters. Education. And then, underneath, we write down what kind of education you want and how to make it happen. Do you want to enroll in college here? What kind of classes do you want to take? Would you rather go to nursing school, or one of those places they teach you to be a court reporter, or what? What do you want to be when you grow up?"

We both laughed at the idea we weren't already grown up.

After a moment, Kate said, "I don't have any money."

"Don't worry about that part yet. Let's just talk about what you want. Then we'll talk about how to get it."

I could tell she'd never even asked herself the question. Probably her mother and father had never asked her the question, because it wasn't a possibility. It wasn't something possible, and so there was no point. It wasn't a subject avoided. It was no subject at all. The same as they probably never discussed how many light years it takes to reach the furthest star, or why our blood comes out red. I thought again about the man in the chair, beaten down by the day, a bullet hole through the top of his foot, in the dark.

I said the words again, "What do you want?"

She looked like a child. "I think I'd like to take some history classes. I always liked history."

I was surprised by her answer, and excited for her. She'd probably never told anybody before, and then a wave of unforseen anger came over me. She'd spread herself naked for men, maybe sucked the dick of Jeff Temple like he said, given herself away in so many ways, and none of those people cared a shit about what she wanted, and maybe I was too late. She was pregnant with another man's baby. Who knew what they'd done to her, all of them, and now I was charting how to fix it. How to fix everything, right down to the details.

I wrote, "History classes, enroll for next semester," and closed my eyes halfway through, the words tailing off down and away.

We stayed up for hours, talking and writing down pages of notes underneath capitalized titles. She had credit card debts. Her brother lived in New Mexico. She believed in God, but thought he'd given up on us and wasn't really paying attention anymore to what was going on.

We circled employment opportunities in the Classified section of the newspaper, weighing the advantages and disadvantages of each type of job. I balanced a hypothetical budget based on what the two of us could make, plus Eddie's share of the rent, and took into consideration a monthly payment toward Kate's credit card debt. The interest accrued at a rate higher than we could pay down, an endless cycle of wasted resources.

She didn't want to see her father again, and didn't like to talk much about her mother in Oklahoma.

"Do you know if you're having a girl or a boy?"

"I don't know. It feels like a girl."

"Do you have any names picked out?"

"No."

"Why not?"

"I'm just now gettin' used to the idea there's somethin' living inside me. I haven't gotten around to naming it yet."

On the pad of paper, I wrote down, Baby Names.

We both stared at the page.

Finally Kate said, "I like the name Gretchen."

I wrote it slowly on the paper. Gretchen. Kate said it out loud again. It was old-fashioned, original. I hadn't heard the name in a long time.

"I like it," I said. No one spoke for awhile as we stared at the word on the page. Seeing the written name made it more real.

"You can't do any more drugs, Kate. And you can't drink. Not just for yourself. For the baby."

"I know," she said.

"Do you need help, or can you do it yourself?"

"I can do it myself. It's just a diversion. I don't need it."

We were sitting very close together, our heads nearly

touching as we leaned over the pad, backs against a mound of pillows stacked at the headboard of my small bed.

She smelled glorious, a clean soapy smell mixed with a soft, feminine scent. I glanced down and could see the top of her breasts, light brown and smooth, leading to the border of the white bra just north of the nipple line. I felt a stir in my shorts. Just a stir at first, but as my imagination slid slowly across Kate's body the stir became a full erection, hidden behind the yellow pad of paper in my lap. I felt my breathing deepen and wondered if she knew.

Her face rolled to my face and I felt Kate's lips brush my cheek and stop. She kissed me. I'd been through it a thousand times in my head. In cars, hotel rooms, open fields. There was almost a familiarity, an expectation, but in reality it was new ground.

I turned my face until our lips touched and closed my eyes. There was a moment, a tiny fleeting moment, when I wondered if it was real or just another vivid, detailed daydream. And I moved against her, and we kissed. And I moved again until I was above, and she was below, and I could feel her breasts pushed against my chest, and our hips together with the pressure in between.

My left hand found its way and cupped Kate's breast, firm, but not too firm, a light squeeze, and the desire to have it in my mouth. I pushed downward, my lips on her neck, and then slowly to the skin of the chest and then up against the place I wished to bury myself, the softness and the smell like nothing my imagination had been able to capture.

I slid back up and kissed her again on the mouth, harder, and felt Kate's legs wrap around my waist. It was actually happening, and I tried not to think about it. I tried just to do the next thing, think the next thought, apart from the whole. And with our clothes still on, Kate started a slow rhythm, our bodies moving together into each other, and God help me it was more than I could control, and the instant came upon me like a wave of water and I raised up with involuntary sounds from my mouth, and Kate must have known because she pulled me to her and held me hard, wrapped up in arms and legs until the shuddering stopped and the embarrassment came quietly down upon me like a dark blanket. It was the sign of things to come.

"I'm sorry." I whispered. "It's never happened before."

When I said it, I was actually thinking it had never happened before in all those vivid daydreams. Those dreams of red panties and short skirts always ended well, the timing perfect.

I rolled off her and we lay side by side, looking up at the dotted ceiling. I felt the yellow pad under me and didn't bother to move. I was afraid to look at Kate, but when her breathing began to come and go in a rhythmic flow I finally looked over to see her eyes closed. I worried about what had happened and felt the wetness in my underwear, but our arms were locked together so I didn't try to get up, and lying next to Kate Shepherd, her breathing slowly put me to sleep.

I woke up alone to the sound of the front door gently closing. The clock showed 1:13 A.M. Kate was gone. I bolted up from the bed and changed clothes quickly. I ran outside and headed in the direction of campus, watching for figures of people moving in the dark shadows or under the lamp lights.

I traveled in the direction of the yellow house, hoping I would be wrong. Hoping there would be a simple explanation, until I found myself on the street of restaurants and bars, looking left and looking right, and there she was, with her back to me, walking in the direction of the yellow house, and the man on the floor, and the burnt doll in the corner of the room.

I followed at a safe distance. Maybe she forgot something? Maybe I'd left behind a dress or a shoe when I zipped up her bag? She turned up the walkway to the yellow house, its windows dark. I stepped into a bar off the street and found a place to stand where I could see Kate and the house. She went inside without knocking. Just walked into the dark house.

Somebody behind me said, "You want anything, buddy?"

It was the bartender. A big guy with curly blonde hair and a t-shirt with no sleeves.

"Yeah," I said, "a cigarette."

He didn't hesitate. The big man pulled a pack of cigarettes from his top pocket and with one hand shook out a single cigarette. He held the pack out to me and I took it.

I never really understood the idea of addiction to cigarettes. I'd smoked off and on but never felt the physical demand. It was just a cigarette, and with a pack of matches from the top of the bar I lit the end and stood next to the open swinging doors, my eyes fixed on the yellow house halfway down the short block.

Ten minutes passed. I glanced back and forth at the big clock behind the bar. How long would I wait? Was Kate in some type of trouble? I picked a number, twenty minutes, and decided I'd go get her if she didn't come out by that point.

I thought about what happened earlier. How awkward it became so quickly, and how she'd fallen asleep without so much as a word about it. Maybe she didn't consider it a problem? Maybe she considered it a compliment? I would, if I could cause a girl to shudder in pleasure with a simple kiss and the mere touch of a breast.

Fifteen minutes passed. I noticed the bartender watching me, suspicious, or maybe just curious about my presence and the importance of something down the street and the passing minutes on the clock.

I decided at seventeen minutes I'd start walking down the block. I estimated, at the twenty minute mark, I'd be standing at the door of the yellow house ready to do whatever I needed to do.

I stepped out of the bar onto the sidewalk as the second hand crossed the twelve. At that exact moment, Kate came out the front door of the yellow house. I took a backwards step through the open door into the bar, feeling the bartender's eyes on me. Kate held nothing in her hands and walked back the way she'd come, eventually passing me in the bar as I moved in a step behind a large plant between us. I couldn't read anything on her face. Her hands were in her jean pockets. I ran out of the bar in the opposite direction, jumped a chain-link fence, and ran in the dark over the railroad tracks around the Arts & Sciences Building back to my apartment. I got inside, took off my shoes, and struggled to catch my breath.

Should I lie down and pretend I was still asleep, or should I confront Kate with what I'd seen? Was it a one-time thing, or would I always wake in the night alone, wondering?

I sat down in the chair in the bedroom. The front door opened, and closed, gently. Kate came around the corner through my bedroom door. She looked at me, and I couldn't tell anything from the look.

"Hey," she said.

"Hey," I said back. I waited, but only a few seconds, and then said, "Where'd you go?"

"For a walk. I couldn't sleep."

Maybe it was true. Maybe she couldn't sleep. Maybe she just had one last loose end to tie up before she changed her life. I wanted very much to believe.

Kate came slowly across the room, bent at her waist, and kissed me on the lips, casual, comfortable, like she'd done it a thousand times before and planned to do it a thousand times more. It was all I needed.

eleven

Eddie never asked me anything about the girl living in our apartment, which was odd, but I suppose not so odd as my going out into the night and bringing the lost girl home in the first place.

In a short time I crossed over some sexual barrier into a place I never knew existed. A place of experimentation, comfort, physical pleasure, and it left me dumb and hypnotized, like an opium addict. We wouldn't leave the room for days, choosing the flesh over reason, another position over food. I had no idea it could be like that, and Kate seemed happy to be locked away and safe. I spent hours exploring every portion of her skin, every fold, especially the parts I didn't have myself.

"I feel like I'm at the doctor's office," she said once, and I felt stupid, so I turned off the flashlight.

Sometimes, when Kate slept, I'd go through the written plan, adding things and marking things off. Kate got a job as a hostess at a restaurant. She enrolled in only two history classes, deciding to take it slow in the beginning until the baby was born.

Eddie failed out, as I knew he would. He packed his things and left on a Wednesday evening without much fanfare. We had more space, but it certainly didn't help in the rent department. I put Kate in charge of the utility bills so she could handle her own money and gain a little confidence. Sometimes, right after we accomplished a particular goal, I'd make a big deal out of pulling the yellow pad from under the bed, turning to a certain page, and marking a dark line though the word on the list. I didn't notice until much later how little Kate really cared about my list, and marking things off, and any of the rest of it.

For a month and a half we were like a happy little married couple, wrapped up in each other in my small bed, taking turns cooking inexpensive meals, even studying together. I felt like it could be that way forever if I could only lock the door, nail boards over the windows, keep out the world and everybody in it. We could be like two humans kidnapped from Earth, taken by aliens to another planet to be observed naked in a homelike setting, except for no telephones or televisions, and nobody else to talk to, self-contained and happy, fornicating and eating ice cream all day. But we couldn't live that way for long, and eventually the world outside would seep under the door and we'd have to pay bills or file taxes or clean out the wad of hair from the sink drain.

Kate's little belly swelled. I could rest my head on top and listen deep inside. It was hard to imagine a baby in there, floating quietly in a sack of warm liquid. And if my head happened to be resting in a particular direction, guilt would mix with lust to form a separate uncomfortable feeling, until the lust would eventually win out.

"I know it's not my baby inside you, but it feels like my baby."

Kate didn't say anything.

"If we get married, she'll have my last name. They'll put me on the birth certificate."

I thought I felt something move next to my cheek underneath Kate's skin. I stayed still and waited to feel it again. Waited for the confirmation.

"Should we tell her?" I asked.

Kate didn't say anything. She had her hand on the top of my head, rubbing lightly through the hair. Maybe she wasn't listening at all.

Sometimes I imagine waking up in the morning to see a giant eye on the horizon. The Earth held up between a huge index finger and a thumb, being examined, the way we might examine a child's marble. And seeing the giant eye, and knowing the Earth is just a single grain of sand on the beach of some planet far away, I am relieved of worry and responsibility for everything and anything.

What a wonderful burden Jesus carried, all of mankind on his shoulders, when I'm allowed to save only two, Kate and the baby. But at the same time, what a relief it must have been to be tortured to death on the cross by those Romans, set free of worry and responsibility, at least for a little while. Some things were only meant to be carried for short distances.

"Let's go up to the courthouse and get married," I said. Kate's hand stopped rubbing my head, and then started again.

"When?" she asked.

"Now," I said.

I couldn't see her face and didn't want to. Hesitation was unwelcome. Inane questions were unwelcome. There was just me, and her, and whoever was inside of her, and the giant eye on the horizon. There was just Jesus, and the Romans, and the wonderful burden.

"Okay," she said, matter-of-factly. Not overjoyed, not sad, but without much hesitation, and naked, with my head resting on her warm belly, pointed in the wrong direction on purpose.

I rose and started to get dressed, very conscious of each muscle, each movement, listening behind me for sounds of Kate rising from the bed, getting dressed for our marriage.

I hadn't told my mother. I hadn't even told her Kate was living in my apartment, or Eddie had failed out, or I was on the verge of changing every single thing about my old life. But as I got dressed I imagined sitting at the kitchen table telling my mother all about it, and having Christine, braless and distant, listen to everything I had to say. And then the phone would ring, and she'd hurry out of the house, leaving me at the kitchen table, mid-sentence, with both of us knowing it was her way of showing me how much she really cared.

Kate brushed her hair. She wore a blue sundress, light blue, loose around her waist so no one could see the bulge. I wanted to ask her if she'd always dreamed of a big wedding, with a white dress and bridesmaids, maybe a band at the reception and shrimp cocktail. But I didn't ask her, because I didn't want to know. I hated the possibility she was disappointed, it wasn't the way she'd dreamed it would be. So we kept getting dressed, brushing our teeth in silence except for a few short sentences.

"Have you seen my other shoe?"

"No."

And then a few minutes later, "Is this your other shoe?"

"Yes."

I'd saved every extra penny for the past weeks. In the car, on the way to the courthouse I said, "Afterwards, we could go out to eat."

"That would be good," she said, but I couldn't tell much from the way she said it. My usual sharp instincts of perception had become dull and self-centered like the opium addict.

I let my left hand sneak down from the steering wheel to my left pocket. The bump in the pocket was my grandmother's ring. She gave it to me when my father died. We were alone in her kitchen after the funeral. She didn't make a big production of it.

"One day," she said, "you'll meet a special girl." And she placed the ring in the palm of my hand and bent my fingers inward into a fist around the ring. Now it was in my pocket, all clean and old-fashioned.

The lady at the marriage license desk asked us questions. She liked to guess to herself which couples were pregnant. I could tell by the way she glanced at Kate's belly from time to time, unsure. I wondered if some of the questions she asked were really necessary or if maybe she just enjoyed knowing things about other people. People getting married. Pregnant people.

We walked upstairs and sat in a judge's office. The secretary was too busy to ask us anything and simply said the judge would be with us shortly.

My stomach felt like I'd swallowed a pinecone. One of those hard green pinecones, and after it sat awhile in the juices of my stomach, the pine cone must have expanded. Kate looked down at her hands. We both thought about the baby inside her. We both had all those natural and unnatural doubts. I thought maybe if the judge didn't come out soon one of us might get up and leave, not in a hurry, but just get up and go outside and heave up a green pinecone.

"The judge will see you now."

We went in the office where he stood in a black robe. The secretary sat down against the wall. She was the witness. There's always a witness.

We shook hands with the judge and made small talk. He looked over the marriage license and then opened a small notebook.

My knees were weak, and I tried to think about the yellow pad under the bed, and the lists, and how good it was to rest my head on her soft belly and listen inside, and my grandmother, and my father's hand holding mine.

Mostly his voice when he told me things I needed to know.

"Marriage is an institution of divine appointment and commended as honorable among all people. It is the most important step in life, and therefore should not be entered into unadvisedly or lightly, but discreetly and soberly," the judge said.

It was like a train beginning to move and slowly picking up speed. Once it started, it would be damn near impossible to stop, and I was glad.

"Into this estate these two persons come now to be joined. If any person can show just cause why they may not be lawfully joined together, let them speak or else hereafter forever hold their peace."

I turned around and looked at the secretary. She was staring blankly at the floor. She'd probably stood quietly by as thousands of ill-suited idiots married each other, only to eventually end up back in the courthouse fighting over kitchen tables and visitation rights.

"Wilt thou, James Early Winwood, have this woman to be thy wedded wife, to live together after God's Ordinance in the estate of matrimony? Wilt thou love her, comfort her, honor and keep her in sickness and in health; and forsaking all others, keep thee only unto her, so long as ye both shall live?"

"I will," I said.

"Wilt thou, Katherine Anne Shepherd, have this man to be thy wedded husband, to live together after God's Ordinance in the holy estate of matrimony? Wilt thou love him, comfort him, honor and keep him in sickness and in health; and forsaking all others, keep thee only unto him so long as ye both shall live?"

I looked at the side of Kate's face. She was crying just a little bit. I wanted to hold her right there, and tell them to leave us alone. Let us lock the door and cover the windows and stay in my room forever with the aliens watching us through the glass.

"I will," she said.

"Please join your right hands."

My hand was wet, and her hand was wet, and we held hands because the judge told us to.

"Repeat after me, please," he said, and I did as he directed.

"I, James Early Winwood, take thee, Katharine Anne Shepherd, to be my wedded wife, to have and to hold from this day forward, for better, for worse, for richer or poorer, in sickness and in health, to love and to cherish till death us do part, according to God's holy Ordinance."

I stopped repeating at the tail end, thinking for a moment he said, "God's holy orifice." I looked at Kate, and I think she thought the same thing because we smiled at each other like no one else could see us, like the judge was a robot.

The judge looked at Kate and said, "Repeat after me." And she did.

"I, Katherine Anne Shepherd, take thee, James Early Winwood, to be my wedded husband, to have and to hold from this day forward, for better, for worse, for richer or poorer, in sickness and in health, to love and to cherish till death us do part, according to God's holy Ordinance."

And right when he said the last part Kate and I looked

at each other again, and she started laughing, and God help me, I'd forgotten what her laugh could do to me. It was a medicine.

The judge said politely, "The ring?"

I reached my left hand deep into the pocket and pulled out my grandmother's diamond ring. Kate held up her left hand with a look of surprise on her face, and I slipped the ring onto her finger.

That was that, I thought. That was the hardest part.

The judge said, "Inasmuch as this man and this woman have in the presence of God and these witnesses, consented to be joined together in the bonds of matrimony, I do now pronounce them husband and wife.

"Ephesians: Husbands love your wives, even as Christ also loved the church and gave himself for it…He that loveth his wife loveth himself.

"May the Lord bless and keep you, may he make his face to shine upon you, may the Lord lift up his countenance upon you, and give you his peace now and evermore. Amen."

And when he was finished saying what he had to say, I kissed Kate Shepherd long and hard in the judge's office, and she kissed me back in front of the witness. It was almost like the act of marriage was the proof we needed that Kate loved me, and I loved her, for all the right reasons, and it wasn't as crazy as it seemed.

There was a sound like a gunshot. And then silence. Through a window we saw men in uniforms running. Heavy footsteps down the hallway.

I looked to the judge, but he looked afraid, and he looked at the secretary who had broken free of her trance. A large deputy sheriff came through the office door.

"Judge, there's been a shooting downstairs. I'm gonna take all four of you through the back entrance, evacuate the building."

The judge asked, "Has anyone been hurt?"

"Yes," he said.

No one wanted to move. It seemed pointless, and the next day, in the newspaper, sitting in my fucked up little room, I read about what happened in the courthouse on our wedding day.

ON TUESDAY AFTERNOON at 2:15, shots rang out in the County Courthouse. Investigators believe Clay Namen (age 28), and his estranged wife, Jamie (age 26), were embroiled in a custody battle over their six year old daughter, Deanna. The case was scheduled for a trial in the Courtroom of Judge Francis, and according to authorities the Court broke for lunch after the wife concluded her testimony.

Apparently, by yet unknown means, Clay Namen was able to smuggle a gun past the security checkpoint and into the Courthouse. A spokesman for the Sheriff's department refused to speculate and stated only, "This has never happened before." According to sources, after lunch Mr. Namen testified in the hearing, acknowledging he had made mistakes during the couple's marriage, but begging the judge for the opportunity to see his daughter regularly. Witnesses report that before the judge issued a ruling, and during another break in the trial, Clay Namen fired a single shot in the hallway in the direction of his wife. The bullet missed Jamie Namen and apparently ricocheted off the wall, striking the six-year-old child in her face.

The child was pronounced dead upon arrival at St. Martin Hospital.

PART II
somewhere in between

It was just a regular day. The doctor's appointment was scheduled in the afternoon. It was the day we expected to see the sonogram and learn if it was a boy or a girl inside. I knew there was a part of me resentful of this baby, but I suppressed the resentment and tried not to think back to Kate's time away from me, and the yellow house and all the other possibilities, but instead to the plan mapped out on the pad of paper under the bed.

We sat in the waiting room with the other pregnant women, some with men next to them. I wondered if they were the fathers, or just men waiting for something in the waiting room. Anything. A place to wait quietly, apart from all the hustle and bustle outside.

"Are you nervous?" I asked Kate.

"Yes, I've got to pee."

We were called to the back, and I sat on a stool in the corner of the room. The doctor placed the stethoscope on Kate's belly, moving the silver circle from one spot to another.

"Excuse me just a moment," he said, and left the room.

Kate lifted herself up on her elbows. "Do you think anything's the matter?" she said.

"No, nothing's the matter. He probably just forgot something in the other room. Don't worry."

But she looked worried, and somehow the silence and the disinfected environment didn't help like it should have.

The doctor came back in the room with a nurse. This time the nurse moved the silver circle around on Kate's belly, listening.

The doctor said, "I couldn't pick up the baby's heart-beat. It's not unusual. Sometimes Shelley is better at it than me."

The room fell silent again. Any second I expected Shelley to say, "There it is, I hear it," but she didn't, and the moment expanded slowly like a balloon filled with warm air until there was a pressure all around us.

The nurse said, "Let me try the other one."

She left, and the doctor followed, leaving us alone again.

"Oh, God," Kate said. "Something's the matter."

"No, it's not. Nothing's the matter. You heard the doctor, it's not unusual."

I believed what I said. I'd imagined the birth of the baby, our lives together, even crazy things like one day encountering the natural father, but my mind had never imagined no heartbeat. It wasn't on the list. It wasn't part of the plan.

But it happened anyway. The baby died inside Kate, never reaching the outside. She cried with a sadness I'd never seen. I tried to hold her, but she was limp in my arms like she was dead, too.

We crawled along through the next days and nights at home and then at the hospital. I tried to imagine what it was like for a doctor to scrape the dead baby off the side of the womb and feel nothing at all, like it was a blister. To ball it all up together in one of those little metal bowls and then throw it away, hearing the thud in the trash can.

We didn't talk much during those days. There was nothing to say. Once, when I was sitting at the kitchen table alone, I felt Kate looking at me. I lifted my eyes, she kept looking, and we just stayed that way, me trying to figure out what she was thinking, and Kate wondering if I'd wished for it. Wished another man's baby to die inside of her, like I had a secret list somewhere, hidden, with such things written on the page. Such things as "I hope the baby dies…"

Looking back, the death of the baby inside Kate seemed to start in her an unstoppable process of decay. Who knows, maybe it was already unstoppable and all I did was slow it down awhile, but nothing was ever the same again. For my part, I was driven to deposit my seed, to put another baby where the last one had been, right the wrong, fix the problem, put everything back the way it had been. But it wasn't so simple. The lightness was gone. She pulled back from my hands, and looked at me like I was a cripple, turning me slowly from a savior to a beggar, leaving me to make ridiculous rational arguments, sometimes out loud.

"For everything I provide to you, the roof over your head, an education, and you can't let me touch you? You can't give yourself to me for just a few minutes? Once every two weeks just isn't enough for me."

And another one. "It's funny, I'm supposed to be strong all the time, like a statue, like a tree, always solving the problems. I can't be weak for a minute, not even weak for you, physically. Even that weakness is unattractive to you."

The arguments always sounded better alone. When I tried them out loud, the whole structure caved in upon itself until I was a blithering idiot and the words had no meaning, only a cutting anger and frustration. Success was rare.

One day I called Kate's restaurant.

"May I speak to Kate, please."

Pause.

"Hello?" I said.

"She doesn't work here anymore."

Pause.

"What do you mean?" I said.

"She's no longer employed here."

We had a gigantic fight that night over the definition of being fired. I never could figure out exactly what happened, and in the middle of the fight the electricity went out. The man on the phone said we hadn't paid our bill, but Kate swore she sent the check.

I could barely function. I found a bottle of vodka

behind a box of tampons. The bank called to say Kate had bounced three checks at the grocery store. The phone started ringing at night, and Kate would go outside and whisper. I'd press my ear to the window and pick up pieces of words, inflection in Kate's whisper, a soft laugh.

And then, one day while I was in economics class, my wife packed her bags and went away. I couldn't concentrate. Everything had unraveled. In just three or four months it had gone from my head resting on Kate's belly to complete and utter chaos. I couldn't focus on schoolwork. I'd slept on the floor, on the couch, or sometimes next to the corpse in my bed. I'd argued with myself, and Kate, and swung from one end to the other, until the day I came home to the empty apartment. Everything had happened so quickly, at least that's the way I remember it now. Life just wouldn't slow down.

The door was unlocked. I thought it might be another one of those nights I'd end up staying awake listening for the sound of her getting home late. But it was different. This time, even her ghost was gone, and the apartment felt like it used to feel when Eddie laid around in his socks watching daytime television.

Sitting on my bed, I closed my eyes and let myself believe for a minute it was all a dream. One of those crazy nonsense dreams you wake up from and you're glad it's over but wish you could get back in the middle of it a few more minutes. But it wasn't a dream. I was married and had no idea where my wife had gone. She didn't leave a note or anything else. Even the tampons and vodka were gone, leaving in their absence a recurring visual analogy of a person drowning in a pool, calling out for help until someone jumps in the pool and pulls them to the side. And then, a few minutes later, when nobody's looking, the person paddles back out to the middle of the deep end and starts to drown again, calling for help, until they're saved again, and so on and so on until finally nobody comes when they call and so the person either drowns or struggles to the side, and by then maybe nobody cares anymore, no matter how beautiful they are or how worthy they may be, because maybe God made some people unsavable on purpose.

I remember one time on the couch, after the baby died. Kate had fallen asleep. I climbed over and crawled in beside her, my front against her back, and smelled her hair. With my top hand I ran my index finger along the skin on her upper arm and slowly let my arm relax downward until I cupped her breast. We were still for a moment, the rain outside falling sideways against the window, and then, with her eyes still closed, Kate said, "You'll be feeling me up on my deathbed."

I remember thinking, as loud inside of myself as possible without anyone else being able to hear, "No, I won't." And knowing what I already knew, saying to myself, "You're not who I wanted you to be. I can't save you. I can't even save myself."

I left the empty apartment and got in the car to drive home. It seemed like the only place to go. I drove past the street with the restaurants and turned the wheel. I could see the yellow house up ahead. It was a cloudy day, thin gray clouds covered the world like a blanket. The front door of the house was wide open, but I couldn't see any-body. I drove past slowly to the end of the street, turned around in a driveway and went by again. Standing in the doorway I saw the man I'd beaten on the floor before, and he saw me. We watched each other and I thought of him on top of Kate, kissing her mouth, her open legs around his waist, the burnt doll in the corner watching, fixated, and then I felt my lungs seize up, and the last free breath leave my body, and the burning panic like I'd felt before.

I didn't stop driving. I opened the windows and got on the highway heading home. It was the middle of the week. I had classes the next morning. I was in the thick-ness of an asthma attack. My wife was gone, everything had come apart. I had no detailed plan for such a day, so I drove, and wheezed, and tried to make each breath just a bit easier than the one before. I thought about my father on the train tracks, and how until I found Kate he was the person I felt closest to, and he was dead. And now the per-son I'd brought closest to me didn't want to be close to me anymore, but my father didn't have a choice.

I pulled into the driveway of my mother's house after hours of driving and driving. It was raining, big drops pounding against the metal roof of the car. I thought about opening the car door, but didn't. I thought about it again, but my hand didn't move, and I wondered if maybe my body had decided not to listen to my mind anymore. Maybe the rebellion had reached my own arms and legs, a complete rejection of any plan I'd made, or would ever make in the future. Maybe my hand would decide if and when it would open the car door, and my legs would decide if and when to go inside the house, and my mind would just have to wait.

I sat for awhile, just listening to the rain, feeling sorry for myself. I saw my mother come to the front window of the house. We looked at each other, and I wondered if she knew instinctively somehow that something was wrong, or if she was devoid of any such instincts and saw only a car in the rain in her driveway in the middle of the week.

We stayed that way for minutes, me and my mother, in a silent conversation, but I needed more from her. My hand opened the door and my legs took me in the house, wet and shivering, and after an awkward continuation of our silent conversation, my mother actually hugged me. She held on long enough for me to know the sacrifice.

"I got married."

She didn't react. I might as well have told her it was Wednesday.

"How about a cup of coffee?" she said.

We sat down at the white kitchen table. My mother's house was always extremely clean. In fact, it reminded me of one of those model homes where no one actually lives. Just a house, with furniture, and books on the shelves not meant for reading.

"I got married to that girl from high school, Kate Shepherd. We went to the courthouse. It was the day the man shot his little girl in the hallway outside the courtroom. We were there that day, upstairs, getting married, me and Kate."

My mother took a sip of her coffee. "I'm not sure what to ask. Why did you wait until now to tell me?"

I felt myself wanting to cry. I hadn't cried but I felt the feeling in my throat and then up into my face and eyes.

"I screwed up," I said, trying to force back the emotion. My mother said, "Everybody screws up, Early. Everybody."

"She left. I don't know where she went."

I started to cry, and when I started I couldn't stop. My mother stood and leaned over me, her hands on my shoulders, her face resting on the back of my neck, and I cried so damn hard I thought the asthma might come back, my body shaking, eyes squeezed shut in my hands.

My mother didn't offer any advice, and I'm glad she didn't. Whatever she said would have cheapened how I felt, and it wasn't the reason I drove to see her anyway. I drove there because it was still my home, good or bad. It was the place where my father used to walk in the front door from work every day, and I'd hear the door open and run like hell to see him, until that last day when he didn't come home at all and the world changed colors.

The agony slowed and I was able to speak. "'I've got to go back to school, Mom. I've got classes in the morning."

She didn't try to make me stay the night. She didn't tell me it was crazy to drive all day to get there in the rain just to turn around and drive all the way back. She didn't tell me everything would be okay, because it wasn't, and we both knew it, and what would be the point of patting each other on the backs and saying, "Everything will be all right?" No point.

Back at the apartment I tried to focus on the next thing only, the next class, the next day at work. I counted on the routine to pull me slowly from the mire, but it was too slow to notice, like the movement of the minute hand on the clock. You know it's moving, you just can't see it, and so you can't really be absolutely sure it's moving at all.

Weeks passed, and then months. Kate didn't come back. She didn't call. One night I found the pad of paper under the bed. Pages of words, all in my handwriting, outlining a life other than my own. No wonder it failed, but as time passed some of the bad things about Kate diluted and some of the good things rose slowly to the top. Maybe she was in a horrible situation? Maybe she needed me? I drove around town, past the bars, past the yellow house, past the bank, the restaurant where she used to work. No one had seen her. She hadn't gone to her classes. Maybe she went back to Oklahoma. Maybe back to Jeff Temple.

On a cold morning I opened my front door and stepped outside. There was a man.

"Are you James Winwood?"

I was startled. My breath came out white in the freezing air.

"Yes."

And he handed me some papers. Divorce papers. Katherine Shepherd Winwood, plaintiff, vs. James Early Winwood, defendant. The papers said Kate was pregnant, and I was the father, and she wanted custody, and me to pay child support, and she planned to marry a man, an older man named Russell Enslow, with a good job, financial stability, who would help her provide a fine home for the baby. And the papers said I had "tendencies of violence," having beaten a man in his home, and I was controlling, "stalking the plaintiff since high school," basically "imprisoning the plaintiff in my apartment," and more and more and more.

I expected to read, "He tried to feel me up on my deathbed." It was like we were in two different relationships, in two different places, with me and my Kate on the faraway distant planet, enclosed in glass, observed by aliens as we ate ice cream and fornicated happily all day, while the other Kate and the other me were locked in a musty apartment strung out on control issues and implied threats of violence waiting for something bad to happen. We didn't have to wait long.

two

My lawyer looked like an idiot, tall, gaunt, with big ears, one sticking out farther than the other. I guess I shouldn't complain. My mother paid his bill.

Kate's lawyer was sharp-dressed and angry. He pranced around the courtroom pointing his finger and raising his voice. Kate's new boyfriend, the rich old guy, Russell, paid his bill.

The judge said, "I'm not entertaining the issues of paternity or custody until the child is born. After the child is born and the DNA tests are completed, we'll deal with all of this, gentlemen. In the meantime, the mother can move to California as long as she comes back after the birth of the child and consents to jurisdiction here."

I tried to stare straight ahead. I tried to look at the judge, the bailiff, a black speck on the top of the table where I sat. I didn't want to look at her. I didn't want to see her. I suppose the man who shot his wife in the courthouse hall on my wedding day must have felt such things. The anger of losing something. The fear of falling to your knees and begging to get it back. The prospect of a lifetime alone.

The falling apart happened so fast. The healing seemed not to move at all. I surrounded myself with the fortress of daily routine. Class and work, brush my teeth, remember to eat, go to the library, don't think. The worst parts were those minutes between the tasks. Forced to acknowledge there would be a baby in the world soon, and I would be kept from her, by a judge, by distance, by a sharp-dressed angry lawyer, by my own stupid decisions and mistakes. And it was all outside my control, happening to me when somebody else decided it would happen.

I started smoking cigarettes again to fill the empty spaces in the routine, but I found myself creating more spaces than the ones I filled.

"What if I'm not the father?"

But the question went unanswered, sitting in the dark on the ground with my back against the wall next to the barbecue grill, smoking another cigarette. Sleeping sometimes wasn't possible. It's when all the loneliness settled in the room until I couldn't breathe. Everything she'd touched, I threw away. The sheets, the shampoo. Everything that smelled like Kate I carried out to the dumpster in the rain. It was impossible to separate her from what was happening to me, from the self-pity, the futility, the embarrassment, the longing. But the options were limited, and I got up again, and did it all one more time, and waited for the healing to begin.

Gretchen Anne Winwood was born in Sacramento, California on April 22. My lawyer called to give me the news. The divorce and custody trial would be scheduled in the summer. I hung up the phone and then sat for a very long time, thinking about my father, and how, if he hadn't been killed that day, things might be different. Trying to go year by year in my mind, from age eleven to the present moment, imagining my father still alive, and how his simply being alive could have changed me. And it made me think about the baby girl so far away born into this world without me being the first to hold her. Some other man being there instead, and how she could get confused by everything and think I didn't love her, which wasn't true.

The DNA test was positive. It was my mindless sperm responsible for locating and penetrating the ripe egg despite Kate's disdain, her limp legs wide open, our relationship smoldering like a bombed-out city. You would think an entity as capable of creating the miracle of life could take a few minutes to grasp the circumstances of the surroundings before deciding to plow ahead and make a baby inside a madwoman. But no. Nature hasn't quite caught up to the complexities of a modern overpopulated world. The crazy sperm blindly twisting and swimming at all costs for the opportunity to further complicate the universe.

My mother walked over to Kate and Russell where they sat in the hallway with baby Gretchen. The same hallway where Clay Namen had accidentally killed his daughter. My eyes scanned the walls for bullet holes, but I couldn't find any. There were sections with slightly newer paint, and I imagined a man on a ladder filling the holes with plaster and painting over the spots.

"May I hold my granddaughter?" Christine said.

I stayed at the other end of the hall, sitting in my suit, listening. She said the words without begging, without sympathy.

My mother sat down next to me, holding the baby. She was pink and quiet, with a nose you could see up inside, and eyes like Kate's. She looked at me like I was just another person in the world. Like it was perfectly normal to meet your father for the first time in the hallway outside of a courtroom. I wanted to say, "Don't you understand what's happening here? Don't you see what's going on?"

The lawyer told me we should reach an agreement. He said I was in no position, working and going to school full-time, to take care of a baby. He said if I agreed to let Kate have custody out in California, which he said the judge would undoubtedly do anyway, they'd agree for me not to pay child support until after I graduated college and could afford it. He said I could visit Gretchen, and talk to her on the phone, and later, if I wanted, I could come back and try to get more visitation, or even go for custody if Kate slipped.

His ears stuck out from the sides of his head like they were pulled by invisible fishing line. I felt myself wanting to reach up and cut my hand through the air along the sides of his head to reveal the clear string, pulling the line tighter with the pressure of my hand, forcing the ears out-ward even further.

My mother told me it was the right thing to do for the time being. We couldn't prove Kate's drug problem. She'd never been arrested and she tested negative on the urine test. She would impress the judge holding the baby in her arms as she testified. Russell's money had bought good legal representation, a nice place to live in Sacramento, California, and I couldn't match their financial stability. What judge would order the baby removed from her mother's arms to be handed over to a part-time barbeque restaurant cook who could barely pay the electric bill?

I couldn't stop thinking about Clay Namen, having the only thing he loved in God's world taken from him, his daughter. Walking past his wife and her smiling fam-ily on his way to the bathroom and knowing they would win and he would lose because everybody knows a father can't be a mother.

I graduated from college in finance and took a job as an investment broker in a national firm. There were three of us in the office and three secretaries. I sent a child sup-port check every month to a central collection office. Sometimes when I'd call to talk to Gretchen they'd answer the phone. More often it would ring and ring and ring and I'd slam the fuckin' phone against the nearest wall. I'd send cards and never know if they were received. Father's Day passed with nothing.

I buried myself in my work for ten years. I remember very little about the efficiency. I bought a small house, with a room set up for Gretchen. The first time she came to visit we sat on her bed like strangers. She was six.

"You've got your own bed here. And look at the sheets. Pink, your favorite color."

She held her little bag in her lap like she might stand up and walk out the door any minute. Like a small replica of her mother.

"There aren't any toys here," she said.

She was right. It was like a picture of a child's room in a magazine. Perfect color coordination. Perfect alignment of the furniture, but no toys, or stains on the carpet, or half-eaten Pop Tarts.

"We'll go get toys," I said. "We'll go buy as many toys as you want and fill up the room."

She didn't move. I expected a fine reaction, a big smile, a hug.

"You don't have any books to read, or movies."

"We'll go to the bookstore. We'll go to the movie store, too. I promise."

We sat silent on the bed. My tie was too tight around my neck.

"Just give me a chance, Gretchen. Please. Just give me a chance. I'm your dad, and I know it's all weird, but we've got to get a chance to know each other."

And I started telling her more than I planned. "My dad died when I was eleven. For a long time I was really mad. Mad at my dad, mad at God. When I got older, instead of being mad about all those years I didn't get to spend with him, I started being happy about the first ten years we had together."

On Gretchen's visits I used my vacation time from work. It always took us days to get familiar again. Every time I heard her call Russell "Daddy" it was like a cold icepick shoved in my ribs. I took her to the zoo, the theater, the park, trying to cram a year into a week, a lifetime into a few days. Each time I saw her she seemed like a different child, older, taller. I stayed away from the subject of Kate but secretly looked forward to fragments of information, stored later inside my mind in a certain place, all together.

"Why don't you have a wife?" Gretchen asked one day.

I hadn't dated much. I'd overheard one of the secretaries at work tell another secretary she thought I was gay. I couldn't even muster the energy to tell her any different. Nearly every woman I met scared the shit outta me. What was behind them? What poison lay just under the skin? What secrets did they hide until it couldn't be hidden any longer, until it was too late? If I'd been so wrong before, I could be so wrong again, and it just wasn't possible to survive another round. Goals at work could be reached. Bonuses earned. On some channel, somewhere, a baseball game, or a boxing match, was happening, pure. I started running. Long distance running. It allowed me to organize my thoughts, discipline my mind to a degree. I looked forward to it, hated it after a few minutes, and then loved it again standing in the shower.

Kate and the old man had gotten married. They'd had another child, a girl. It's all I really needed to know, but I knew a lot more. Through bits and pieces from Gretchen the picture had come together. Russell was the father figure I couldn't be. The father figure Kate always needed. She felt safe, secure, and it didn't matter if she loved him, or if he loved her. She was a long way from the house in the woods down the dirt driveway. A long way from the old man sitting in the darkness. But both of us knew, both me and Kate, she was never too far away from where I found her.

Gretchen asked, "Why does your house smell funny?"

If it smelled funny, I didn't know it. Ten years of living alone does strange things. Empty refrigerator, hair on the soap bar, too much fast food, too much sausage. Nobody to point out all the obnoxious habits until they build on top of one another and sooner or later you're not fit to be around people, unable to smell your own smells. Some people might say those ten years were wasted time. They weren't wasted. They were lonely, necessary, but not wasted. There was a time I thought I'd never heal.

And then one day I was in the grocery store. There was this woman, about my age, up ahead of me in the cereal aisle. I don't know what it was about her that made me stare. There was no ring on her left finger. She was buying food kids would eat. I liked the way she moved. Quietly and gently, like she was quiet and gentle inside. Her hair was clean and short, sandy blond. She dressed casually, but carefully.

There was a rhythm to her existence. It's hard to explain. A simplicity.

I passed her and took a deep breath through my nose, trying to smell her. Not too much perfume. I lagged behind at the oatmeal until she passed me by again. I hadn't felt such a way since Kate, light like a boy. Like anything was possible.

"Hello," she said.

"Hello," I said back, too quickly. Premature response.

She smiled. A good smile. An inviting smile. A new light at the end of a long tunnel.

three

I went to the same grocery store every day at the same time for a week. I saw her again. There she was next to the milk. I'd planned the moment. She needed to see me first. I'd be able to tell everything from her immediate reaction, before she had time to be polite. Would she be glad to see me? Would she be pleasantly surprised? Or would she not even recognize my face, turning away to check the expiration date on the milk?

I stood in front of the cheese ten feet away. So many different kinds. White and yellow, shredded and block, Mexican, mozzarella. Out of the corner of my eye I watched her put a small carton of half-and-half in the buggy. She stared at something level with her eyes, and then glanced at me to her left. My timing was perfect. I turned a split second after her glance and we were looking at each other.

She smiled again, like before, except this time with recognition. She remembered me and was glad I was only ten feet away next to the cheese.

I forgot my line, betrayed by the exhilaration, and instead said, "There's lots of cheese."

"Yes, there is," she said.

"My name is Early Winwood," I said, and stuck out my hand like I was meeting a guy at the lumber yard. She stuck out her hand and we shook, awkward but nice but just the same.

Her hand was very soft and well-manicured. She was smaller than I remembered, relaxed with herself, and me. I abandoned the master plan altogether. The coy little conversation I'd rehearsed in front of the mirror. She liked me. There was no need to beat around the burning bush. I was over thirty years old, not seventeen. We were grown-ups, in the grocery store, liking each other.

"Would you go to dinner with me tonight?"

She didn't flinch one way or the other. Just stood there, smiling. I tried to put myself in her place. I could be a murderer, a rapist, a con man. She not only had her-self to protect, but probably children. The children at school, looking forward to drinking milk when they got home.

So I said, "I'm thirty years old. I'm an investment broker. I've never been arrested. I've got a ten-year-old daughter, Gretchen, who lives in California. I'd like to be more coy and mysterious, but we wouldn't be able to have dinner tonight, and it would be at least another week until we ran into each other again. And then I'd probably say something stupid like, 'There's lots of cheese', so I was wondering, would you like to go out to dinner with me tonight?"

She listened to all my goofy crap with the same pleasant smile. Her eyes were good and blue. A deep blue. Almost gray, and her skin looked extra-soft. I was struck by the desire to reach out my hand and touch her on the face, but I didn't, thank God, and instead waited patiently for her answer.

"Yes, Early Winwood, I would like to go to dinner with you tonight."

I went home in a new mood, feeling things I hadn't felt in a very long time. I called Gretchen on the phone, not to tell her about my date, but just to talk to her, connect my good things with each other.

"Is it a beautiful day out there in California?" I asked.

I didn't expect her to question my upbeat mood, or even notice it. Gretchen sometimes struggled with the obvious. I had, however, detected in her some perceptive ability. She was shy in new surroundings. Watching. Noticing. And picked up on things about people.

"I can't wait until Thanksgiving," I said. It was Gretchen's next planned visit. Christine and Gretchen had a bond. It was subterranean and strong. They seemed to have an understanding, sometimes looking at me like I was the weak link in the chain. I was jealous of the bond at the beginning. It seemed I'd never be as close to either one of them as they were to each other. But the jealousy went away, and it was healthy, appropriate, and provided me a glimpse into my mother I couldn't get otherwise.

"I've got a date tonight," I blurted out to Gretchen on the phone.

I hate to think I said it hoping the news would get to Kate, my ex-wife of ten years, the wife of Russell Enslow, the woman who packed up and left me while I was sitting in economics class. But who knows why I said it. Maybe the motivation was pure. Maybe I just wanted to share it with my girl.

"Daddy's got a date," she said out loud to someone in the room with her. I couldn't hear what the other person may have said.

"Where are you taking her?" Gretchen asked.

"You got any ideas?"

"You're the Plan Man," she said, and laughed like the other person in the room with her shared the thought.

"Maybe not anymore. Maybe it's time to stop planning anything at all, just wake up and go through the day. Whatever happens, happens. Carefree. You can call me Mr. Carefree. Who knows? Maybe I'll buy a horse and become one of those people who rides the horse real fast around barrels."

"That would be fun," she said. "I think you should get a horse."

I should have kept Kate locked away in my mind. I shouldn't have ruined her with all that impossible reality. Some things need to be left alone. The memory, the memory of her before that night outside the bar on the street curb could have been a great thing to visit. A place to go when I needed her, in between parts of my life, anytime I wanted.

I stood at Samantha's door, as nervous as a bird. The house was huge, in a fancy neighborhood. My modest car looked pitiful in the driveway next to the white Mercedes. Samantha Kilborn was rich, or at least somebody was.

I knocked on the door. A boy, maybe ten years old, Gretchen's age, opened the door. He was dressed neatly, and we looked at each other for a moment.

"Is Samantha Kilborn here?" I asked.

The boy turned and walked away, leaving the door open. I heard him call out, "Mom." There was whispering, and then Samantha and the boy came to the door together.

"Early Winwood, this is my son Allen, Allen Jr.," she said. "Allen, this is Early Winwood."

"Hi," I said, again too eager, like a big, over-friendly dog.

We all stood there. Allen Jr. said, "Early? That's a weird name."

Samantha scolded him. "That's not a nice thing to say."

I tried to be funny. "Better Early than late."

It was brutal. Nobody laughed. We stood there like three well-dressed mannequins in a window. I ended the brutality with a simple, "Okay, are we ready to go?"

Samantha and the boy retreated inside. More whispers. I caught a glimpse of a third person, a babysitter maybe. And finally we were outside in my modest car going to a restaurant. I wanted to know everything about her. I could feel myself begin to surface from the disconnection. Someone new. The excitement. The sexual undercurrents.

We laughed a lot at dinner, which is good. She remained relaxed, gentle, and told me she was divorced from Allen

Kilborn. Allen Sr., she called him. They'd been divorced for three years and she really hadn't dated much. She didn't work outside the home because Allen Sr. wanted her to raise their only child, Allen Jr., who was eleven years old and struggled with his parents' divorce.

I told her about me, leaving out most of the weird parts. I dwelled on simplicity and Gretchen, skipping all the stuff about Kate, and the oddness of my conception, and my father's death, and my vow to be average and invisible. As I edited my responses I wondered how much Samantha edited what she told. I looked for signs of mental instability, pent up anger, propensity toward misery. I analyzed and over-analyzed everything she said, but at the same time tried with all my might to keep it light and fresh.

At one point, when she had a piece of chocolate cake on her top lip, I wanted to kiss her. I wanted it more than anything I'd wanted in a long time. And my mind took off on its own with a quick sequence of imagined sexual events, starting with the kiss in the restaurant, and my hand sliding underneath her shirt, and me falling to my knees with my head under her skirt, and finally the two of us up against the far wall next to the painting of the Italian landscape, knocking the painting off the wall.

"Where does your ex-wife live?" Samantha asked.

"She lives in California. Sacramento."

"Do you get along with her?"

I thought about the question. "We don't really talk. Gretchen's old enough to talk for herself, so we don't need to. What about you? Where does Allen Sr. live?"

"He lives outside of town."

Her face revealed the slightest sign of tension when she spoke of her husband. Just enough to show.

"Do you get along?" I asked.

"Yes, I suppose," she said, and wanted to say more, but didn't.

After dinner we parked downtown and walked around looking in the windows of the shops. Maybe it was the wine, maybe the cool evening, but there was no discomfort between us. No sense of wanting to get away from each other to assess the situation and organize thoughts. We were walking along and came to a crosswalk. Samantha took my hand as we hurried across ahead of the cars. When we arrived on the other side of the street, she left her hand in mine, and it felt really good. I kept my mind on the moment. Tried not to let it slip into the fear that I'd misjudged again, and it might be good for awhile, but then confusing, and eventually unbearably painful, and I'd be rolled up in a ball again on my living room floor crying until I coughed.

Driving home I wrestled with the idea of the goodnight kiss. Should I try in the car? Should I wait until we're at the door? But I didn't want to freak out the kid. He already seemed freaked out enough by his mom going out on a date. Maybe skip the kiss. Ask her on a second date. Plan the kiss. Location. Circumstances. Eliminate the possible complications.

I walked Samantha to the door. She reached for the knob and the door swung open. Standing in front of us was a large man. Maybe six foot three, two hundred thirty pounds. His face was hard, and that's the way he seemed to like it. I felt the potential immediately. The posture of the confrontation. I knew it was Samantha's ex-husband. The man she wanted to tell me more about, but didn't.

Samantha wasn't prepared.

"I didn't see your car," she said to the man.

"I guess you didn't," he said back, in a voice matching the body. A crushing tone over the words as he looked down at us.

"Did you leave Allen with a babysitter again?"

Samantha's demeanor had changed. She was more childlike, apologetic, like she'd been caught sneaking a cookie.

I stuck out my hand. "My name is Early Winwood."

He looked down at my hand and left me standing there.

"Early Winwood?" he repeated, like he was making a mental note of the spelling. Like he'd be checking me out and needed to remember the name.

My hand was still out. I decided to leave it there.

"Do you see this house?" he asked me.

I looked across the door frame. "Yes," I said.

"I bought this house. Just like I bought that car in the driveway. Just like I bought everything inside the house. I don't know who you are, and I don't really care."

He'd been a bully all his life. I could tell. And all his life it worked. People did what he told them to do. He'd raised intimidation to an art, believing himself superior in size and intellect. It must have scared away so many competitors. So many potential problems. Like one of those big black gorillas in the rainforest pounding a fist against the dark flesh of his chest and howling.

If I shrunk away, Samantha and I would never see each other again except perhaps with uncomfortable sideways glances in the grocery store from time to time. It was terribly early in our relationship for such a test, but there it was before me, and I decided to leave my hand extended in front of him, without moving. There was no way to pull it away with dignity. I was back at the cafeteria table so many years ago with the senior leaning over, emptying a mouthful of chocolate milkshake on my lunch tray.

"My name is Early Winwood," I repeated.

The big man looked over my head to the street. I turned to see a car pulling up in front of the house under the streetlight. He walked past me, past my outstretched open hand, toward the car.

I stared at the back of his head and had a clear vision of the future. Something bad would happen, and it would be me, and not him, to make it happen. I heard the first click of the machine in my head, the first microscopic movement toward a plan. A detailed, mapped-out, absolute plan. The man walking across the green lawn would ultimately affect my life, perhaps more profoundly than any other single person.

Samantha and I watched him. Allen Kilborn looked back at me over the top of the car before he climbed inside and went away. My hand was still outstretched.

"I'm sorry," Samantha said. "I should have told you."

"Can I kiss you?" I asked. It came out quickly, before I could think about it.

She seemed surprised by the question. She seemed surprised I hadn't run away like one of those smaller gorillas in the jungle, looking over my shoulder.

"Yes," she said, "you can kiss me."

And so I did.

Samantha at home and out of the workplace, he not only limited her contact with the outside world, he also kept her financially dependent. He paid the bills. He paid the house mortgage. He doled out money with so many strings attached they hung in the air like kite tails.

The control didn't stop with money. The man used his child, and the threat of taking his child, as the trump card. The kid worshipped his fucked-up father like a god, believing the suffocating control was a powerful version of love. The power and manipulation was sometimes subtle, sometimes not, and my hatred of Allen Kilborn Sr. grew with each day.

The most obvious area of control was physical. He was a large man with a constant edge of volatility. Samantha would never tell me if he put his hands on her, but it didn't really matter. With every movement he instilled the belief the next moment may hold a fist up against the side of a head or a hand wrapped around a soft throat. He seemed to show up at odd places at odd times. Samantha told me he cheated on her more than once. He was obsessed by the idea another man might notice his wife, and yet felt entitled to break his vows. And like everything else, Allen Kilborn ultimately took control of the entire divorce process, setting his own terms, his own rules, despite being the one to violate the sanctity of the marriage. It made me wonder what part of him was broken in order to need such control. What had happened to make him feel so inadequate? But those questions could never be answered. The man had buried any vulnerability underneath a lifetime of debris. Besides, what could possibly justify twisting your child in a knot to serve your own purposes? What could possibly justify treating a woman like Samantha as if she was a possession?

The idea of Samantha underneath him sickened me. Underneath him physically, thrusting himself into her, and underneath him mentally, afraid she might wake up in the night with the man standing above her in the darkness. Worried her son might be taken away, or the house sold, or the electricity turned off. I felt a jealousy, wrapped around anger, and the old secret desire to protect, fix, and save, began to mix together with the jealousy and anger to form a new emotion.

After three or four months of seeing each other, I was at Samantha's house on a Saturday. Allen Jr. kept me at a distance. Our conversations were always short and meaningless. I'd never walked the line of stepparent, or potential stepparent, and therefore decided to walk slowly, particularly under the circumstances. Where did I fit between mother and father, between the role of big brother or no role at all?

Little Allen, as he was sometimes called, stood in the kitchen. Samantha was somewhere in the back room. Without provocation, Little Allen said, "I don't have to listen to you."

It caught me unprepared, obviously something his father had told him. I said, "Well, I suppose nobody has to listen to what anybody says."

He looked at me. Eleven years old, but already beginning to look like a version of his father, staring with purpose, head tilted back just enough to notice.

"I'm just saying, legally I don't have to do what you say. That's the law."

I thought about it. "What if I married your mother? What if we all lived in a house together? Don't you think you'd want to listen to me then?"

I didn't intend it as a threat. It was just a direction for the conversation. A hypothetical situation. Allen Jr. looked at me until his face hardened, and he left the room in a hurry. I knew he'd call his father. After that, I wasn't sure what would happen.

Ten minutes later my uncertainty was answered. I was in the front yard trying to start the lawnmower. Samantha and the boy were inside the house. The large white truck pulled up to the curb and stopped with a jolt. Allen Kilborn slammed the truck door and headed in my direction. I stood my ground and waited on the far side of the lawnmower. It was the space I might need if the man took a swing.

He was dressed well, like he'd just left a business meeting. He stopped on the side of the mower, and we stood there looking at each other.

"You think you're the first guy to hang around here?" Samantha told me she hadn't dated much.

"I don't know," I said.

"You're not," he said. His voice wasn't loud, but the words had the same crushing tone as before. Like everything he said was more important than anything anyone else could say. It was my turn to speak.

"Okay," I said.

He leaned his heavy frame over the lawnmower and

merely whispered, "You'll stay around here as long as I let you stay around here. Understand?"

I considered my options, having run through this scenario many times in my mind. If I told him I'd stay around as long as Samantha let me, it would only push the pressure back on her, and eventually she would fold under the weight, unable to stand against him, unable to choose me over the alternative. It would be easier, even if she loved me, not to face the threat of losing her only child, or the house she loved, or going back into the workforce, or being afraid every day, every time a white truck passed her office or the phone rang in the middle of the night.

I looked at the man and felt the second click of the machine in my mind, the second microscopic movement toward a plan. It was justified. He'd justified it himself by his actions every day. By choosing himself over his marriage, his wife, his child. Choosing bad over good, evil over cleanliness, the deadly sins over God's choice. Allen Kilborn would never stop. He would eventually force the end of Samantha for me. Force me back inside the hole where I'd spent the last ten years. Force his son to hate me, and to hate his mother, and eventually the entire world, until the boy got married himself, and had his own boy, and felt entitled, and followed the endless circle back around. Allen Kilborn would never end the cycle on his own volition, and therefore, someone else had to do it.

All those thoughts, and more, passed through my mind in the few seconds we stood looking at one another. How much he knew of my thoughts I wasn't sure, but he seemed like a man too busy with his own intentions to figure out other men. I knew much more about him than he knew about me. It was only one of my advantages. He would underestimate me, and I would let him.

Allen Kilborn walked away and got in his big truck. I turned to the house to see Samantha and Allen Jr. standing at the window of the living room. It reminded me of the time I sat in the car in my mother's driveway in the pouring rain and looked at her for a long time. Samantha could probably no longer even contemplate what was best for her. And the boy, God knows the boy understood nothing. He probably thought his father looked tough walking across the front yard back to the big white truck.

On a Friday evening when I knew Allen Kilborn was at a local football game with Allen Jr., I drove to his house. The road off the highway was long and newly paved. There was one streetlight at the beginning of the road, a mile from the house, and one in front of the driveway leading to the house. The driveway was also paved, which made things easy. No tire tracks could be left behind in the dirt.

I drove past the house and turned around. The closest neighbor was a quarter mile away. I saw an older man working in a flower bed. He didn't see me. The name on the mailbox was Welty. No dogs barked. The trees between the houses were thick. I doubted the Weltys liked Allen Kilborn much.

On the way back past Allen's house, I slowed to a stop. Again, no dogs barked. I took out my notepad and drew a crude draft of the house and surrounding area. From the driveway to the front door there were walking stones, which made things easy. No shoe prints left behind.

I sat in the car and smoked a cigarette, glancing every few seconds in the rearview mirror to make sure Mr. Welty wasn't going out for a drive. The house was two stories. Ostentatious, like the man who lived inside. I made a note to shoot out the streetlight above a few days before I'd come back. I could use Little Allen's pellet gun.

The second part of the plan was to gather certain information from Allen Jr. through questions hidden in the flow of a conversation. I read a newspaper article once about how the vast majority of murders in America are heat-of-passion. Domestic violence. Alcohol-related. Bad drug deals. Late night fights in barrooms. The defendant gets convicted by eyewitness testimony, or the statement of an accomplice, or leaving behind evidence like DNA, or fingerprints, or a murder weapon. It seemed to me, with proper planning, ninety percent of those problems were easily eliminated. Wear gloves, don't have an accomplice, never talk about your plan or what you've done. Use a weapon that can't be connected, have an explanation for anything you might leave behind, be thorough, prepared, completely destroy everything afterwards that could possibly become a link back. Such as shoes, clothes, gloves. Just be smart, and patient, remove the emotion from the equation. Consider it a mathematical formula.

"Your dad's not home, Allen," I said, one afternoon in the yard. "Unless you've got a key, we can't take you over there."

"I've got a key," he said. "Dad gave me one."

"What about the house alarm?" I asked.

"He doesn't use it. Dad says it's stupid. He says the .357 magnum is a better house alarm anyway."

The boy was mimicking his father's words. I could detect a change in tone, a puffing up.

"Your dad's got a gun?" I asked. "I bet you've never shot it."

"I have so. We went to the pistol range. He lets me shoot it anytime I want."

I considered the next question carefully.

"I bet he didn't give you a key to the safe where he keeps the gun."

"Now that's stupid," the boy said, again mimicking his father's tone. "What good would a gun be locked up in a safe if somebody busted into your home? He keeps it in the kitchen drawer next to the refrigerator. It's a special place made just for the gun."

I have to admit, when I first drove out to the man's house, and even much later, it was just an idea. A crazy idea that rested in the back of the mind like a tiny seed. Something to think about alone in bed at night. Something to occupy the dead minutes of the day, to mollify the anger. I just toyed with the idea, kinda pushed it around to see if it would move on its own. I kept notes in the notepad. Before too long, it became truly necessary. More than possible, it became truly necessary. Necessary to me and Samantha having a life together. Necessary to Samantha getting out from under, becoming herself again. Necessary for the kid to have a chance in this screwed-up world. And there was something even bigger than all that. Some necessity to prove the angels right. Bad people should never prosper, and until I got involved, Allen Kilborn prospered like a king.

In another conversation, clearing off the dinner table, with Samantha in the bath, I said, "You need to go to bed early tonight."

"Why?" he asked.

"Your mom said you and your dad stayed up late last night talking on the computer. You've got school tomorrow."

"Dad stays up sometimes all night on his computer. That's how he gets his work done. He just fixed up the little room at the top of the stairs as the computer room. He's gonna give me my own new desk and new computer next to his. A lot nicer than the one here, that's for sure."

I wanted to say, "Of course it's a lot nicer, you idiot. He makes sure your mother can't ever win. The game is rigged, and you fall for it every time."

But with this last tidbit of information, everything fell into place. I'd long since passed the point of questioning the morality. It was now just a question of precision. With proper precision, the legal consequences didn't seem relevant. I never considered anything else. How it might change a man's life when he kills another man. Any man. Even a bad one.

four

I looked forward to seeing Samantha. She spent the night at my place whenever Allen Jr. was staying with his father and Gretchen wasn't in town. It was our time, alone, without distraction, free from ex-husbands and ex-wives, free from the complications of children and potential stepchildren. It was always the time I knew for sure I wanted to marry her, and live together, and not be on my own anymore.

She was funny. And in the bedroom Samantha didn't just wait around for things to happen. I'd forgotten how wonderful it could be with the doors locked, a few glasses of wine, a mischievous look in her eye as the panties come off.

But even at my own home, with the doors locked tight, I found myself peering out windows expecting to see Allen Sr. sitting in the big white truck outside my house. I knew he wasn't the kind of man who would ever allow another man living in the same house with his son, taking his place as a father figure, taking his place as the husband he could never be to the woman now outside his control, no longer dependent upon his money.

My plan was slow and patient. I took a business trip to Chicago. It was a seminar on new investment opportunities. On a Tuesday afternoon I skipped a class on alternative fuel source investments and rode a taxi to the far side of the city. At a Salvation Army store I got a pair of brown cotton gloves, khaki work pants, a button-down flannel shirt, a pair of thick dark socks, and a pair of cheap boots. I made sure none fit me well.

Next door, at a hardware store, I had a key made. The morning before leaving home I had taken Little Allen's key to his father's house and slipped it in my pocket. While the man in the hardware store cut the key, I made small talk.

"I've never really figured out how that machine works," I said.

"It's easy," the man said. "You just stick it in here."

I didn't pay attention.

"Can you tell where a key was made?" I asked. "I mean, if I found a key on the street, would there be any way to tell what machine, in what state, at what store, cut the duplicate key?"

"Naw," he said, "there's not a secret number on it. It's just a key."

When I arrived at the airport, I put the shoes, pants, shirt, socks, and gloves in the trunk underneath the spare tire in the wheel well of my car. That evening, over at Samantha's house, I waited for Allen Jr. to go outside and then replaced the key to his father's house back where I'd found it, later hiding the spare in my own house.

While in Chicago I toyed with the idea of buying bullets for a .357, but I couldn't get them home on the airplane and didn't want to risk sending a package through the mail. Surely Allen would keep his gun loaded. He was the kind of man to have a loaded pistol in his house, or at least bullets nearby in the special drawer in the kitchen.

I hadn't seen Eddie Miller in years. He still lived in town and worked for a rental car agency, but we never seemed to be in the same place at the same time until we ran into each other at a doughnut shop one morning.

It was good to see him again. He'd gained weight, probably from hanging out too often in the doughnut shop. We talked about being kids and the stupid stuff we did. We talked some of college days, but not a lot, and I told him all about Kate. He already knew most of it, but shook his head and listened anyway. He seemed happy for me finding Samantha.

We left the doughnut shop promising to go drink a beer together soon. We exchanged phone numbers and shook hands. His smile was the same as it always had been. Wide but reluctant, like he wasn't sure it was appropriate to laugh at certain things. Like maybe the world wasn't supposed to be a funny place, even if he found it funny sometimes.

The days kept passing and the plan kept moving forward by itself. On Samantha's calendar hanging on the refrigerator, a date was marked in red. I pointed with my finger and said, "What's happening here?"

Samantha leaned over to see. "Oh, Allen's father is taking him deep-sea fishing. They leave at five A.M. and get back around seven at night."

It was three weeks away. Suddenly my plan had a date, a day on the calendar marked in red. It became more real. Part of me hoped something would happen to change the course of events. The other part of me knew there were no alternatives. The next night, perhaps purely by coincidence, I was reminded of this fact.

Samantha and I were having one of our nights alone at my house. We had candles around the bathtub, and a bottle of wine, and the blinds closed tight. She bent over for me in front of the big bathroom mirror, and I was grateful for the chance to see us that way. A few minutes later, after midnight, while Samantha stretched out in the bathtub, I snuck out my back door to the secret porch in total darkness to smoke a cigarette. I was naked, and it felt good to be naked in the cool evening, the backyard surrounded by a privacy fence.

I kept a pack of cigarettes and a book of matches hidden in a crack between two boards above the door. Samantha didn't know I smoked a cigarette every few days. I'm sure she wouldn't have cared, but it wasn't how I wanted her to see me. I never smoked in front of anyone else, and sometimes went months between buying a new pack.

I reached up, fished out a cigarette, and lit it quickly. I held the menthol smoke inside my lungs, breathing out slowly, thinking about the woman in my bathtub, surrounded by candles. Thinking about the look on her face in the mirror, bent over with me inside her. I closed my eyes and let the smoke roll freely from my nose.

In the quiet, from the darkness twenty feet away at the far end of the screen porch, the voice said, "That's some sweet pussy, wouldn't you say?"

The shock of not being alone, the instantaneous outright fear, shot like electricity up my legs and into the core of my naked chest. I spun around, lost my balance, dropped the cigarette on the floor and fell against the door leading back into the house. It wasn't until I got through the door I recognized who it was, the voice.

I ran to the hall closet and grabbed a baseball bat. From the bathroom Samantha said, "What's going on?"

"Nothing," I answered quickly, and then pulled on a pair of shorts, the fear hardening into a brick of anger. How long had the son-of-a-bitch been there? Did he watch us through the tiniest crack in the blinds at the bathroom window? He had seen me smoking, naked, on the back porch, eyes closed?

I flicked on the kitchen light and swung open the back door to the porch, now lit from the lights through the windows. He was gone. My cigarette still lay on the tile floor, smoke rising slowly up and circling.

I heard Samantha coming up from behind. Before she could see, I picked up the cigarette and shoved the butt into the dirt of the big houseplant by the screen door.

She was wearing only a towel and carrying a glass of white wine.

"What's going on?" she repeated.

I decided not to say.

"It smells like somebody's been smoking out here," she said.

"I know. I thought I heard somebody. Probably just kids." I turned my head away so she couldn't get a whiff of my breath.

She stretched her neck to look around the doorframe.

"You've got a bat," she said.

I wondered whether Allen Kilborn was somewhere out in the darkness watching us, maybe even close enough to hear our conversation. The moment solidified my resolve. He deserved to die. He earned it. Sitting on my back porch in the middle of the night. I wasn't Samantha. He wouldn't intimidate me with his bullshit. And I remembered Allen Jr. was staying at his house that night. The man had left his eleven-year-old son alone in the house. What if the kid woke up? What if he had a bad dream and went to his father's bedroom for comfort? His father wouldn't have been there. Instead, he would have been on my back porch talking nasty about the mother of his son. Scaring the holy shit out of me.

Two days before the date marked in red on the calendar, I drove in the very early morning hours to two designated spots. I put on the Salvation Army boots and walked approximately fifty yards to each place into the woods. I took a small gardening shovel I'd found a few weeks earlier at the local dump. With the shovel I dug two holes, one at each location, about two feet deep, in the soft soil. I piled up the dirt around the backside of the holes, careful not to leave any mud or dirt around the front of the holes, and careful to remove any dirt from the bottom of the over-sized boots before the boots were placed back in the wheel well. No cars passed on the secluded backroads while I dug the holes.

Later that day I burned all my written notes and plans, along with the diagram of Allen Kilborn's house, and the maps of the backroads. I lit them on fire inside a ceramic pot, and after each piece was burned, I poured water into the pot, stirred it around into a black mess, and poured it on the flowers in the backyard. I burned the entire notepad in case anything I'd written or drawn had traced onto a bottom page. The diagrams reminded me of the drawings I'd made so long ago of the drugstore—locations of mirrors, the pharmacist, the candy bars, Eddie's lookout point. I'd forgotten the janitor, and learned from my mistake.

The day arrived. I didn't sleep well the night before.

Looking over at the red numbers on the clock by the bed. Thinking, and rethinking, every part of the plan. Allowing myself to overthink and find flaws where no flaws existed. It was almost like the plan stood alone, outside of me.

I knew the boy would be picked up by his father around five in the morning. At five-thirty I drove over to Samantha's house and let myself in the back door. She'd gone back to sleep like I knew she would and the house was quiet. I went to Little Allen's room and got his pellet gun. I drove to Allen Sr.'s house and pulled up at a spot on the road with a clear shot at the streetlight. I took aim at the light, pulled the trigger, and missed. The gun wasn't very loud, but I felt stupid missing the entire streetlight. I shot again. And then again. On my fifth shot the light busted and glass crashed to the ground. I drove away in a hurry, checking the rearview mirror for any cars coming from the direction of the Weltys' house down the road.

Back at Samantha's, I replaced the pellet gun in Little Allen's room, wiping my fingerprints away while she slept.

I took Samantha to breakfast and we spent the morning shopping at the mall. I tried to focus on little things, bacon, a kid sitting on a wood bench, swinging his legs, waiting for his mother to try on another pair of ridiculous shoes, a dog outside lifting his leg on the back tire of a new car, and then the front tire a few seconds later. I tried not to think about how the plan would ultimately end, only the next step. The next thing to do on the list in my mind.

I called Eddie Miller and set up a time in the afternoon to drink a beer together. He picked me up around three o'clock. Down the road on the way across town to the sports bar to watch the Saturday game, I said, "Do you mind swinging by Samantha's ex-husband's house? It's on the way. I'm supposed to see if the kid's back from fishing."

"Yeah, okay," Eddie said. He didn't care anything about the game.

As we pulled up near the front of Allen Kilborn's house, I pretended to notice the broken glass for the first time.

Eddie said, "Looks like somebody busted the street-light."

I told Eddie to stop at a spot on the street where he couldn't see the front door. His windows were up and the radio was playing. Eddie was the kind of man who enjoys air-conditioning and music.

I walked on the pavement and then across the steps to the door, glanced back to make sure Eddie's car was out of sight, knocked on the door three hard times, and then opened the front door with the key cut in Chicago. I hurried to the kitchen and opened the drawer using the tail of my shirt between my fingers on the knob. Inside was a .357 pistol, just as Allen Jr. said, in a special wooden rest. It was loaded.

I went to the foot of the stairs and walked up slowly, stepping near the middle of each step. The seventh step squeaked in the middle. The right-hand side made no sound. At the top of the steps, straight across the hall, was the computer room. The back of the chair faced the stairs, with the computer in front of the chair, and a big window to the left. I went back down the stairs, again slowly, and avoided the middle of the seventh step. I ran to the refrigerator, grabbed two beers, stepped outside, locked the door, and walked across the stones and the pavement to Eddie's car, careful not to step near any broken glass.

"The door was unlocked," I said. "They're not back yet. I don't think he'll miss a few beers."

Eddie drank down nearly half the beer like he was

thirsty. In only a few minutes I'd accomplished a good chunk of the plan. I tested the key, verified the location of the gun, made sure it was loaded, and got the layout of the house. I checked out the stairs, saw the design of the computer room, made Eddie a witness to my visit to the house of Allen Kilborn, as well as the unlocked door and the busted light. Most importantly, I now had an explanation for any hair, fingerprint, glass shards in the shoe sole, stray eyelash, or anything else I could leave behind or take with me from the crime scene. I simply stopped by to check on the boy. He wasn't back yet. The door was unlocked, so I called inside, walked up the steps to see if they might be upstairs, grabbed a few beers, and left. And who could say the door wasn't unlocked? Allen Kilborn? He'd be dead in ten hours, according to the plan.

At around seven o'clock in the evening, according to schedule, Allen Sr. dropped off his son at Samantha's house. The boy was exhausted. He told us all about the day. He went to his room after a shower and talked with his father on the computer. By ten o'clock, Allen Jr. was sound asleep.

By eleven o'clock, Samantha was on her fourth glass of her favorite Chablis. I brought over two bottles, and every time I poured a glass for myself I'd fill it half with water. We watched a movie, and around twelve o'clock, midway through her fifth glass, Samantha fell asleep. I carried her to the bedroom and she was snoring like a sailor in just a few minutes.

I entered the boy's room quietly. He was hard asleep.

The computer in his room was turned off. I closed his door and then sat down alone in the living room. I could have laid down on the couch and just fallen asleep. I could have let the Saturday marked in red on the calendar pass by. Sometimes I wish I had.

I got the clothes from under the wheel well and changed in the front seat of my car. I drove the posted speed limit to the road leading to Allen Kilborn's house. The light was on upstairs in the computer room. The Weltys' house was dark except for a light on the front porch.

I parked away from the broken glass on the dark street. I could have driven away. I could have gone home and stood on the back porch smoking a cigarette. But I didn't. I closed the car door quietly, walked over the pavement and across the stones to the door. No matter how much you plan, no matter how precise and careful, luck demands a role. Allen Kilborn could've been standing in the kitchen in his underwear drinking milk out of the carton when I opened the door. He could have been at the top of the stairs looking down on me. But he wasn't. He was sitting, just as I envisioned, at his computer, with his back to the stairs, when I arrived behind him, holding the man's loaded pistol in my gloved hand. He didn't hear the squeak from the middle of the seventh step, because I didn't step in the middle. He didn't hear anything at all.

I was behind him. I could've gone back down the stairs. I could've avoided the squeak on the way down, replaced the pistol in the special drawer, locked the door on the way out, and climbed in bed with beautiful, drunk Samantha. But I didn't. I held up the gun and thought of her on her knees with her mouth on him, with him looking down on her, and her eyes looking up at him. It disgusted me, and I felt my chest tightening inside. Suddenly, I couldn't draw the next breath, just like the day at the pond with my grandfather. My lungs seized. I felt the panic rise through my body.

Allen Kilborn's fingers stopped on the computer keyboard, like he sensed someone behind him. Like he knew I'd gotten the best of him. And according to plan, even in the middle of a full-blown asthma attack, just as I knew I would, I pulled the trigger, exploding the back of Allen Kilborn's head like a ripe melon across the room.

I bent over at the waist and tried to concentrate. The air sucked in, and I stood, arms outstretched, praying I wouldn't collapse on the floor in the dead man's room. Listening for my grandfather's words of comfort. Trying to rationalize the irrational, and in time, the air came more freely. I didn't look back at him. I kept the gun, ran down the stairs, rubbed both doorknobs with my gloved hand, and left the door unlocked on my way out. I stayed on the stones, and then the pavement, and avoided the shards of glass. I drove carefully, my hands shaking on the wheel like a man with Parkinson's, my breath still short and forced, to the first designated location on the backroads. I turned the car so the headlights would shine in the woods, walked in my Salvation Army clothes to the hole I'd dug, and dropped the gun into the hole. With the shovel I'd left near the hole, I pushed dirt and mud inside until it was full and covered the top with dry leaves. I walked back, careful not to step in any mud, and removed my boots before entering the car. I changed clothes in the front seat. At the second designated location, after parking the car again with the headlights shining my path, I walked in sock feet to the second hole. I dropped the shirt, pants, gloves, and boots into the hole, filled the hole, and again covered it with leaves.

Before entering the car, I removed the heavy dark socks and put my regular socks and shoes on my feet. A mile down the road I threw one sock out the window. A mile further, the second sock followed. And a mile later, the little shovel ended up in a gully and the spare key flew through the air and landed in a farmer's field.

I parked outside Samantha's house and opened the back door quietly. Again, Samantha, or even worse, Allen Jr., could have been standing in the kitchen getting a glass of water. But they weren't. Allen was still sleeping hard after a day fishing in the hot sun. Samantha still snored like a sailor. It was done. It was over. I stood in the shower and felt the hot water down the back of my neck, felt the shaking in my hands slow to a pulse, took long steady, deep breaths, in and out again.

I climbed in bed in my underwear and waited until my body warmed beneath the blankets. I touched Samantha and woke her with a kiss. If she only knew what I'd done for her and her boy. If I only knew how it would occupy my mind for the rest of my life.

She smiled. "You're staying the night?" she asked softly.

"Yes," I said. "I'm staying the night."

six

That night I dreamed again of the scary black circle on the floor. I hadn't had the dream in years, but it came back just as before, except this time in the dream I was an old man. I was alone in a bedroom, sitting in a wheelchair, watching television. I was very tired. The circle appeared slowly on the hardwood floor by the closed door. I watched it form, beginning as just a slight discoloration, and then taking shape until it was the same circle from my childhood dreams.

The black circle began to move toward my wheelchair. The movement was steady and slow, getting closer and closer to me. I couldn't move my arms. I was too tired to move my arms to roll away from the circle, and it got closer and closer until the edge reached the outer wheel of the chair, and the chair began to tip into the hole, and I woke up covered in sweat.

Believe me, my various motivations for what I'd done to Allen Kilborn did not completely escape me. I'd built a fortress of justification, but it was impossible to ignore my savior complex rearing its ugly head. The jealousy and anger held deep roots, and regardless of whether the world, and Samantha, and Allen Jr., were better off, I would forever struggle with untangling the necessities.

I lay in bed, thinking of the circle and waiting for Samantha to open her eyes and see me in her bed, see the clock, and know I'd slept with her throughout the night. I backtracked through my mind, making sure I hadn't forgotten anything. The explosion of the man's head was difficult to believe. How quickly he went from alive to dead. How suddenly I was alone in the house, his brains and blood across the computer and the wall. The next morning, it was hard to believe I'd done such a thing.

"Good morning," she said. The clock showed 8:07 A.M.

"Good morning. How do you feel?" I asked.

"Like my head got stepped on by a giant."

She went to the bathroom, and I put on my pants. While she took a shower and tended to her headache, I banged around in the kitchen until Allen Jr. wandered in for breakfast.

"What are you doing here?" he asked.

"I fell asleep," I answered.

The boy made a face of disgust. He went back to his room, and I knew he would send a message to his father telling him I'd spent the night. Tangible confirmation of my alibi. See, even the boy knows I spent the night in the house. I was there the next morning, in the kitchen, with no shirt.

Allen Jr. and Samantha arrived back in the kitchen at the same moment. She avoided eye contact with the boy, recognizing the anticipated repercussions from her ex-husband for allowing a man to spend the night in his home with his son in the other room.

Allen Jr. said, "Dad's not answering on his computer."

"Maybe he's still asleep," Samantha said.

The boy picked up the phone and dialed a number. I poured a cup of coffee and imagined the phone ringing in an empty house, the dead man upstairs in a cake of his dried blood, stuck to the floor. My stomach felt weak. The smell of the coffee was suddenly sickening.

"There's no answer," he said.

"Well, maybe he had to go out for something," Samantha offered. "We're gonna go to church this morning. We missed last week."

"Can I go?" I asked. I'd never been with them before.

Samantha seemed pleasantly surprised. "Yes, you can," she said.

I drove home, washed my clothes in the washing machine with hot water, took another long, thorough shower, washing my hair twice. On the way to meet Samantha and Little Allen at church, I stopped at a self-service car wash and vacuumed the car, including the trunk and under the spare tire. I sprayed down the car, concentrating on the tires and underneath.

The church was big and white. We sat near the front, and I was glad. The multi-colored, stained glass window of Jesus on the cross glowed in the morning sunlight, high above.

The Episcopal priest stood to deliver the sermon. He was a small man, thin, with not much hair left on his head. He spoke of our limitations, and how we shouldn't be disappointed in our inability to always behave like God would want us to. He said that's the very reason we need a God, to forgive us, to teach us, to help us find our way. What would be the role of God in a world full of God-like humans? None. Just like the Devil would have nothing to do in a world of sinners who fail to recognize their sins, or fail to repent. I tried very hard not to fidget or look around too much.

Afterwards, on the way out, I shook hands with several people I recognized, and knew they'd remember seeing me for the first time in their church. I shook the priest's hand at the door, but didn't overdo it or bring attention to myself. He hugged Samantha, and told her he was praying for her. I wondered how he had enough hours in the day to pray for everyone he knew, or even everyone he knew who needed praying for.

On Sunday night, alone on my back porch, I sat in the dark smoking a cigarette. All day I'd waited for the phone to ring, the news of Allen Kilborn's death, the suspicion cast on the ex-wife and her boyfriend. The coming down of everything upon the discovery of the dead man. I hoped it wouldn't be Samantha or the boy to see him first.

The phone rang. It was Samantha. "Allen wants me to take him over to his father's," she said.

"It's a school night," I said. "His father's probably not

home because he's stalking one of us again. Maybe he's hiding in my bushes right now, or putting sugar in my gas tank."

She laughed a little, but not really. It was more a nervous giggle, kinda like it was risky to say such things over the phone. Like there was nothing Allen Kilborn couldn't hear, or tape-record, or find out about.

It was impossible to sleep. I kept hearing the priest's words in my head. I kept going over and back over every detail of the plan, every unforseen mistake, and the black circle waited for me. Waited for my eyes to close, the cover of darkness, peaceful sleep, to sneak back into my room and maybe swallow me completely, sucking me down. But eventually I must have fallen asleep, because at 6:48 in the morning the phone rang, loud like a fire alarm.

"Hello," I said.

"Oh my God," the woman's voice said.

"Hello," I repeated.

"Allen's dead," Samantha stuttered. "Somebody killed him."

"Jesus," I said. "Little Allen?" I asked.

"No, no. Not Little Allen. Big Allen. They found him shot in his house. His business partner was supposed to meet him there at six-thirty this morning. He just called me. The police are there."

"Oh my God," I said convincingly. I knew the phone records would show Samantha called me immediately after hearing the news. I knew the investigators would jump to the conclusion we killed him together, and Samantha was calling me to tell me the body had been found.

"You need to go over there," I said. I figured her emotions would be genuine in front of the investigators. She had nothing to fake, because she knew nothing, and never would. The first impression she would leave with the investigators could be invaluable.

I needed to be seen at work, composed, yet concerned about Samantha. I ended the conversation telling her to go to Allen's house so she could give the police any information about the fishing trip, and her son's return Saturday night, and Allen Sr. not answering his boy's calls all day Sunday. I didn't want to be there with her, following the old pattern of the murderer returning to the scene of the crime.

I shared with the people in my office what had happened, appearing amazed and shocked. Later that morning, about lunchtime, Samantha called from the police station. She asked if I'd come down. The investigator wanted to ask me a few questions. I didn't hesitate or hurry, arriving at the police station and asking to see Samantha Kilborn.

A man introduced himself to me.

"I'm Frank Rush, the investigator on the Allen Kilborn homicide."

"I'm Early Winwood. Is Samantha here?"

"She's in the back talking to my partner. Would you mind stepping in my office? I was hoping you could answer a few quick questions."

"Absolutely," I said.

He was mid-fifties, slightly overweight, with a mustache and a patient way about him. I sat down across his desk. Behind him there was a picture of a woman with three grown kids, maybe college-age. The youngest looked very much like his father sitting in front of me, except without a mustache. The woman was remarkably unattractive, her face reminding me of a rodent.

"How long have you and Samantha been going out?"

"It's been months. She called me and told me what happened right after the business partner called her this morning. Has anybody told the boy yet?"

Frank Rush studied me for a moment. All of his thirty years of instincts were focused on my eyes, the inflection in my voice, the movement of my hands in my lap, my breathing. What if I had another asthma attack? An involuntary shut-down of my lungs in the office of the homicide investigator?

"The boy's in a safe place," he said. "You mind if I tape-record our conversation? It just helps me later when I have to put all the information in a report."

"No, I don't mind."

He pressed the button on a hand-held recorder, whispered the date and time and my name, and asked me, "Mr. Winwood, you know anybody who might want to kill Allen Kilborn?"

"Well," I hesitated, "no." I intentionally left a space between the words to invite the next question.

"You seemed to hesitate with your answer."

"Well, I don't know how much you know about Allen Kilborn, and I don't want to speak ill of the dead, but he was the kind of man someone might want to kill."

I could almost see his mind reeling inside. "How so?" he asked.

"He was…abrasive."

"Abrasive?" he repeated.

"He was a bully. I guess that's the best way to put it."

Frank Rush sat perfectly still, arms crossed on the desk in front of him. "Did you ever want to kill Allen Kilborn?" he asked.

"No," I said. "I never wanted to kill him. I would have liked to kick his ass a few times, but I wouldn't want to kill anybody."

"Do you have a key to his house?" he asked.

"No. I don't even think Samantha has a key."

"Have you ever been inside Allen Kilborn's house?"

I pretended to think. "As a matter of fact, yes. This past weekend. Saturday afternoon around three o'clock or three-thirty. I stopped by to see if they were back from deep-sea fishing. I knocked, nobody answered, the door was unlocked, so I went inside and called out for the boy. They weren't back yet, so we left."

"Who is 'we'?" he asked.

"My friend, Eddie Miller, was driving. We were on the way to watch a football game at a sports bar."

Frank Rush leaned back in his squeaky leather chair. "Is it just a coincidence, Mr. Winwood, that the first and only time you've been in Allen Kilborn's house was the same day he was murdered?"

I paused. "I guess so, but he wasn't home. They weren't back from the fishing trip. I'm sure you can verify that with the charter boat."

The man stared at me. I waited the required period of time. "You act like I had something to do with this," I said.

"Did you?" he asked.

"No, I didn't."

"Whoever it was who went to see Allen Kilborn this weekend went there to kill him. It wasn't a robbery. It was an execution. Do you own a gun?"

"No, I don't have a gun. I've never had a gun." I showed a touch of anger at the implied accusation.

Frank Rush said, "You wouldn't mind if we searched your house, or your car, would you? I mean, you have the right to say no, but if you don't have anything to hide…"

He shrugged his shoulders. It was a test.

"I don't have anything to hide. You can search all you want."

My car was taken behind the police station to a garage. I rode with Investigator Rush to my house. Two other officers met us there. I sat down on the couch as they combed through my house. Shirt, pants, socks, and shoes, all touched and replaced in drawers and on hangers. One guy crawled around in my attic with a flashlight and another sifted through the garbage in my garage. There was nothing to find.

My car had an odd smell, a chemical smell, when I got it back. After I left the police station I drove to see Samantha. Allen Jr. was with his grandparents. They'd searched Samantha's house, specifically asking about Allen Jr.'s key to his father's door. They took the boy's computer.

I tried to ease Samantha's concerns.

"This is routine, Sam. When somebody gets killed, the first place they look is the ex-wife or ex-husband, and whoever they're dating. Don't worry, we didn't do anything wrong. They've probably already figured out we're not involved. You know as well as I do the son-of-a-bitch probably had a dozen enemies who'd blow his head off if they had a chance."

She said, "They asked me if you spent the night Saturday night. I was embarrassed, but I told them the truth. They looked through my car. They took Little Allen's key and his computer. The man with the mustache said he was killed around midnight Saturday night. He said the only thing stolen was the gun. They think he was shot with his own gun. And they said the door was unlocked."

I went home that night. The highly trained police officers had failed to find my hidden cigarettes. I could've had the gloves hidden there, or the spare key, or a snapshot of the dead man sprawled across the floor, and they'd have missed it. As I smoked my cigarette in the dark, I wondered if Frank Rush was sitting in the bushes in my backyard watching. Maybe sitting in the same place Allen Kilborn sat weeks earlier after scaring the holy shit out of me.

On Tuesday afternoon Investigator Rush stopped by my office unannounced. I didn't act rattled, expecting to hear from him soon. This time, we sat across from each other at my desk instead of his.

"I just had a few more questions I wanted to ask you. You mind if I tape-record the conversation again, just to help my memory? I wouldn't want to get anything wrong."

"Okay," I said, and looked him directly in the eye.

"Where were you Saturday and Saturday night?"

"Allen Jr. went fishing with his father. I went to

Samantha's in the morning and took her to breakfast. We went shopping at the mall. After that, Eddie picked me up around three. We stopped by Allen Kilborn's house, like I said, looking for the boy. He wasn't there. We went to the bar and watched the game. I drank maybe two beers. I got back to Samantha's around six-thirty. Allen Jr. got dropped off by his father at seven.

"After that, Allen fell asleep somewhere around ten. Me and Samantha stayed up, watched a movie, went to sleep around eleven. I usually don't stay overnight when the boy is there, but I fell asleep and woke up the next morning around eight. I fixed coffee. I saw Little Allen in the kitchen before I went home to get dressed for church. And we went to church later that morning."

For the first time in my dealing with Frank Rush, I saw some doubt in his eyes. Doubt that I was involved in the death of Allen Kilborn. Doubt that solving this case would be so easy. Or maybe I imagined it.

"Did you notice anything odd, or out of place, at Kilborn's house that afternoon?"

"Yeah, as a matter of fact, the streetlight outside the house was busted. There was glass by the driveway."

"Anything else?"

"Only that I thought it was strange for the door to be unlocked in the middle of the day with nobody home. But then again, he lived out in the country. Maybe he didn't lock his doors. I don't know."

The investigator looked down at his notes. "There was a calendar on Samantha's refrigerator. Had Saturday marked in red."

"I think Little Allen did that. He was looking forward to the fishing trip."

"How long you and Eddie Miller been friends?"

"All our lives. We grew up together."

"When's the last time you and Eddie went to watch a game together, or drink a beer?"

"Before Saturday?"

"Yeah, before Saturday."

"Probably ten years ago. College."

He watched me closely again. "Is it just a coincidence, again, that the first time, the only time in ten years, you go have a beer and watch a game with your lifelong friend, Eddie, happens to be the same day, and the only day, you ever go inside Allen Kilborn's house, which happens to be the same day Allen Kilborn gets his head blown off in that same house?"

Conscious of the tape recorder spinning round and round on the desk between us, I said, "I guess so, Mr. Rush, but I'm not a killer, and neither is Samantha."

Frank Rush leaned over and turned off the tape recorder. "Would you mind, Mr. Winwood, providing me a written statement of your whereabouts on Saturday and Sunday? Just for the file."

"No, I wouldn't mind," I said.

"Oh, by the way," he said, "Eddie told us about your ex-wife. We pulled the divorce file, and called Kate to verify a few things. Did you ever get charged criminally with assaulting the man you assaulted in that house off-campus?"

For the first time in our conversations, I was caught off guard.

"No," I said, "and it didn't happen the way she said it did. People will say anything in a custody battle. Did she mention she was strung out on crack?"

It was near the end of our conversation. He accomplished his goal of shaking me up, but it wouldn't make any difference. He stood to walk out the door, and then stopped in the doorway. "Oh, one last question. How many times have you been to church with Samantha and her son?"

We looked at each other. "Once. Sunday was the first time."

He reached his hand up and scratched the back of his neck. Frank Rush said, "Another coincidence?"

But he didn't want an answer, and didn't wait for one.

The funeral was on Wednesday morning at the Episcopal church. Allen Jr. was the same age I had been when my father died. Watching him cry made me feel the way I'd felt twenty years earlier as I stood in front of my father's casket and wanted to wake him. Just wanted to touch his arm and remind him it was time to go throw the ball in the front yard. Watching Allen's body shake in front of his father's closed casket made me doubt what I had done. Maybe it wasn't for me to decide. Maybe the bad would outweigh the good, for all of us.

I looked up at the stained glass window above, Jesus on the cross, multi-colored and all-knowing, glowing in the sunlight of a Wednesday morning, and I began to wonder about who I was, and what I had done, and whether anything would ever make sense again.

seven

Two days after the funeral I had my first experience of leaving myself. It sounds crazy, I know, but the way it sounds is nothing compared to the way it felt.

I was driving down the four-lane interstate alone in the afternoon. Traffic was light, and up ahead in my lane, two or three hundred yards in front, I saw an old pickup truck. The bed of the truck was piled high with picked corn, still in the husk, and on top of the pile of corn sat a Mexican boy, maybe fifteen or sixteen years old. I found myself, within the drone of the radio, fixated on the truck ahead, and the corn, and the boy with the faded red t-shirt and black hair. I got closer and drifted into the left-hand lane to pass the old blue truck. I couldn't seem to remove my eyes from the face of the boy. It was like I was hypnotized or something. And he looked back at me, no expression, with dark eyes against smooth brown skin, the color of wood.

We were nearly side by side, my car and the truck, me and the Mexican boy, and then I saw myself. I saw me, driving my car, from the eyes of the Mexican boy sitting atop the pile of picked corn in the back of the pickup truck. I saw me staring, my hands on the wheel of the car. I looked down at the brown hand resting on the ear of corn next to blue jeans, and looked up again to see myself for just a split-second longer behind the wheel of the car. Just a split-second, and then I was back inside myself again, seeing the Mexican boy, and him seeing me, and passing the truck, trying to figure out what had happened. Looking in the rearview mirror to see if the boy would turn his head around to the front, recognition that something had happened to him also. It wasn't just me. But he didn't turn around, and I kept going, speeding up to get away from the blue pickup truck.

It happened maybe five more times after that through the years, after that day, but never so profoundly, never with such stark images and clarity of perspective. To see the world through someone else's eyes, if only for a second, and then return to yourself, moving away, never to see that person again. I've often wondered what happened to the boy. Where his life took him.

The fallout from Allen Kilborn's murder was immediate. There were possibilities I'd failed to consider. A week before Gretchen's next scheduled visit, I bought tickets for a play and made dinner reservations. I fixed up her room, wondering if I'd picked the right colors. Knowing I was only guessing what girls her age liked, or didn't like, or thought was stupid. I'd missed so much. I'd missed waking her up in the morning, holding her hand on the way to school, the bond that can only come from the repetition of one goodnight kiss after another.

She didn't come. The day before she was supposed to arrive, a deputy from the Sheriff's Department knocked on my door. I sat on Gretchen's bed, on the new quilt and clean sheets, and opened the envelope. My visitation was suspended. Kate's lawyer called me "the subject of a murder investigation," and said I was "cohabitating with a member of the opposite sex not related by blood or marriage." Overnight visitation with my child should be suspended temporarily, they said. There was an affidavit from Investigator Frank Rush cleverly worded to call me a suspect, and at the same time call everyone in the world a suspect.

I called Kate's house. No answer. I hung up before the machine picked up. I called again, and again. I wondered if Gretchen knew it was me, and didn't pick up because she didn't want to talk to me. Because she thought I was a murderer, and a cohabitator, and some strange man she didn't really know, or even want to know, who lived a million miles away and sat in a room that wasn't really hers, on a bed she didn't really want to sleep in.

What judge would order a child to fly across the country to sleep in the home of a man suspected of blowing a man's head off sitting at his computer, in his own home? Not me. What's more, I did it. I wasn't just a suspect. I was a murderer. A man capable of such a thing, even if I was the only one who knew.

I loved Gretchen. I wanted everything I'd missed. I would have been a good father. Better than good. If the judge had given her to me so many years ago, I would have fixed her breakfast every morning. Gotten her dressed. Taken her to daycare or pre-school and made sure no one was mean to her. We would have played in the backyard, and had things together. Like words we both laughed about, or stupid little songs only the two of us could sing, because we'd made up the songs. They were ours.

But she didn't come home with me. She went to California with her mother and her rich stepfather and now they wanted to cut the string of what was left. Maybe it was all a part of the investigator's strategy. Put pressure on me. Take away my little girl. Watch it eat me up inside until I told the truth, all of it, for a chance to see my girl again, or a pack of cigarettes, or a promise of redemption and everlasting forgiveness.

Eddie called and wanted to meet me for a beer at the same place we met before.

When I arrived, he was already perched at a stool, a cold frosty mug of draft beer in his hand. I sat down next to him. He didn't waste time with small talk. "This guy Rush has come to see me three times, Early."

He held up three fingers and repeated, "Three times."

"I know," I said. "He's been to see me, too."

Eddie took a sip of his beer. He said in a low voice, "He's asking me about you, and shit from college, and Kate, and the day we stopped by the dead guy's house."

He looked straight ahead while he talked. It occurred to me he might be wearing a wire. Frank Rush might be sitting in the back room of the bar, listening. He sent Eddie to see me. He squeezed Eddie with threats of arrest, co-conspirator accusations, and now, here we sat, me and my childhood friend Eddie Miller, not so far removed from the drugstore.

"He's asking me the same questions, Eddie. I guess they can't figure out who killed the man, so they just keep asking us the same things over and over. Since we didn't do anything wrong, we don't have anything to worry about. That's the way I look at it."

Eddie looked over at me and took a little sip of his beer. We were quiet for awhile. I glanced around the room looking for anything out of the ordinary. Maybe some-body watching me, a tiny camera lens. Maybe I was paranoid, I thought. Maybe I'd be glancing around rooms for the rest of my life wondering who was wearing a wire or why somebody was looking at me.

Eddie said, "When I was a little kid, why did you tell me there was no such thing as Santa Claus?"

I thought about it. "I don't remember, Eddie."

"That was a shitty thing to do, Early. Shitty. We only have so much time to believe in things like Santa Claus, and after that, it's bullshit and bills to pay, sittin' around knowin' we're gonna die at the end anyway. You shouldn't have told me that."

He was sincere. I began to doubt Frank Rush was hid-ing in the back room with earphones. The bartender walked over to us.

"I'll have what he's having," I said. "And bring him another one, too."

Eddie looked down at his glass.

"I'm sorry," I said.

Somebody slapped my shoulder from behind. It was Jake Crane, my other childhood friend, the polar opposite of Eddie Miller. The guy who laid on the roof next to me watching his cousins take showers. I hadn't seen Jake Crane in at least ten years. He was bloated, puffy in the face. I imagined ten years of cigarettes and whiskey, pool halls and local jails.

"It's like a reunion," Jake yelled. "Bring me one of those beers," he called out to the bartender.

In my paranoid state, I immediately wondered if it was a coincidence. Maybe Jake was in over his head with some drug charge. Maybe he was willing to wear a wire, accidentally run into his buddies, try to start a conversation about Allen Kilborn. Maybe Frank Rush had decided Eddie was involved in the murder, and me and Eddie did it together. My mind spun in circles and eventually came to rest on the puffy face of Jake Crane. He pulled up a stool between us.

I asked him, "Where you been the past decade?"

"Well, let's see," Jake said. "I been married twice, fixin' to be three. I spent a little time upstate after my fourth DUI. I got me a damn good job now, and I gained fifty pounds. That's about it."

I lied and told Eddie and Jake I had to be somewhere. The fallout continued in directions I hadn't envisioned. My two best childhood friends, and I couldn't trust either one of them to have a simple beer and a simple conversation at a bar. I left them sitting next to each other, and I knew when I walked away I'd never meet with either one of them on purpose again. I walked out and got in the car. I sat there thinking about the Mexican kid and the idea of fate. The idea that, if I left the parking lot ten seconds later, or ten seconds earlier, I might find myself in the path of a dump truck running a red light, or find myself not in the path of a dump truck running a red light, and how do I know when to start the car, and when to pull into traffic, and how fast to drive to avoid the dump truck that may not exist, or may very well crush me in my car on the way home?

Reasonable doubt. The very foundation of the American judicial system. A standard a jury must utilize to determine guilt or innocence. If you have reasonable doubt, a doubt for which you have a reason, then you cannot, according to the American judicial system, declare someone guilty. The standard, of course, exists to protect the innocent, but also harbors the well-organized, the well-prepared, the man willing to sacrifice. Maybe one of those sacrifices would be Eddie Miller and Jake Crane. Maybe the sacrifices would never end. Gretchen, then eventually Samantha, and finally, myself. Maybe fate would take it off my shoulders.

I wanted to marry Samantha immediately. I wanted her next to me every night, but it couldn't be done. A wedding so soon after Allen Kilborn's death would brighten the spotlight on me and Samantha. Her focus since the funeral had been on Allen Jr., which is where it belonged, but it left me utterly alone night after night on my porch smoking cigarettes in the dark.

I was finally allowed to talk to Gretchen on the phone. Her voice sounded like she was in the bottom of a deep hole. At one point in the conversation she called me "Early." I knew she'd been calling the old man "Dad," but she rarely slipped anymore. The worst part is, when she slipped on the phone, she didn't even catch it. It went right on by, the low voice from deep in the hole mumbling something about feeling sick, or not being able to miss cheerleading practice. After she called me "Early" it didn't matter anymore.

My mother called. "Why isn't Gretchen coming to visit?"

I couldn't tell her. I couldn't say it.

"She's sick. She can't miss cheerleading practice," I lied.

"That's a lie, Early. What's going on?"

I hesitated. "They filed something with the Court to suspend my visitation."

"For God's sake, why?"

"It's Kate, fuckin' with me. Taking advantage of the situation. They told the judge I was a suspect in the murder of Allen Kilborn."

"Are you?" she asked.

"No," I nearly yelled. "No."

There was silence on both ends of the phone. I could hear her breathing.

"What about me, Early?" Christine asked.

"What?"

"What about me, Goddamnit? Me and Gretchen? Our relationship? Forget about you for a minute. Why do I suffer because you end up in screwed-up situations? I miss the girl. Every day. She's my best friend."

More fallout. More unintended consequences. It didn't seem to make any difference if I got caught by Frank Rush or not. Even my mother would end up hating me. My father would know what to do. If he was still alive, things would be different. I would have married a nice, pear-shaped, stable girl from a stable family and lived securely in a well-built house. No savior complex. No rich stepfather or courthouse marriages. Smooth sailing, it would have been, if only my father had left the parking lot ten seconds earlier, or ten seconds later, crossing the tracks ahead of the train. It was just a matter of moments, like it's always been, and like it will always be.

Strangely, as the weeks passed, and then months, I felt a change in Allen Jr. Before it was always them against us. Little Allen and Big Allen against me and Samantha. The lines were clear. Now, he was just a boy. A boy without a dad. His dad died and left him alone with his mother, and me. The man who hangs around his mother.

"Are you gonna play baseball this year?" I asked.

We were sitting in the living room. Me in the chair and Little Allen on the couch. Since his father died, the boy was quiet most of the time, just like I'd been.

"Maybe," he said.

It was getting late. Samantha was in the bathtub. Every night, before Allen went to sleep, I said goodnight and went back to my house. He had enough to deal with in his world without seeing me walking around the house in my underwear or imagining me and his mother doing it in the bedroom.

"I think you should play. If you want, we'll go look for a new glove. You need a new glove."

He looked at me as I spoke, like he was seeing me for the first time. He didn't respond to the comment about the baseball glove. We sat quietly for a minute. I raised up in the chair to leave.

Allen said, his eyes staring at his hands, "You don't have to go home every night. You could stay here some nights."

It made me smile. It was justification, small, but justification nonetheless. Before, he would never have considered such a thing. I was the enemy. Not anymore. Now I was just a guy. A guy who liked baseball, and anybody who loves baseball can't be all bad. No matter what they've done.

eight

On the third ring, I said out loud into the phone, "Pick up the fuckin' phone." Before I'd finished the sentence, somebody picked it up. There was silence, and then Kate said, "What if Gretchen had answered?"

"Sorry," I said, and I was actually sorry. The frustration was maddening. To have no control over something so important, so simple as having somebody pick up the phone on the other end of the line.

"Nobody answers over there, Kate. I've called ten days in a row. I can't talk to your machine anymore."

Kate said, "We've got caller ID, Early. Gretchen can tell who's calling."

There it was. What I didn't need to hear. "Don't say that. Even if it's true. What pleasure could you possibly gain in saying that? You should see what it's like to be on this side. Why don't you send Gretchen down here? You can have three visits a year and maybe we'll pick up the phone, maybe not, and I'll be sure to rub it up in your face whenever I get the chance."

There was silence again.

"Don't hang up," I said.

I wasn't sure she was still on the line.

"I'm getting married," I said.

There was nothing do but wait for her to answer.

"To who?" she asked.

"Samantha."

"The dead man's ex-wife?"

"Yes. But it doesn't have anything to do with Allen Kilborn. She's a good mother. She's got a boy Gretchen's age."

It was strange, but Kate's voice still held me. There was something pleasant inside of it. I wondered if it was the voice itself, or some memory attached to it. If I'd never met her before, would the voice make me feel anything beyond the words?

"Will it be a big wedding?" she asked, revealing more curiosity than I expected, and maybe more than she expected.

"It didn't start out that way. At first we just had a list of about twenty people. A month later, it was two hundred. Now we've got two cakes, a band, shrimp."

She laughed. "A little different than the first time."

"Yeah," I said. "A little different. I think that's why Samantha wants the whole show. She did it like ours the first time."

It was the most normal conversation I'd had with

Kate since the day she lost her baby. Our baby. The baby inside her that died and made her hate me.

"I want Gretchen to be in the wedding," I said.

"I've got a court order."

"I know what you've got. I haven't seen her for eight months, Kate. I'm gettin' married. She's my daughter. I can't wait until she turns nineteen and then hope she sends me a Christmas card every year. Hope I can undo nineteen years of unanswered phone calls."

I tried to keep the tone of my voice level. Frustration seeped out between the sentences. I took a deep breath, soundless, so she couldn't hear my desperation.

She said, "Did you kill that man, or what?"

"What do you think, Kate?"

She didn't answer, and I imagined her standing in her high school home next to the man in the chair with the hole in his foot, a dim light and a dog at the screen door. A bottle of vodka by the chair. I could see it plain as day. She was wearing a dirty white apron.

"Is your dad still alive?" I asked.

I'm not sure what I meant by the question. Maybe I meant to remind her she had no relationship with her father, and maybe that was part of the reason she'd been so screwed up. And how could she want the same thing for Gretchen?

She finally said, "If Gretchen's going down there, I'm going with her, and we're staying in a motel. I'm gonna be there with her at the wedding, too."

It was unsettling on a number of different levels. Ex-wife at the new wife's wedding. Mostly it was unsettling to me personally. If her voice still held me, how would I feel about her in the same room? At my wedding? But I was in very little position to challenge. Another court battle could take months, and money set aside for other things. Just another conciliation in the great compromise. Wishing I'd left her on that damn street so many years ago didn't help, because there'd be no Gretchen, and then I'd have no idea at all what I'd lost.

"Okay," I said, and we ended the conversation.

People gathered in the church. I stood in a back room at the mirror with Allen Jr., tightening our tuxedo ties. I couldn't stay still.

"Are you nervous?" he asked.

I wanted to be the strong, silent type. I'm sure his father never looked nervous a day in his life. "Yeah, I'm a little nervous," I confessed.

Allen said, "I would think the nervous part would be asking a girl to marry you. That's when you really make the promise."

He was right. The hard parts were over. Minutes later we stood together at the altar waiting to watch Allen's mother walk down the aisle with her father on her arm. My eyes scanned the faces in the crowd. People from work. Not really friends, just people who work in the same place. Allen's grandmother on his father's side. Her face hard like her son's face had been. My mother, Christine, her eyes on Gretchen across the aisle from me. And Frank Rush, the investigator, his face near the back, uninvited. We looked at each other, and I moved along to the next face, and the next, but I felt my chest tighten, the breath stopping at a shallow point in the top of the lungs, refusing to go down deep.

I glanced at Little Allen, and he smiled up at me. He seemed genuinely happy about the marriage. His smile gave me comfort, and I realized that his was the only face in the crowd to bring the feeling. In the far side of my field of vision I saw Kate. For the past two days I'd managed to avoid the moment, but now there was nowhere to go. I didn't have the endurance to look away. She was beautiful. A woman now, not just a lost skinny girl with no home. Her presence made me weak in my legs. A moment longer, even one more moment of looking at her, and something bad would have happened. Instead, the music started, and my new wife turned down the aisle as pretty as any bride could be, her elderly father smiling wide just like the boy next to me, while the stained-glass Jesus looked down upon all of us.

And it happened again. Only for a few seconds, but it definitely happened again. I saw myself from Allen Jr.'s eyes. It was just a blink, the side of my head, the wedding song, and I could feel what he felt. An excitement. Not nearly as clear as with the Mexican boy, but real just the same, and I was grateful for the interruption this time. Not as shocked as before.

At the reception I focused on Samantha. All the other distractions had no place in the day. When I slipped away to the bathroom I thought I'd found a minute to smoke a cigarette and clear out my head. I was wrong. Before I could get the single cigarette out of my inside jacket pocket,

Frank Rush came through the door. If it wasn't an accident, he sure made it seem like one.

"Congratulations," he said.

I washed my hands. "Thanks."

It was like he was the gym teacher, and I was the kid who smoked cigarettes in the bathroom, and he almost caught me.

He stood at the sink, washing his big hands.

"I just wanted to see it for myself," he said.

I played along. "See what?"

"See if you could go through with it. Standing up there next to that boy. Knowing how much he loved his daddy."

We looked at each other in the mirror. I decided not to say anything.

Frank Rush dried his hands on a brown paper towel. He never took his eyes away from me.

"I know you killed the man, Early. I know it down in my bones. We can't prove it yet, but we will. Sooner or later you'll tell somebody, or the gun'll turn up, or your wife and Little Allen will figure it all out, and I'll get a call, like I always do. And when that day comes, I think you'll be glad to get it over with. You don't seem like a bad man to me. Hell, maybe we're all better off without that abrasive son-of-a-bitch around anyhow."

The bathroom door swung open. Eddie Miller walked in. He stopped dead still. There was a minute when we all looked at each other. I almost laughed. Don't ask me why, because I don't know why. It just seemed so ludicrous, the three of us standing in the bathroom together.

"Hey," Eddie said.

"Hey," I answered. I turned and left.

Maybe, like I said before, it was fate. Leaving the parking lot ten seconds too early, or ten seconds too late, and getting pulverized by a train, except in my case, it was extreme violence so close in time and location to my conception. Maybe somehow the sound waves of the violence, the gunshot and the blood spatter against the wall, traveled through the small space of air from the window to my mother's womb, wobbled the egg sac somehow. Maybe I would kill again, and again, and no one would be safe around me, including Samantha or Little Allen or Kate or Eddie Miller. Or maybe I was right in what I did. And there's a place for violence, controlled violence, in a civilized world.

I drank too much champagne at the reception. Everywhere I turned there was stilted conversation with the mother of the man I murdered, or Frank Rush eating a piece of chocolate cake, or Kate's red dress on the other side of the room. So I drank another glass of champagne, and another, and for some godforsaken reason I decided it would be funny to snap a picture with somebody's disposable camera up the skirt of a stiff, middle-aged woman with black hair and a tight bun on the back of her head, until she turned around at exactly the wrong moment. And her husband saw me do it. And then somehow somebody apologized to somebody else and Samantha and I were whisked away to our honeymoon to have sex, anytime, in almost any way I wanted, for four days and four glorious nights. That's the way I remember it.

PART III

middle-aged anarchy

Our lives are not defined by the wide radical swings, but instead, by times in between, the leveling off. After the death of Allen Kilborn and my wedding, I tried very hard to smooth out my life into normalcy, the daily routine of living. After all, that's why I did what I did, so Allen Jr. and Samantha could level off. So our lives would not be wide radical swings every day.

The first step was committing myself to my career like never before. I was in my late thirties, a time in a man's life when he should hit his stride. Working for a national investment company had it advantages, I suppose. There were plaques on my office wall. Corporate trips to San Francisco and New Orleans. If I jumped through the right hoops I got a bonus, or a new title, or a call from some big shot in Seattle who told me I was "the lifeblood of the organization. The personification of the values that set the company apart from competitors."

I remember sitting at my desk staring at the back of the closed door for God knows how long. I remember feeling I was on the verge of slipping into some sort of cataleptic state, able to hear and see the world around me, but unable to make the decision to move a muscle.

The voice from the phone said, "You're the kind of man who moves this business forward, Early, and I don't just mean the business of our company. I mean the stock market itself, the free enterprise system, America. You're innovative, energetic, willing to work outside the lines, and you'll be rewarded in the short run, and of course, in the long run."

The words were like morphine. A dead warmth spread through my body. I remember saying, "Do you mean Heaven?"

The voice hesitated. "Heaven?" it repeated.

"Yeah, the long run. Do you mean all my innovation and hard work will get me into Heaven? Eternity with God and all the other people who earned a spot?"

The voice hesitated again and said, "Well, I was thinking more along the lines of district manager, but I suppose God likes hard work. It certainly can't hurt."

The back of the office door was off-white, the color of margarine. It looked good enough to lick, shiny. I began to imagine, in my cataleptic state, with the voice purring in the background though the phone, what it would be like to become part of the door, virtually melt into the off-white black hole of another object, until the voice said in a slightly louder volume, "Congratulations, Early Winwood."

"Congratulations to you," I said, which of course made no sense at all.

My relationship with Allen grew in direct proportion to the deterioration of my relationship with Gretchen. He looked forward to seeing me in the afternoons. We talked about sports. I taught him the secrets of baseball. Gretchen wouldn't return my calls. On one rare occasion when she answered the phone she told me she hated the idea of me sleeping in the same bed as Samantha.

"She's my wife," I said.

"I know. I was at the wedding. Remember?"

"Your mother sleeps in the same bed with her husband."

"No, she doesn't," Gretchen said.

"What do you mean?" I asked.

"They've got separate rooms. Anyway, it's not your business anymore. You didn't want to be married to Mom, so now you've got a new wife…"

I stopped her in the middle of the sentence. "What do you mean I didn't want to be married to your mother?" I said.

She hung up the phone. It was an odd revelation, Kate and her husband in separate rooms. I didn't know what to do with the information. Maybe I wasn't supposed to do anything with it at all. Maybe I was just supposed to not think about it one way or the other. Maybe I was supposed to be satisfied with my life, my job, my wife, and not reserve a corner of my mind for Kate Shepherd. The same corner she'd always occupied, maybe smaller now, but pretty much the same general location of the brain. The back left corner. Next to the part that thinks about food and oxygen.

Of course, there wasn't enough room in my mind for Kate Shepherd, or anything else for that matter, since Allen Kilborn Sr. crawled around inside every hour of my day. It got so bad I created a mechanism inside myself to cope with the problem. An automatic switch. When I'd catch myself thinking about the man, or what I did to the man, I'd switch to something else immediately. I started with Samantha, and then Little Allen, but it didn't work well. My thoughts would circle back. I tried unrelated subjects, like the batting averages of third basemen, or listing the presidents of the United States in chronological order, but the relief was temporary. The only subject I found successfully distracted my attention was sex. The images inside my mind were vivid enough to start a chain reaction throughout my body, and the natural instinct seemed to take over.

This caused new problems in the house. Since about a year after we got married, the sexual opportunities with my wife began a slow, steady decrease. There were plenty of excuses, and I began to obsess on the subject. It seemed like such a small sacrifice for her to make. I worked very hard. I provided. I was loyal and dependable. How could she let weeks pass without providing for me? I walked the line between beggar and brooder, and not very well. I might add. A line I'd walked before, and just as poorly.

"Samantha, it's important to our relationship. I don't understand."

Sometimes, when she would give in, I'd find myself on top of a dead body, warm and supple like a new corpse before the onset of rigor, with her head craned way to the side, probably thinking about grocery shopping, like an animal pretending to be dead until the predator moves along. As much as the situation disgusted me, I wouldn't stop until I was finished, and satisfied, if only for a few hours. Sometimes, while we were doing it, I'd think about him on top of her and wonder if it was the same. Wonder if maybe with him she writhed and bucked and moaned.

The value of sex for a man in a marriage far outweighs the five-second orgasm. It's the ultimate reassurance. The ultimate display of complete trust, loyalty, and respect, to allow someone to enter you, literally, to physically enter your body. It's an act of appreciation that can keep a man getting up in the morning and going to a job he doesn't like, at least for a while.

I found myself creating a new mechanism. An automatic switch away from sex and nasty fantasies of my wife doing things she'd never let me do. I started thinking about nothing. Started visualizing a blackboard at school. On the blackboard were words like Allen Kilborn, Kate, district manager, Gretchen, cigarettes, step #7, and Frank Rush.

I would lie perfectly still on my back, eyes closed in the dark room, and start with ten deep breaths. Then I'd visualize the blackboard with the words written haphazardly from top to bottom. One by one the words would be erased, and with each disappearing word, my body would relax. Finally, all the words would be gone and I'd be left thinking of absolutely nothing. Dark, black, nothing, surrounded by thick metal walls to keep everything else away from the nothingness.

The front page of the paper said: SUSPECT ARRESTED IN MURDER OF KILBORN. The picture of Eddie's face these years later made him look blank and hollow. It was a booking photograph from the jail. His eyes seemed to look directly at me and no one else.

The article didn't give many details. I can still recall my first clear thought after reading the headline. It had to be a trick. A ploy to get me to come forward. There couldn't be any evidence against Eddie. He was innocent. All he did was drive me to the house earlier in the day. He couldn't confess to something he didn't do. He couldn't lead them to the murder weapon, or the clothes, or the key.

I sat at the kitchen table staring down at Eddie's picture. Samantha must have been looking over my shoulder.

"Oh my God. Isn't that your friend?"

I didn't react.

"We were friends in grade school. I haven't seen him but a few times since we grew up."

"He was at the wedding!" she yelled.

Allen Jr. ended up in the unhealthy conversation.

"He killed my father? Your friend killed my father? Why?" he asked me.

"It must be a mistake, Allen. I've only seen Eddie a few times since college. He always seemed like a good man. It must just be a mistake."

Samantha read the article. "I hope they execute the bastard."

Little Allen started crying. All the emotions came upward from wherever he'd locked them down below.

"It's just got to be a mistake," I said again. It was the only explanation I could offer. My mind started spinning around back to that day.

Frank Rush must have convinced himself that Eddie was involved. Out of desperation, he must have finally decided to make a move, try to shake things loose. Rush probably figured if Eddie was involved, certainly now, sitting in jail with no bond, and facing execution or spending the rest of his life in jail, he would tell what he knew. What if he made things up? What if he told more than he knew, or could know, just to give Frank Rush what he wanted, which was me?

The police car could pull up to my office any day, or maybe come to the house in the middle of the night, and they'd pull me off my limp wife and drag my sorry ass to jail. It could be me next week on the front page of the paper, with a washed-out photograph, and other people sitting at their kitchen tables saying what a nice guy I always seemed to be.

There was nothing for me to do but wait. It was ironic, if that's the right word. I would depend on the same judicial system for Eddie, an innocent man, as I depended upon for myself, not innocent, but prepared. If the system provided protection for a guilty man, even a well-planned guilty man with good intentions, then certainly it would protect Eddie Miller. If it didn't, what would I do? And was it possible Eddie was in on the trick?

That night, on the way home from work, I took a longer route through town. Nobody seemed to be following me. I drove south and then looped to the backroads where I'd dug the holes out in the woods. It was hard to tell exactly where they were. The area was being built up, new subdivisions, box houses one next to the other. I didn't turn my head to look into the woods as I passed. I just aimed straight ahead in case Frank Rush stood behind the line of trees waiting for me to pass. Waiting for me to coincidentally be on the wrong road, looking into the woods at the wrong spot, on the day after the wrong man was arrested.

I stopped at a convenience store and bought a pack of cigarettes. My first pack in over a year. At home, after Samantha fell asleep in the middle of a conversation, I checked on Allen. His light was off down the hall. On the screened back porch, in the dark, I lit a cigarette with matches hidden by the grill. I could feel the thick smoke fill my lungs and then disappear invisibly into the night. I let the silence come down on me, and I listened for any sound. A dog barked down the street. An airplane roared way above in the sky, taking people I didn't know to see other people I didn't know, and I imagined each of them thought of things like me, but different from me, and they didn't even know I was down below smoking a cigarette in the dark.

The back door swung open. My head spun around to see the silhouette of Little Allen, not so little anymore as a teenager, standing in the doorway. I dropped the cigarette to the brick floor and stood on top of it with my bare foot, twisting as I turned to Allen.

"Is everything okay?" he said.

"Yeah, yeah. I thought I heard something. It was just a dog."

He was in shorts and an oversized t-shirt. He was a good boy. Honest, with a full heart. It was the people around him who were crazy and disjointed.

"A dog? What kind of dog?" he asked curiously.

"I didn't see it. I just heard it."

"Is there something burning?" he asked.

It should be the other way around. It should have been me catching a teenage boy sneaking a smoke on the back porch at night. It should have been me at the door in my boxers asking the questions. Instead, I felt a burning on the bottom of my foot. The pain built to a point I nearly cried out, then slowly lessened until there was a sound in the bushes to the left of where we stood. We both turned to look.

"What was that?" Allen whispered.

"Probably the dog again," I said calmly, but we both knew it was a lie. It didn't seem like the sound a dog would make. It seemed more like the sound a man would make in the bushes. A man who watched me when I didn't know it.

two

I was in my office, daydreaming about nothing, when the speakerphone on the corner of my desk said, "Mr. Winwood, there's a Frank Rush here to see you."

The daydream ended abruptly. My secretary must have thought she was talking to an empty room.

"Are you there?" she asked softly.

"Yes. I'm sorry. I was in the middle of something. Send him in."

The door opened a few seconds later and Investigator Rush stood in the doorway. He was a bit larger than the last time I'd seen him, but the face was the same. Heavy.

He sat down, and as was the custom between us, I waited. A brown briefcase rested in his lap.

He said, looking around the room, "You've done pretty good for yourself."

The panorama of framed certificates seemed impressive, but it was all bullshit. Seminars where I sat in the back not listening to the boring guy stomping around the stage. Training sessions I didn't actually attend.

"Did you see Eddie in the newspaper?" he asked, focusing on a gold-leaf diploma to my left on the wall.

"Yeah," I answered.

I felt a line of sweat sneak from my left armpit down my ribs beneath the blue button-down shirt. Mr. Rush watched me, and I watched him, the usual dance. I'm not sure what he expected from me. I'm not sure what anybody expected from me.

In the silence between us I heard someone laugh in the outer lobby. It was the laugh of a woman, unrestrained, tickled by something, with no time to muffle the response. It was genuine, and I wished I was sitting next to her, whoever she was, instead of sitting across from the man with the briefcase in his lap, a thin line of cool sweat inching downward to my hip.

Frank Rush opened the briefcase and casually placed a large pistol on the desk between us. He closed the case. It was Allen Kilborn's pistol, or one that looked like Allen Kilborn's, only older, weathered, dug up from its grave.

"You recognize that?" the man asked. He pointed at the gun but started directly at my face. I leaned up a bit in my chair to see the pistol, and then leaned back again.

"No," I said.

The investigator leaned up in his chair also and looked at the gun like it was the first time he'd ever seen the thing.

"We found it at a construction site off Highway 33. It's a pretty remote area back there, but over the last few years neighborhoods have popped up. They were puttin' in the foundation for a house. It was buried about a foot and a half."

I glanced from his eyes back down to the gun.

"It's cleaned up now," he said. "It was in pretty bad shape. At first, I figured there was no chance a fingerprint could survive, but we sent it off to that fancy lab up in Virginia, the FBI lab."

In my mind, I watched myself put the gloves on my hands. I saw the gloved hand open the drawer and remove the gun from the special wooden rest. I saw the hole I dug, about eighteen inches deep. Two feet at the most.

"They found a fingerprint. One fingerprint."

I didn't flinch. I didn't swallow. I just looked him in the eye.

"Guess whose fingerprint?" he said.

The woman in the lobby laughed again. Almost identical to the first laugh, but longer. She let it linger at the end, trailing away.

Frank Rush said, "Eddie Miller's."

It was a lie. I knew it was a lie, and he knew it was a lie. Eddie never touched the gun. It wasn't possible. But I was the only person to really know for sure, and the investigator across from me looked so hard into my face for anything at all, anything, I began to feel physical pressure along the top of my eyes and down to my cheekbones, like his big hand was touching my face, holding my face like a soccer ball.

"I don't believe it," I said.

He studied my answer. "Why not?"

"Because Eddie Miller doesn't strike me as the kind of man who would kill somebody. And why would he kill Allen Kilborn? I don't think he even knew Allen."

Frank Rush said, "You can't always tell a killer by how he looks, Mr. Winwood. I believe we all have it inside us. The ability to kill, I mean. A man who wouldn't kill to protect his child, or his family, is a coward. We all have a reason, a reason worth killing over, most of us just never get to that point. I guess Eddie Miller got to the point, for whatever reason, and now he has to face the consequences."

I said, "I don't know much about you, Mr. Rush. When I was younger, I could see people a lot better. I don't see 'em so good anymore, but you don't appear to be the type of person willing to send an innocent man to prison just so you can close an old file."

The gun was directly between us and I tried very hard not to look at it again.

"What makes you so sure Eddie Miller is an innocent man?" he asked sincerely.

I turned my chair slightly to look at the gold leaf diploma displayed so proudly.

"Because when we were kids, maybe twelve years old, we planned an elaborate heist from the drugstore. A candy bar heist. Eddie's job was just to be the lookout."

I glanced back from the framed diploma to Frank Rush where he sat.

"He couldn't do it," I said. "He couldn't even be the

lookout for a candy bar theft. He started shaking all over and looking for excuses. He wouldn't be a very good murderer."

Frank Rush seemed to consume the story I told, and as it digested he shook his head up and down like he understood.

He said, "What exactly was your role in the candy bar heist?"

I thought of the countless diagrams I'd drawn. Diagrams with locations of mirrors, and employees, with an X marking the spot where the candy bars were displayed. Frank Rush stared so hard at the side of my face I felt he could steal the thoughts right out of my head.

My secretary's voice blared out from the speakerphone, startling the hell out of me, and in turn startling Frank Rush.

"Mr. Winwood, I'm sorry to disturb you, but Gretchen's mother is on the line. She says it's an emergency."

It was Kate. Something about a seizure. Something about Gretchen in the television section of a big store, she had a seizure, fell into a TV, she was at the hospital. Kate was crying. The doctors weren't sure what caused the problem. There were tests to do.

I hung up the phone.

"I have to go to California, Mr. Rush. My daughter's in the hospital. I need to be there. I hope I'm right. I hope you're not the type of person willing to keep an innocent man in jail, for whatever reason."

I stood and walked out of the room, leaving him in the chair, brown briefcase in his lap and the pistol resting on my desk. I walked past my secretary and the lady laughing in the lobby. She weighed at least three hundred pounds. Her blue dress was like a bed sheet draped across her massive body. She smiled at me and I smiled back.

Samantha helped me pack my bag. She wanted to know details, but I didn't have any details. She wanted to know exactly what Kate said, but I couldn't remember the exact words, and it seemed like a strange time to be thinking about herself. I looked at Samantha across the room, my eyes red from crying at the thought of Gretchen dying in a hospital in California, and it occurred to me Samantha wasn't capable of giving me comfort. She loved me when I was strong and dependable, because that's what she loved about me. There was no place for me to be needy. When I needed comfort, affection, sexual reassurance, I was no longer strong and dependable, I was weak, and she didn't love weak, so why would she want to have sex with a weak man, or put her arms around me and tell me she loved me?

I wanted to tell her right then and there that I killed Allen. Right in our bedroom, me standing by the closet, her standing by the bed, my suitcase open, my eyes full. I wanted to tell her what I'd done for her, Allen Jr., and all of us. Ironically, one of the primary purposes of killing the man was to remove all impediments in the relationship between myself and Samantha, but the guilt and suspicions, the underground doubts, had built a wall even larger, an emotional barrier we couldn't seem to cross. I created unreasonable expectations.

I turned away, but she knew something had clicked

inside me. She watched as I packed my bag. The picture of my father was in my sock drawer, down at the bottom, and until I saw it, I'd forgotten where it was hidden. I'd forgotten again exactly how he looked, smiling, his head turned a bit to the side. The white t-shirt had a dark stain near the belly like he wiped his hands across his shirt. Maybe working on his car. Maybe working in the yard.

Samantha watched me put the photograph in the suitcase. She let me walk out the door to fly to California to see my daughter in the hospital, without a kiss good-bye. Without putting her arms around me and telling me everything would be all right. Even if it wasn't going to be all right. Even if it was going to be bad.

I stepped inside one door of the waiting room just as the doctor stepped in the other. Kate and her old husband, Russell Enslow, stood. There was no one else in the small room. The doctor explained he believed it was pancreatitis. Rare in young people. The pancreas becomes inflamed, shuts down, wreaks havoc on the body. There would be more tests. It was a very serious situation. Gretchen was asking for her mother. The doctor took Kate with him, leaving me and Russell Enslow alone in the small waiting area.

I'd spent the last eight hours in airports and taxicabs. I could smell myself. The smell of self-pity and body odor. I hadn't spoken a word, just walked up in time to hear the explanation from the doctor. I sat down across from Russell Enslow. We'd never had a conversation. Not one. We'd passed each other in the hallway of the courthouse seventeen years earlier. He answered the phone sometimes and handed it off to Gretchen. But no conversation. I knew nothing about the man, and all he knew about me was the venom he'd heard spewed from Kate's mouth. He probably thought I smelled bad all the time.

We nodded to each other. There was no real anticipated relief. Kate's return might ease his anxiety, but not mine. I took a deep breath and closed my eyes. It was hard to believe earlier in the day I was sitting in my office with Frank Rush, a gun between us, and now I sat in a hospital waiting across from Russell Enslow, nothing between us except a coffee table covered in old magazines.

I was exhausted. All of it, Eddie in jail, the gun, the fat lady in the lobby, Samantha's indifference, pancreatitis, all of it on the same day. Just another seemingly random day empty on the calendar where circumstances converge and take the wheel of your life out of your hands, the feeling of falling, free-falling into the future.

I let my head go back on the chair. I let my eyes close. The sound of pages of a magazine turned by Mr. Russell Enslow created the only sound I could hear, until he spoke.

"My wife is in love with you," is what he said.

I thought I must have dreamed it. Could he have said anything less expected? Maybe, "Do you mind if I take a dump on the carpet?" or, "My left ear is on fire."

I swear to God I thought I dreamed it, maybe I'd dozed off, and without actually seeing Mr. Enslow in my dream, heard him speak. But when I opened my eyes, the man was looking at me, and I knew it wasn't a dream. He was angry, not because he said what he said out loud, but because it was true, and looking at me half-asleep on the other side of the coffee table, he just couldn't figure it out.

"What did you say?" I asked, just in case.

He spoke succinctly, "My wife, Kate, is in love with you."

We were in full-disconnect. I began to wonder if I was having one of my episodes, but even weirder than usual, seeing a world that didn't exist instead of just seeing the real world though another set of eyes.

"I don't understand," I said.

"Believe me, neither do I, but our lack of understanding doesn't change the fact."

He appeared resigned to the situation, like years had passed since he found it out and surrendered to the knowledge.

"I'm married," I said.

"No shit," he said. "Me too."

It was no place to laugh. There was a strange comraderie. We were in it together, destined to share equally in the misery, both free-falling through the experience, no more in control than a butterfly in a storm.

We looked at each other for a long time. Me at him, and him at me. Russell Enslow was in his fifties, well-dressed, not overly handsome, but not ugly either. He had a slight paunch under his shirt and a sureness I never had, not even in my best moments.

"What are we supposed to do now?" I said.

"I don't have the slightest idea. I thought you'd know. I'm not unhappy. I love Gretchen. I'm excited about her going off to college in a few months. Kate respects me. She appreciates what I provide, financially and as a father.

You'd think it would be horrible to share your home with a woman who is in love with someone else, but it isn't so bad. I'd rather be me than you."

I wanted to stand up and punch him in his little head, but maybe he was right. Our first conversation hadn't really helped me in any way. There was a youthful excitement to it all, but I had a wife, and a young man at home who needed me, maybe more than anyone else in the world. Eddie Miller was in jail for a murder I committed, and I had an office covered in framed certificates and fancy plaques. Even if Russell Enslow was correct, and I couldn't imagine why he'd lie about such a thing, what would it mean in real life? It was all some crazy crap the world conspired to place on my doorstep at exactly the wrong moment, as if there would ever be a right moment.

Kate came to the door. Russell and I stood.

From across the room Kate said, "They think she's going to be okay."

"Thank God," Russell said.

Kate seemed to be looking at a spot between me and her husband, some comfortable middle ground with no eye contact. Maybe the fictional place she envisioned we should all come together in our concern over Gretchen.

"She wants to see you," she said.

I turned my body toward the door.

"No," Kate said, still looking at no one, "She asked for Russell."

He looked at me, but I saw no spite or satisfaction in his face. It just was what it was, no matter who was at fault. Right and wrong, good and bad, have no place in the present. They exist in the past and in the future, to be pre-dicted and judged. Different-colored highways on a map leading to some seemingly random day on the calendar, like the day where I stood in the place where I stood wait-ing like the butterfly waits for the storm to blow itself out.

Later, when I was alone in the room, I rooted my hand around through the clothes in my bag until I found my father's picture. I could see Gretchen in his face. Very clearly I could see her outline superimposed upon my father, two people a generation apart. Never allowed to be in the same room together, connected only by me.

three

I've always had a real need for permanency. A fundamental clinging demand for believing the idea that some things are forever, set in timeless stone, dependable certainties. Maybe it's a human characteristic, or maybe it's only a characteristic of me. The difference is difficult to distinguish sometimes.

It might derive from the shake-up of my father's death and the blunt-force realization at age eleven of the eventual loss of all things. It's a complicated concept, and even more complicated to overcome. The constant need to rotate around something permanent. Another person, a job, the vows of marriage, even the certainty of the arrival of the Sunday morning paper.

It wasn't until I was able to break through the idea of permanency, set it aside and see the world as it is, every minute changing, evolving, temporary, unable to make or keep a promise for tomorrow, that I set myself free. Unfortunately, the cost of this freedom became a prepossession with suicide. The idea of it. The balance. The reasons for and against. The manner of the deed. Not for attention, nor for the purpose of some grand statement to the world, but to be dead, at ease.

Maybe suicide, and the idea of it, was my mind's attempt at replacing the concept of permanency. When all else seemed beyond anyone's control, maybe my mind clung to the idea that at least I could control how long I remained.

They say thoughts of suicide are supposedly symptoms of mental illness, but I didn't feel mentally ill. I doubt seriously I suddenly suffered a rapid chemical imbalance. It wasn't a knee-jerk reaction, an impulse to run outside and hang myself from the nearest tree. Instead, it came as a coldness, a vague narrowing of reason, and the idea, like a billowing white cloud, slowly took shape, and then began to flow from day-to-day virtually the rest of my entire life.

My mother was out of town and asked me to stop by her house and water the plants. It was a good chance to climb up in her attic and look for those baseball cards I'd been telling Allen about. I found a box in a wooden chest, and opening the box of baseball cards was the closest thing to actually going back in time. The smell. Bent corners I remembered. Batting averages I'd memorized, with the numbers so ingrained in my memory they came back instantly, like addresses or phone numbers of childhood homes.

I took the box and started to close the top of the wooden chest, but something made me stop. There was a small bundle of paper. Letters and envelopes, yellowed and held together with a rubber band, in the corner of the chest. I sat down under the hanging attic lightbulb and began to read.

They were letters from my mother to another man, and from the man back to my mother. His name was Bruce. The postmarks on the envelopes told me they were sent and received before my parents were married, before the night Bobby Winters was shot in the head outside the window of my conception.

He loved her, and he told her so in the words of the handwritten letters. And she told him how she thought about him all the time and wondered what her life would be like with him. There was a photograph of them standing together in front of a house I didn't recognize. He was a big man, much bigger than my father. His arm was around my mother's shoulder and she was looking up at him with a smile I'd never seen on her before.

I started to read another letter, a long one, and stopped. We never really know our parents, the events that shaped them before we were born. The first kiss. The first person who ever loved who didn't love them back. The choices they regret, and can't change, because time has pushed them beyond the chance to go back.

And so it goes that Gretchen and Allen will never really know me. They will know what they see of me, those parts shown, but not the rest. Because I couldn't tell them about the night that I sat staring at Kate passed out in the backseat of the car, or how good it felt to beat the man on the mattress into a bloody mess, or my fear of becoming my mother, or the idea I had yesterday morning of swimming out into the ocean, putting a gun in my mouth, and floating slowly away. And they wouldn't want to know those things anyway, just like I didn't want to know about Bruce, or the letters my mother kept, or the smile in the picture.

I was becoming more like my mother, and it was hard to decide how I felt about it, mostly because it appeared her detachment was based on fear instead of strength. And learning this fact removed yet another delusion of permanence. My mother was getting older. Her mortality was becoming clearer to us both, and it didn't seem to sit well with either one of us, for different reasons of course. She would never remarry, and we both knew that. Not Bruce or anyone else. She would hold bitterness for me, choosing to lay the blame on me for Gretchen being so far away. And I would accept the blame, the guilt so thick between us it sometimes seemed visible, like a fogbank.

Gretchen's illness got better, and my relationship with Allen continued to grow. We spent an entire week together looking for a car for him. He was genuinely a good kid, growing up, ready to become a man. He fought with his mother on occasion, and she expected me to be the disciplinarian. I walked the line between best friend and stepfather, and I must say I walked it well. We avoided using the "step" word whenever possible. I introduced him as my boy, and he was truly my boy, with the hint of something unseen nearby. I couldn't describe it, but Allen

Kilborn Sr. still occupied a place inside our home, our lives. We never spoke of him, Samantha and Allen Jr. avoiding the subject in my presence. I imagine they spoke of the man when I wasn't around.

My relationship with Samantha reached a routine oddness. We seemed almost uncomfortable around each other, but so dependent the oddness was endurable, inevitable. It was a constant struggle of miscommunication and unfulfilled expectations mixed with reliability, trust, and commitment. It occurred to me I might be entering a phase in a long-term relationship I'd never entered before. The leveling off I've spoken of. An apparent profound compromise, but without effect. Expectations settled like an old dog going round and round, coming to rest on the same comfortable pillow. There would be no more nights of unashamed passion. There would be no more flutter in the chest at the sight of her in the backyard planting flowers. But so what? I thought. Until the letter arrived.

It came to the office. The stack of mail was left on my desk. Maybe a dozen envelopes. There was one different than the others. Handwritten. I recognized the handwriting before I saw the name on the left-hand corner. Kate Enslow.

She hadn't written me a letter since the day she left. Not so much as a note. I held the envelope in my hands. If there was something the matter with Gretchen, Kate would have called like before. I remembered Russell Enslow saying the things he said in the waiting room at the hospital. I remembered Gretchen telling me they slept in separate rooms. I turned the envelope around and held it to my nose. There was no smell. No words written on the back. There was nothing to do except open it.

Early,

How are you?

I know it must have been strange to see this letter mixed with your business mail. I'm not very good at explaining myself. I just felt like writing you a letter.

Last night I found a shoebox on the top shelf in the storage closet with pictures of you and me. I knew it was in the house somewhere, but I hadn't been able to find it for the longest time. Getting older is different than I thought it would be. Watching Gretchen leave for college was harder than I imagined. But I didn't cry, which is hard to believe. I cry now at the drop of a hat. I sat down in the closet and looked at the pictures. I could hear you and feel your touch, but then it was time to put you back in the box. I left a little crack in the top.

Kate

I read the letter. Then I read it again. And again. I'm not sure what I thought I'd see different each time, but there was so much to think about. All those many years had passed, but one letter, written by her hand, could still tie me up in knots.

I hid the letter in my file cabinet, in a file I knew no

one would look for. The next day I pulled it out to read again. It took a lot for her to do it. As much or more as it would have taken for me to sit down with pen and paper. Write the words. Fold the letter. Address and stamp the envelope. Put the letter in the envelope. And finally, drop it in the mail. Each part of the process as difficult to finish as the one before. More than enough time between each level to throw it in the trash. Reconsider. But she didn't. She finished every step, and now she knew I held the short letter in my hands. And undoubtedly she understood what it did to me.

She'd been looking for the pictures of us in her house. The feelings were strong enough to hear my voice and feel my touch, or at least to say she did in writing, which was equally amazing. And the part about the crack left in the top of the box. Just a little space for the possibilities to breathe. But I told myself, "She's going through a down time. Getting close to forty years old. Mid-life crisis. Her only child leaving the nest. A lull in her marriage, discontent."

It's easy to remember only the good things. It's easy to toy with the idea the grass is greener, and maybe life would have been different. Just like my mother, and Bruce, and the letters she kept in the chest in her attic.

Days passed. I felt guilty around Samantha for something I hadn't even done. At the baseball game, watching Allen, I knew I'd never leave him, no matter what. It wouldn't make any difference if Kate showed up at the front door and delivered the letter herself.

I agonized over what to do. Write back? Don't write

back? Pretend I never got the letter? But I ultimately couldn't do it to her. I imagined Kate going out to the mailbox each day. Worried she'd done the wrong thing. Full of regret one minute and the next minute wishing for my response to arrive.

Dear Kate,

I got your letter. It was a surprise, but a good surprise.

Seeing your name in the corner of the envelope on my desk made me smile. Like we used to smile a long time ago. I wish you'd send me copies of those pictures. Somehow I didn't end up with any. It would be nice to remember, and have my own box, with a crack left in the top.

You're right. Getting older is different than I thought.

Early

I sent it four days after I received hers. Not too eager, but also not purposefully cruel.

My letter made no promises, but at the same time, invited a response. A chance to see another one of her letters, handwritten, in my stack of boring business mail on the desk. A chance to let my imagination run wild on Kate Shepherd, and be back in my apartment in college, and see all those imagined moments in high school, but still remain totally under control. Letters were one thing. Calls or meetings were altogether something else. I would control the situation this time. I would decide the rules. The next day I threw her letter away, and wished to God I'd never sent my own. What if Russell Enslow got the mail? What if Kate called the house and told Samantha she loved me, and that I loved her, and we were gonna be like those crazy-ass people who leave their husbands and wives for each other out in Hollywood?

It was upheaval, but pleasant upheaval. I would keep her inside my mind where she belonged. At least that's what I told myself.

four

I read somewhere that not a single cell in our bodies is the same as the cells contained inside us at birth. Our bodies are constantly regenerating and replacing old cells, and so, technically, we are completely different people than the day we were born. If this is true, and I believe it is, who are we? Are we strangers to ourselves? Is it just our invisible souls holding us on a certain track of identity until we die?

The call came from the hospital. "Mr. Winwood, this is Sherilyn McNally. I'm a nurse. It might be a good time for you to come down and see your mother. She's asking for you."

"I don't understand," I said. "My mother's at home."

There was silence on the end of the line.

"Hello?" I asked.

"I'm still here," she said. "Mr. Winwood, your mother's very sick. She's not home, she's here in the hospital."

On the drive it occurred to me that I hadn't seen my mother in months. I worked. I concentrated on Little Allen. I paid bills. I walked in and out doors all day long, watching the stock market, worrying about Gretchen, agonizing over letters. My mother had her own life. It's the way she wanted it to be.

I was absolutely amazed at how different she looked in the hospital bed. She was in her sixties and looked like an eighty-year-old woman I'd never met before. My mother's face was gaunt. Her hands on the outside of the white sheets were hands I didn't recognize, bony and wrinkled, the skin dry, her fingernails longer than I'd ever seen them.

"Jesus, Mother. What is happening?" I whispered, like it was a secret. Like no one else could see what I could see.

"I'm dying," she said calmly.

"No, you're not," I answered.

She waited a moment, probably to allow the ridiculousness of my answer to resonate in the room.

"Yes, I am, Early. I'm dying."

It made me angry. While I'd been paying bills and smoking cigarettes on the back porch in the dark, something was happening to my mother, the last remaining vestige of my permanence on this Earth. And now she looked like a dead body resting in an open coffin, except her eyes were open, and she was speaking.

"Four months ago the doctor told me I had pancreatic

cancer, in an advanced stage. I decided against chemotherapy. I'm ready, Early. I've been ready for a long time now. Don't be afraid."

I heard myself say, "What if I'm not ready? Did you think of that? Did you? What if I'm not ready for you to die?"

At the moment, where I stood in the cold hospital room, it seemed impossible. All of it. Like a crazy dream where you tell yourself it's only a crazy dream. And then you wake up, and you're glad it wasn't real.

I left the hospital room and drove around for hours and hours. I thought of every memory of my mother. Every single detail I could recall about her, and me, and my father, and I cried like I didn't know I was capable of crying. Wiping my face at stoplights, ashamed, clear juices running from my nose down over the top of my lips, hyperventilating at times to the point of dizziness. I ended up in a full-blown asthma attack in my grandfather's backseat again. I pulled over to the side of the road and tried my trick of the blackboard full of words, each one slowly erased in my mind, until there is nothing to think about and the air began to flow freely again. The man on the radio said to expect lots of sunshine. He said tomorrow would be beautiful.

I had never taken the time to imagine my mother dying. After all, she was strong, removed, artistic, and detached. She wasn't like me or my father, weak to the world around us. My mother was immortal, almost unnatural.

It must have been nearly two o'clock in the morning when I pulled back into the hospital parking lot, all cried out. My soul was dry. There was nothing left to remember. Sherilyn, the same nurse who'd called me earlier, let me back in my mother's room. She was asleep. I sat in a chair by her bedside and looked around the room. This idea came to me. This idea of taking flying lessons, and renting a small plane on a clear spring morning, and taking off into the rising sun, turning south toward the Gulf of Mexico. In a bag on the seat next to me would be a bottle of good whiskey, a few books, and a large bottle of pills. As I cleared the coast, the white sands like snow on the beach below, I would start taking pills, swallowing each down with the hot whiskey, and reading passages from the books, my headphones off, the sound of the engine of the small plane drowning out everything. Not everyone is meant to live seventy or eighty years. Not with a soul as dry as mine.

"I thought you might come back," she said.

Her eyes were opened in thin slits. The liquid dripped down the tubes into the place in her arm. Tape covered the needle to keep it secure in her dry skin.

"I just don't understand, that's all. Why wouldn't you tell me?"

"You have enough going on, Early. And what would you have done anyway? It's better this way."

I felt the anger rise. "Says who? Who says it's better this way, Mother?"

She smiled a little bit, something I hadn't seen in a long time.

"I do, Early. It's my life, not yours. I get to decide."

The nurse entered the room and changed the bag of

liquid hanging above. We were all silent while she did her job.

"I have a million questions," I said.

"I'm sure you do," she whispered. "I wish I had a million answers."

And then she started to talk, for maybe the first time in our lives together. And I started to listen, maybe for the first time.

"I wasn't born with a lot of motherly instincts. To be honest, I really didn't have the slightest idea what to do with you."

I remembered what I'd read about none of us having a single cell left in our bodies from the day we were born. The person who came out of her was literally someone else.

"Your father knew," she said. "He knew from the first minute they put you in his arms. With him around, I could count on someone knowing what to do, how to raise a baby. When he died, eleven years with no practice, I was just as lost as the day you were born.

"I can't really apologize. God made me who I am. God and my own mother. The eternal victim. She died before you were born. I promised myself when I was a little girl never to be like her. She went from one crisis to the next, almost each self-created, and blamed everyone around her. She lived off sympathy and guilt, and killed herself on her thirtieth birthday. I was nine years old."

"How?" I asked.

My mother looked at me, aggravated by the interruption.

"Pills," she finally said.

It was quiet again. Unbelievably quiet.

"Maybe that answers some of your million questions," she said. "Maybe not. You know, we like to believe we get better every day. We like to believe we wake up every morning a little better than the day before. I'm not sure it's true. Maybe we peak long before we get old."

The quiet seemed to settle around us, and my mother's eyes closed slowly. She whispered, "Why don't you come back tomorrow and we'll talk some more."

I sat in the hospital room for at least another hour and watched my mother sleep, and then I watched her die. There was no shouting or convulsing. No struggle to hold on for one last word. She just died, and left me very, very alone in the big world, with a dry soul, a family history of suicide, a guilty conscience, and tears rolling down my cheeks.

She also left me a letter, folded neatly in an envelope:

James Early Winwood,

From the day you were born you were taught to be strong. As tiny men, even learning to walk on your little legs, you are all told not to cry. Crying is weak, and men are never to be weak.

Men stand tall, they wear uniforms, they fight on battlefields, real and created, and they provide for their families.

At some point, some critical point, in order to truly know God and yourself, you must separate what you have been ingrained to become from what you must do. We must be weak to truly know anything. This weakness will let you say, "I love you," to those you love, to cry for no real reason, to reach those places inside your heart I was never able to reach until the end. You see, it isn't really weakness at all, is it?

The greatest debate inside every human in the history of civilization is the debate over the proof of the existence of God. But there is no debate. No need to argue or require. There is a God, because there must be, and that is all to be said.

I thank God for you and your father. Without you two I would have never known love, spoken or unspoken, never known the reason for this life. God will bless us both, now and forever. I know this to be true. He has told me many times when I have been tired and needed to hear His whisper.

I love you,
Your Mother

As you might imagine, she left her affairs in perfect order. The house was packed up, everything in boxes, with notes where each box should go. I never found the letters from Bruce, but she left me a box of things about my father, and it was like getting to know him for the first time.

Inside the box I found his little league baseball trophies, pictures of me as a baby in his arms. The three of us on the beach. The same snow-white sands, building a castle at the edge of the surf. My mother was smiling in the picture, the same smile I'd seen with Bruce's arm around her shoulders.

There were poems my father had written, and letters to my mother, and little, odd things like an old bullet, three baby teeth in a small, black, cloth bag, a firecracker, and a picture of a dog that I'd never seen before, and all those other things that reminded me how little we know our parents. And now there was no one left to ask the million questions. Those people who created me, those with the closest connection, were both dead. And Allen Jr. held me so tight, and watched me like a grown man watches a child.

He stood next to me at the funeral and put his hand on my shoulder when I couldn't hold myself together. Gretchen sat two rows behind with her mother and Russell Enslow. She looked at me with misunderstanding, perhaps the same way I had always looked at my mother.

Samantha was lost in the role of providing comfort to a crying man, but I will never forget Allen coming home from college and sitting up late at night with me. Calling the office every day for months, pretending he needed this or that, when it was me who needed. The very boy whose father I murdered. The very boy who turned to me after his own daddy's funeral and asked if I would be the one to throw the ball with him in the front yard from now on. And with this very boy, who had become a man, I would forge the strongest bond I would ever have with another person in my lifetime. Perhaps even stronger than the bond that I held with my long-dead father.

How the current of life flows as we struggle in the waters to get to one side or the other, to control our own destinies, when all along the current will decide. The current will take us, willing or not.

five

If my first marriage was like the lighting of a match, quick and bright, burning out as soon as it began, then my second marriage was the opposite, a slow rot. After Allen moved out and my mother died, there was an unforgivable onset of loneliness. At least it seemed Samantha was unable to forgive me, for anything, but particularly my hints of insecurity. She had hated Allen Kilborn Sr., but at least she respected the man.

I couldn't figure out how to fix things between us, or if I wanted them fixed at all. I couldn't even figure out how to get laid in my own house, with my own wife, in the bed I paid for. It was more complicated than sex with a complete stranger, and my mind began to drift to the idea of other women. Kate, or the lady across the street getting her mail from the box on a Saturday morning, short pants and gardening gloves. I had a particular fantasy where I walked over to her garage, we didn't say a word to each other, and she simply positioned herself bent over the hood of her black BMW, and then pulled down her shorts to her ankles and watched me over her right shoulder.

I felt guilty about it. The Bible says the sin is committed with the first thought of lust, but my mind wouldn't leave it alone. It was easy to shift the blame to Samantha. She was cold, unproviding. She'd rejected me so many times, how could I expect anything different? But still, I struggled with the immorality of it all. I knew if I took the first step toward making it real, more than just a fantasy, it might actually happen. If not with the woman across the street bent over the BMW, another woman, somewhere else, bent over something else. It wasn't the fear of getting caught. It was the fear of not getting caught, and becoming like those men who cheat on their wives every time they go out of town, like it's just something men do, they can't help themselves, regardless of vows, or promises. I think if you do it once, it becomes easier the next time, and the next.

The letters from Kate kept coming. All full of innuendo and code. She was unhappy, I was unhappy, so I wrote back, in the same code and innuendo, imagining her husband would see the letter one night when Kate drank too much red wine and got caught taking the box down from the top shelf to peek inside.

Early,

I keep remembering those days locked up in your apartment.

It was a long time ago, but not so long. I also remember the first time I ever saw you out by the cemetery where we used to go back in high school to see Onionhead. You kept staring at me, and now it's me doing the staring. Maybe you could explain why I need to send you letters. I have several theories, but I'd like to hear yours. Maybe you could explain why you wrote me back after all those years, especially when I did all I did to you.

It's hard to even figure out why anymore.

Kate

I would lie awake on the couch and imagine sending a letter saying, "Meet me in Kansas City, next Saturday, in the lobby of the airport Sheraton Hotel, and stop asking why." I'd buy a plane ticket, invent a reason to go to Kansas City on business, and spend a weekend of naked bliss in a hotel room. Would she show up in the lobby, or was she only willing to dance around the words of handwritten letters? If I actually sent the letter, and got on the plane, and sat in the lobby pretending to read the paper, and Kate actually got on the plane and showed up through the front door with a red dress, how would our lives change? It was like the fantasy with the lady across the street, or suicide, or the murder of Allen Kilborn. Once it became more than just an idea. Once it began to happen, it was like the current, out of control, deciding for itself.

Besides, I would tell myself, "It was a mirage." One of us needed to be smart enough to remember how bad it was and how bad it probably would have gotten. I was a kid. I fell in love with my own imagination. A girl that didn't exist. How long can such a thing last? Not long, apparently. So how could anyone expect it to work itself out twenty years later? But still, the Kansas City hotel weekend was worth all the hours thinking about it.

As my mind drifted and my marriage crumbled, Samantha scheduled counseling. We sat in the office of Dr. Paulette Long. She kept us at a safe distance across her antique cherrywood desk. The woman was entirely pointy. Thin, her face coming quickly inward to the sharp nose. I didn't like her the moment I saw her, and I don't think she liked me either.

"So, why don't we start with you, Mr. Winwood. Tell me a little bit about your marriage."

"I think it would be better if Samantha starts."

"Why?"

"I just do."

There was an awkward silence. She reminded me of a big pencil.

"Okay, Samantha, would you start?"

It seemed to me they'd met in the office before, without me, and discussed their strategy for proving I was to blame for everything wrong in all of our lives.

Samantha said, nervously but rehearsed, "There's a distance between us. I don't feel the closeness we had before."

It got quiet again. Apparently, it was my turn to say something.

"There's no closeness because she sleeps as far away from me in the bed as she can get without rolling off on the floor. My wife hasn't touched me in three months, and before the occasion three months ago when she nearly fell asleep in the middle of intercourse, it was about four months before that."

Dr. Paulette Long stared at me with her dark, beady eyes.

"I think, Mr. Winwood, Samantha was speaking of emotional distance, emotional closeness. Not physical."

"No shit?" I said.

It came out wrong. Sarcastic, impatient, like a man in the room with two conspiratorial women and seven months of locked-up sexual tension.

Samantha said, "Are you having an affair, Early?"

I thought to myself, if imagining the lady across the street bent over the hood of her black BMW with her white panties around her ankles constitutes an affair, then I'm guilty. But it doesn't. It might be a sin, but it's not an affair.

"No," I said.

Dr. Long asked, "Why would you ask that, Samantha?"

It sounded like they were actors in a bad movie. They each knew exactly what to say.

"Well," Samantha spoke, "it may sound silly, but I read about certain clues when your husband is having an affair. There are just things I've noticed on the list."

"Like what?" the doctor asked.

"Well," Samantha spoke again, "he stays late at the office for one. He recently got a haircut and new shoes. He doesn't try to kiss me or touch me anymore. Those things are on the list."

I couldn't listen to much more. "You know what? This is stupid. Maybe eating is a clue also. Or scratching my ass. That could be a clue."

The doctor looked down her runway nose. I didn't wait for her to ask another question.

"I stay at work late so I can afford our oversized house in a rich neighborhood that my wife can't live without. I haven't tried to kiss or touch her because after you've been turned down fifty times in a row with stupid excuses like falling asleep at eight o'clock, or having PMS two weeks before her period, you'd stop trying, too. Who likes being rejected over and over?

"And the haircut. I get about four or five haircuts a year, every year, since I've been a grown man. I had no idea the timing of the haircut and new shoes had such significance. Maybe I should grow my hair down to my asscrack and wear these shoes until my toes stick out the holes."

Samantha was crying. The doctor hated my guts.

"Mr. Winwood, you have a great deal of anger. We need to find the source of that anger."

"Let me just ask you this," I said, "are we searching for the source of my anger for my benefit, or for the benefit of this marriage? Because honestly, Samantha, do you want to stay married to me?"

We were all struck with the possibility that she might say no, but after only the tiniest of hesitations, Samantha said, "Yes. I wouldn't be here if I didn't. Allen loves you.

We're a family. If you're going through some mid-life crisis, get a motorcycle, write a book, whatever."

For ten weeks we met once a week with Dr. Paulette Long and explained every facet of our relationship at two hundred dollars per hour. I learned a lot about people, myself, women, and other worldly pursuits. At the end of ten weeks Dr. Long announced our marriage would have a better chance of surviving if I moved out of the house and continued to pay all the bills. So that's what I did.

In the back of the newspaper there's a section for dead people. A section with photographs, sometimes old photographs above obituaries of people who have recently died. I've always stopped in those sections and looked at the people's faces, read about their lives.

On a winter morning, sitting at my desk, I saw the picture of Eddie Miller above his obituary. It was an old picture, maybe from high school, with his eyes full of light and hope. It didn't say how he died. I hadn't talked to Eddie since he was arrested. They only held him in jail a few weeks, probably like I said, to see if they could put the pressure on him or me, break open the case.

People told me how Eddie went downhill after that. He got a divorce. The wife took the kids. He drank a lot, spent time sitting in barrooms. And now he was dead. A picture on a page full of pictures of dead people.

The Catholics believe the only unforgivable sin is suicide. It seemed impossible to me that God would turn his back on the very children who needed Him most, until I figured it out. It's a good rule, but it's not for the people who actually kill themselves. The rule is for the people who just think about it. Religion is the ultimate slippery slope. We're told to believe in the comfort of a God who loves and provides, but we're told not to completely embrace the idea of Heaven, because if we did, everyone would be killing themselves to get there. Why not? It's wonderful. No worries. Surrounded by the warmth of God's love. It's Heaven.

So they made a rule. A bump on the slippery slope to stop us from going all the way to the bottom. Believe, but don't believe too much. Doubt, but don't doubt too much. Float around in the middle until you die of natural causes and get your picture in the paper.

The letter went like this:

Kate,

Saturday. January 20. Kansas City airport Sheraton hotel lobby at two o'clock in the afternoon.

Two days. Room service. Hot baths. Never leave the apartment.

Wear a red dress.

Early

I even put it in the envelope, a stamp in the corner, and drove through the post office parking lot. I sat in my car, the window down, in front of the big blue mailbox with the envelope in my hand. And then, believe it or not, I dropped the damn thing in the box. It was like my hand, and then my arm, just decided for themselves.

There was immediate regret. Immediate. I sat in my little ugly rental house and drank a half bottle of Jack Daniel's before I came up with the brilliant idea to go back to the post office at two o'clock in the morning to retrieve the letter. As are most decisions made at two o'clock in the morning after a half bottle of Jack Daniel's, it was a mistake.

There was no one around. The parking lot was empty under the glowing lights. My hand couldn't get down the hole. The same hand, and the same arm, that earlier decided to send the letter, now couldn't get it back. I decided to steal the entire mailbox. It was huge. Too big to fit in the car, and as an added problem, it was bolted into the cement.

That's when the police car arrived. I tried to explain.

"There's a letter in here I need to get."

"Have you been drinking, sir?"

With a noticeable slur I said, "How is that relevant?"

At the police station, under arrest for public intoxication, I sat in the holding cell with my face in my hands, already feeling the beginning of a hangover. When I lifted my head, Investigator Frank Rush was sitting across from me on the metal bench. I hadn't heard him come in. At first I thought he was a hallucination, like a story by Edgar Allan Poe or something.

"Did you read about Eddie in the newspaper?" he asked.

I took a long, deep breath, trying to gather my wits before I spoke.

"Yeah."

We were quiet. He watched me breathe.

"How'd he die?" I asked.

Frank Rush seemed to think a moment.

"Some people just die, Early. They don't really die, it's more like they just stop living. Other people, like Allen Kilborn, don't get to decide. Someone decides for them, like you did."

"You're wrong," I said. "Allen Kilborn made his decisions, not me."

He felt the weakness.

"It's time Early. It's time to get this off your chest. It's time to tell me how it happened. We both know he was a son-of-a-bitch. I never said he didn't deserve it."

It was like the whiskey evaporated from my bloodstream in a split second. It was like my mind rose up from the fog at the exact right moment. I leaned back against the cold cinder-block wall and waited. From his face I could see that Frank Rush was watching the moment of weakness pass. His chance for a confession disappearing before his eyes. I remembered the letter in the box. I thought of Allen Jr. with his arm around me at my mother's funeral.

"Eddie was a good kid," I said. "We grew up together."

"I know," Frank Rush answered.

And that was it. I closed my eyes and let the exhaustion carry me under. I woke up alone.

six

A few days before January 20th, Little Allen called. His voice was the voice of a man. He had something he wanted to tell me, but not over the phone. At first I was worried, but his laugh gave away the goodness of whatever it was he wanted to talk about. We decided to meet at my little rental house the next day.

Allen was living and working two hundred miles away. We talked on the phone often, but he came home less and less. Not out of anger or anything negative, but simply his life pulling him in the direction it was meant to go. I missed him being around. He had taken the news of me and Samantha's separation better than I would have. He seemed to already know it was coming and prepared himself.

When we talked, we mostly talked about baseball, and

work, and things like that, gently veering away from the subject of his mother. I found the conversations comforting, stabilizing, and I wondered if he could see our roles changing ever so slightly, almost unnoticeable, like a child growing from one day to the next.

I watched around the curtains through the front window as he pulled into the driveway. There was a woman in the passenger seat, young and pretty. I watched them walk together toward my front door. They were a couple. Comfortable with each other. The comfort that only comes from being in love. She held his arm, and he smiled at the touch. Allen was bringing a girl home to meet me, and not just any girl. I remembered bringing Kate home to meet my mother. Now it was my turn to learn how my mother felt that day. Happy, concerned, maybe a little jealous.

I opened the front door and acted surprised to see the young woman. Her smile was absolute and genuine, like she hadn't figured out yet how fucked up the world really is. A smile you could look at and believe everything would be okay. I immediately envied Allen, and immediately wondered if my mother had felt the same about Kate, or whether it was obvious to everyone except me that Kate's smile hid things we were all afraid to see.

Standing at the door, Allen said, "Dad, this is Emily. Emily, this is my dad."

Since the beginning, we had mostly stayed away from words like "dad" or "son." I would overhear him call me his "stepdad" on the phone with his friends. After all, he had a real father, and our last names were different, and I didn't show up in the boy's life until he was half-grown.

But now, standing at the door, he introduced me as his father, and I shook Emily's small hand. It made me wonder if Gretchen, on the other side of the world, might be introducing her boyfriend to Russell Enslow and calling the man her father like I didn't exist. I suddenly remembered I was leaving on a plane early the next morning bound for Kansas City. Maybe I wouldn't show up. Maybe I'd just go to work like a regular day.

Allen wasn't the kind of man who would bring just any girl to meet the family. I could see they were way beyond the awkward stage. Sitting in the living room, every now and then she would glance at Allen, probably wanting the same comfort he provided to me in our telephone conversations. She would grow old and the beauty would fade like a painting, but there was something strong about her. She didn't need saving. Neither of them did.

"We're getting married," Allen said. She watched my face carefully, looking for the reinforcement of an instant smile, and that's what she got. I didn't need to fake it. There was a light around them, and I hoped it would never go away.

Before I could catch myself I said, "I hope you have children."

Emily and Allen looked at each other. I had the feeling she knew my story, or at least the parts Allen knew to tell her.

"We hope so, too," she said.

I could feel the tears fill up my eyes, and I continued, "Because children are the best thing this world has to offer."

It occurred to me I was getting old. She saw me as an old man, lonely, exiled to a stranger's house, looking across the couch at the embodiment of youth. And then it happened again. I came outside of myself. There we were, in the living room of my little rental house, me in the chair, Allen and Emily sitting on the sand-colored couch across the coffee table, except I was seeing me from Emily's eyes and feeling Allen's hand on mine. I was afraid and calm at the same time. Wanting it to stop and continue together.

One second became two and then three, and I wondered if Emily was inside of my body, or if it was just me, and then I wondered if it would never go back to normal, stuck. But then in a blink I was back in the chair and there was no hint of awareness in Emily's eyes. Certainly, if she'd suddenly floated into someone else's body, there would be some reaction, some recognition of the odyssey.

When they left I felt a little shaken. I sat down in the same chair and searched around inside my mind for a foothold. My second marriage was collapsed. The hollowness of my career was beginning to reveal itself. My daughter was distant, and now I was planning a weekend of debauchery with my first wife, who was married to another man, and I'd just gotten a close-up look at myself through the big, brown eyes of my stepson's fiancée. The stepson whose father I killed, and who now introduced me as his dad, and who was getting married, starting a family of his own, and drifting further away.

I went to bed. It was three o'clock in the afternoon. I was exhausted, but couldn't sleep. I got up and packed, and then went back to bed. I got up and ate, and then crawled in bed again. I went over in my mind everything we could possibly do in a hotel room over two days and nights. I got up and made a list: champagne, chocolates, a red rose. I tore up the list and took a shower, colder than usual.

It was after midnight before I finally fell asleep. The alarm went berserk at three-fifty in the morning. I was in a whirlpool of doubt on the drive to the airport. Turn around. Don't turn around. Are you stupid? What are you doing? It might be fantastic. Maybe we were always right for each other, we just needed to grow up. Maybe these years with Russell and Samantha made us appreciate each other. Maybe I have a chemical imbalance that allows me to drift into the bodies of other people from time to time, but doesn't allow me to stop doing stupid shit. Like killing people and meeting my ex-wife in Kansas City.

When the door slammed shut on the airplane, I felt the way I felt weeks earlier when my hand dropped the letter in the big blue mailbox. Panic and exhilaration. Much like I imagine it would be shooting up methamphetamines for the first time. Waiting for the feeling to start.

I checked in the hotel at 11 A.M.

"One bed or two?" the man said.

"One. King-size."

"Will you need a key to the minibar?"

"Yes."

I put my bags in the closet and inspected the room. The bed was big and soft, covered in pillows. Six big pillows, I counted. The tub was large enough for the two of us. Little bottles of shampoo and bubble bath, sky blue.

I opened the curtains to see the airport in the distance, planes landing. Maybe Kate's plane. Maybe it was touching down. I ran downstairs to the lobby. It was big. Lots of couches and chairs. I found a couch with a view of the front door and the check-in area. It was perfect.

There was a newspaper on the table. I began to read, holding the paper up to cover my face. What if someone from home spotted me, started up a conversation, just before Kate arrived? What if Samantha's cousins wandered into the lobby and saw me reading the paper, looking suspicious? I would probably stand up and scream, "I'm a fornicator. I'm a sinner?"

It was eleven thirty-three. I could still go home. I could run upstairs, grab my bags, and be back at the airport. Fly home and make it to the office before it closed. I could sit in my favorite chair across from the couch at night and drink the rest of the bottle of Jack Daniel's. Lock myself in the house. Sift though the mail every day to get the letter from Kate. The letter that says she went to Kansas City to see me, and I wasn't there.

Out of all the people I didn't expect to see, my childhood friend, Jake Crane, was probably on the top of the list. But there he was, standing in the line to check in. He looked out of place. I lifted the paper to cover my face, peeking around the edge of the sports page. He was looking around like he'd been sent there to find me. Sent by Frank Rush. I closed my eyes and suppressed the pure paranoia. It was just a coincidence. A weird coincidence. Surely he would leave before Kate arrived.

It was eleven-fifty. Any minute the red dress would walk through the big glass doors. We would act like we didn't know each other, accidentally end up in the same elevator. Exit separately on the same floor, and then run giggling down the hall to the wonderful room waiting for us.

Out of all the people in the world who knew Kate, and all the people in the world who knew me, Jake Crane was unfortunately one of the few who knew us both. One of the few people on the entire planet who would know it was no accident we were in the same elevator together. His presence was a dirty omen. What were the chances? I began to feel the paranoia press down, but I held my position. Regulated my breathing. Finally, Jake finished checking in and walked past me to the elevators. I carefully maneuvered the paper to cover my face as he passed and turned to the left. It was five after twelve. Thank God she was a few minutes late, I thought. The omen was no longer nasty, but humorous instead. A good story to tell someone later, I'm not sure who.

I think it was twelve-fifteen when the possibility fully occurred to me Kate might not come. Maybe she made it as far as the airport. Maybe she actually got on the plane and ran out before the door slammed shut. It's possible she got as far as Kansas City and just got on another plane back home. Maybe she ran into Jake at the airport coffee shop, panicked, and went back to California.

Then it occurred to me there were two Kansas Cities. Kansas City, Missouri, and Kansas City, Kansas. Maybe there were two Kansas City airport Sheratons. Maybe she was waiting in another lobby for me, her legs crossed, the edge of the red dress at her knees.

I asked the lady, "Excuse me, are there two Kansas City airport Sheratons?"

"No, sir. This is it."

"What time is it?"

"Twelve thirty-four."

The lady patiently waited for me to speak again.

"Have you seen a woman with a red dress? A pretty woman with a red dress? Mid-forties, brown hair?"

She smiled like she knew everything about me and why I was there.

"No, sir. Sorry."

I sat back down on the couch in my spot with the perfect view, and then went back to see the lady again.

"Do you have any messages for Early Winwood, room 833?"

She tapped around on the computer keyboard. Shaking her head, she said politely, "No, sir. No messages."

The elevator ride to the eighth floor was long. No one was accidentally in the elevator with me. No one ran down the hall giggling. The bathtub and the bed were big and empty. I ordered room service and ate alone, falling asleep in the middle of a repetitive pornographic movie. It's a sure sign you're getting old when you can fall asleep to the grunts of a pornographic film, but that's what I did, and to tell the truth, I slept like a baby. It was one of the best night's sleep I'd had in my life. I woke up the next day at noon to a knock on the door.

Noon. A knock on my hotel door. The Kansas City

airport Sheraton. Had I gotten the wrong day? Had she gotten the wrong day? And I realized my first feeling was fear. Fear that Kate Shepherd would be at the door, and make me feel the way she always made me feel. Sky-high, on top of the world, and then waiting for the fall. And waiting. And waiting.

A voice came from the door. "House cleaning," the voice said, and on top of the fear, above all else, I was disappointed.

seven

The letters stopped, mine and hers. From time to time, late in the evening, I'd sit at my desk, in front of an empty piece of paper, and imagine, far out in California, Kate doing the same. But neither of us had the courage or weakness to send anything.

There was nothing left of my marriage to Samantha, and both of us seemed beyond blaming. I can't remember who called who, but we met over dinner to negotiate the end. I remember seeing her sitting alone at the restaurant when I arrived. She was staring out the window holding a glass of white wine. Her face was very still, resigned. I just watched her for a moment, wondering what I would eventually feel, and then feeling nothing.

She turned to look at me, and we stayed that way, both of us sure now, until I tried to smile. It was a childish smile.

The fake kind, but openly fake, purely to bring an end to the moment before. A transition to the next moment.

On the walk to the table, escorted by a waitress, I thought to myself, "It's not my job to make everyone happy. It can't be done. Where did I ever get an idea it was possible anyway?"

"What do you think of Allen's girl?" was the first thing I said.

It was our common ground. It was the only thing we liked about each other. I watched her chew a piece of bread slathered in butter and wondered what it was that I ever liked about Samantha Kilborn. She watched me take a sip of water, and I knew from her eyes she felt the same way about me. I was conscious of my lips on the edge of the glass. Too much, not enough. We had moved beyond love, beyond hate, to the land of annoyance. We didn't even care to purposefully annoy each other anymore, it just happened, and I swear I wouldn't have touched her naked body if we stood alone in the Garden of Eden, which is saying something.

"Do you want your tools out of the garage?" she asked.

"Yeah. I guess so."

"I like Allen's girlfriend. She's different than I expected."

"How?" I asked.

"It's hard to explain. Just different, that's all. Not like I expected."

It was at least her second glass of wine. She kept staring out the window at nothing in particular.

"You can have the house," I said. It was the same house she had when we met. Every year was a new renovation project. Guest room. Island in the kitchen. Always something new and expensive, but I didn't care. I never wanted to go back there. I never wanted to set eyes on the island again.

After the first sip of her third glass of wine, Samantha said, "Let's make this the last true conversation we ever have. After this, let's just be cordial when we run into each other at the grocery store, or end up in the same place with grandchildren, but let's not talk about anything important."

She was distant and serious.

"Okay," I said. "Can I get some copies of the pictures in our photo album?"

And then she looked at me and said, "Early, did you kill my husband?"

I wasn't ready for the question. If I'd been ready, the answer would've flowed. But I wasn't ready, and maybe she planned it that way. Other than Frank Rush, no one had ever asked me point blank.

She wasn't staring out the window anymore. She was staring directly across the table at me. Maybe it was over-due.

Then I grasped the wording of the question. "Did you kill my husband?" Allen Kilborn Sr. wasn't her husband when I shot him in the head at the top of the stairway. They were long since divorced.

"No," I finally said, the word coming out a little too quickly.

She held the stem of the wine glass between her index finger and thumb, twisting it slowly as the base rested on the white tablecloth. I looked down at the golden liquid, and then back up to Samantha's face.

"Did you cheat on me?" she asked.

It was amazing the woman would consider the questions equal in her mind. Executing a man in his own home and bending the neighbor lady over the hood of the BMW. It was amazing I was capable of a moral transgression at the level of murder and then concerned with finding a loophole in the wording of a question in order to tell a lie.

"No," I said, less quickly than before.

Her eyes drifted back out the window.

"Do you want your golf clubs?" she asked, her words flat.

My answer was yes. I really did want my golf clubs. I hadn't played in five years, but I wanted them anyway.

That night, when I was alone in bed at my rental house, I thought of something I'd completely forgotten. It came back to me like a brand-new memory, alive and sharp, as if it happened the morning before.

Gretchen was about six years old. I looked forward to our time together like a man in prison looks forward to seeing the sun. Not just pleasant, but life-giving, like water.

We went to the ice cream parlor. It was next to the movie theater and we had tickets to the matinee. Gretchen was shy, whispering in my ear the flavor of ice cream she wanted instead of telling the lady herself.

It was early spring, cool but not cold, and we sat outside on a glassy blue day at a table under a big white umbrella. Gretchen had birthday cake ice cream in a cup made of white chocolate with colorful sprinkles covering the top of the ice cream.

She took her first bite and a smile came across her little face. A real smile, the opposite of the one I gave Samantha from the other side of the restaurant. Gretchen's smile was so genuine, so pure, I remember I started to cry. I don't believe I've ever seen anything as important.

I sat there and started to cry. I had to look away from her. Put the napkin to my eyes. Pretend to cough. The girl was so perfect and so happy, and so far out of my life. That little smile over something so small as colored sprinkles left me unbearably alone, like the day my mother died.

She looked up from her ice cream.

"Daddy," she said, "how much does the sky weigh?"

"I don't know, baby," I said.

She took another bite of ice cream covered in tiny bits of color.

Gretchen said, "I think it weighs a million miles."

I wanted to hold it forever. The ice cream, the smile, the sky, the day. All of it. Just hold it close to me. The weight of a million miles.

I sat in the church at my daughter's wedding. Two hours earlier I met the man she'd marry for the first time, and I didn't like him much. He was plain and hard, a face like stone. He'd never know the Gretchen who sat with me outside the ice cream parlor, and I'd never know the woman he was about to marry. All I had was snapshots of her life. Little pieces that didn't fit together.

Russell Enslow gave her away. I guess she was his to give, but it left me sad anyway. Kate was aloof. I watched her at the reception. She never looked my way. Never smiled to acknowledge Kansas City, or the letters we once wrote to each other, or the night we'd conceived the child who just walked down the aisle and exchanged vows with the stone-faced man with big hands.

I wasn't sure what I expected. Maybe I hoped something miraculous would happen, or maybe I just hoped the sight of Kate would change everything. For the most part, that's what happened. Seeing her made her real again, if just for a few hours, and there's nothing quite like reality to douse the fire of fantasy. She was looking older. I didn't like her hair. It was too short. And she was skinnier than I remembered.

It was deflating. I wanted to feel that feeling again, if only for a few minutes. The way she always made me feel in her presence. Just to know such a thing still existed. But she wouldn't look at me, at least not while I was watching, and I stood alone by the big plate of shrimp, not knowing a single soul at the wedding reception for my only daughter. Not able to muster the energy to cause a scene, or maneuver Kate into a conversation, or do much of anything. I felt listless and average.

Less than a year later, I stood at the window of the nursery at the local hospital with Allen. His wife had just given birth to a fat, healthy boy, and the nurse held up the baby for us to see.

"Jesus, Allen, he's beautiful."

Allen touched his hand to the glass, fingers outstretched, finding himself in the middle of a miracle.

"He is, isn't he. Guess what we named him?"

"What?" I asked.

"Early James Kilborn."

I couldn't really say anything back to him. The boy named his son after me. It was even better than a white chocolate bowl of ice cream covered with sprinkles, and I smiled like Gretchen smiled, like all was good with the world, and might be forever, but I knew better.

eight

I slid gently into the disillusionment of my career. My job simply was not capable of providing any permanent identity. It helped temporarily, sometimes for stretches of years, but ultimately it was only a job, even when I loved it. Just a means to survive, refined and diluted by civilization. The cavemen may have loved the hunt and loved the meat from the hunt, but the purpose was much higher. The purpose was to feed the children, keep the mate, survive another day. Those purposes really no longer existed for me. Going to work every morning was just part of the routine. A diversion from imagining strange ways to kill myself or obsessing over my lack of sexual opportunities.

Nearly a year and a half since I'd seen Kate at the wedding, she called one night out of the blue. I knew immediately from her voice it wouldn't be good. There was no lazy, sexy cadence of too much wine on a lonely night, no nervous introduction before strolling down memory lane. It was business. Something was the matter.

"It's Gretchen," she said. "He beat her up. It's the second time, and this time it's bad, Early. Real bad."

It was the first time I'd heard her speak my name in many, many years, but the feeling was overshadowed.

"What are you talking about?" I said.

"Mike, her husband, the asshole, hit her in the face. Her eye is black. He's a drunk. He stays drunk."

"Jesus Christ, Kate. Why haven't you called me before?"

"For what? What could you do halfway across the country? We put him in jail, and he got out. We got a restraining order, but she went back to the asshole. She's here now with me, but he knows where to find her. A piece of paper won't stop him."

"What can I do?" I asked. "Do you want me to come out there?"

"No," she said quickly. "I want Gretchen to come stay with you. At least for a little while. She'll be safe there. Talk to her. Tell her to leave him. Tell her it'll never end. He won't change. Nobody changes, Early. We all know that."

I thought of Kate's father, the man in the chair with the rotten foot propped up. Sitting in the dark. A bottle of vodka in his hand. I remembered the smell. Old cigarette smoke, the odor of dog. Gretchen had probably never met the old man, but somehow, deep inside her, she carried the pain of her mother, and probably the pain of her mother's mother. It would never end.

"I think that's a good idea," I said, and as the words

came out of my mouth I felt an old familiar feeling. My mind began to form the beginnings of a plan. Just a seed. A seed of redemption, freedom, and just a little bit of revenge.

Maybe that's what Kate wanted. Maybe she knew, she always knew I was capable of such a thing, and now, after so many years of not needing me for anything, raising Gretchen with Russell Enslow, now she needed me for something. And maybe it was my purpose on this earth to kill people like Mike Stockton, and Allen Kilborn Sr., in order to set other people free.

I lay in bed almost the entire night thinking. It was more complicated than the time before. Mike Stockton lived far away in California. Unfamiliar territory, both geographically and otherwise. No built-in murder weapon or alibi witness. No hazy motive. If I was anywhere in the vicinity I'd be the first suspect.

When I fell asleep, the dream of the black circle came back. It was there on the floor between my bed and the door. Bigger than before. Even blacker somehow, with a gray ring around the edge.

In the dream I heard a noise and sat up in bed. The only light in the room came from the streetlight out the window. I could barely see the doorknob turn slowly, and the door began to open. In the crack I saw something. At first it was just a form, near the knob between the crack. Then I could see Gretchen's face. She was a little girl again, around five or six.

The door opened wide and we could see each other. She was wearing the same little shirt and pants she wore the day at the ice cream parlor. And then she smiled. The same smile I remembered.

"Daddy?" she whispered.

I couldn't speak. I opened my mouth, but I couldn't speak. I saw her lean forward. I saw her take the first step running toward me, but I couldn't yell. I couldn't tell her about the black circle on the floor between us. And then it was too late.

I woke up angry. What kind of man hits a woman? What kind of man chooses alcohol over his family again and again? Such a man deserves no respect. In my mind I could see the back of his hand come down against my little girl's face. I could hear her crying, balled up on the floor, wondering what existed inside of her to create such a situation, to deserve such a choice.

The dream led me to the next step, a blank piece of paper, a pen, a plan written out, a first draft. Written on the hard desk instead of a pad of paper, to be sure the sentences didn't bleed through to the pages below. Written left-handed, and mostly in words that reminded me of other words, so the plan only really existed inside my head.

Gretchen arrived at the airport. She was skinny, like her mother. Her bones seemed to be held together by only her clothes. Underneath the makeup I could see the blueness around her right eye down to the edge of her nose.

I took a deep breath and smiled. We were mostly strangers, but maybe we wouldn't be anymore. Maybe there was an opportunity to find out about each other, without judges, or Kate, or even Samantha, in the way.

I cooked supper. When she was a kid her favorite was

spaghetti and meat sauce. No meatballs. They were gross. And the meat sauce couldn't have onions, or peppers, or anything weird.

At the dinner table she asked, "Who's the child in the picture on the bookshelf?"

"It's Allen's little boy."

"He's cute," she said quietly.

"I made you spaghetti and meat sauce. No meatballs. No onions. Just the way you like it."

She started to say something and changed her mind. Maybe she started to say "I'm not a little girl anymore. I have other favorite foods now. Adult foods. And I've smoked cocaine, and given blow jobs, and lied intentionally to hurt people, and married a man who treats me like a possession. All because you were a shitty father."

But she didn't say anything like that, and I was glad. We talked about good things we remembered about each other. We talked about the weather, and her mother, and then ran out of things to say in a short period of time. I locked the doors, checked the windows, and pulled the curtains closed.

I took a vacation from work. Gretchen slept the first night in the guest room. The next morning, when she was in the shower, I went to make her bed. Under the pillow I found a gun. It was small and loaded. I put it back under the pillow and left the bed unmade.

Gretchen and I spent the next three days together. We found things to talk and laugh about. We ate lunch in restaurants and visited Allen and his family. There wasn't much left of the child I'd once known, my little girl, but I liked the person she'd become. She was smart and fragile like her mother, but without as much outward defense. There were shimmers of vulnerability and silence, but I chose just to watch and learn for awhile.

After our third day together, I decided to start a conversation about her predicament. "Why don't you move here? You can stay with me until you get on your feet."

She seemed displeased I would talk about anything unpleasant.

"I can't," she said.

"Yes, you can. It doesn't have to be forever. The guest room is yours. You can stay as long as you want. I'll help you find a job. Maybe you could even work at my office."

Gretchen looked down at her hands. She was still wearing a wedding ring. She wanted all the badness to just go away magically. She wanted everything to fix itself without confrontation.

She said, "There's a picture of a man next to the picture of Allen's little boy. Who is that?"

She didn't even know what my father looked like. She didn't know anything about him, or what he meant to me.

"Stay here," I said, and I went to my bedroom closet for the box my mother had left me.

Sitting down across from Gretchen at the table, I said, "It's my father. He died when I was eleven. I still miss him every day. I still think about things we did together, places we went. I remember words he used."

I handed her the photographs of me with my parents at the beach. I had no actual memory of the day, but the pictures were like their own memory. Gretchen looked through the pictures slowly, smiling back at the smiles. She loved my mother. They were important to each other. But just like my mother, Gretchen seemed to hold some resentment over my interruptions in their relationship, warranted or not.

"Is this your dog?" she asked.

It was the picture of the unidentified dog.

"No, I don't think so."

"Whose dog was it?"

"I don't know."

Gretchen looked at me for an explanation.

"I'm not gonna throw it away," I said. "It's in the box. It needs to stay in the box."

I handed her a picture of my father holding me in his arms. I wasn't more than a few months old. She looked at the photograph a long time before she said, "I like his face. He's got a good face."

That night, Gretchen went to bed early. I stayed up late at my desk thinking about Mike Stockton. Almost anybody is easy to kill if you don't mind getting caught. It's the loose ends. Gretchen couldn't know. Kate couldn't know. I had to pinpoint a location. A time. A way to be two places at once. What else could I do? Sit back and watch my girl crawl home to the man who'd eventually beat her down like a dog? The man who'd find a way to keep her from leaving him again, through babies, guilt, sympathy, promises. Lots and lots of broken promises.

"I'll never do it again."

"I swear there won't be any more drinking."

"I love you."

"Just this one last time."

"I'll be home at five o'clock."

A sea of broken promises and days strung together by lies. What kind of a father can wait around and watch it happen?

I closed my eyes and thought about what had to be done. In the silence, the very clear silence, came a pounding on my front door. BAM, BAM, BAM. Hard, strong, crazy, and purposeful.

I looked at the clock. It was two-thirty in the morning. There was only one person it could be. Mike Stockton. He found her. He came a very long way and found the right house.

I ran to the guest room. In the dark I whispered, "Gretchen, Gretchen."

No answer.

My eyes adjusted. The bed was empty. The pounding on the door came again.

"Bam, Bam, Bam." Three times. Even harder than before.

I heard a noise in the room with me. A low sound. On the other side of the bed, crouched in the corner between the bed and the wall, Gretchen held the gun.

"It's him," she said. Her voice cracked in fear. It was hard to see her face in the darkness, but she was crying, the gun held tight in both hands near her cheek.

A figure passed the window outside, a shadow from the streetlight across the white curtain of the bedroom.

I ran through the house, turning off the lights in the office and then the living room. I grabbed the phone and brought it back to the guest room.

Gretchen was where I left her. I got down beside her, our faces only inches apart.

"Listen to me," I said. "Do exactly what I tell you to do. Exactly. Do you understand?"

She didn't answer.

Without raising the volume of my voice, I hardened the tone to get her attention.

"Do you understand?" I repeated.

She looked at my mouth, the place where words had come from, and then moved her eyes to my eyes.

"Yes," she whispered. "I understand."

"Give me the gun."

I took the gun from her hand and replaced it with the telephone.

"Is it loaded?" I asked.

"Yes, it's loaded."

Slowly I said, "Now listen, call 9-1-1. Tell them what's happening. Mike's trying to get in the house. Tell them what he did to you before, and how you had him arrested, and how you got a restraining order. Tell them you came here to get away from him and now he's tracked you down, trying to break in the house."

She waited a second and said, "Okay."

"It's very important, Gretchen, you tell them everything so they'll understand the seriousness of the situation. So they'll send someone immediately."

I stood up with the gun in my right hand. It was smaller than Allen Kilborn's gun. It felt like a toy in my palm.

"Stay here," I said. "Don't leave this room until I tell you to come out, or the police tell you to come out."

She seemed very much like a child huddled against the wall, small and afraid, waiting for me to fix it all.

I walked cautiously down the hallway to the living room, listening for any sound, trying to determine if he'd found a way in the house yet. There was nothing.

The living room was dark. Very gently I turned the knob on the padlock to unlock the front door. Very gently I turned the little button on the doorknob to unlock everything.

I stepped back from the door about ten feet, careful to negotiate the coffee table, and stood in the small space between the coffee table and the couch, the same couch where Allen and his girlfriend sat when they gave me the news of their wedding, when Allen called me "Dad." It seemed like a long time ago.

I could hear Gretchen's voice on the phone in the bedroom. It was low and muffled, but every few words came clear. She was doing as she was told, and I imagined the dispatcher relaying the information to a police officer on night shift, bored, patrolling the quiet neighborhoods, and now with an emergency call. A home invasion. Blocks away. It was just a matter of minutes, and I waited, the way I've always waited, listening to the clock in the kitchen tick and tick. Listening to my little girl's voice on the phone down the hall. Taking deep breaths to keep my hands from shaking.

It happened amazingly fast. No warning. No small noise followed by bigger noises. The door just swung open and slammed hard against the wall.

Mike Stockton stepped into the doorway. He seemed huge, the light behind his back illuminating his frame. Large arms hanging at his sides. Far off in the distance there was a siren. The bored officer, adrenaline now pumping through his veins, on the way. Only seconds now. Only seconds away.

I raised the gun and fired. The sound was loud, but not like before. Not like the explosion at the top of the stairs that blew Allen Kilborn's head into small pieces.

Mike Stockton didn't move. I fired again immediately, and then a third time after that. Three shots, ten feet away, into the man's chest.

I heard Gretchen scream. I saw the body fall to the floor. The flashing colored lights of the police car appeared. Through the open front door I could see the officer exit his vehicle, gun in hand, assessing the situation, wide-eyed.

I reached over to the wall and flicked on the living room light. Gretchen was standing by the kitchen, the phone still in her hand. I set the gun down on the coffee table.

It was done, I thought. It was all done. There was no choice. What choice could there be? All those years of failing my daughter were brought to an end in a few seconds.

It would be a new beginning. A clean slate, as they say.

But then I watched Gretchen run to the man on the floor. I watched her wrap her arms around him in a way I've never seen, like she could pull him back from death, hold on so tight he wouldn't slip away to wherever he was going.

She turned and looked at me with a hatred I couldn't understand. A black disdain, total and complete, for me and what I had done to the man in her arms bleeding out on my carpet.

"What did you do?" she yelled. "What did you do?"

She waited for an answer. Just looked at me and waited for an answer.

"I shot him," I finally said.

The walls of the room seemed to close from all sides. It was just Gretchen looking at me for an explanation, her arms around the dead man on the floor.

I remember closing my eyes and concentrating on breathing, slowly in, and then slowly back out again. Trying with every piece of my brain to reconstruct the memory of Gretchen outside the ice cream parlor, remove myself back to that certain day, outside of my living room, away from the demand to explain to my broken daughter why a father might kill the man who beat her senseless and tracked her down thousands of miles away, until it dawned on me.

I opened my eyes and asked her, "You told him where I lived, didn't you?"

PART IV
the golden years

I found myself alone in a room at the police station. Mike Stockton was dead, three small caliber bullets to the chest and a pond of thick red blood at my threshold. It was done, and I couldn't say I was sorry, no matter what happened to me.

Frank Rush came through the door into the cold room. I think I almost saw a smile on his face. He sat down across from me at the table, two files in his hands, one thick and one thin. He placed the files next to each other between us, carefully lining up the edges. I could see the labels. The fat one was the file on Allen Kilborn Sr., and the thin one had "Mike Stockton" written across the top.

I waited for him to speak.

"Well, James Early Winwood," he said, "here we go again."

As before, I tried to concentrate on my breathing, in and out, slowly and as deeply as possible without sound or movement. It made me wonder how we are able to breathe at all. What force exists inside us to suck air inward and then push it out again? To regulate the speed and pressure?

"Usually, Mr. Winwood, I'd let the suspect talk first, tell me what happened, but this time, I think I'll go first."

I chose not to say anything and waited.

"This is how it looks to me," he said, "people around you end up shot. Not just random people, but now we have a pattern. Do you see the pattern?"

I think he just wanted to hear me speak. He wanted to hear my voice in the cold room.

"No," I said.

"Well, I do. Bullies. Specifically men who bully women."

He waited for me to say something, but I let the air go a little deeper in my lungs than before. Let it fill a pocket usually left unfilled, vacant.

"Allen Kilborn bullied your wife—your ex-wife, Samantha. And Mike Stockton bullied your daughter, Gretchen. You found a way to bring it to an end each time. A permanent end."

He continued, "Now granted, you picked two very different methods, but still there's common ground. Each was a shooting. Both times you used someone else's gun. And each time you succeeded."

I said, "The man came all the way from California to hunt her down. He beat on the door, came in my house. Gretchen is still black and blue from the last time he beat her up. You would have done the same, Mr. Rush. You would have done what needed to be done in order to protect your child and yourself."

We were quiet for a time. I was exhausted, almost a chemical exhaustion. The results of a pill I didn't take.

"Maybe," he said. "Maybe, but there's a few unanswered questions I have."

He leaned back slightly in his chair, an older man now. A little heavier, less hair, more lines around his eyes.

"Why was the door unlocked?" he asked.

"I guess I forgot to lock it. I was still awake, sitting in my office, when he started banging on the door."

"It's just hard for me to believe, Early, that a man like you, a cautious man, a smart man, knowing what Mr. Stockton did to your daughter, would leave the front door unlocked at two-thirty in the morning. I checked. All the other doors were locked tight. The windows were all locked. But somehow you forgot the front door."

"I guess so," I said. "I guess I forgot to lock the front door."

Frank Rush raised his arms and put his hands behind his head.

"I'm curious how he found the house. You're not in the phone book."

"I don't know," I said.

"Gretchen says she didn't talk to him. She says the only people who knew where she was were you, her mother, and her stepfather. If we take a look at your home phone records, will it show any calls to Mike Stockton's phone?"

"Not from me," I said.

"You didn't call the man and tell him where she was, did you, Early? You didn't lure him down, leave the door unlocked on purpose, make sure the gun was loaded, tell Gretchen what to say when she called 9-1-1, did you?"

I listened to his words. We knew each other better this time around.

"No, Mr. Rush, I didn't."

"Because Gretchen says you were very calm. She says you brought her the phone and told her exactly what to say. You calmly turned off the inside lights, told her to stay in the bedroom, and went to the living room alone to wait. All while a crazy man was beating on your door and circling your house."

I wondered how he knew Mike Stockton circled the house, leaving the front door for awhile. I didn't have to ask the question.

"Gretchen wasn't the only person to call 9-1-1. One of the neighbors heard the banging, watched out their window, saw Mike try the doorknob, walk around the back of the house, and then come back to the front door. Only this time, the door was unlocked. He was able to step inside. Into the dark room. Where you waited for him."

I asked in a monotone voice, "Am I under arrest?"

Frank Rush stared at me, and I stared back. I think he wanted to rip my head off and look inside, like the answer would be floating around in there, easy to see.

"No, you're not under arrest. Right now, you're free to leave any time you want."

"Is Gretchen here?" I asked.

"No."

"Where is she?"

He said, "She gave a written statement and asked if she could go back home. I told her yes. She packed up her things and left in a taxi."

I suppose it was unrealistic to believe Gretchen would stay with me in the house where I killed her husband, but I hadn't imagined her leaving, either. The sun was probably rising outside. A new day beginning.

"It must be difficult," he said.

He wanted me to respond, but I didn't. I also didn't get up to leave.

"It must be difficult," he repeated, "doing something to help someone else and having them not appreciate you. I mean, you kill the man who abuses your daughter, and she hates your guts for it. You kill the man who makes Samantha's life hell, and she divorces you anyway. Kicks you out of the house where you paid the bills."

Sometimes you can't see how much open space there is down below until you get up in an airplane. I started to rise above myself and look down on my situation. The balance is delicate between who we are and who others believe us to be. It is the greatest struggle a man faces between birth and death, the endless process of separating the threads of your individual identity from the expectations, needs, demands, and imaginations of all other humans. Who would I be if I was the only person in the world? Who would I have killed, and who would I have protected? Would the open spaces be so much easier to see?

There was the possibility I'd been used, by Gretchen, or more likely Kate and Russell Enslow, purposefully or subconsciously, but used nonetheless, to accomplish a purpose. After all, it was my fault. Everything was my fault. Gretchen's father issues. Kate's lifeless marriage. Samantha's intolerance. They were my problems to fix, and so I fixed one, at least temporarily, but then again, everything is temporary, isn't it? Sticking band-aids on the cracks in leaking dams, each leak proof of the impossibility of permanence in this life, a reminder that everything we care about goes away, as well as everything we don't care about.

I started to get up from the chair to leave the ice-cold room, but my legs were hollow, the physical weakness beyond anything I'd ever experienced. It was like I was Mike Stockton, all the liquid from my body drained dry. I kept my hand on the table to steady myself.

Frank Rush pulled a piece of paper from the file. It was my written plan, left on the desk in my house, found by Frank Rush, and a now a part of the permanent file. As permanent as a file can be.

With his stubby hand the investigator pushed the piece of paper across the table in front of where I stood. He turned it around so I could see my words right-side up. They were written left-handed. Words used in place of other words. A code.

"I found this," he said, "in your house, at the desk, the ink pen still on top."

I worked very hard at not letting my knees buckle. I leaned over, pretending to look at the piece of paper, transferring part of my weight onto my hands, braced against the tabletop. The weakness had nothing to do with what he showed me or the conversation. It was an independent weakness.

Frank Rush looked up into my face. "Does M.S. stand for Mike Stockton?"

The code was no code at all. I had written the words expecting them to burn long before any other eyes would search the page. But they were the words of a different plan, a plan never to be executed, in a faraway place.

He began to read, "M.S., CAL., Kate, miles, time, ice cream, R.E., Kate again, weapon?"

I needed something to drink. Maybe orange juice would replenish the blood.

"What do the numbers mean, Early?"

I looked from the paper to his face and said slowly, "They don't mean anything, Mr. Rush. Nothing does. Just scribbles. Can I go now?"

Allen was waiting in the lobby. He stood when I came to the door, and I wanted to collapse in his arms like a child. Like I was sick, and he was my father, strong and sure, and I could fold into his arms and sleep it all away.

He led me to the car, and we started the drive back to my house. I wondered if it would be surrounded by yellow police tape. I wondered how I would step across the stain of blood into my home, if I had a home at all.

"Who called you?" I asked.

"The lady across the street. She said you shot somebody. By the time I got there, they'd already taken you to the station. The investigator told me it looked like self-defense. He just wanted to ask you a few questions."

There was still no strength in my legs. The weakness was an actual feeling, its own separate, dull ache centered in the knees.

Allen said, "What happened?"

Looking out the window at a girl riding a red bicycle, I said, "I killed a man. Gretchen's husband. He beat her up. She came to stay with me. He found her, and I killed him."

The girl on the bicycle was pedaling like mad. She was late for school. Maybe fourth grade, or fifth. Her hair was very black, tied in a loose ponytail up top near the crown of the head. She wore dirty tennis shoes. The girl saw me look at her and looked away in the direction she was going, down the sidewalk.

"I didn't even know you had a gun," Allen said.

I looked at him and said, "I don't. It was Gretchen's."

We rode along. I didn't pay any attention to our direction.

"Where is Gretchen?" he asked.

"She's gone. She went back to California."

We rode along in silence. It was a beautiful morning. I noticed things I never noticed before. It seemed like I'd been gone a long time, and while I was gone they planted new trees and built new houses in empty lots.

We pulled up in front of Samantha's house. The house I'd lived in for years, helped raise Allen in, paid to update, then renovate, in order to keep up with people I'd never met.

"What are we doing here?" I asked.

"Mom's out of town. You don't need to go back to the

rental house right now. I'll go there this afternoon, clean up, get some clothes. You can stay here a few days."

"Where's your mother?" I asked.

There was hesitation. He didn't want to say. She was probably with another man. On a trip with another man to some Caribbean island covered with palm trees and surrounded by water the color of emeralds. In fact, as we sat out in front of the house, she was probably down on her knees in the bathroom of a beach bungalow giving the man great pleasure. I smiled. After all, she was no longer my wife. I was a man without a wife.

"Nevermind," I said.

It was strange being in the house again, especially without Samantha's permission. After Allen left, I crept around like a burglar. On the screened-in back porch, behind the potted plant above the door, I found my stale cigarettes. The matches were damp. I had to light the cigarette off the stove and run outside to make sure the smoke didn't seep into the flowered wallpaper and raise Samantha's suspicions.

I sat on the wooden chair. The same mystical force allowing me to breathe oxygen pulled the cigarette smoke deep into my chest, releasing the whiteness ever so slowly until I could feel the nicotine reach the center of my mass. It had been a while since I'd smoked, and during the first three drags I remembered how much I loved it. Toward the end of the cigarette I realized how it always left me unfulfilled. The expectations too high and the results too average.

But I lit another one right after the first anyway and

sat alone thinking for hours about what I had done. Trying to figure out what part of me was responsible, and what part of me wasn't.

two

Most of my suicide scenarios included a common theme. Apparently, subconsciously, I was concerned about offending the person who might find my body washed up on the beach, or bloated and smelly three days in the bed, or even lying peacefully in the backseat of my car in the garage. I'm not sure exactly what this means.

I kept thinking about digging a hole. Finding a secluded place down on the beach about ten yards up from the water's edge. Around noon I'd go out with a shovel, ice chest, and a few books. I'd begin digging a deep, deep hole, piling up the sand on the side of the hole facing the water. Between digging, I'd have a cold drink, lay out on the towel reading my favorite books, watch the seagulls and pelicans frolic along the shoreline.

If anyone passed, walking along the beach, I'd keep my face in the book and pretend I didn't speak English. I would intentionally select the day of the month with the highest tide, a full moon, I suppose.

After the sun went down the water would begin to rise, creeping up the sand a little further with every breaking wave. When the waves began to touch the pile of sand in front of the six foot hole, I would remove the gun from the plastic bag inside the ice chest. The metal would be cold on my hands, and I'd be careful not to set the gun down in the sand.

I'd throw the shovel, ice chest, and my favorite books down into the hole. Then I would position myself at the far end of the hole, standing upright, leaning slightly forward. The gun would be in my right hand. I would look one way and then the other down the beach, to make sure there were no flashlights. No families walking the beach, or young lovers, or people unprepared for the horrors of finding a dead body late at night.

At that point, I'd be ready. Standing stiff, I would lean forward until my body, a victim of gravity, would begin to fall. In midair, the gun pointed at the side of my head, I'd pull the trigger, ending my life and allowing my body to end up in the very bottom of the hole next to the shovel, ice chest, my favorite books, and the gun.

The moon would exert its strange force upon the water, pulling it upwards, opposite from the gravitational force plunging my body into the deep hole, and eventually the waves would push the pile of sand down into the hole on top of me, burying my dead body far below the surface of the pristine beach. I would be allowed to rot in peace, going back to the earth the way God intended.

Maybe I'm not really concerned about those people who could find my lifeless body. Maybe it's a control issue. I don't like the idea of my body being flipped around, drained of fluid, dressed up and locked down in a dark, sealed casket.

I spent so much time thinking about dying, I never considered the possibility of slowly falling apart. The doctor said the tingling sensation down my right arm was caused by the impingement of a nerve in my neck. The impingement was caused by the herniation of a disk, probably the result of the constant pounding of jogging, or maybe my insides were rotting for no reason.

"You're getting older," he said. "You can put up with the pain, or we can replace the disk."

I tried to put up with the pain, but it just got worse. One morning I woke up with my head cocked to the side. Something had shifted inside my neck during the night and fire shot down my arm if I tried to straighten my head. It made me wonder how people in chronic pain coped before modern medicine. Did they pray every day for their chance to die? Did they spend hours thinking about killing themselves and ending the pain?

Waiting for surgery, nearly naked with my head still cocked to the side, I felt the same loss of control a dead body might feel. The same lost feeling I had the day they told me my father died. The medicine began to drip and the warmth slowly rose through my pitiful limbs. For some reason, I started to tell a story that wasn't true.

"I hated my wife's Yorkie. It was a pain in the ass. Bark, bark, bark. We lived out in the country on fifty acres, mostly woods. One night I was eating dinner and the damned dog just wouldn't shut up. So you know what I did?"

The overweight nurse said, "What?"

The warmth had invaded my head. I don't remember anything else. I woke up in a hospital room with Allen and Emily standing by the bed. The overweight nurse was busy in the room. I was convinced death was upon me. From the outside, I was sure I looked the way my mother looked the day she died.

"That was a horrible story you told," the nurse said.

I didn't know what she was talking about. Maybe I'd recounted the excruciating details of the murder of Allen Kilborn, or my trip to Kansas City, or the time I thought I had herpes and it turned out to be a spider bite.

"I love dogs," she mumbled, her face tight like a ball of rubber bands.

"What story did you tell?" Allen asked me.

My mouth was dry. "I don't know," I managed to say.

The nurse couldn't leave it alone. "He told a story about his wife's Yorkie, and how he hated it, and how one night at the dinner table, after his wife left the room, he rubbed gravy on the dog and put the poor thing outside in the woods so the coyotes would eat him alive."

Allen laughed. "I never heard that before."

I noticed Early, my grandson, my namesake, sitting off to the side. He was around five years old at the time, and he was listening to the story. His eyes were red.

I gathered the energy to say, "It isn't true. My wife never had a Yorkie. I've never even seen a coyote in my life."

The doctor entered the room.

"Everything went well, Mr. Winwood. We ended up removing two disks. Just like we talked about, I scraped out the leftover material and replaced the disks with cadaver bone. We didn't have any problems with the titanium brackets. I think the screws are secure."

After the doctor left, and the dog-lovin' nurse closed the door, Early came over to give me a hug. He smelled all fresh and wonderful, and held me tight.

"Grandpa," he said, "what's a cadaver bone?"

Allen answered for me. "It's the bone of a dead person. Sometimes the doctors use cadaver bones to help fix people who are hurt."

Early seemed to think about it for awhile. There was much to consider.

"What dead person?" he asked.

It was an interesting question. I hadn't thought about it much.

Allen said, "Well, we don't know."

That night, with the morphine rolling steadily through my veins, I dreamed I was a black man named John Evans. The people in my dream knew who I was. They hugged me, and called me by name, but I didn't recognize their faces.

One woman in particular, an older woman, black as coal with a big smile, kept saying, "John, where'd you leave the key? I told you ten times not to take the key. Now where is it?"

I looked down at my hands. They were the hands of a working man, like my grandfather's, the hands of a carpenter. But I didn't recognize them as my own. I'd never seen them before.

I woke up several times in the hospital room, and each time slid gently back into the same dream, with the same people who recognized me, but I didn't recognize them.

I remember saying, "Why do you call me John?"

And the woman in the dream raised her voice, "Don't be a fool. Now give me the key, John Evans."

She was mad, but not really. The way old women sometimes act mad at their husbands, but it's all just part of the relationship. The anger is for show.

The dreams continued for months. I started to wonder if maybe the dead man's dreams were somehow trapped in his bones. I liked the idea of having a carpenter's bones in my neck. It made me think about my grandfather, the same grandfather who saved me at the lake that day.

Paw-Paw had a basement. In the basement he had a workshop full of tools, and saws, and pieces of wood. I can still smell it. The fresh-cut cedar. He built things like birdhouses and little cabinets, and everything in the basement was in a particular place. The place it belonged. I never saw the hammer anywhere except in my grandfather's hand or on the wall hanging on the hammer hook.

I loved the order. I loved the feeling of being in the basement, just me and my grandfather, making something no one else was making. No one else in the whole world.

He would say, "Early, mark this spot right here with the pencil. This is exactly fourteen inches."

And I would mark the spot, watching his hands drift across the surface of the wood, imagining my grandfather could build just about anything in the world.

Lying in the hospital bed, in my mind I began to draw a diagram of my grandparents' house. Beginning at the front door, down the hallway, each of the bedrooms, and back to the kitchen. I was able to close my eyes and see the house exactly as it was so many years ago. A house now lived in by strangers, my grandparents long since buried in the ground. It occurred to me, with my death there would be no one with any true memories that my grandparents had ever lived at all, ever existed, and my mortality, lying alone in the hospital room, became unbelievably certain. I would die also, and be remembered, and then forgotten, like every person who ever lived.

It was a turning point of sorts. Difficult to explain. Certain things became enormously important while others lost all value. I turned my attention to my grandson. Maybe it was for his sake, and maybe it was for mine. What difference does it make?

Behind my rental house was an old building. At one time it may have been a garage. It was a perfect size for a woodworking shop, and I dedicated myself to the idea of creating a place like my grandfather's basement. A place of simplicity, and order, with no telephones or televisions. A place filled with the smell of cut cedar.

I took my grandson with me to the hardware store to buy all the tools, and saws, and pieces of wood. We picked out hammers and nails, screwdrivers and wire, a tape measure and a set of wrenches. We loaded up a cart, and then another cart, asking questions and settling on a plan to build a doghouse for a dog we didn't have. It was Early's idea, maybe as a way to equalize the imaginary murder of a certain Yorkie.

The man at the cash register said, "You two sure did find a lot of stuff."

Early stood behind my legs, peeking around the edge of my pants at the man. He found the courage to move forward enough to see the items being scanned, one by one.

"That your grandson?" the man asked.

"It is," I said.

"I can see the resemblance."

I smiled and paid the man.

We spent the whole weekend building the workshop. On the wall above the wooden table I hung a piece of plywood just like the piece of plywood above my grandfather's wooden table. I made hooks for all the tools and tried to place them in the same order I remembered, the hammer on the far left, the hacksaw on the far right, a row of paintbrushes. Over the table hung a light, a single bulb with a switch at the base of the bulb. On the left edge of the table we secured a metal clamp designed to hold things tight so the piece of wood wouldn't slip as the saw pulled back and forth.

"Mark this with your pencil," I told Early, and he did, exactly where I told him to make a mark, and we cut the wood at the line, the first board for the doghouse.

There was one moment, one I remember, when Early

looked at me the way I looked at my grandfather so many years earlier in the basement. His eyes seemed to understand and focus, etching the grooves of a memory to last his entire life. I reached out and touched my hand to his face, holding my fingers to his cheek, and he let me do it, without pulling away, like he knew how important it was for me. Like he was me, and I was him, and we were together in my grandfather's basement, making something new.

On Sunday, after Early went home, I laid on my couch. I wished I was Mike Stockton. I wished I could go outside and then come through the door and have someone waiting for me in the dark. I didn't want to, but I started thinking about buying a small fishing boat. Taking the fishing boat up to the lake on a Monday morning. Bringing along fishing equipment, a cooler full of cold drinks, my favorite books, a cement block, a rope, and a pistol.

I'd fish in the cool morning, watching the fog burn away in the rising sun. Catch a fish, maybe two or three. Nothing big. Little fish, bream, hold 'em in my hands, let 'em swim away back to wherever they lived. I'd have a drink, take off my shirt in the midday heat, maybe read a little if I wanted. And after the sun set beneath the tall pines to the west, I'd start making preparations.

I'd sit on the side of the boat, careful to balance myself, the cooler and the tackle box placed on the far side of the boat to offset the weight. I'd tie one end of the rope to the cement cinder block and the other end around my waist, pulling the knots tight and tying double-knots.

Then I'd lift the cinder block to my lap and let it rest across my upper thighs. It would be dark. I wouldn't have a single light on the boat. My eyes would search the horizon to make sure no other boats were near. Then I'd cock the pistol, stick the barrel in my mouth, lean back slightly to the edge of tipping over, and pull the trigger.

The force of the bullet would help the inertia of my body falling backward into the water, the cement block rushing to the bottom of the lake, and the rope pulling tight, carrying me down. The boat would drift through the night coming to rest the next morning on the muddy bank. The fish would eat my flesh and gnaw my rotten bones over the summer months until nothing remained except a cement block with a rope weaving in the current.

three

I knew it was a clean killing, if there's such a thing. The man had a history of violence, a history of threats, and entered my home illegally. The neighbor corroborated my story. She heard Mike Stockton beat on my door. She saw him stalk around the house at two-thirty in the morning. There was no evidence I purchased a weapon in anticipation of killing. There was no witness to testify I'd bragged of my intentions to kill the man who beat my daughter. It was self-defense, and defense of Gretchen. A man's house is still his castle, and so did Frank Rush, but it didn't change our history. It didn't change what we knew.

My fiftieth birthday came and went without much fanfare. I was twice divorced, estranged, and living alone at the scene of a crime, more or less. I fell silently into a routine, occasionally interrupted.

Keith Perkins worked in my office. He was a few years younger than me, and for the most part we didn't pay much attention to each other. He was pleasant and bland, a forgettable combination. The man seemed to smile a lot for no identifiable reason, and sometimes I detected the slightest smell of alcohol around his person. Like maybe he kept a little silver flask in his desk drawer, and when nobody was looking, took tiny refreshing sips of warm vodka.

One evening, out of sheer loneliness, we ended up together at a downtown bar after work. Over the course of several hours we both drank too much, and the conversation went from stilted to strange.

"I don't ask for much," he said. "I really don't. I work hard. I provide my wife and kids a nice house in a nice neighborhood. She's got a closet full of shoes. How could anybody need seventy pairs of shoes?"

"I don't know," I said.

We were quiet for a long time. Keith Perkins seemed to be wrestling with something. I really didn't give a shit what it was, and truthfully I had no intention of listening to him unburden himself. I hoped he would wrestle with his problem and then decide to talk about the baseball game on the television behind the bar.

"I love baseball," I said out loud to myself.

"You know what?" he said. "I don't need to feel guilty about anything. Why should I? Do you know how many hours I work every week? I don't care about clothes or a fancy car. I don't smoke pot or gamble."

Whatever it was he wanted to talk about was only a sip or two from sneaking out into the open. He turned and looked at me.

"You're a single man, right?"

"Yes."

"You've been married before, right?"

"Twice."

"Well, then I'm sure you understand. Kids?"

"Yeah," I said, and finished my bourbon and water.

"Let me get you another one," he demanded, and I let him do it.

Keith leaned toward me and said in a drunken whisper, "I've got this girl. A call girl, I guess. Whatever you want to call her."

He stopped talking. It was a little test to see how I'd react. I didn't react at all, just stared at the baseball game. Keith moved his body back straight on his stool. I looked at the side of his face and saw something sad about him. I was nearly a stranger, and yet he needed to tell me something. Something he probably hadn't told anyone else. Not his brother, or his parents, or his wife—nobody except me.

"She's beautiful," I heard him say in a low voice, looking over the drink he held in both hands. "And she does things for me."

I was curious. "What kind of things?" I asked.

He turned back to me like a puppy excited at the sound of my voice. "Anything you want. And she smiles while she does it. Smiles the whole time."

We were quiet again. The barroom around us was

loud, glasses clinking together, the sound of pool balls slamming against each other. I wanted a cigarette.

"It's not like having an affair or something. I work hard. Last year I was only sick two days. Only two days. Did you know that?"

He was nearly begging for my approval. Something, anything from me to ease the guilt.

"Seventy pairs of shoes," he said. "That's a hundred and forty shoes."

So I gave him what he wanted. "You deserve it," I said. I could tell he loved the word, "deserve." He loved it. It spoke volumes. It was the word he was afraid to use. The word that somehow didn't sound right.

"I tell you what," he said, "I'm gonna give you her number."

"That's okay."

"No, I'm gonna give you her number. You don't have to call her if you don't want to, but you'll have it."

Keith scribbled the number on a napkin, folded the napkin, and slipped it to me like a drug dealer.

"Tell her you know me," he said. "It's worth it. You deserve it, too. I've got to go home. I'll see you tomorrow."

I stayed at the bar for an extra drink. I unfolded the napkin. Her name was Gina, or at least that's the name he wrote on the napkin.

I was drunk. Certainly too drunk to drive home, but I did it anyway, concentrating like a madman on the road ahead, radio off, seatbelt firmly fastened, thinking the entire time about Gina and all the things she could do with a smile on her face. I wondered the price, and whether it was too late to call.

"Hello," she said.

"Hello."

I froze. I froze like a boy in high school confronted with a girl's voice.

"Hello," she said again, and then I was unfrozen.

I managed to talk. "May I speak to Gina?"

"This is Gina," she said, and her voice was exceptionally soft and smooth. It ran my imagination into a frenzy.

"I'm a friend of Keith Perkins."

She hesitated, and then said, "Okay."

"Is it too late?" I asked.

It sounded like she was eating something. Maybe a grape, or a tangerine wedge. Something juicy.

"No," she said.

I fumbled around with a plan. A standard motel. I'd call her with the room number. And the next thing I knew I was back in the car concentrating on the road again, making my way to the motel across town.

I felt like a fugitive at the front desk, started to give a wrong name, and then panicked at the prospect of being asked for my driver's license. I paid cash, yawned, talked about being on the road all day and looking forward to a good night's sleep, and then called Gina with the room number.

I sat on the edge of the bed in the motel room, waiting. The idea a beautiful woman would knock on the door, take off her clothes, and do anything I asked, was dynamic. The thought of unconnected sex was foreign to me. No undercurrents of guilt, or love, hatred or compromise. Just two people in a small motel room fornicating, shaking hands, and walking out the door afterward.

I took off my jacket and then put it back on. I removed a shoe, smelled my sock, and then took a quick shower, dressing again. It was all very odd. Several times I stood to leave and then sat back down.

The knock on the door was light. Keith Perkins was correct. She was beautiful. She reminded me immediately of the sixteen-year-old girl at the beach so many years ago. The girl who took me by the hand to the pool. The similarity was something in her eyes and cheekbones.

"How old are you?" I blurted out.

"Twenty-two. How old are you?" she asked, with a genuine smile, looking around the room.

My drunkenness had given way to a slight headache and a numb feeling around my face. I sat down in the chair, and she stood in front of the television. Gina wore a short dress, not too revealing, but perfectly formed around her hips. She was extremely aware of her body, but she didn't overdo it. Her hair was brown, medium length. She could have been a college student.

"Aren't you afraid?" I asked.

"Afraid of what?" she answered.

"Afraid somebody might kill you or something. I mean, it's the middle of the night and you're in a strange man's motel room."

She smiled again and put her hands on her hips. "You're not a strange man," she said.

I leaned forward in the chair and rubbed my tired face

in my hands, pressing small circles at each temple in unison. The pressure relieved the pain momentarily. When I opened my eyes she was still standing there.

I said, "When you're finished, I mean when you're finished having sex with a man for money in a room like this, a man like me, how do you feel?"

She made an expression of disappointment. Not disgust. Not anger. Like it wasn't the first time she'd been asked the question.

"You're one of those guys," she said, looking down at me.

"What guys?" I asked.

She took a few steps forward and pulled my face against her stomach. Her hand felt small and light on the back of my head. We stayed that way, and I could feel her heartbeat, gentle and rhythmic. My right hand reached and touched the inside of her thigh. Slowly, I moved it upwards, aware of the short distance between the tips of my fingers and the magical place nestled between her legs. My hand moved so slowly upwards I could barely detect it was moving at all. The skin was smooth and accepting, sure of itself, and I moved again, now only a whisper from the warm place. She waited patiently, waited for me to do as I wished. And for a moment I thought I could do it. I thought I could be a man who could enjoy the bodily pleasures of a strange and gorgeous woman. But I was wrong. A wave of nausea rose from my stomach, and I leaned back in the chair, looking up at the girl above me.

I was old enough to be her father. Who was she to trade intimacy for money? Who was she to mock the myth of love? The strongest, most organized and essential myth in the history of mankind, and for a few hundred dollars she'd let a man touch her and pretend she loved him.

It was me who was disgusted, and without a word I stood up and laid face-down on the bed. I never heard another sound from her. I must have fallen asleep in only a few minutes. She could have killed me, or hit me with a baseball bat, or anything else she wanted. Instead, I suppose she decided to leave my kind alone in my own misery, untangling the reasons for being unable to move my hand the final inch.

I woke the next morning and didn't know where I was. I arrived at work two hours late and people stared at me like I was covered in blood. Keith Perkins winked when I passed his office door, and I was glad to close the door of my own office and sit in silence.

On the desk was a stack of mail, and on top of the stack was a handwritten envelope from Kate. It was the first letter since the Kansas City proposal. The letters had stopped, and after a while, I stopped looking forward to the daily mail. Stopped rifling through the business envelopes searching for her handwriting.

But there it was, the envelope in front of me. I held it in my hands and wondered if it was a coincidence, Kate's letter arriving the morning after my night in the motel room alone. The mistakes in this life are all patiently waiting to be made, but I opened the letter anyway.

Early,

Whether it is true or not, I've come to believe you are the only person who has ever really known me. I was a daughter to my screwed-up parents, a wife to Russell, a mother to Gretchen. With you, I was simply me. It was raw, and right, and scary, which is probably why I ran away. It was like running away from myself.

Meet me Saturday, June 10, at the Kansas City airport Sheraton hotel lobby at 2 o'clock. Two days. Room service. Hot baths. Never leave the apartment like before. I'll wear a red dress.

Love, Kate

God help me, but I felt like a teenage boy. Just a few words on a piece of paper written by her hand held the power to bring me back to the way she made me feel. A lightness. Clear-headed. Ready to face the day, and June 10th was only two weeks away. The world was good again.

four

The definition of success doesn't always include longevity. I mean, we think a restaurant in business twenty years is successful based solely on the period of time, or a fifty-year marriage, or a man who spends his life employed at the same place. I looked back at my own life and realized many of the most pleasurable experiences were short-lived. Most people would think my marriage with Kate was a failure, but that's not true. My feelings for her, good or bad, were as intense and concentrated as any feelings I have ever experienced. I learned more about myself through Kate in a short period of time than maybe any other span of my life. And despite my best efforts, I still loved her, or at least I loved the thought of her. The idea of Kate Shepherd still existed as a separate entity, like a painting on a wall in a museum.

If I'd been thirty years younger, pride would have kept me from going to Kansas City. I would have left her sitting on the couch in her red dress watching the glass door the same way she left me years earlier. But I wasn't thirty years younger, and I never would be again. I was becoming an old man, and one of the benefits of being an old man, besides watching your body fall apart and thinking of suicide constantly, is recognizing why pride is included in the list of deadly sins.

I had two weeks and a plane ride to think. I suppose I should have waited to marry Kate, at least until we got to know each other, but youth isn't for waiting. It's for doing. Blindly doing. What else could it be for? Would we prefer to spend youth rationalizing and contemplating, preparing for retirement and eating low-cholesterol bran muffins? Such a small percentage of my time on this earth was spent in Kate's presence, but so much time was spent thinking of her.

I hadn't made a reservation at the hotel. Since Kate was the one who invited me, I left it to her. I wouldn't have the opportunity to prepare the room, set up champagne and strawberries. I'd just arrive, and let things happen. No written format. No forcing one planned moment to follow the next planned moment, drowning in the anxiety of possibilities. Like the possibility Kate wouldn't show up again, or if she did, we'd quickly learn we'd both become very different people. Too much in between to overcome in a few short days. Maybe we'd even hate each other, one person leaving the other in the middle of a bitter lunch, storming out, packing a bag, no strawberries.

It was a long flight. I had a drink to calm my nerves. My thoughts flowed from fear to pure and divine lust. In my mind, Kate's body was the same as it had been before. The same as it existed so clearly in my memory, naked and brilliant, her breasts firm and round, but it dawned on me they may no longer be firm and round, but instead elongated and elastic, attacked by gravity. Maybe her face would show wrinkles, and her hair would be peppered gray. And how would she see me? Would I look like an old man in the bedroom, a walking skeleton, my testicles distended?

So I had a second drink and thought about the prostitute. She was young and beautiful. What stopped me from touching her, but allowed me to kill people? Who is responsible for the moral minefield inside me? Jesus was allowed to save the world. The ultimate Savior Complex. Did God make some people unsavable, even for Jesus? And if so, why? Why would He create such a person to live a life without hope? And is it true that people who live their lives to save others, like myself, are truly the people who need saving the most?

I stared out of the taxi window on the way to the airport Sheraton Hotel. It was only 1:40. I was twenty minutes early. I considered asking the driver to ride around for the next half hour, but I didn't. It was raining. Clear strands of water spread like long fingers across my window from front to back, witch's hands shaking in the breeze. I became lost in thoughts I can no longer recall, and the driver had to speak before I realized we were in front of the hotel, on the other side of the glass door.

I paid the man and stood on the sidewalk in the rain,

my bag over my shoulder. Through the glass I could see the lobby and the couch where I sat before. The couch was empty. Nothing red inside. I entered the door, looking left and then right on the way to the couch, and sat down with my bag at my feet.

At five minutes until two I felt the way I'd felt before. Was I an idiot? Sitting in a hotel in Kansas City, waiting for no one again? The same clock on the same wall. It seemed the same people, besides Jake Crane, were milling around the lobby on the marble floors. How long would I wait this time, and would I spend the night alone or fly home?

For some reason I looked to the right at the golden elevators fifty feet away. The elevator door opened and Kate stood alone inside. We were looking at each other, me on the couch in the lobby, Kate in the red dress, standing alone. No one around us could know we were together. We'd always been together, no matter how far apart, and no one needed to understand, not in high school and not now.

She held up four fingers. The elevator door closed slowly. I smiled to myself. She'd come all the way from California. Our room was on the fourth floor. Now it was just a matter of controlling expectations. Navigating the great abyss. Reconnecting without consequence.

I stood casually and walked to the elevator. On the fourth floor I turned the corner to look left, and then right, down the long empty hallway. There was no one. I must admit, for a minute I questioned myself. Had I seen her at all? Had I wanted so badly for Kate to show up I'd created her in the elevator, a mirror image of the woman inside my mind, a delusion? Was I standing in the hallway once again, waiting for no one?

I heard a door open. I saw a flash of red. Kate's head peeked out. I walked her way. The door was cracked, and I went inside. She was standing in front of the television. We smiled at each other. A knowing smile, and she opened her arms. I dropped my bag, and we held each other. It was just a matter of who would let go first. Tears came to my eyes behind her back, and I didn't want her to see them. There was still the part of me that needed to be seen strong. The part my mother's letter told me to leave behind. But it's not so easy. I was a man, after all. If not for our strength, who are we?

I started to speak.

"Shhhh," she said quietly.

On the table I could see a bottle of champagne resting in a silver bucket of ice, two crystal glasses next to the bucket, and a single red rose in a long slender vase. I'd brought nothing.

Kate pulled away. She closed the curtains on the window and turned off the only light in the room. The bathroom light allowed me to see her.

I started to speak again.

"Shhhh," she said quietly. My silence was necessary for her somehow.

Kate was barefoot. In the near-darkness she unbuttoned my shirt. I touched her face with my fingers, and she smiled like she remembered something good.

My body below reacted even before Kate removed my

pants. It took every molecule of control not to touch her, but just like my silence, it seemed important to wait. Necessary.

Kate's red dress dropped to the floor around her feet. She stepped out, and we stood naked in silence, thirty-five years after the last time we'd been naked together in my college apartment, when days passed wrapped up in each other's bodies. The darkness, the silence, the patience, were all necessary now when they hadn't been before, but it felt so much the same. The same out-of-control desire I'd always felt in her presence. The need to harness and explode at the same time. Touch and deny myself simultaneously.

She took me by the hand and led me to the bed. The sheets felt clean and cold. Side by side, we kissed gently, I wanted to lick every single inch of her body, but I waited, and eventually, she touched me. It seemed the entire purpose of my desire my whole life was Kate Shepherd. At the moment of my conception, that crazy moment with Bobby Winters watching outside the bedroom window, my DNA was programed with Kate Shepherd in mind. It seemed she was the reason for my existence, the intention of my pleasure, and now she let me, wanted me, to kiss every part of her skin. So that's exactly what I did. I started at the top of her painted toe and moved upwards. There was no hesitation. The silence solidified the simplicity. Kate made low noises when I stopped at certain places, her hand light on the back of my head.

There was nowhere else to go. We were exactly where we wanted to be, and neither of us spoke for hours until it was like going back in time. The covered window could be any covered window, anywhere. The light from the bathroom could be any light, anywhere in the world, like the light in my college apartment bathroom, and with no words or sights to provide context, we were twenty years old again.

Afterwards, we found ourselves lying next to each other in the bed. One of us, at some point, would speak. Lights would be turned on, our flaws revealed, but I didn't want it to end. I could hear a television in the next room. Someone walked down the hall rubbing the bottoms of their shoes against the short carpet. The thin line of light between the curtains was yellow.

"Do you remember," Kate said, "the list you made of everything I needed to do to change my life?"

I remembered the list. Education. Finances. Spirituality. Baby names. I remembered it was all in my handwriting, not Kate's. They were all my ideas, not Kate's.

"I remember," I said.

Just the words, the words spoken in the air, changed everything. The context had been established. The borders of time had framed the moment. We were forced to remember.

I reached out and turned on the lamp. Kate was on her back. The sheet was pulled up to her neck. On the outside of the sheet, Kate's hands were folded together. I noticed her fingernails were chewed down to the quick, and I was just as surprised as I'd been in high school when I'd first noticed.

I looked at the side of her face. It wasn't the same. We weren't the same. I thought of the burnt doll in the yellow house. The shirtless man on the mattress who had touched Kate before me. Jeff Temple, the baseball player who told the story of Kate Shepherd on her knees behind the concession stand, his dick in her mouth. And that day at the courthouse, my baby in the arms of Russell Enslow, my baby in another man's arms.

Without speaking, or looking at Kate, I got out of bed and went to the bathroom to take a shower. Under the warm water something occurred to me. Something I'd never acknowledged before. My life, my entire life, had been more affected and directed by unrequited love, by the people who couldn't or wouldn't love me as much as I loved them, than by those who loved me the most. Kate, my mother, Gretchen. My life was a reaction to their rejection, and I prayed to God Kate would be gone when my shower ended.

I turned up the hot water and felt it cascade down my back. The rain was probably still falling outside. Kate would need time to gather her things. Maybe she only wanted to stir up her life a little. Keep it from settling in the bottom of the glass. Maybe her reasons for coming to Kansas City on June 10th were very different than my reasons. Maybe it had always been that way, and I was too stupid to know the difference.

In that shower, praying to walk into an empty room, I was more alone than I'd ever been before. I dried my ugly body and listened for a sound outside the bathroom. Any sound. A door closing. The zipper of a suitcase. I wrapped the towel around my waist, took a deep breath, and walked out of the bathroom.

She was gone. Her clothes were gone. I was alone in the room, and again, immediately, I regretted my prayer. Wished I could take it back. Unpray.

The champagne was open. She drank a glass before she left. Next to the rose, at the bottom of the slender vase, was a ring. I picked it up and held it to my eyes. It was my grandmother's ring. The ring I'd given Kate so long ago. She left it for me. She returned it.

five

Nothing compares to the present. Nothing. How could it? Yesterday, how could we possibly possess the imagination necessary to paint the tiny details of today? And tomorrow, how could we possibly possess the memory to resurrect every point of light, every sound, from the exact moments of the day before? Knowing this, I tried anyway, but losing the idea of Kate left me floating out into the universe. Allen was the only person who knew me well enough to notice.

"Is everything okay with you these days?" he asked.

My house smelled funny. Like men, we talked around the issues.

"Yeah. Everything is fine. Just workin' too hard."

"Early wants you to come to his baseball game tonight."

Sitting there in my living room, I started thinking about Allen's father. I started thinking about those last few seconds before I pulled the trigger, standing behind him at the top of the stairs, when his fingers stopped on the computer keyboard. He sensed something in his house, someone behind him, and then the gun went off.

Maybe there was no justification. Maybe it wasn't my decision to make, just like it wasn't my decision to kill Mike Stockton.

"How's your mother?" I asked Allen, trying desperately to change the track of my thoughts.

"She's doing pretty good," he answered. "I took her out to the grave. . . " And then he stopped himself.

They'd been out to the man's grave together. They probably brought flowers and talked about things they could never talk about in front of me. I wondered if Early was with them. If they told him it was his grandpa's grave, and he'd been murdered, and they never caught the person who did it. Murdered in his own house, with his own gun, by a coward.

When other people complain about being depressed it sounds like horseshit, but something was the matter with me. Nothing seemed good. Ice cream. The beach. A cigarette. Even building something with Early in the workshop. My mind floated from Kate to Allen Kilborn Sr. and back around again in an endless cloudy circle of doubt and regret.

I think there are still active volcanos somewhere in Hawaii. I imagined planning a trip, flying to Hawaii, staying a week in expensive hotel rooms, eating roast pig and drinking pineapple juice. I could spend every last dime on whatever I wanted to, maybe leaving a small trust fund for Little Early.

On the last day of the trip I could rent a car to drive out to the volcano. I'm sure there must be tour guides and hiking trails. I could make plans in advance and act nice and normal, like nothing was up.

Later, people would say, "He acted nice and normal, like nothing was up."

But when I'd finally reach the crest of the volcano, and the tour guide would turn his back, I'd jump down into the red molten lava. My body would disintegrate instantly into the intense heat, disappearing for eternity. No bones to find later. No cakes of dried blood. Just a bewildered tour guide standing at the edge wearing a backpack wondering if I'd fallen accidentally or purposefully incinerated myself. There would be no need for explanation. I'd be dead.

So I asked the question. "Did you and your mother go out to your father's grave?"

Allen looked down at his hands. Maybe he thought it was disrespectful to talk about the man in front of me, or maybe he'd just gotten used to the idea of keeping us separate inside himself.

"Yeah," he said.

I wanted to know more. I wanted to know all the details.

"Do you go there a lot?"

He looked up from his hands. It wasn't my business. Allen's relationship with his father, and now with his mother, wasn't my business anymore, and maybe never was.

It was that moment I decided I needed to tell Frank Rush the truth somehow. At least Frank Rush, if not everyone in the world. I didn't want to spend the rest of my life locked in a prison cell, but what was the difference. I had to get it off me somehow, and Frank Rush was a man who might just understand why I did what I did. Maybe he could even help me see things I didn't see before.

So when I was alone, I got out my pen and paper again. This time to plan something good. I started a fire in the little fireplace, a tiny volcano, and sat in front in a wooden chair. In longhand I began to write the words I would use to tell Frank Rush the truth. Not just the words, but where we would be for the conversation, and when, and how it would all be arranged.

If possible, I wanted to confess my sins without repercussion, an unrealistic goal, but a goal nonetheless. I didn't want to lose Allen or Emily. I didn't want to die in jail. I didn't want Gretchen sitting in the back of a courtroom staring at me like I was Charles Manson. I didn't want to see Kate's envelope in a stack of prison mail. I didn't want Early standing over his grandpa's grave hating me, his namesake, for killing the man he never got to know. A man, so many years later, remembered as someone he wasn't.

The planning went on for weeks and then spread into the next month. I decided to learn Frank Rush's routine. I'd pick the right date to accidentally find myself sitting next to him on a park bench or at a movie theater, away from his office, away from his little tape recorder. He'd know why I was there. He'd know it wasn't an accident.

The words would come to me, a combination of all the best parts of each written confession I'd tossed into the fire. And then we'd talk about it. Man to man. Father to father. He'd tell me what he knew, and I'd fill in the blanks, holding back any information that might lead to physical evidence. After that, I was unsure what would happen.

I'd tell him, "I won't plead guilty, Frank. I'll deny we had this conversation. I'll never tell you where to find the other buried things, or the spare key."

On a Tuesday morning I picked up the newspaper at the end of the driveway, like usual. I sat in my office with the door closed, reading. In the obituaries I saw a picture of Frank Rush. It was right there, in color, amongst the other faces. He was smiling. He was dead. Died of a heart attack. The article under his picture said lots of good things about him. Frank Rush was retired. He'd served in the United States Navy, had eight grandchildren, and loved model airplanes. It didn't say anything about me.

I suppose, if you wait long enough, everybody dies. It's just the way it is. Like when I was a boy and asked my mother about my father dying. She told me we never really figure it out. We just become more comfortable with the mystery somehow. I wasn't comfortable with the mystery at all. I'd never planned for Frank Rush to die. He was like a mountain. He died never knowing. I wondered if he thought about me, and Allen Kilborn, and Mike Stockton, the day before he died. Probably not. He was probably thinking about his grandchildren, or model airplanes, or whether it would rain, leaving me with visions of volcanos and no one to talk to.

I went to work like normal the next day. Since the night in the bar with Keith Perkins, every time I passed his office he winked at me. We were co-conspirators, forever linked by Gina, the woman he enjoyed, and I couldn't.

This time I stopped at his office door. "Keith," I said.

His eyes grew wide like he feared I would reveal our secret. Scream across the office, "Keith loves whores," in my loudest, angriest, stock market voice.

"Yes," he said meekly.

"Don't wink at me anymore."

He seemed relieved and confused. I didn't wait for him to answer.

I stopped by the grocery store on the way home after work. I always loved the grocery store. I kept finding myself roaming around up and down the aisles instead of going home to my empty house. The store was so well-lit, and colorful, with the smell of baked bread, and I didn't have to talk to anybody if I didn't want to.

I stood in front of the cheese in the dairy section. My attention was drawn toward a figure to my right. Ten feet away, in front of the milk, stood Samantha. The scene was exactly as we'd stood years ago when I'd orchestrated our meeting. When I went to the grocery store every day for a week at the same time until I saw her, and stood in front of the cheese, and waited for her to turn around and look at me, and then forgot the lines I'd rehearsed. Dumb-founded like a school boy.

This time I hoped she wouldn't look at me, but I couldn't seem to move. I couldn't seem to stop watching her as she squinted over her reading glasses to read the labels on the milk jugs. I'd seen her from time to time at Early's games or other events, but not so close. Her hair was shorter. She'd gained a few pounds around the middle.

So long ago the sight of Samantha had left me speechless. The thought of her nakedness cleansed my mind of everything. But now it was like we'd never known each other. Like we'd never shared anything at all. Just two people in the grocery store, struggling to read labels on dairy products.

She turned to see me and for a moment seemed not to recognize my face.

I spoke first, automatically, without expression. "Hi," I said.

She smiled politely, like she promised she would do. "Hi," she said, and then turned and walked away with a milk jug in her hand. I watched her go.

I left the store, buying nothing, and drove to the little league baseball park. Early played shortstop and was one of the best kids on the team. He was more aggressive and competitive than his father had been, watching the score-board over his shoulder, nervous.

I waved, and he saw me take my place in the aluminum bleachers next to Allen. Emily was home, pregnant with their second child. A girl. A baby girl on the way into the world. A world that seemed too angry and confusing for a little girl, but who was I to say?

A ball was hit hard to Early. He dove and missed, out of reach, and then banged his glove on the red dirt, mad at himself.

"Good try," a man yelled below me.

I smiled. It was really a very pleasant place to be, the baseball park. It was well-lit like the grocery store, with kids, and peanuts, and the smell of hot dogs. They smell much better than they taste, the red texture always disappointing.

I wished my father could be there. He'd be an old man. I did the math in my head, eighty-one years old. If it wasn't for the train, or any other tragedy between the train and the ballpark, my father would be sitting next to me in the bleachers, probably wearing a jacket, maybe a hat to cover his gray hair, eating peanuts. He would have liked Little Early, the competitive spirit, slamming his glove down in the red dirt.

He would have said, "Good try, boy," and patted me on the leg, choosing not to acknowledge the horrible things I'd done after I'd sat down next to him on the park bench and confessed my sins to him. The plan to kill Early's grandfather. The squeak on the seventh step. The man's head exploding like a balloon, blood and bones sprayed across the computer screen. Mike Stockton's black figure in the doorway, the light from the streetlight behind him, maybe just waiting to talk to his wife, straighten things out, apologize.

But my father would have understood why I did what I did. And in the last inning, when Early hit the ball to the fence and scored the winning run, my father would have stood up and yelled for his grandson, dropping his peanuts, and putting his arm around my shoulder.

six

I took the death of Frank Rush as a sign from God. A sign to pursue my childhood vow of being average and invisible. My life became measured by baseball seasons. Going to work, stopping at the well-lit grocery store, locking the door behind me in my little house, not answering the phone, and then going to work again, looking forward to Early's next game, or even the next season.

I took to writing letters to Kate about virtually nothing, and she never responded. Usually the letters were written late at night, after I'd had too much to drink.

Dear Kate,

Come to my funeral when I die. I don't know why it's important, but it is, and I don't care to figure it out. Just tell me you'll be there.

Early

Most of the letters were never sent, piling up in the bottom drawer of my desk, but sometimes, burdened by the knowledge the sobriety of morning would dampen my courage, I'd venture out late at night to the mailbox. The same mailbox I once attempted to steal.

Kate,

Do you remember the time we were at the park for my visitation with Gretchen? She couldn't have been more than four or five years old. You and I walked away to argue about something, who knows what now, and left Gretchen alone.

When I turned around she was standing in a bed of fire ants. They were all over her sandals and biting her little legs, her eyes were filled with tears, her arms outstretched to us.

I remember the helplessness. The total and utter understanding I couldn't protect her from the bad things in this world.

Why is it our minds hold certain moments, certain conversations, certain words spoken, or visual images like Gretchen's outstretched arms, and yet dismiss huge pieces, events, entire years of our lives? Why is it we're not allowed to forget certain moments, and then not allowed to remember others?

Early

At first, when I sent the letters, I spent time wondering about Kate reading my words. Standing at the mailbox on a beautiful California morning. Smiling, or not smiling, as the case might be, alone in her bathroom, door locked, afraid of what I didn't mention. But slowly, as the years passed along, I didn't think any more about Kate reading the letters. It didn't much matter. They weren't for her anyway.

On a Monday morning I went to work as usual, and as usual, the office door was locked and the lights were out. Most of the time I was the first to arrive. On this particular Monday morning, I flicked on the lights to see my co-workers standing in the lobby around a large cake on a table. Balloons were tied to the four corners of the table and somebody had written on a white poster: HAPPY BIRTHDAY OLD MAN.

It was my sixtieth birthday. I was sixty years old. Sixty years had passed since my moment of mis-conception.

They began to sing, off-beat, awkward, most of them wishing they were still in bed. And as they sang, I thought about how much I hated everyone in the room. Keith Perkins with his nasty little secret. Debbie Cunningham with all those extremely black nose hairs. Chad Driskall and his political comments on everything under the sun. "I believe beavers would be Republicans if they had a choice, don't you? I mean, they're industrious, conservative creatures."

I didn't really hate them, and so we all stood in the lobby at seven in the morning celebrating my sixtieth birthday and ignoring the absurdity of it all.

I turned my head away from Debbie Cunningham as she gave the obligatory birthday hug, and then as we parted, tried to stare directly into those dishwater eyes and keep myself from glancing at the newest nose hair sprouted overnight. Keith Perkins wanted to wink at me so badly his face twitched, and I swear to God I heard Amber Sullivan pass gas standing next to the cake during a quiet moment. I imagined her stink absorbing into the white frosting and almost dry-heaved at the idea.

I had dinner that night with Allen and his family. Emily cooked a grand meal. Little Early was a young man, grown up before my eyes. His sister, Jessica, looked just like Gretchen to me, which was genetically impossible of course, and made me feel I might be losing my mind.

During dinner, I started to think again about killing Allen Kilborn Sr. It would flash in my mind, and I'd try to switch quickly to something else, but it would come back again and again, making my head actually hurt. There was really only one question left. Would I tell Allen I'd killed his father or not? Would I go to my grave unforgiven, or risk losing the love of the person in my life who probably loved me more than anyone ever had?

How would Allen react if I told him, and would his reaction be a product of who he was born to be, or who I made him? After all, ultimately, don't we become a combination of every important person in our lives, taking pieces of them as we go?

I looked around the dinner table. They had no idea who I was. To them I was Early Winwood, old man, builder of doghouses, stockbroker, ex-savior. They didn't see me at night at my desk next to a glass of brown whiskey, scribbling pitiful letters to a woman who never loved me. Or sitting in my office wishing Keith Perkins was dead. Or remembering my fingers on the inner thigh of the whore in the motel room. They didn't know how much I missed my mother and needed my father. They didn't know because I didn't tell them, and there was no way for them to know such things.

For days after my birthday I sat around thinking about telling Allen. I decided it wasn't a choice. It had to be done, maybe more than anything I'd ever done before. So I smoked and thought, thought and smoked, and tried to work out the details of my confession.

It would be done in person. A letter would be too cheap and easy. I should leave out gruesome details and not provide too much explanation either. It wasn't a moment for justification or self-pity. It was my gift to Allen, for him to do with as he chose, and I would need to be prepared for the worst. Prepared to spend the rest of my life without him, or Emily, or Jessica, or Little Early's baseball games. In some regard, it was much like one of my suicide scenarios, with less finality and more serious consequences. It also happened to be real life instead of volcano fantasy, and for months I couldn't think of anything else.

Kate,

A long time ago, in high school, we left a party one night to take you home. You made Jake drop you off blocks from your house late at night under a streetlight. I can still see you standing there under the light. We drove away and I watched you out the back window of Jake's car.

You waited until we turned the corner.

I'm sixty years old.

Early

It happened around midnight.

I was alone at home, as usual. The house was quiet. The house was quiet. I remember standing slowly from the wooden chair at my desk.

It was like the lights went out. It was like God turned off all the lights in the universe with no warning except a tingling sensation in my brain.

I woke up on the floor beside the desk. I knew where I was, but I couldn't seem to move my body. The inside of my head pounded and pounded like my brain was swollen against the bones of my skull. It was very hot, and I tried to decide what had happened to me.

I couldn't collect my thoughts, almost like being on the edge of sleep, or drugged, or chained to the floor of a smoke-filled garage watching blackbirds fly against the walls.

I would tell my arms to move, but nothing would move. I would tell my mouth to speak, but no words would come out. The room smelled like burnt hair. There was a telephone on the small table a few feet away, but a few feet was like a mile, and I began to imagine ants on my body. The same ants that bit Gretchen's feet and legs, leaving raised white welts on her skin and wet tears in her little eyes. I could feel them crawling on me, in my cracks, under my shirt.

Maybe it was a heart attack, I thought, but my chest didn't hurt. Maybe I'd been shot or struck by lightening. Maybe I was in Heaven and this was what Heaven was like, lying on a floor with my head pounding and ants crawling on my body, unable to reach the phone two feet away, as helpless as the day I was born into the world.

I could hear a clock somewhere, ticking, ticking. After a while the room began to lighten, the morning sun rising outside somewhere, and I guess I started to cry. I could feel the cold teardrop slide downward from the corner of my eye and slowly across the skin on the side of my face to a resting place in the hair around my temple. I knew I was crying, but it was more like someone else was crying and I was only watching.

My arm moved. Not so much moved as jerked, spasmodic, knocking my hand into the leg of the small table, the phone falling to the floor. The dial tone was a relief at first, a noise, proof I was still alive, but then the noise changed to a beeping sound, and I was trapped in the shell of my body. Unable to defend myself. Unable to separate my thoughts from the beeping sound.

Two days later, they tell me, I woke up in a hospital with Allen above my bed. It was a stroke, the doctor said, and I could hear him but couldn't answer his questions. I was in my house for twelve hours on the bloody floor. I'd cracked my head on the desk on the way down and bled all over myself waiting to be found, jerking on the hardwood.

It was Allen who found me. Keith Perkins called him from the office. Said I was never late, never missed work, something was the matter. The black-nose-hair lady and her farting friend were worried. Everybody was worried about Early Winwood. So Allen went to the house and found me on the floor next to the desk. He said he thought I was dead.

When the doctor left and we were alone, I looked up at Allen. The words came to me from nowhere. The perfect words to tell him what I had done and why, written neatly across my mind, words I'd never found before in all those moments of thinking and smoking, smoking and thinking.

I opened my mouth to tell him what needed to be said, knowing he might turn and walk from the room, but the words wouldn't come out. Nothing came out. Nothing at all. And I wasn't even sure my mouth had opened because Allen looked down at me in the way my father must have looked down at me in the white crib of the hospital the day I was born, wearing the t-shirt he wore in the picture I kept in my sock drawer.

I absolutely know my father's last thought was of me. Nothing else, and no one else but me. I absolutely know it, but I waited too long to tell Allen the truth, and now I'd come full circle. Back to the beginning.

seven

I so longed for my chance to die, and then it got complicated. I woke up in a hospital basically unable to speak, with the right side of my body basically useless. When Allen's family had gone home, a nurse came into my room. She talked to me the way people sometimes talk to pets.

"Well, does somebody need a little bath?"

I watched her scurry across the room, marking off chores on the checklist inside her mind. She was short, but her ass was wide and flat. I think she preferred to work with patients who couldn't possibly blurt out, "No, I don't want a bath, and by the way, your ass is wide and flat."

"It'll feel really good," she said. "Nice and cool," she smiled and wrapped her arms around herself pretending to shiver when she said the word 'cool'.

The woman pulled back the blankets and began to

undress me. I didn't have the energy to stop her and heard myself mumble a few words. Not really words.

"You're welcome," she said, misinterpreting my sounds.

I was naked and had the feeling drool was escaping the corner of my mouth and dripping off my cheek to the pillow.

The cold sponge touched my chest. I stared directly into her face. There were lines around her eyes. A fever blister on the top lip was visible under a smear of skin-colored makeup. She was lonely. No wedding ring. Her hair was going gray despite the best efforts to dye and pluck, probably standing in front of a mirror until she was sick of who she was, memorizing every blackhead and undesirable blemish on her generic face.

When I was young I was so sure my potential lay in a special awareness I possessed. The ability to notice and dissect other people and the world around me. Somehow, I'd lost touch with it through the years of my life. Too busy to notice, I suppose.

The wet sponge, no longer cold, slid across my arms and beneath my neck. She wouldn't look at me. All work. Just another chore to mark off the list, her eyes following the sponge as it ended up at my hips and then gently wedged between my thighs. I felt the beginning of an erection.

I was far beyond the point of embarrassment. What would be the point? Naked, spread out in the bed, unable to feed myself, shitting in a pan, drool most certainly in a thin clear line from the corner of my mouth to the white pillow. But regardless, being cleaned by a woman not remotely attractive, my body prepared itself for procreation anyway.

"Something seems to be working just fine," she said as workman-like as possible, hopefully finding an ounce of joy in the idea she could still cause such a reaction in another living thing.

She avoided any further contact with my private parts, dressed me, pulled up the covers, and left the room humming a song I didn't recognize. I was left alone to think about the irony of spending each day imagining my death, even wishing for it, only to find myself with a reason to live. I wondered how long it would take in rehab, how many months, to speak the words clearly to Allen. Because once they were spoken, I would be free to go, one way or the other, with or without forgiveness.

Doctors and nurses came and went through the night and into the next day. After lunch, the door opened slowly. A head, Gretchen's head, appeared, and as the door opened I could see Kate behind her. They'd come from California. Allen must have called. They'd flown together to see me. If things had been different, my wife, Kate, would have been the one to find me on the floor, waking in the other room to the sound of my head cracking against the wooden desk. She would have cried quietly at the kitchen table when they took me out on a stretcher, afraid of the idea I might die and leave her all alone.

My good hand tried to pat down my hair and once again I had the feeling of drooling. Gretchen stopped a few feet away from the bedside, unable to hide her shock at my appearance. If I could have seen myself, I imagined

I looked like the Hunchback of Notre Dame, eyes bulging, saliva glistening on my thin lips, strands of antenna-like, wiry gray hair in every direction.

Kate stepped up ahead of our daughter. She seemed strong, prepared, and took my hand in hers with no reaction to my appearance except a soft smile. Even if I had possessed the power of speech, there is nothing I would have said.

"Allen called," she whispered.

Behind Kate I could see Gretchen lost in the situation. It was the first time in her lifetime she was alone in a room with her mother and father, just the three of us, and it had to happen in a hospital, with her father drooling on himself like an idiot.

Gretchen roamed around the room, in and out for a few days, never knowing what to say, a ball of anger and sympathy rolled tightly together. She left to go back home. Something about her job. "Inventory," she said. It wasn't true, and it didn't matter. Kate stayed.

She hugged Gretchen and sat back down next to the bed. It was outside the realm of possibilities, so I'd never taken the time to imagine such a thing. She read out loud to me deep into the evenings from books she knew I loved. She talked to me like we'd never been apart. Like I'd dreamed all the bad things and we'd been married forever. Smiling. Taking care of me. Telling Allen and Emily she'd be staying a while longer. Whatever I meant to her, she was afraid of losing it.

I watched her face as she read out loud. It was a pretty face. The years hadn't changed it all that much. Still full of mystery and surprise. She'd been the love of my life, my whole life, and I wouldn't have it any other way, because either you believe in the concept of love or you don't. There's no middle ground. No compromise. It's all or nothing, and if it's all, there are no limitations other than those you set yourself, and a broken heart doesn't count.

She was reading from *The Catcher in the Rye*, and it was making me feel the way it always made me feel, how difficult it can be sometimes to squeeze any real purpose from the day. I started to think about finding her on the street that night, sitting on the curb, her head resting on her knees wrapped in her arms. I watched her face as she read the words, and at the same time I saw Kate as I'd seen her that night, from the back, unsure if it was her at all. She was humming softly to herself. I couldn't hear the words. And when a car passed, the lights showed me a part of her cheek, just enough for me to know it was Kate Shepherd I'd found, and rescued.

Those days and nights she stayed with me were dreamlike, and I can't be sure they ever happened. On the day she left, Kate kissed me on the cheek and touched her hand to my hair.

"I have to go home now, Early."

She said it like she knew it was the last time.

"Through the years you probably thought I was crazy or something."

I just listened, glad I couldn't speak. Glad I was able to listen without expectations. She struggled with the words.

"I guess…" she stopped herself.

We both waited a moment. I knew I'd have plenty of

time to cry after she left. "I guess," she said again, "I just didn't understand how you could love me so much. It was more than I could figure out. Maybe it still is."

Sometimes it's harder to identify the problem than it is to solve it. If I hadn't had a stroke, if I wasn't speechless and bedridden, I don't know what I would have said or done. Probably nothing. She figured it out. There was a hole in each of us, and I watched her pick up her purse slowly and then walk out the door for the last time.

It was what it was, and I'd cried about it too many times. There was only one thing left. One thing left to do. I went home to Allen's house. Emily quit her part-time job to stay with me and they turned the guest room into a place they hoped I'd like to be. Pictures of the kids were on the walls and Allen had thoughtfully packed up every-thing in the little house, selecting certain items to decorate my new room.

Little Early made the high school baseball team. Every evening after practice or a game he'd sit down in my room and tell me everything that happened.

"It was the last inning. We were tied six to six. Toby Raines was on third. There's two outs, and two strikes on me. The first one was high, but the second one I just missed it. No excuses.

"Anyway, the kid pitchin' was the coach's son. He throws about eighty-five. Some people say ninety, but I don't think so.

"He pulls up in the stretch, and you wouldn't believe it. The ump calls a balk, with two outs, two strikes, tie game, the ump calls a balk.

"That kid wouldn't come out of the dugout to shake our hands. He just sat in the dugout."

I went through rehab every day. I didn't give a shit about walking across the room or holding a fork. I just wanted to talk again. Coherent. Make my tongue move the way I wanted it to move, and my mouth, and the muscles in my face, to form the words.

The wheelchair didn't bother me. They even loaded me up in the car and took me to a few baseball games. I tried not to look at the people who looked at me. Especially Samantha. It would have been better for someone just to stand up and clear the air.

Someone could say, "This is Early Winwood. He had a stroke. He's not the man he used to be. Now, who wants popcorn?"

Everybody could look at me openly for a few minutes, get it over with, and go back to watching the game. Little kids could ask, "What's wrong with your face?" or "Why does your hand look like that?" and I'd have Allen answer their questions calmly.

My speech therapist was named Jackie. She had more patience in the tip of her nose than I had contained in all my bones combined.

"Say corn."

And I would make a noise similar to "corn," but since the word corn wasn't likely to appear in my conversation with Allen, I really didn't give a damn about the word.

I missed being alone, believe it or not. I missed my little house, and my desk, and the late-night drives to the post office.

I didn't miss my work, but I missed the office. The half-hour each morning I sipped my coffee and read the newspaper before I heard a key enter the lock and turn the deadbolt.

I missed the woodshop. The smell. The purity of cutting straight lines and hammering nails, making something from nothing, using my mind for a single purpose.

But none of those things changed my plan. At night, alone in the bed, the neighborhood quiet, I arranged scenes. It would be just me and Allen. I would give him a route to escape after the conversation. A door to walk through. A chance to think about what I said.

I'd be prepared to answer questions. Why? How? And explain if he wanted a further explanation. He deserved whatever he wanted, and I deserved whatever he put upon me. If he just chose to sit and listen, it would be relatively short. No more than two minutes to say everything I needed to say, and then I imagined a moment of silence. A moment when neither of us was sure how he'd react.

On a piece of paper I scribbled a note to Jackie, my speech therapist. "I'll give you $10 for a cigarette."

It didn't sound good to me, but I wanted it anyway. Since the stroke I'd lost my taste for meat, peanuts, and ice cream. My favorite foods were suddenly disgusting as feces and caused the same reaction. I prayed God had saved for me the pleasure of tobacco, but I didn't hold much hope.

Jackie wouldn't get me a cigarette, but I bought one from a wrinkled-up old bastard with six bypasses and a tube in his throat. He could barely draw the next breath, but he loved cigarettes with a lust rarely seen.

I waited until Early went to the grocery store and wheeled myself out onto the back porch. I struck a long fireplace match and lit the Marlboro. A wave of nausea began deep in my bowels and moved upwards. I vomited in a potted plant before I could take the second drag.

The days moved slowly. On the calendar I marked the day I believed I'd be ready to tell Allen. It was only four weeks away. I was able to talk to people, and they were able to understand, but I wasn't quite ready. On the other hand, I didn't want to make the same mistake I'd made twice before, waiting too long. The doctor said I was at a much higher risk of another stroke than the average person. He said I was lucky the first one didn't kill me, and maybe I wouldn't be so lucky the next time.

I worked on pronouncing certain words. "Sorry." "Controlling." Even small words were hard to say. "Gun." "Mom."

Emily and the kids went out of town for Thanksgiving to see Emily's parents. Allen stayed with me. I insisted he have Thanksgiving dinner with his mother, and I'd be fine. When Allen left, I decided to find a little whiskey. It was off-limits of course, doctor's orders, but I hadn't had a sip since the day I woke up in the hospital.

I found a bottle, and a glass, and sat in my wheelchair in the living room, feeling sorry for myself. I thought of Kate, and Gretchen, and the day marked on the calendar. I drank down almost the entire bottle and somehow made my way back to the bedroom and laid down on top of the covers.

I remember crying. That's mostly what I remember. Just crying, without stopping. My body shaking. Everything running together. Wishing I'd died and then feeling guilty. Waiting to reconcile the irreconcilable, a sin of the highest level, a life unlived.

I remember looking up from my bed to see Allen standing above me. His presence in the room made it full and complete, and it was clear the moment was upon me.

I looked up at him and said, "I killed your father, Allen."

That's all I said. The other words I'd practiced and performed avoided me, but those five words, "I killed your father, Allen," were as clear as any words I'd ever spoken, and as I expected, they were followed by agonizing silence.

eight

I can't be sure where the dream started and the world stopped.

The next thing I remember is the black circle. Just like before, on the floor between my bed and the door in my childhood bedroom. A deep black hole with a gray ring around the circumference, maybe an arm's-length across, no more.

In the dream, if it's a dream at all, I'm sitting up in my bed in the dark watching the closed door. I have a certainty the door will open, it's just a matter of time, and the wait is excruciating. I'm just a boy, maybe eleven years old. It's the day Mr. Walker told me my father died on the train tracks. My mother took me home from school early, and I remember it started raining right after dark. A steady, heavy rain.

I sat in my bed, waiting for my father to come home. He always came to my bedroom when he got home late from work, and I always, always, always, waited for him before I fell asleep. From my bed I could hear the car door slam in the driveway, and then a few seconds later the front door would close quietly. He always closed the front door quietly so he wouldn't wake my mother. She went to sleep early, and it wasn't good to wake her up, so we didn't.

After I'd hear the front door shut, I'd wait, smiling in the dark, for my father. The doorknob would turn. I could see it, and in the dream it turned so slowly, but I didn't move. After all, it was the day they told me my father died. It was the day I was asked to believe he'd never come home to me again. Never take my hand in his hand, or throw the football in the front yard, or tell me about baseball. It was the final test between a child's life and God's real world. A world where people die and just never come back, like a butterfly in a storm.

I can't move. It's like I'm frozen again. The doorknob turns. My father's coming home and the black hole on the floor waits between him and me.

The door opens slowly, and there he is. He looks perfectly normal. No bandages or blood. No scratches on his face from the glass shattered by the impact of the hundred-ton locomotive barreling down the tracks to places unknown.

He smiles at me. The same smile from the picture. Mischievous, like we're in on something together. A secret. But I want to tell him about the black hole. I want to warn him before he walks to my bed to hug me the way he does every night. I can't speak. All I can do is sit there and look at him.

The door opens wider and he takes two steps to me. I'm not allowed to close my eyes, only watch my father begin to fall into the black circle on the floor, and in an instant he is gone, the room quiet again, rain coming down on the roof of the house. I am alone.

The next thing I remember is waking up in the hospital. The light is dim and the window dark. Tubes are hanging down across my chest. Next to the bed, on my left, sits Allen. His face is down resting in his hands. It's just the two of us in the room.

At first I want him to know I'm awake, but then I remember what I've told him. I want to reach out and touch his hair, but I'm too far away, and maybe he doesn't want me to touch him. Maybe there's a black circle between us, unseen by me, but between us nonetheless. Just resting in the short distance between my hospital bed and his chair.

I watch Allen in the silence. The marrow of life exists in the moments in between. Those moments before and after the violent upheavals and admissions of futility. For the birth of a child is meaningless without expectation, and the death of a parent is hollow in the absence of memory. And though we are forged by a handful of events, some dramatic, it is those moments in between, waiting for life to happen, when we discover who we have become. When the violent upheavals and admissions of futility resonate, harden, and reveal themselves for what they are.

I must have fallen back asleep, or maybe not, but I am in my workshop with Little Early. He looks at me the way I remember looking at my grandfather, and I reach out to touch his face, holding my fingers to his warm smooth cheek, and he lets me do it without pulling away. Like he is me, and I am him, and we're making something together in my grandfather's basement, the smell of cedar soft in the air.

But before we can start, I am off again, in and out, coming to rest at the high school baseball field. The grass is amazingly green, and I sit in the aluminum home field bleachers, alone, on a bright blue day. Across, on the other side, sits Kate. She has a textbook open in her lap and looks out into center field, freshly mowed. We are the only two people in sight, and I watch Kate Shepherd close her eyes and take a deep breath.

I am in the kitchen with my mother, just a few days away from leaving for college. She is standing, leaning against the refrigerator, arms crossed over a long, faded blue nightshirt.

"Do you ever think of Dad?" I ask.

She studies me and then smiles just a little bit. It gets the best of her, just like he did, and she goes ahead and lets the smile remain.

"Sometimes," she says, and I know it's true, but more importantly, she allows me to know.

There's a far-off flash of light, like lightning in the distance too far away to hear the thunder, and I am with Gretchen at the ice cream parlor, sitting outside under a big white umbrella. We're waiting to go the matinee. Just enough time for ice cream. Gretchen has a scoop of birthday cake ice cream in a cup made of white chocolate with colorful sprinkles.

She looks up at me and takes her first bite. A smile comes across my little girl's face, genuine and pure, and I start to cry. I can feel the tears roll slowly down my face, and instead of wiping them away I just let them roll down.

"Daddy," she says, "how much does the sky weigh?"

"I don't know, baby," I say. "I really don't know."

I wake up again. It's daytime. Feels like early morning. Allen is standing at the window with his back to me. We are very still, and I wonder if I am dying. Wonder if all of it has come to this, waiting for Allen to turn. Waiting for his decision.

One moment I see Allen's back, and the next moment I am looking out of the window of the hospital, seeing the world for the last time through someone else's eyes. Allen's eyes, looking across the parking lot to the buildings on the other side, watching a tall pine tree sway in the morning breeze.

This time it goes further. This time I can feel what Allen feels. The forgiveness is an entity. It exists like a stone, heavy and solid, inside his body, and it is the only thing in this world worth knowing.

I turn from the window and look at myself in the hospital bed, tired and gaunt, much like my mother when I was called to her bedside, but Allen sees me differently. He sees himself in me, and as I walk slowly across the room, the past, the present, and the future melt together to form something entirely new for me. I am not alone anymore, and never will be again.

Allen places his hand upon my shoulder, and I am allowed to feel the touch on both the shoulder and the hand. A gentle squeeze. Assurance. Resurrection. With no words spoken, I am forgiven, and Allen's hand on my shoulder is the last thing I remember before the beginning of the gentle slide into light, when everything you ever wondered makes sense. When the enormously personal journey ends in the reflection of God on the surface of the cool water.

ACKNOWLEDGMENTS

David Poindexter, Kate Nitze, Sherilyn McNally, Scott Bidwell, Shauna Mosley, Steve Johnson, Michael Dasinger, Sharon Hoiles, Sonny Brewer, Michael and Jillian Strecker, Kevin and Carolyn Shannon, Kip and Shannon Howard, Frank and Virginia Hollon, Sara and Skip Wyatt, Sally Hollon, Hoss Mack, Marion Bolar, Austin McAdoo, Gladden Statom, Fred White, Rich Green, Allison, Dusty, Mary Grace, Lilly, Smokey Davis, Chris D'Arienzo, Robbie Boyd, Kyle Jennings, Aleta Dasinger, Paige Benson, Tank and Janet Dasinger, Melissa and Julie, Weber, Joel Stabler, Stephanie Wheeler, Russ Copeland, Will Kimbrough, Joyce Miller, Helene Holmes, Joshilyn Jackson, Brietta, Hilary, Anne, Pete Ware, and Pat Walsh. Thanks.